SANDRA CARMEL

EVERNIGHT PUBLISHING ®

www.evernightpublishing.com

SANDRA CARMEL

Love recognizes no barriers. It jumps hurdles, leaps fences, penetrates walls to arrive at its destination full of hope.

—Maya Angelou

SANDRA CARMEL

LAST HOPE

Intertwined Love, 1

Sandra Carmel

Copyright © 2021

<hr/>

Chapter One
Scaling the Heights

Hope Fede stood at the summit of Tasmania's Federation Peak, gasping for air through burning lungs. "Amazing. Beyond amazing!" The climb, the views, the company.

Cole Sparks's brilliant smile and shimmering cobalt-blue eyes were filled with mischief like he was some sort of sexy mirage. Hope slipped in beside him, still trying to catch her breath, and leaned her forearms on the warm, jagged rocks, her sweat-beaded skin sliding against his.

The view overlooking Hanging Lake had a magical, almost surreal feel. The serene blue sky and sharp surrounding ridges were reflected in the mirror-still water. A hidden treasure amongst punishing, rough terrain. A bit like finding Cole in the challenging business world of fake, ruthless, beautiful people.

"Thanks for this. All of it." She couldn't believe

she'd nearly missed such an incredible experience. When he first sprang the five-day break on her, she thought she'd have to decline.

His eyes flashed with that devilish spark she loved. "My pleasure." And with Cole, he never disappointed, especially not sexually.

As CEO of his own game software development company, Cole had the flexibility to escape just about whenever he wanted. She, however, worked for an uptight, inflexible television network and had to constantly make a good impression.

Unspoken, palpable pressure convinced her she had to be available for their busy filming schedule leading up to Christmas if she aimed to get more major television gigs in the future.

Sweaty tendrils of hair clung to her face, and Cole reached up to push them away. His big, manly hand lingered on her skin, the pad of his thumb creating soft circles on her heated cheek. "You were stressed. You needed time away. We both did. Together."

So he'd spoken to her station boss and promised he'd do an exclusive interview with Hope about his business success and recent Cosmo Bachelor of the Year title, third year running, in exchange for a week's holiday for Hope. And like with anything he set his mind to, he succeeded.

"See, I told you I'm a caring boyfriend." His eyes and tone were full of cheek, but absolute truth rang in his words. He was real, and he got her. What he'd said and done, since they met just under a year ago, proved that.

Hope had gone to one of those dreaded pre-Christmas business dinners she'd sworn never to attend, full of arrogant, mind-numbing, self-absorbed chit chat. If she'd heard one more person say how flawless they were, she'd have blocked her ears and screamed like a tantruming two-year-old ... with taste.

That night, though, the moon, twinkling stars, and heavenly planets must have aligned, because she had the great fortune to be seated beside him at the table. She introduced Cole to eggnog and her long-term love of the stuff, and their conversation continued to flow as though they'd been friends for years. Friends with a lashing of lust and flirtation.

His smile went from mountain-climb high to downright dirty. "Race you to the lake. Winner chooses their pleasure."

She turned to face him, gravitating like a flower to the sun. She squeezed her thighs together to stem the growing ache between her legs, to try to control her desire, which tended to be pretty impossible whenever they stood within touching distance.

Hope conjured up her most convincing pout. "Unfair. You always win." Honestly, she loved it when he won. He never failed to shower her with attention in all the best areas. Landscape and body. Her experience with Cole confirmed his number one priority—seeing her hit the heights of earth-shattering, out-of-this-world orgasmic bliss. Every. Single. Time.

How had she gotten so lucky? Up until him, her love quest had been littered with endless Jason-and-the-Argonaut-style trials leading to the elusive golden fleece that she started to think she'd never discover. However, with a name like Hope, she had refused to give up, the idea almost blasphemous.

Cole kissed her, teasing and sweeping her mouth with his adept tongue, cupping her butt with his large hands and pressing her against his hard, impressive length. An explicit taste of what delights were in store. An enticing sample of what was to come.

Using his regularly demonstrated Dom-style

control, he ended the kiss. The sudden loss of intimate contact left her head buzzing like she'd drunk too much champagne. And God he smelled so good, like mountain and man. Tipsy and intoxicated on him, she stumbled back.

He snagged her waist, keeping her upright, grounded. "I'll give you a head start." Meaning he'd catch her, pass her, pleasure her.

Her whole body zinged with anticipation. The sooner they reached their destination, the sooner they could indulge in an assortment of naked delights. And without having to hurry to meet some dreaded work deadline.

She pulled out of his grasp and started her descent to the track below, leading back to the lake. Hope glanced up at her strong, athletic man, his muscles bunching and straining against his charcoal and black fitted t-shirt and pants. A rush of desire shot down to her core. His butt alone would have made Rodin weep. A flesh sculpted work of art.

They reached the track several slow-going hours later, and he held her hand in a powerful yet warm, loving grip. Hope had lost the drive to beat him to the lake, instead savoring his closeness, their time-consuming trek like extended foreplay or, as they called it, *mountain-high play*. She dragged her feet, exhausted, but he urged her to keep going, promising an ending with a bang.

Lugging her backpack sapped her strength, but she focused on the end result, using her last, second-wind burst of dwindling energy to make it to the camping spot. They dumped their gear and he ran—actually ran—to the lake's edge. The man was superhuman.

Hope took off at a staggered, stop-start jog and conked out a couple meters behind him. She bent forward, hands propped on her burning thighs and sucked in lungfuls of crisp, high-altitude air.

"Naked. In the lake. Now." His eyes flared with desire, his tone dropping from calm and encouraging to pure, direct Dom. And she loved it.

Hope's heart rate dialed up to danger-of-exploding. She pushed to her feet and surveyed the stunning view. Cole, with his potent, piercing blue eyes and rich caramel-flecked hair, now dark and soaked with sweat, stood against a backdrop of steep, majestic mountain shards, green and brown brush, and still, tannin water the color of golden syrup.

Daring, rugged beauty.

She redid her disheveled ponytail, pushing her long hair high up on the back of her head, and began to peel off each protective layer of clothing, her legs weak and wobbly.

Even though they'd been a couple for just under a year and had off-the-charts sexual chemistry, he hadn't once hinted about a more permanent commitment. He hadn't even told her *I love you*. Her heart said he was the one. But what about his heart? Did he feel the same about her? Should she confront him about it?

No. She didn't want to risk scaring him away with her over eagerness. She'd give him a bit more leeway, a bit more time, and just hope he hadn't ruled her out of serious relationship contention now that he knew her confident, well-put-together façade hid self-doubt and insecurities.

Were her looks and talent good enough to succeed in the entertainment business? Was she special enough, exciting enough for him? She preferred tracksuits and runners over designer clothes and thousand-dollar shoes and couldn't be the pretty, stereotypical TV bimbo or accessory on his arm.

Not that he'd want that. He definitely needed mental stimulation as well as physical and emotional, or he'd get bored and move on to the next challenge. Just like with mountain climbing.

Hope glanced up.

He didn't say anything, just watched. His sizzling stare drank in her slowly revealed bare body like she represented a revitalizing glass of cool water on a steamy, hot day.

Right now, she shouldn't overthink. Right now, they should use the opportunity to enjoy each other. Thoroughly.

The small, warm patch of sand shifted under her aching, blistered feet. She stepped past him, his gaze like a caress, lingering on her face, breasts, and hairless sex. His intense, I'm-gonna-do-you look gave her goosebumps, made her nipples hard, not the cool water or soft breeze buffeting her skin.

Cole shucked off his clothes, his Adonis-like body glistening in the afternoon sun. He dove into the lake, emerging right in front of her, and slicked back his thick, drenched hair. Drops of water clung to his eyelashes and some trickled along his strong, angular jaw. "On the rock, legs spread."

Her juices joined the water lapping at her inner thighs. Hope pushed herself up onto the heated rock ledge and lay back along its water-smoothed surface.

"Knees up."

With her pulse thrashing in her throat, she did as he asked, planting her feet on the edge of the rock and exposing her pussy. Propping on her elbows gave her a great view of him and the spectacular surrounds. She didn't want to miss a single moment of his breathtaking seduction.

His gaze connected with hers, then drifted down

her body as he swam forward. The water swished with his approach, and it was the hottest thing ever, even hotter than the sun's rays baking her body.

He pressed an open-mouthed kiss to her mound, along each inner thigh and finally, *finally* licked the length of her seam. She cried out and he gripped her hips, his calloused hands rough against her skin. This was why she let him win.

Hope threaded her fingers through his wet hair, guiding him closer to her clit, which he loved avoiding until he'd worked her right up. Control. He had plenty of it. It radiated from him like an aura. Nothing defined drop-dead sexy more than a confident, skilled, self-assured man.

He took his time exploring her folds with his expert tongue, then circled her entrance and thrust inside.

She arched up into him. "Cole!"

"Mmm … you taste so fucking good." His breath came in hot bursts and he thrust faster, deeper, a prelude to later.

She dug her fingers into his scalp, her clit throbbing with need. So close to the edge. "Please." The almost unbearable ache swelled in her core.

"Knees up to your chest, and keep those gorgeous legs spread."

She almost sobbed in protest, greedy, desperate for an orgasm, but obeyed. The more he delayed, the longer and more intense the climax. Over the time they'd been dating, he'd proven it to her consistently.

Cole kissed her opening and slid his tongue to her back hole. In the past she would have freaked out. She'd always considered it a no-go, forbidden, non-sexual spot. Well, not so forbidden anymore, not since she met him and he introduced her to the pleasures of anal.

He rimmed her, still avoiding her clit, and she

considered finishing herself off, like last time. He'd unloaded spurt after powerful spurt of cum all over her breasts and stomach, watching her masturbate.

She reached down with one hand and he grasped it and placed it back on his head. "Uh-uh, impatient girl. Try that again and it'll be orgasm denial."

Hope nearly cried. She needed the release like she needed to breathe. "Please, Cole."

"Please what?"

Always such a tease. "Make me come."

He groaned. It had started getting to him too. She imagined his cock as hard and solid as the rock she lay against. "Please."

His mouth on her clit stalled her shaky intake of breath. He swirled his tongue and sucked her swollen nub and she screamed, climactic aftershocks reverberating through her bucking body.

Cole didn't stop. Instead, he trailed one hand up her torso, tugged her pointed nipple, and continued to lick and suck. His other hand slid along her inner thigh, and he inserted two fingers inside her. He zeroed in on her G-spot and rubbed. Hard.

Exquisite pleasure exploded in her core and she squirted, actually squirted, for the first time—something she thought she'd never achieve—the sensation so mind and body altering, she came again, and again, ejaculating every last drop of ecstasy.

She dropped her hands from his head and collapsed back against the rock, panting, beyond satisfied. The man was the king of cunnilingus. Before him, she'd struggled to get decent oral, rarely orgasming once, let alone multiple times.

He kissed her sensitive clit, then her navel. "How you doing?"

Coherent thoughts deserted her. She scrambled

for words to describe the indescribably incredible experience. "Ah… Amazing. Worn out." Not even close to covering what she felt, but the best her post-climax, inarticulate brain could come up with.

"Worn out? We've only just started. I've got a special friend here who's very excited to join you."

Hope laughed. "Yeah, I bet." She tried to direct some energy back into her sated muscles and slipped into the water, her body sliding against Cole's massive erection.

His gaze swept over her exposed breasts, her nipples dipping into the rippling waves. He looked up into her eyes and caressed her cheek. "Fuck, you're beautiful."

She leaned into his big palm. "Look who's—"

His urgent kiss smothered her reply. He thrust his tongue deep, her taste still lingering on his lips, driving her wild. Even the bliss-induced coma from only moments ago couldn't stem the blossoming need to come again.

Hope wound her arms around his neck and wrapped her legs around his waist. She rubbed her clit along his length, tingles racing up her spine and right down to her curling toes.

They both groaned.

He stepped closer to the rocks, his strong hands holding her butt above the water. With her heart about to thump out of her heaving chest, she reached between them and stroked his smooth, rigid cock.

"If you don't stop right now, I'm not going to last."

Poor man, on the verge of losing the last frayed threads of his control. The power to drive him crazy with lust and longing was heady. She pressed the head of his cock to her entrance and eased down, savoring the thick feel of him filling her up.

Dark desire blazed in his eyes, turning them midnight blue. "I need to move."

"Yes!"

He withdrew, then slid in, withdrew and slid in, his face taut with the strain of holding back.

She kissed the rapid pulse thumping in his neck and licked up to his ear. "Harder." She nipped his earlobe. "Faster."

He let out a tortured breath and slammed into her, setting a pounding pace. "Touch yourself."

She ran her hand over the sprinkling of caramel hair on his muscular chest and traced the lines of his eight-pack abs that flexed under her touch. She lowered her hand to rub her clit, her circling motions matching his frenetic pace. "Ohhh…"

That delicious, pre-climatic tingle built between her legs.

"Come for me." Cole's command pushed her straight into paradise. She ground down onto him, riding the euphoric wave, her insides clenching and releasing his cock over and over.

"Fuck. Hope!" He dug his fingers into her butt cheeks and pumped once, twice, then stilled, grunting out his release.

Her arm went limp around his neck and she dropped her head on his shoulder, her other hand crushed between them, Cole still inside her.

"So fucking fantastic." He kissed her hair, his ragged, recovering breath caressing her skin. "Let's get back to the tent and get settled."

He slipped out of her, and she whimpered at the loss of him. Somehow, he not only still stood, but also had the stamina to continue carrying her, his heart already back to its strong, steady beat. He took a step toward the shore, and she twined both arms around his neck, clinging tight.

They collected their discarded clothes, and that evening—after feasting on salami, two-minute noodles, and trail mix—they sat under the bright, shining stars, in front of the fire. Once the sun disappeared behind the horizon, the temperature dropped and the wind whipped up, carrying with it significant bite.

She shivered and wrapped her arms around his waist, nestling her head into the crook of his neck. He ran his hand along her thigh, up and down, up and down, up and down. His steady, tender touch made her feel valued, cherished. And she fell for him even harder.

Hope glanced up and their gazes locked. "I love you."

Cole just stared, silent, penetrating, but didn't say it back. He never did. The first time she'd said it was around the six-month dating mark. She hadn't expected him to reciprocate then, but now…

He bent his head, capturing her lips in what felt like a genuinely loving kiss. His usual response in place of those three special words. Did he ever plan on saying them to her out loud?

A twinge of disappointment seized her, yet she couldn't deny the potency of his touch. She grasped his cling-wrap-tight t-shirt in the center of his chest and slipped her tongue into his mouth, deepening the connection.

Hope lost time, passion drunk in his arms. Then he slowed things down, pressed a kiss to her forehead, the tip of her nose. "We should get some sleep. It's going to be another long day tomorrow." He patted her bottom. "Come on, up you get."

"Yes, Mr. Adventure Man, Sir." She couldn't help but inject a little cheekiness into her tone. Some might call it topping from the bottom, but she'd worked out the subtleties enough to just get away with it. Mostly. Behaving a little bratty, she knew, would get the expected response.

He growled, but she could see the hint of humor in his eyes, the twitching smile on his lips. Looked like she could lure the Dom but not his heart. And that was something she aimed to rectify.

Her muscles rebelled against moving, still sore and heavy from their exhausting day of hiking and other more intimate activities. Reluctantly, she peeled herself off him, entered the tent, and changed into some sexy red lingerie. The tent flaps parted and she turned, goosebumps rising on every bit of exposed skin. He stood in the gap, the fire glowing behind him.

His gaze roamed all over her. "You know the rules—no clothes in the sleeping bag."

"But—"

He held up his hand to stop her resistance. "Don't even try to use the but-we-need-to-keep-warm argument, because skin on skin is the best producer and conductor of heat. And then there's that extra friction I had in mind."

Extra friction, aka, another round of mind-blowing sex. *Oh God.* Naked rubbing against Cole never failed to create fire in her blood, like their skin was sexual kindling.

Hope shivered, images of them making love and falling asleep snuggled up in each other's arms flooding her brain. "Right again, Sir," she said, with just a hint of sass, and started to undress.

He slapped her ass, the sharp crack splitting the silence, the sound making her jump more than the exquisite sting.

"You have a smart mouth, babe. And I think you

enjoy the punishment."

She stared up at him, dazed with lust. If he chose to discipline her further, she hoped it would consist of more smacks strategically placed across her butt, the top of her thighs, or between her legs, and not something excruciating like orgasm denial.

He soothed the throbbing hot spot on her butt with his warm, wicked hand. "You better not be wet." His playful, slow-burn smile suggested he already knew the answer.

The man knew how to turn her on, particularly when he went into full-on Dom mode.

He slid his hand between her legs and stroked her wet panties. "Fuck. You're drenched."

Always for him.

The look in his eyes and tone of his voice suggested he was impressed and debating whether to punish or reward her. "Hmmm… I think I might drag things out, let the tension, the anticipation build. I promise it'll be worth the wait."

Sounded perfect. Exactly what she'd counted on. Hope slipped out of her panties and packed them away with her negligee. She honestly hadn't intended to argue about whether or not to wear clothes to bed.

Her intention with the lingerie had been to look sexy, desirable. Maybe make him think of offering her forever. Not that she had any problems being nude. They spent a lot of their time together that way.

She'd wanted to try something different, show him she refused to be complacent, that she wanted to continue making an effort. She wanted to prove she didn't take him or their relationship for granted.

A soft, flickering amber glow brightened the tent's interior and she glanced up. Cole had lit a couple of lanterns, which had the added benefit of highlighting his impeccable, masculine form.

She drank him in, his smooth, erect cock hitting his abdomen, taunting, teasing her, and her core clenched. He set the lanterns safely aside, crouched down, and unzipped the double sleeping bag.

Under each other's heated gazes, they got in and cuddled together. He reached around her, zipped them in, and initiated a slow, sensual make-out session. But before she could get too worked up, he wound things down to affectionate, heart-melting caresses. Although she loved the sex, this was deeper, more meaningful. Is that what he'd intended?

An overdose of oxytocin surged through her veins, making her feel closer to Cole, not just physically, but also emotionally. Calm, safety, and comfort seeped into her brain and body, encouraging her to open up. "You know I love you, but do you love me?"

"Of course. Where did that come from?"

"You never say it, so…"

Cole tucked his fingers under her chin and tipped it up until her eyes met his piercing stare. "People say a lot of things, but you can't rely on words. Actions are what count. Actions show how a person really feels."

He had a point. His actions constantly showed he cared. However, words and discussions still held some real value. "Some things need to be spoken about, though, like our long-term plans, kids…"

Was that a flinch? "They do."

"How do you feel about them?"

His hand froze on her thigh. "Kids or long-term plans?"

Had the air gotten colder? "Both. Are they something you want, with me?"

"Are they something *you* want?"

"Yes. Definitely. I'm getting close to mid-thirties,

Cole."

"You've got plenty of time."

Not *we've* got plenty of time.

"How about you? You haven't answered my question." Her eyes searched his, trying to extract the truth from their churning, conflicted depths.

"I'm working on the whole long-term plan thing." Were his muscles extra stiff, extra tense, or had she read into their stilted conversation? "As for kids, they're not a deal breaker." Did that mean he preferred to have children with his partner or that he'd rather not?

His replies were so politician-like at times, avoiding direct answers, talking around an issue, particularly when it involved the heart, emotions. "Having them or not having them?"

"Hope, honey, enough of the interrogation, okay?" His words were sweet, but his breath was harsh against her skin. All traces of the heart-warming connection and arousal they'd had only minutes ago— obliterated. Just like that, with a few simple words.

"But…"

The expression in his eyes said *don't push me.* The subject and his responses were important to her, though. She needed to know whether he considered her marriage material, whether kids featured in his future plans. If not, she'd have to reconsider their situation, possibly break things off and move on, even though it would be the hardest decision of her life.

"There's something I want to ask you."

A jolt of excitement skittered along her spine and spread like a happiness virus, killing off the negativity, the assumptions. Maybe he'd been nervous, not resistant. Maybe he'd finally decided to say the words she'd been longing to hear. To propose they spend the rest of their lives together.

"I'm away next week. The weather's finally going to be perfect to do the Kosciuszko climb."

"Oh." Him and his I-must-climb-the-highest-mountain-in-each-place-I-visit obsession. At first, she'd thought it quirky, endearing. Now, it seemed he cared about that more than anything else. Anyone else.

It was already hard to spend decent time together. Their work lives were so hectic, her with her erratic television schedule and him with his game software-development company … and fitting in his passion for mountain climbing.

"I realize it's not the best timing, but you know how much I've wanted to do this. And I'll be back by Christmas. Will you be free Christmas Eve?"

Was that his question? No *I love you*, no hint at wanting a more permanent commitment. Disappointment sank like a heavy stone in her heart. "Um. Yes." Even though frustration simmered beneath her skin, she couldn't say no to him. Yet. She'd give him until Christmas Eve. If things weren't any clearer by then, she'd press him for answers.

The tension in his body seemed to drain away. He relaxed against her, his hand restarting its strokes up and down her thigh. "Good. Keep a look out in your inbox for an e-mail from me. I have something special planned."

Chapter Two
Dark Descent

Hope sat alone at her desk, in between filming, and checked her e-mail for the fiftieth time today. Cole had been away less than a week, and she missed him like they'd been separated for months.

The first day he arrived at Mount Kosciuszko, he'd sent her a text to tell her he was okay and would be in contact again soon, but he'd been silent ever since. She couldn't quite decide whether to be angry or worried.

Something special planned. That's what he'd said when he booked their Tassie trip too. Knowing him, it'd be some other climbing expedition they could do together, followed by hours of lovemaking to celebrate. Not that she minded, but at thirty-three her biological alarm clock had gone off, and the dysfunctional snooze button no longer gave her relief.

Their relationship had progressed to a serious point, or at least she thought so, and now she needed more. She loved him; however, she needed to know whether they had a long-term future.

"Hope, you're back on in five."

She swung around to the open doorway, the station runner already gone. "Thanks," she called after him.

Hope got up and checked her hair and makeup in the dressing room mirror, perpetually glowing with golden, flattering light, and prepared for her ten-minute segment on *The Travel Bug* that would probably take the rest of the day to film.

Ding.

Her phone. She rushed back to her desk and

snatched it up. A personal e-mail. She clicked on it, and Cole's gorgeous face popped up, with a message, as promised.

Have you been naughty or nice?

Hopefully naughty, but not too naughty ... until you're with me ;-) My hand's tingling just thinking about spanking your gorgeous ass. And my cock, well, you can imagine...

Hey, Hope. Miss you so much. Can't wait to hold you in my arms again, and command you in the bedroom (or up against the wall, on the sofa, bent over the kitchen bench...) like I know you love.

So far, the climb has been everything I'd hoped. My only regret is you couldn't be here to share the experience. But believe me, you won't miss out. I'll make it up to you.

Right. Now, onto Christmas Eve.

I've arranged a car to pick you up at 4 p.m. Pack light. I've organized for us to stay in the city overnight, but most of the activities I have planned don't require clothing. ;-) Just wear something casual, comfortable for during the day, and bring a sexy dress and shoes for the evening.

Once you've checked in, the driver will take you to the pre-arranged special spot. I'll meet you there at 6 p.m.

I'm so looking forward to seeing you.

Cole x

Hope squealed like a teenage girl. She would be reunited with her love soon and maybe, just maybe he'd take the next step.

****

Sir Stamford Hotel, Circular Quay. Presidential Penthouse Suite.

Wow.

Cole had arranged some amazing accommodation for them before, but the penthouse... Another level altogether. A first. She traveled up in the elegant lift with her overnight bag, unable to tame the ridiculous, oversized grin on her face. Maybe this trip was extra special.

She entered the striking, antique-style suite with high ceilings, mahogany wood, and cornflower-blue lounge chairs. So rich and elegant. Almost too beautiful to touch. Italian silk wall hangings, a grand piano, classical paintings, and a marble fireplace made the space look even more untouchable, museum-like.

So sumptuous, so breathtaking, so sublime. Hope rolled her small case into the bedroom and left it near the window beside the king-size bed. She stared at the white sheets, picturing her and Cole making love.

An hour later, she returned downstairs and climbed back into the passenger side of the car Cole had pre-booked. After a short trip, the driver pulled up in front of BridgeClimb Sydney. She entered the office and lined up to speak to one of the ticketing staff. The eager-looking teenager confirmed Cole had reserved tickets for them to do a twilight bridge climb.

So Cole. Then again, maybe he'd make it memorable, romantic, and propose at the peak?

Hope sighed and checked her watch: 5:45 PM. Only fifteen more minutes, and she'd see him. Her heart swelled with excitement, and she took a seat with a clear view of the front door.

She waited.

And waited.

And waited.

Six fifteen.

Six thirty.

Late. He'd never been late. Not for the entire time

they'd been together. Panic chewed through her nerves. She rummaged around in her handbag and retrieved her phone, but no message. Something must have happened to him. It could be traffic, but if he were held up, he'd have let her know. Unless his phone battery died.

Hope selected his number from the top of her favorites list and stared at the screen, waiting for the call to connect. His phone rang and rang and rang, then went to voicemail.

"You've reached Cole Sparks of Sparks Fly Enterprises. Leave me a message and I'll get back to you as soon as I can..."

Beeeeep.

"Cole, it's Hope. Where are you? Are you okay? I'm worried. Please give me a call when you get this message. Love you." She pressed the red "call end" button and focused on the front door, scrutinizing every person who entered.

"Miss? You're scheduled for your climb in fifteen minutes."

She jerked her head to the side, the silent phone still clutched in her shaking hand. The eager ticket boy from before stood patiently awaiting her reply. "Okay."

"You'll need to come with me for your orientation."

"What about my boyfriend? He hasn't arrived yet."

His smile looked kind and reassuring. "We'll send him up as soon as he gets here."

She followed the lanky young man upstairs, and he handed her a blue-grey-and-black jumpsuit. "You can get changed in the dressing room, then put your bag, clothes, watch, and any tissues in the combination locker.

"Once you're done, come back out and go into the projection room where there's a short safety video.

Your guide will then come and collect you, get you all harnessed up, and you'll be ready to go. Any questions?"

Yes. Where's Cole? But the poor kid couldn't answer that. "Do I have to leave my phone?"

"Yes. Sorry. It's for everyone's safety."

"I understand." Sort of. Rationally, it made sense, though not so much emotionally.

She couldn't stop trembling. The vibe felt totally wrong. She had no clear evidence to support her unsettled feelings, and yet, she couldn't ignore them. Fear prickled under her skin like cactus needles.

Hope changed, checked her phone one last time before locking it away with the rest of her possessions, then joined the small group of climbers in the projection room. Instead of watching the video, she stared at the door, willing Cole to arrive.

The film ended and they were ushered out to grab their harnesses.

Still no Cole.

The group lined up at the entrance to the tunnel, and she made sure she connected last to the safety line. They passed through the original bridge foundations before stepping out onto the iconic Sydney Harbour Bridge.

Most people would have been impressed, overjoyed. But not Hope. Instead of enjoying the experience, she kept turning her head, only half listening to the guide.

They scaled the outer edge of the bridge, stopping at various points to admire the view of the Opera House and the harbor, and to take the obligatory, professional photos for later purchase. Probably the real reason why mobile phones weren't allowed.

But no matter how magnificent the view, she couldn't relax, couldn't appreciate it. Not without Cole.

Not when he'd organized the whole thing and said he'd be there, right alongside her.

Had he tried to call while she climbed over Circular Quay? Instead of making the most of the climb, she fixated on getting back to her locker to check if he'd left a message.

The golden sun disappeared over the pink-purple horizon, and darkness descended over the city. Artificial lights blared, replacing the day's soft, natural sunshine. She hurried down the last few steps, disengaged her harness, and raced to the change room. Hope fumbled with the combination lock, yanked open the locker door, and grabbed her phone.

A text. From Cole. Thank God!

Can't make it. Can't see you again. I'm so sorry.

"What?" She stared at the ten simple, devastating words. Can't see her again? No. Didn't make sense. Not after he'd gone to all this trouble, all this effort. Maybe it was a predictive text error.

She had to speak to him and sort this out, give him a chance to explain. She selected his number and called.

Straight to his sexy-voiced message bank. He could be on another call. She tried again. Straight to voicemail. And again. Maybe he'd dropped out of range or his phone battery went flat. Tension coiled in her stomach, and her pulse raced like she'd had an EpiPen of adrenaline stabbed straight into her heart.

The drive back to the hotel blurred into lights and commotion and confusion. Insecurities edged their way into her jumbled thoughts. Maybe he'd met someone while away. Someone who wouldn't push him for kids and commitment.

Tears stung her eyes like acid. Assumptions,

fueled by fear. She shouldn't jump to conclusions until she had facts. Easy to say, though not so easy to convince her emotions.

As soon as she entered the suite, she switched on the lights and searched every room, her last hope of him showing up there shattered. She snatched her phone out of her handbag and tried him again.

No ring, just the sound of his deep, husky voice, assuring he'd call back as soon as he could. But it had been hours now. She slumped onto the huge, cold, empty bed. Normally he responded quickly, returning messages—especially hers—within thirty minutes max.

The high ceilings that had seemed so romantic and luxurious in the late afternoon sun now made the space feel cavernous, hollow, lonely. She pushed herself up, flicked on the lamp, then trudged back through each room, turning off the glaring overhead lights.

A shower. That's what she needed, to wash off the dirt, worry, and disappointment of the day. She brought her phone with her into the massive bathroom and left it on the vanity. The hot water soothed her tense muscles and drained the negative energy out of her pores and down the plughole.

Bzzzzt. Bzzzzt.

Her phone.

She jumped out of the shower, water still running, and dripped a trail across to the bench. She snatched up her mobile and checked her messages.

You're probably too busy to answer this. Ewww. Don't even want to think about it ;-) Just wanted to hear how your special date went with Cole. The clean bits. Any special news to announce?

Not Cole. Her brother, Brody. Oh, she had some special news to announce—her supposedly kind, considerate boyfriend stood her up. But she wasn't in the mood to talk about it. Not yet. Not until she had a clear explanation, one that made sense.

Hope turned off the water, dried herself, and threw on the only nightwear she'd brought—a barely-there black number she'd hoped would bring Cole to his knees, literally and figuratively.

She placed her phone on the bedside table and lifted the covers. *No clothes in bed.* His commanding voice, the one that set her libido skyrocketing, sounded in her head. How she loved that rule, the heat and rub of his skin turning her into a shameless, wanton hussy.

Not tonight.

She shivered, afraid and bewildered and alone. She plucked her phone off the bedside table and called him again. And again, straight to voicemail. She hung up. He may be her boyfriend, but she didn't want to sound like a stalker. Instead of leaving another worried message, she sent a text.

Hey Cole, your phone keeps going to voicemail. Is everything okay? Please let me know you're all right. I miss you. Love always, Hope xox

She pressed send before she could overanalyze and change her mind, then checked her social media accounts and e-mails. Nothing too exciting. Nothing from Cole. She closed her eyes and tried to sleep. Maybe she'd wake up to a message.

****

A shaft of early morning sunshine sliced through a split in the curtains like a blowtorch. Hope clawed her way from dozing to conscious. It took her a few disorientating moments to remember where she was, to remember yesterday's strangeness.

She patted her hand over the comforter until she found her phone, face down. She gripped it, her heart pounding, eager for a message, though unsure she wanted to read it if it contained bad news. Whether it did or didn't, she needed to know the truth, even if it hurt.

She flipped her phone over, and the notification light flashed a steady green. Hope stared at the black screen, pressed a button to deactivate sleep mode, and refreshed the display. Thirteen notifications. Three from Facebook, five from Twitter, two from Instagram, two from her personal e-mail, and one text. From Cole.

Ambivalence crammed her chest and she clicked into his message.

Please don't call or text anymore. It's over between us. I'm so sorry.

The phone fell out of her hand and hit the bed with a soft *thud*. Over? No. It couldn't be. Everything had seemed fine on the twenty-first. Something must have happened after that. But what? And why wouldn't he confide in her? She had to talk to him. She picked up her phone and selected his number.

One ring, then straight to his voicemail. Did he see her name and cancel the call or was she … blocked? She tried a second time. After one ring, it went to his voicemail again. Then she called his home phone.

Disconnected. What the hell…? It was like she'd dropped down into an alternate reality, transforming her positive, wonderful life into a nasty, negative nightmare.

Had her questions about kids and the seriousness of their relationship scared him off? Sent him running into another woman's arms? Could that be why he'd shut her out? Guilt? Fear? What else could explain his actions?

One minute he'd planned an intimate weekend away and the next it seemed like he'd tried to do everything he could to avoid her, to eradicate her from his life like she, all of a sudden, meant nothing to him.

And if that's what he'd aimed for, he'd

succeeded.

Drained of all hope, she gave up.

Chapter Three
Reinvention

Six months later…

Fuck.
Fuck, fuck, fuck, fuck, fuck.
Cole folded forward in his new, electric-adjusting, king-size bed. His legs shook, spasmed. He'd only been discharged from the hospital a few days ago and had already established a routine.

Stretch. Catheter. Shower. Breakfast. Catheter. Work. Lunch. Catheter. Work. Dinner. Catheter. Work. Catheter. Bed.

Or the alternate day, like today—toilet and shower. Three hours of agony and frustration. Although not quite the electric chair, his shower commode definitely met the definition of an instrument of torture.

He pressed into his bloated stomach. Yep, time for the toilet. He grasped his leg and lifted it onto the wheelchair footplates, pushed one palm into the mattress and the other onto the far side of the wheelchair seat, raised his butt off the bed, and swung into his wheelchair.

After he positioned himself all the way back, he pressed on his abdomen again. A sudden, sharp pain sliced through his bladder and shot down his legs, starting off another shuddering spasm.

Sweat erupted on his forehead, and just as the pain began to settle, a slight tingle, a ghost of the I-need-to-piss sensation he used to feel, zinged in his bladder, increasing the urgency.

Strange. Maybe it was a different sort of spasm—or the start of another urinary tract infection?

Welcome to his new disabled life.

No longer did he have the luxury of spontaneity. Before that last, life-changing climb, he'd totally taken his freedom for granted. Now every activity, everything he participated in, revolved around his physical needs. It was fucking frustrating, but he'd quickly learned he had to get his basic requirements met first or else he wouldn't be able to function. He wouldn't be able to survive.

Cole propelled into the charcoal-and-white wet room, grabbed a catheter from the mirrored medicine cabinet, peeled off the sticker, opened the packet, and pressed the sticky attachment onto the side of the cistern.

He returned to the basin and used hand sanitizer to clean his hands. Then he exposed his limp cock and tucked the waistband of his black boxer briefs underneath his balls.

The cruel irony. His dick made an appearance more now than before the accident. Using a medical-grade wipe, he cleaned and sterilized the tip of his cock, returned to the toilet, and inserted the catheter. Urine started to flow.

At least the accident hadn't impacted his work. As CEO of his own game software development company, he only needed computer access. And since his fall, he'd stayed hidden, working from his hospital bed until the spinal rehab team discharged him home. No one could know what had happened. He'd paid to make sure of that. The last thing he wanted was pity.

The creation of his virtual reality game, *Intimacy World*, had shown he could continue to succeed… Just not in the romance department. He shouldn't complain. In fact, he should be grateful. He'd met some wonderful women over his lifetime and had indulged in some sensational sex.

And that year with Hope, right before everything

went to shit, had been the best year of his life. He may not ever feel his cock again or the incredible elation and post-release euphoria, but at least he had the experiences, the memories.

He flushed the toilet, washed his hands, and had some breakfast in his wheelchair-accessible, black-and-stainless-steel kitchen. Prior to the disastrous mishap, he'd chosen fittings and furnishings for their aesthetics, whereas now his choices were all about functionality, practicality. Adjustable benches and sinks, pull-out drawers and baskets, and Lazy Susan corner cupboards were required for maximum accessibility and independence.

After he did the dishes, and his agonizing toilet-shower routine, he pushed to his computer to make the final adjustments on *Intimacy World* before his physio friend, Jeb, arrived.

His phone buzzed. Time for a pressure lift. He braced his hands on either side of his seat and pushed up, so his butt lifted off his pressure-relieving cushion, allowing blood flow back into his blood vessels and preventing skin breakdown.

After two minutes, he immersed his butt back into the pressure-care cushion and reviewed the recommended game changes. Not a day passed where he didn't question what he'd done. Pushing Hope away. He'd been a blockhead in how he'd handled things, but he justified his actions by convincing himself he hadn't wanted her to suffer long term. He loved her too much.

There were consequences to every decision, and now, outside of his work, he was fucking miserable. He kept trying to assure himself he'd learn to live with the massive changes to his situation. However, she didn't have to. Hope shouldn't have to pay the price for his poor choices.

He clicked into his Web browser and did a search for Hope. A page of photos flooded his screen, all with her looking glamorous, though he preferred her in her natural state, with no makeup, her long dark hair cascading over her bare shoulders, her emerald-green eyes filled with desire and love and focused solely on him.

If his dick worked, right now he'd have a mega hard-on.

The stunning designer range of clothes she wore for work made her look super sexy, though he preferred her in casual gear or, even better, naked. The real Hope. In all the shots she stood alone, *thank fuck*, outside of a few past pictures of them together.

God, they made a great couple. *Made*, past tense. He had no right to be glad she still appeared single, seeing he'd given her up and supposedly wanted to see her happy. However, his head and heart disagreed about what was best.

He closed the page, leaned his elbows on the height-adjustable desk, and dropped his face into his hands. His accident hadn't only caused physical changes. It also morphed him into a fucking emotional mess.

Hopefully, between the intensive home rehab program he intended to start, and his work, he'd have little time to think of much else. He aimed to focus on improving, on recovery and getting his life back on a fulfilling track.

Given his fucked-up situation, he'd had to move on, both relationship and location-wise. The good thing about shifting to Edgecliff, Sydney, was no one knew where to find him.

The reason why he'd relocated from his Neutral Bay historic home had nothing to do with that, though. He could never have returned to his old place. Not now that he relied on a wheelchair for mobility. Too many stairs, and he couldn't do stairs. Not anymore.

One thing the move didn't do—stop the memories of Hope waking up in his bed all disheveled from a night of lovemaking and little sleep. His changed mobility restricted so many things, created so many more far-reaching effects. One stumble, one short moment, had fucked up his whole life.

A knock on the door broke his descent into despair. He lifted his head and pushed away thoughts of the past. He'd spent most of his first few months in the hospital pulling himself out of that dark hole with the help of Jeb, the spinal team, and especially the psychologist.

"Cole, it's Jeb."

Ten already. Shit!

He set his computer to sleep, propelled to the door, and opened it. His long-time physio friend greeted him with a large, contagious smile and ducked his head to step inside. The guy was always on time, always around when he needed him. Had helped him through plenty of mountain-climbing injuries and women troubles over the past few years.

Not that Jeb gave away much about his relationships. With the snippets Cole had pieced together, he deduced that the guy had pretty much been celibate since he lost his fiancée a few years ago. He got it. He could empathize with his mate, but Jeb was well overdue to get back on the dating horse and definitely due to get laid.

His friend's pale blue, almost silver eyes studied him, then the surrounds. A mountain of a man, muscled and tanned and fit all year round, he stood out. Add to that his unusual eye color and the badass bleeding-heart tattoo on his left bicep and he became even more imposing, striking. "How are things? How's the new place? You all settled in?"

Settled in. Interesting concept. Would he ever settle into his new lifestyle? "Is this twenty questions or a physio session?"

Jeb's laugh shook his entire six-foot-four frame. An easygoing, no shit, perpetually happy guy, his laugh spread joy through his whole body and radiated out to anyone within a fifty-meter radius. "Both."

"The place is good. Great location, allows me to be pretty independent, self-sufficient. I can work from home." *Keep hiding from society, from Hope.*

"Good to hear. Though, doing some community access stuff with you would help heaps. It'd build your physical and emotional strength and endurance."

"Not happening." No way. Cole could hardly cope with his circumstances, so he absolutely did not need more negative attention from others. And that included showering him with sympathy, or standing by him out of pity, a sense of obligation. "Would you like a drink before we start?"

"Nice deflection. No, thanks." Jeb sat on the black leather, three-seater lounge, put some TheraBands beside him, and leaned back. With his long legs and size sixteen shoes eating up the space, Cole's living room seemed to shrink. "Hopefully you'll soon change your mind about getting back out into the world."

Look who was talking—Mr. Self-Imposed Monk, unable to move on himself. Seemed like he and Jeb would be working on each other.

"To have the best chance of a good recovery, I suggest two one-hour sessions a day. We could keep this one at ten and do the afternoon one at three. What do you think?"

"I'll do whatever you recommend … as long as it

entails me staying at home. You're the expert with this stuff." Money wasn't an object, and he'd known his sincere, honest friend long enough to know he wouldn't take the piss.

"All right. I reckon we start with some stretches. I'll go through them passively with you first, and we'll work up to you doing them actively wherever you can. It's important to retain your muscle strength and range as much as possible."

Actively? Did that mean Jeb believed there could be partial, possibly even full recovery? He fucking hoped so, but it wasn't always about hope. Most of the time it came down to hard facts and figures. And he had to remember that, had to remember to remain a realist or else risk another retreat into the sinking depths of depression. "I agree."

"Then we'll do some core and upper limb strengthening exercises—"

"Shouldn't we be working on my butt and legs? My arms and shoulders are okay."

"We will. But it's important to prevent injury in your shoulders and wrists in particular. At the moment, you're reliant on them to push you around in your chair. Anatomically, they're not made for such high usage, so pushing technique and shoulder and wrist strengthening and protection are essential."

"Makes sense."

"I'm assuming you got your gym room set up."

"Haven't christened it yet, though. Thought I should wait for you." He'd been itching to resume some fitness work, but wanted to get his mate's professional opinion first. He couldn't afford to be impulsive, *again*, causing further injury and setting himself back. "I know how much you enjoy a new setup ... only to defile it with hard work and sweat."

Jeb laughed, a deep, hearty belly laugh that rumbled through the room. "It's all part of the fun."

"Physio sadism."

"You betcha." He clapped and rubbed his hands together, then grabbed the TheraBands and stood. The guy had always towered over Cole, but now he really looked like a giant. A giant, buff basketball player. He wore his standard physio getup—long shorts and a tight t-shirt—no matter what the weather. "Lead the way. Let's get started."

After forty minutes they still hadn't gotten to butt and leg stuff. "We'll stop here and focus on butt and legs this afternoon," Jeb said, as though reading his mind. "How are you feeling?"

Sweat poured down Cole's face and rolled between his bare shoulder blades and pecs, even though he'd done less than five percent of his pre-accident workout. "Tired, but good." Well, as good as could be expected for someone who couldn't feel his legs or cock.

"Can you show me your bed?"

Cole schooled his most serious facial expression, struggling to stop his lips from curving up into a smile. "All these years and I never realized you felt that way. I thought I made it pretty clear payment for your services would be through a monetary transaction."

He chuckled and slapped a meaty hand on Cole's shoulder. "Come on, mate. I promise you won't regret these last fifteen minutes."

"So, there'll be a happy ending?"

"If you're good." Jeb's eyes sparkled with mischief, his innuendo-filled retort matching Cole's. Thank fuck they could still joke around, still be the buddies they always were. Their friendship hadn't changed after the accident, unlike his relationships with so many others. And he was so fucking grateful.

They entered his bedroom at the far end of the hall.

Jeb pulled back the bedspread and pressed his hand onto the mattress. "Is that latex?"

"Yeah. The occupational therapist said it provided good pressure relief."

"It does. You don't need anything too high level, because you're pretty fit and mobile. It's got some firmness in it, too, which is perfect. It'll allow me to do your remedial massage here. Then you can stay in bed for a bit after I leave and relax, maybe even have a short nap."

He stepped back so Cole could position himself alongside the bed. "As you heal and build up your endurance, you'll be less tired. Now, let's see how you transfer on."

Cole did as he asked and got some "good" and "that's it" positive reinforcement from his friend. It was the most encouraged he'd felt since the fall.

Jeb grabbed the bed remote. "Lay near the edge of the bed, on your stomach, no pillow, arms by your sides, your head either facing me or pointed away. Yep, stay right there." After adjusting the bed height, he started with some firm yet soothing strokes on Cole's upper back, relieving muscle tension he hadn't even realized he had. "So, how's work going?"

"Good. Great, really." It had been the one steady thing, the one reliable routine that helped keep him somewhat sane through the whole fucked-up situation. Not his parents. Not that he could ever rely on them. They'd lived up to his emotionally absent expectation, too busy on their European holiday to return.

His mum had asked if he needed them and he didn't. He'd grown up pretty much looking after himself, so why would he require their tokenistic support now?

They meant well, but they'd never been the overly affectionate type.

"Did you finish the virtual reality game you were working on?"

"Just about. I received the last bit of feedback from testers this morning. All the components I tried seemed to work. Though, one I couldn't test myself."

Jeb increased the pressure and moved along Cole's spine, zeroing in on tight spots and trigger points. "Which one?"

"I created a cock sleeve."

Jeb's hands stilled. "A cock sleeve?" He sounded surprised but fascinated.

"It works like the gloves I told you about. Basically, you put the sleeve on and the sensors correlate to the game so you feel anything you rub or touch. But because I can't feel my cock…" He cringed and hoped his mate didn't notice.

Jeb resumed his skilled massage. "You needed someone who could, to trial it and give you final feedback."

He appreciated his friend's matter-of-fact response, that he didn't go into counselor mode and ask how he'd been coping with a defective dick. Talking about it wouldn't change reality.

Apparently, Cole could still have sex, but wouldn't feel a damn thing. And the chance of coming was close to zero. So, instead, he focused on living with the limitations and finding alternative routes to pleasure. "Exactly."

"Sounds to me like three-D porn."

Cole laughed. "Some people will probably see it that way, mate. But no. It's so much more than that. This is about the player starring in his own fantasy, not just imagining it, not just watching, actually participating and feeling … where possible."

"How come you didn't ask me to be a tester? I'm happy to help out wherever I can." His teasing tone also incorporated a dose of truth. Most guys Cole knew would line up for the chance to give it a try.

"I bet. Sorry to disappoint. I only use qualified testers to assess the software and game experience overall." Hope's gamer brother, Brody, would have been ideal. Spina bifida had put him in a wheelchair, and he was totally switched on when it came to game technology. Brody and those in similar situations formed the core of his target group.

He'd agonized over whether to contact the guy and ended up deciding against it. Even though Brody could have helped him with fine tuning the game and possibly given him some tips on how to deal with being in a chair, he couldn't have any link to Hope. She already provided support to her brother, so Cole didn't want to add to her burden.

"What about women who want to play?" His mate's question jolted him out of his excuse-filled thoughts. Trust Jeb, Mr. Equality, to be the first bloke to ask about options for the ladies. Maybe he had someone in mind he wanted to go a few sexual rounds with via virtual reality. At least it would be a start.

"I've got an idea for a clitoral hood and vaginal dildo-style device, but they're still in the design stage."

"I'd have been disappointed if you didn't." The muscle kneading increased, heating up Cole's skin and further relieving the tension. "So, tell me about the game."

"It's made up of dating worlds that a player works their way through, from meeting someone, to going for a walk on the beach, to kissing, hugging, fucking. They come up against challenges along the way, like rejections, nasty exes, car breaking down, etcetera."

"Does it cater for sexual and gender diversity?"

Cole wanted to make the game as accessible as possible, and so had asked himself those sorts of questions and conducted a consultation with a diverse range of gamers and non-gamers. The feedback turned out to be invaluable.

"Absolutely. A player chooses their sexual preference, age, gender, and personality, based on the sixteen Myers Briggs types, and what they're seeking in a partner—age, appearance, personality—and the game configures accordingly."

"And does that include a variety of sexual practices such as BDSM, threesomes, foursomes, orgies..." Jeb didn't even miss a massage beat. Not unusual. The guy had a history of asking all sorts of open, curious questions; he just avoided answering them when they were directed at him.

"All of the above and more. You can play on your own or go online and compete against or pick up others. But the aim isn't just so people can get off, though that is pretty important. It's also to challenge beliefs and build some skills and confidence, especially around problem solving and dealing with diversity and rejection that can then be used in the real world, to achieve real success."

Big, warm palms paused on the middle of Cole's back. "That's pretty incredible, Cole. Groundbreaking. It's going to help so many people."

Including himself. Cole's situation had been a massive driver in starting the project.

Jeb recommenced the rubdown.

"That's the plan. Playing, learning through fun. Best way to learn."

A jolt of sharp pain seized Cole's muscles and he stiffened. Jeb kept going and the tension and agony eased, the guy's hands shifting between aggravating discomfort and a soothing balm.

Cole's game was on track, but his life lagged a fair way behind. If he had a clearer prognosis, it would make it easier to plan. Rationally, if not emotionally. "Can I ask you a recovery question? And I need you to be totally honest with me."

"Sure. Shoot. But I can't guarantee I'll be able to give you the most accurate answer." The guy's fingers and thumbs were no longer gentle, now digging in like weapons of torture. Digging in to try to unearth function.

"Your physio perspective is all I ask. I'm six months post accident. What's the best I'm... Owwww! Fuck. Sorry. That bloody hurts."

"I know." Jeb's calm, mellow voice sounded almost meditative. "But it'll improve the pain. Eventually. In terms of your condition, it's hard to know how much more improvement to expect. Each spinal cord injury is unique to each person, so tends to have a unique path of recovery. My recommendation is to keep going with intensive rehab to maximize results.

"I've heard stories of people who've had spinal shock for over a year, and as the swelling subsided, they regained function. Even if you have permanent damage at L-five, there's still room for further muscle reconditioning."

Jeb's hands pressed and kneaded lower along Cole's hypersensitive spine, his legs jumping and jolting with reactive spasms. Even with the discomfort, he persevered. He pushed through, hoping his friend would press the right button for a magical fix.

Magical fix. If only. The odds were less than winning the lottery. Success really came down to hard work, mental toughness, and resilience. Mountain climbing and his stint through inpatient rehab had taught him that. Short-term, fucking-excruciating pain led to long-term, function-building gain.

Cole's head pressed into the mattress, and his hands grasped and twisted the black satin sheet. Cold sweat broke out on his skin, and his heart hammered. The pain magnified, shooting through him like an electric current, and he stifled an agonizing groan.

Jeb finally stopped prodding, and a wave of relief rolled through Cole's body, like the rush of endorphins when he reached the pinnacle after a treacherous, testing mountain climb.

A testing mountain climb. So much more than just the physical, so much more than man versus nature. Each rock-climbing expedition had given him a chance to prove to himself and show his parents, and the world, he was worthy, in control.

A man worthy of love, a risk taker, overcoming challenges, obstacles, destined to achieve great things not attributed to his wealth, good looks, or social standing. Little did he know, his thirst for ever escalating challenges would lead him to the greatest, uphill struggle of his life.

"How do you feel?"

How did he feel? Like he'd been hit by a truck, then pumped with some high-grade painkiller. "Exhausted."

"How's the pain?"

Cole closed his eyes and did a mental scan of his body. "Less. Though I'm not sure if that's because you've stopped your physio torture disguised as remedial massage."

He laughed and placed a calming hand on Cole's shoulder. "A combination of that and therapeutic touch, I'd say. The positive effects should last a few hours. As long as you take it easy. No heavy lifting, no bending into awkward positions, no overreaching, and keep transfers and pushing yourself in your wheelchair to a minimum. And that also means no additional workouts at the moment. Can you do that?"

"Anything you say, boss." His tone sounded brash, but he'd follow recommendations. He'd do whatever it took to get the best results. Except re-enter society.

"Good to hear you know who's in charge."

With his head turned the other way, Cole couldn't see his mate, but knew the exact self-satisfied grin he'd be sporting.

"Urgghh." His over-the-top theatrical groan earned him one of Jeb's contagious chuckles.

"Seriously, the main aims of your program will be joint protection, pain management, and to build strength and endurance to increase your safety and independence with everyday tasks. So, it's essential you don't overwork or you'll go backward instead of forward.

"It's about balancing activity with rest. If you overdo it, you need to promise me you'll be honest. I need to know how you're feeling and what's contributed to that so I can review and adjust your sessions."

"Makes total sense. I promise to be good. Well, as good as I can be." Something about mucking around, about using humor, helped distract from the pain.

"We'll see." He removed his hand, and cool air hit Cole's clammy skin. Jeb grabbed the bedspread and lifted it over him, shutting out the cold. "Stay underneath. It'll keep you warm, help you relax, and allow you to rest. Make sure you get up and eat something at least an hour before our afternoon appointment. I'll check in with you when I get back. As I said, I'll let your pain and fatigue guide treatment."

Water gushed in the basin. His friend had to be in the en suite washing his hands. The squeak and groan of floorboards announced his return.

Drowsiness hit Cole like when he'd taken Valium together with a sleeping tablet in the hospital, and he couldn't even lift his head. "Casch-you-lader." His voice sounded soft and slurred and faraway, and he fell into a comatose sleep.

Chapter Four
Difficult Decision

TV studio, September

"Hope. Hope!"

She jolted her head up and all her colleagues around the boardroom table—scattered with pens, papers, and take-away lattes—stared. At her. With an are-you-crazy look. She tapped her pen onto her notepad covered in dark, scrawly, jagged doodles. No discernible notes. *Shit.*

Hope's boss stood at the head of the table, in front of the white Smart Board with inbuilt projector, her presentation whirring in the awkward silence. Hope knew that glare.

The woman used her signature look, the one that said no one's indispensable, on those not paying attention, not pulling their weight. Hope had seen it directed at several others, the known slackers, though never at her. She'd always been so conscientious.

Until that fateful Christmas Eve.

Cole changed that.

She'd lost her drive when she lost him.

A sea of frustration and rage seethed inside her. Her body tensed, protested. She hated to admit he'd meant so much to her, still did, but it was true. "Sorry. Um, yes?"

The woman advanced on her like an army general leading troops into battle. "I said, I put you forward to present the Innovations in Virtual Reality award at the Excellence in Software Development ceremony in December."

What? One minute the woman looked like she'd

fire her, and the next she offered her best gig to date. "Thank you, um…"

"*Intimacy World* is one of the strong contenders and…"

Intimacy World. Cole's virtual reality game? The game he'd gone on to finish with rave reviews after he split from her, while she only just managed to tread minor TV personality water. Her chest tightened, espresso-coffee-scented air straining to pass in and out of her suffocated lungs. Had the oxygen suddenly been sucked from the room?

She stared at a serene garden spot through the window beside her boss and focused on regaining control of her breathing before she hyperventilated.

No. She couldn't do the presenter job. Not that one. Any job but that one. She couldn't possibly see Cole. Not in person, not after how things were left between them.

A tremor shook through her like a Richter scale seven earthquake. Her pen dropped out of her hand and clacked on the glass-topped table. All she could manage was a vehement shake of her head.

"Hope. Hope? Stop gazing out the window and look at me." Her boss pulled the autocratic voice out of her performance management arsenal.

Hope's dry throat made it almost impossible to swallow, and her breathing bordered on panic attack. She glanced at Ms. Power Dresser, shoulder pads and all.

"You're perfect. You two have a history. It'll make great television, especially if he wins." The woman's eyes lit up wide with excitement, like her money tree had finally flowered.

"I … can't." The words squeezed out through her strangled windpipe.

"Yes, you can. And you will." She spoke to Hope

exactly how a person spoke to a five-year-old or mentally unstable patient. "Remember you lost us the exclusive interview with Cole. You owe me. You owe the station." In other words, don't do this and I can't offer you the promotion to lead presenter on *The Travel Bug.*

"But…" *You promised.* The whole thing screamed of blackmail. Not that she could prove anything. And arguing wouldn't get her anywhere.

The woman's steely, unwavering gaze was disconcerting, like she was studying Hope under a microscope. For a millisecond, her boss's eyes flashed with pity. Possibly even … empathy? "All right, I'll let you think about it."

Within moments, her demeanor returned to her trademark cold ruthlessness. "However, you'll need to give me your answer by five PM Friday. No later."

Hope sank into her seat. How generous. Tomorrow. She had until tomorrow to decide if she wanted to advance her career and break the remaining pieces of her heart, or refuse and lose years of sacrifice and endless hours spent building to this moment.

****

"Brodes. Brody. Answer the door. It's Hope." Okay, it was ten PM, but she had to talk to someone about her disastrous day. And who better than her younger brother, her confidant … who'd probably already gone to bed. Maybe with a woman… *Oh, shit.*

The door eased open, a sleepy-eyed Brody on the other side, still dressed in his characteristic hipster gear—black jeans, white t-shirt, and black shirt with rolled-up sleeves. But no woolen beanie today. "Come in, sis." He rolled back in his wheelchair to let her pass.

"Did you fall asleep in your clothes, in your chair? How about your skin…" He should know better after spending six months in bed trying to heal a pressure injury on his bony butt.

"Please don't go all Mum on me. I just dozed off for a few minutes."

His huge TV screen blared with screensaver images every few seconds. Eiffel Tower, Colosseum, Big Ben…

He'd been gaming. He spent way too much time on it these days. Brody needed to get out there, into the real world or else he'd never get any intimacy—without paying for it—never meet a decent woman. Yeah, like she could lecture him on that when she refused to take her own advice.

Snowscape, colored beach boxes, gondola in Venice…

Instead, she'd been just as guilty of delving into the computer world. Not a day passed where she didn't check the Internet for Cole news. Outside of a couple of print stories about *Intimacy World*, there'd been nothing on him since the day he broke off their relationship.

Not one new photo, candid or otherwise. He'd seemingly vanished behind the high-security-prison-style gates of his business, like Willy Wonka, and she was Charlie Bucket searching for a golden ticket.

Who did that? Tormented themselves, unable to let go after someone they loved made it clear they didn't want them anymore. Only a masochist. And she took top spot on the emotional-pain-provides-a-warped-sense-of-pleasure list.

Lush forests, Great Wall of China, Machu Picchu … where she and Cole had dreamed of going. Together. A selfie of her and Cole smiling, giddy with happiness when they reached Federation Peak…

"You should remove that," she said, choking back a restrained sob in her suddenly constricted throat.

Brody rolled in next to her. "Remove what?" The

screensaver had moved on to more pretty, non-Cole pictures.

"The photo of me and Cole. Any photos of me and Cole. It's over. We're over. It's been nearly a year." Okay, more like nine months, the gestational period for the baby they'd never have.

Mounting tears prickled behind her eyes, but she refused to cry. She'd already done too much of that. All part of the grief cycle, except she kept cycling between denial, anger, bargaining and couldn't get past depression.

If she didn't sort herself out soon, she'd have to see a psychologist. Speaking to a mental health expert to learn new strategies and challenge any lingering, dysfunctional thinking was her last resort to help break the Cole spell.

"I think you need a drink." Alcohol was his best deflection technique. Spirits. Well, they worked on her. Every time. Lowered her inhibitions, loosened her lips. Brody knew that, too, knew she'd spill the details after just a few sips.

Before she could reply, he wheeled into the kitchen and came back a couple minutes later nursing two neat scotches between his spina-bifida-withered thighs that he'd learned to hide behind cool pairs of jeans. He handed over a glass. "Scull."

Hope threw her drink back and reveled in the cleansing alcohol burn down her throat. She put her empty glass on the coffee table, and he put his next to it.

"Better?"

"Give me a minute." By the height of the scotch in her glass, she guessed he'd poured her a double shot, so it should kick in… *Ah…*

Brody angled himself toward her, grabbed a cushion off the couch, and put it on his lap. He propped his forearms on top and searched her eyes. "What's going on, sis?"

"My boss asked me to work at the Excellence in Software awards in December."

His face beamed with a proud smile. "That's awesome."

She slumped her shoulders forward and sighed. "To present the Innovations in Virtual Reality award, where Cole's been nominated for *Intimacy World*."

"And?"

"I can't."

He rolled in closer, grabbed her hand, and squeezed. "Yes, you can."

"What if he wins?"

"You can handle it. You're professional. It's a chance to show him how well you're doing."

"I'm not, though. And he'll know." Cole could always read her state of mind, except her desire to have children and hear him say *I love you* and propose. But maybe that's because he'd planned to break up. He didn't seem to know what it took to work in a successful, long-term romantic relationship.

It's not like his parents had demonstrated a deeply loving partnership. She'd never even met them, and her relationship with Cole had supposedly been serious-ish. From what he'd said, they'd hardly been around while he was growing up, too preoccupied with themselves and their independence and freedom.

He'd been raised by a nanny and had spent his life taking risks, desperate for attention, desperate to prove himself, thinking his strength of character and self-sufficiency would make him lovable. And it did, but he offered so much more than that. She'd tried to tell him, show him but...

"Well, thank him then."

What? "Thank him?"

"Yeah." Brody gestured toward the massive wall-mounted screen that had now gone into sleep mode. "His game, it's revolutionary. It's changed my life."

"Changed your life? How could a game…"

His chest puffed out, a super-pleased smile on his face. "I'm off my antidepressant meds."

"Should you… I don't know whether… Have you checked with the doctor?"

His hazel eyes shone with a mixture of pride and gratitude. "My doctor, my psychologist, my specialist, and they're all happy about it, happy about my positive progress. And it's all because of Cole.

"The thing is, sis, I know you try and understand my situation, what it's like to be in a chair, but you don't *really* know. And I'm glad you don't. There are a lot of things that suck, make life pretty hard. Don't get me wrong. Overall, things are good. I have great parents, fantastic friends, an amazing sister. And I've learned to focus on the things I can do. The only thing I'm missing is…"

In the dim lamplight, his cheeks went all rosy pink. He squirmed in his wheelchair. "A woman, regular sex." He swallowed, took a breath, and met her gaze. "What's so amazing about Cole's game is it's like he understands. Especially the sexual frustration side."

Hope took in the game-centric room. The now black screen, some sort of special visor-headset thingy, a wireless controller, a long black tube, a couple of black insulated gloves on the coffee table.

"Tell me about the game. How does it work?" How did it help sexually?

"See those two small black boxes mounted on the walls on either side of the screen? They're called base stations and track the movement of the gloves or controller. There's a small link box that connects with the base stations to help with tracking moderation. The headset puts me into the game world."

Hope edged forward on her seat and surveyed the deceivingly simple-looking setup. "Wow. Sounds so high tech."

A wide smile spread across his face and crinkled the corners of his eyes. Joy emanated off him any time he spoke about technology, gaming. "You know me and computers. The great thing about virtual reality is it actually feels real, especially with the gloves. They sense everything you touch. That's how advanced the technology is. And it keeps getting better."

"Incredible. I'm intrigued. Can you give me a rundown of what actually happens in *Intimacy World*?"

Dots of pink reappeared on his pale cheeks. "Ah … well, it kind of works through the dating stages. Meeting at a bar, going for a walk along the beach, holding hands, hugging, kissing, right up to sex."

Now it was her turn to blush. "Right."

She and her brother weren't prudes, but they rarely spoke in depth about the mechanics of sex or what they specifically got up to. Her brother had patchy sensation, and could only manage standing transfers, so sex would be tricky unless he moved into the right position. And found the right woman.

What Brody had explained about the game piqued her interest. She needed to know more, her curiosity driving her past embarrassment. "I'm a bit scared to ask, but what's that long black piece, next to the gloves."

Redness spread like an out-of-control fire along every visible part of his skin. "It goes over my cock. Works like the gloves. So when I—"

"I get it."

A look of amazement and excitement replaced the

awkwardness on his face. "It's so real. You know how hard it is for me to meet interested women so … this helps. It's even helping to build my confidence. I've started chatting with some lady players online, through the game, and I'm thinking of trying the bar scene again and attending events in the real world."

She'd never seen her brother so animated, so happy, so full of hope, and all because of Cole and his ingenuity. How did he know? Maybe one of the designers he worked with or people he consulted in the focus groups had a disability?

Brody held both her hands and looked her in the eye. "You have to present this award. I know the way he broke things off sucked, but it was out of character. He's not a prick. He loved you. He may not have said it, but I could see it in the way he looked at you."

Tears welled in her eyes again and blurred her vision, but she blinked and blinked, trying to force them back.

"Sis, there's no way he'd have done what he did just because you asked him about your relationship and his thoughts on kids. I think something major happened to him and he couldn't cope."

"Something major like what? I spoke to Jeb, and he didn't mention anything."

Brody's eyes widened with disbelief. "You called Jeb, his best mate?"

Oops. "Yeah." One desperate night, after a couple of wines, it seemed like a good idea. She'd just wanted to hear something, anything that might at least give her some closure. But he gave her nothing. Just confirmed Cole was okay. "So, if something serious had happened to him, you'd think he'd have told me."

"Maybe he couldn't. Maybe Cole put a gag order on the guy."

"Maybe. But then what is such a big deal that Cole couldn't tell me himself, tell the person he was so intimate with in every other way?" Anger rose like acid reflux, and she snatched her hands out of his grasp.

"If he'd had a significant change in his circumstances and wasn't coping, I should have been one of the first people he told. I would have offered assistance, provided support, whatever he needed."

"I know. You know. But different people deal with things differently. From the few times I met him, he seemed like a pretty in-control guy. So, I reckon he'd struggle to ask for help. I still struggle to ask for help. I don't want to burden you, and you're my sister."

Hope touched his knobby knee and held his gaze. "You're not a burden. How many times do I have to tell you? I love you. I'd do anything for you."

"Then present this award. If Cole wins, thank him for me. Use the opportunity to find out what happened, even if it's just to get closure." Turbulent waves of worry tossed around inside her stomach and reared up, ready to crash. She didn't want to wuss out and disappoint Brody, but she equally dreaded confronting Cole.

Hope left her brother's house after one AM, more confused than ever. Should she really be entertaining the idea of taking the presenter job, seeing Cole again? Her heart swelled with anticipation at the thought, while her mind stalled with indecision.

How could she ever make it to the acceptance stage in the grief cycle if she allowed herself to nurture hope for an unlikely reconciliation? And if he rejected her, she'd be right back to where she started a year ago, but even more dejected.

She got in her car and drove home to her cold, dark apartment on the fringe of the city, hardly remembering the trip. After a quick shower, she slipped into bed and stared at the silver rays of moonlight shining on the ceiling.

Maybe she should sleep on it, let her subconscious do the work and decide. Should she protect her heart, go with the safe answer and say *no*, or go with her gut, live in hope, and say *yes*?

.

Chapter Five
Facing Challenges

Cole held himself up between the parallel bars in his home gym. His arms shook, taking most of the weight.

Jeb stood in front of him, checking the muscle engagement in Cole's bare legs. "You're doing great."

Bright sunlight shone through the floor-to-ceiling windows and lit up his pasty skin. More muscle flickers seemed to twitch in his quads. Though that could just be his view of the situation through a skewed, high-hopes lens. "I. Need. To. Sit." His voice came out all staccato, weak, raspy.

With his large, solid hands, Jeb braced Cole's hips, blocked Cole's knees with his own, and assisted him into his wheelchair at the edge of the bars. Sweat dripped off Cole's face and created a damp patch on his chest and between his shoulder blades. He gulped air into his stinging lungs and scooted back in his seat.

Jeb crouched and looked him in the eye, the most serious Cole had ever seen him. "There was more movement. There's been improvement. Slight changes, but noticeable, from last week to this week. Have you noticed any other changes?"

Cole glanced down, his distended stomach bulging against the waistband of his black cotton boxers. The washboard abs he'd worked so hard to create—gone. He shook his head, his breathing almost back to a steady rate. "Still no sensation, but more pain. Different pain. Not the burning so much, more like hurting from an injury. Am I making any sense?"

For the first couple months post discharge, the afternoon physio session compounded the positive benefits from the morning, and he regularly went to bed at night rejuvenated and relaxed. But by early morning, his legs and feet were on fire, burning with neurogenic nerve pain.

If the pain meant his sensation was returning, he wouldn't mind. However, it just showed nerve damage, similar to phantom limb syndrome in amputees. Then in the last few weeks, the burning had receded, replaced by other pain. Still severe at times, it continued to impair his sleep but affected his body in other, less consuming ways.

"Total sense. Sounds like there might be some nerve regeneration."

Could he allow himself to hope? "So, the new pain's not a bad sign?"

"Nope. In your case, it's a sign of progress. Though we'll need to continue to monitor it. Although it suggests positive changes, it's important to keep pain under control or else it'll make everyday tasks hard. It'll have an impact on your general enjoyment of life. And we want to keep you moving in the right direction."

"We do. So ... what's next?"

"I thought we'd finish this afternoon with thirty minutes of TENS machine treatment. Depending on your response, I'll play around with the settings and see if it makes a difference, particularly with the new pain." He stood and stepped out from between the bars, leaving Cole a clear path forward.

"No worries. Sounds good." Trial and error meant possible results. Different things worked in different circumstances when it came to pain and its highly subjective nature. And he was willing to try anything that might help.

He pushed ahead, leading Jeb to his bedroom. The search for effective pain relief had almost become an obsession. It started in the hospital, but he soon exhausted all the options. He came to the conclusion that not all pain could be resolved, especially the unrelenting ache in his heart from losing Hope.

Persistent, scalding nerve pain didn't even have half the agonizing intensity. But her absence wasn't her fault. It was his. All his. And all totally self-inflicted.

Cole transferred onto the bed and lay face down.

His mate set up the pocket-sized TENS machine unit beside him on the bed and placed four electrodes on Cole's back, two on each side of his spine. "Right, we're ready to go. Just going to switch it on ... now."

Tingles buzzed through Cole's skin, and he melted into the mattress. Somehow the electrical nerve stimulation tapped straight into the relaxation center of his muscles and deflated the tension. Although he knew what to expect, Jeb made sure to warn him every time anyway. Always the professional, responsible physio and reliable friend.

"How's that?" Jeb pulled up a chair and sat beside the bed.

Cole closed his eyes. "Good."

"Pain out of ten?"

"Four."

"Not bad."

A large shadow moved across Cole's eyelids and triggered them open.

His friend held the TENS machine and fiddled with the setting adjustments. "I'm hoping by the end of the session it's a three and stays a three for a good thirty minutes or more afterward."

"Me too." He slid his eyes shut.

"So, how's software world domination going?"

The mattress muffled Cole's laugh. "On track. *Intimacy World* got nominated for an Excellence in

Software award."

"No bullshit."

"I even got an invite to attend the ceremony. But I'm not going."

The chair legs scraped across the timber floor, indicating his mate had shifted closer. "You're kidding. You declined?"

"Yeah."

"But it's an excellent opportunity to promote your business—"

"I don't need further promotion." He snapped his eyes open, and his functional muscles stiffened with renewed stress, all the TENS machine benefits undone in seconds. "I'm already doing great, better than great. I can hardly keep up as it is." His defensive tone slashed the air like an ice axe.

Jeb scrutinized him with his all-seeing, almost-silver eyes. "Sounds to me like you're scared."

The truth stabbed him in the heart. There was no point denying it. His mate could see through him like a clear sheet of cellophane. "I am. Hope's one of the presenters."

"Perfect. You should use the situation to speak to her. Tell her the truth. Pushing her away was a major fuck-up. She's a great girl."

His heart clenched so tight it almost fossilized. "That's the problem. She's too kind, too accepting. Too wonderful."

"What's the problem? I don't see a problem."

A long sigh spilled from Cole's lungs. "She'd have stood by me."

A crease of confusion marred Jeb's forever-tanned forehead. "And? What's wrong with that? It's part of a good partner's role description."

"I don't want pity."

The look on Jeb's face said exactly that. Pity mixed with a firm edge of frustration. "She loved you, Cole. Anyone could see it. So, yeah, she would have supported you. She would have wanted to help you through this. But you didn't give her a chance. You didn't give her a choice. Was that fair? For either of you? Unless you didn't really love her."

"Of course I did. Still do. Very much. And that's why I set her free. I didn't want to chain her to me. I didn't want her to feel forced to stay. I'm no longer the man she fell in love with." Yet, he couldn't stand the idea of her with anyone else.

"Rubbish. Fucking rubbish. And you know it."

"She loved Cosmo-Bachelor-of-the-Year Cole, Mr. Adventure-Man Cole, successful-businessman Cole."

Jeb studied him like he was the biggest, stupidest idiot. "Your accident has affected your body, but it hasn't changed who you are. You're still the driven, hard-assed CEO success story I call a friend. Except unlike the majority of successful businessmen, you have a heart."

"And that's why I couldn't lump this on her. I want her to be happy. She wants kids, and I don't even know if I can give her that anymore." It took his accident and the high possibility he couldn't be a father to realize just how much he did want children. With Hope. A woman he wasn't afraid to tell the whole world he cherished and loved.

But only if she still felt the same about him. He didn't want a partner to stick around out of a sense of duty and obligation or because of his status and wealth. And baby-wise, he promised himself he'd be a present not distant parent.

Cole didn't want kids as ornaments or because society said he should. If he was fortunate enough to have them, he wanted to play a significant part in their lives, to be a role model they could look up to, love, respect, and emulate. He wanted to be a parent who made a positive difference, who staunchly showed unconditional love.

Now he regretted downplaying the importance of children in his life—their life—when Hope had asked his opinion about them during their Tassie trip. He'd planned to address her question about the future of their relationship over dinner, after the bridge climb in Sydney, but his fall totally fucked that up.

Cole had continued trawling the Internet daily to check out Hope, fishing for gossip. Still no pictures with any blokes on her arm and, thank fuck, no mention of any new guy's name supposedly linked to her. He couldn't explain the warped pleasure he got, knowing she likely hadn't hooked up with anyone else. Yet. His reaction may be irrational and wrong, but try telling his heart.

"Do you miss her?" Jeb's question broke Cole's rabbit hole of thoughts.

"Of course. So much, I can't even…"

"You can't even what?" His mate's dark gold eyebrows rose, the left always higher than the right when he tried to ram home a point. "Talk to her? Tell her the truth? Listen to me. Explain your concerns. See where it leads. You owe her that. You owe yourself that."

Just the idea had his heart racing so fast he thought it might explode like a bomb in his chest. "I don't know. I'll see."

"Which means you won't change your mind, you stubborn bastard." He pressed a palm on Cole's closest shoulder and stared him straight in the eye. "You still have a chance to redeem yourself. Don't blow it a second time."

Jeb switched off the TENS machine, peeled off the electrodes, and packed it away. "Time for me to go. But I'm not giving up on this. I'm not giving up on you. We'll talk more tomorrow." His tone was don't-mess-with-me stern. He covered Cole with the bedspread and strode from the room.

The front door clicked closed behind his retreating friend. He flopped over onto his back and straightened out his shuddering legs. Cole couldn't have Hope. Not anymore. No matter what his mate said, no matter what Cole's heart craved, he couldn't contact her, couldn't ask her back ... unless he chose the selfish-prick road and took advantage of her love, loyalty, and empathy.

He frequently fought his selfish need to beg her to return, but he refused to admit that out loud, refused to admit he missed her so fucking much it physically hurt. It wouldn't be right getting her tangled up in his car wreck of a life. He wanted her to be with him out of love. And how could she still love him when he was now only half a man.

Chapter Six
That New First Step

Christmas Eve

Cole's alarm sang out some edgy, alternative electronica number, shattering his erotic dream. More like a memory of him and Hope, working their way through the Kama Sutra on a mountaintop. If only he could go back there. If only he had made different choices.

He dipped in and out of dozing, until his gaze slid to the slashed red numbers blazing in his black alarm clock: 9:01. *Fuck*. Jeb would arrive in less than an hour. No time for a shower. He'd have to wait until later.

Cole shot up into sitting, setting off a string of seismic spasms that shook through his paralyzed legs. When they finally settled, pain remained, a combination of throbbing and stabbing that had continued to worsen. At least the burning had reduced. *Thank God.*

He rubbed his eyes, still heavy with a disturbed night's lack of sleep. Just over a year since his life changed forever. Though not in the way he'd planned.

The top bedside drawer beckoned. He slid it open, rummaged past his neatly folded boxer shorts, and reached right to the back. He closed his hand around the small black velvet box and lifted it out. Hope's engagement ring sat inside, taunting him. He flipped the lid open and stared at it, willing time to reverse, to give him a second chance.

He had planned to propose. Instead… The box seemed to burn a hole in his hand, like a charred hot coal. He closed the lid, dropped the ring box back onto his pile of underwear, and slammed the drawer shut. Like he'd slammed shut the relationship door with Hope.

He forced his thoughts away from the spiral into negativity and focused on the distracting task of getting dressed. What used to be a mechanical act took a lot more thought, organization, and planning these days.

With his tracksuit pants and t-shirt on, he transferred onto his wheelchair and did a catheter. Then he propelled himself into the kitchen and put some bread in the toaster. No time for his usual stove-cooked porridge. Maybe he'd make it for lunch. Fuck he hated being behind, hated being a slave to his physical limitations. However, he had no choice.

He pushed to the fridge, and his gaze snagged on the invitation to the software awards. Jeb had worked on him to change his mind and attend the ceremony, but he couldn't be convinced.

His stomach clenched and churned with guilt, unease, disappointment. If he'd done the right thing, why did it feel so wrong? He yanked out the invite from under the *Master of My Own Domain* magnet.

When he'd found out *Intimacy World* made it into the top five nominations for an Excellence in Software award back in September, he was thrilled. His invention was so much more than just a game. It encapsulated a positive, life-changing achievement for him and, he hoped, for many others. Putting it together had been cathartic, a needed diversion, a sort of broad-healing therapy.

His toast popped up.

He shoved the stiff, white invite under his thigh and made his breakfast. Although he'd declined the e-mail invitation, only a couple days later, a hard copy arrived by post. And he'd flipped out.

Not only did he not want to go, not want to see Hope after what he'd done, how he'd changed, but also someone at the station knew his address, knew where he lived. And that someone worked at the same station as Hope.

A secret part of him wished she'd find out, turn up on his doorstep, and surprise him. She hadn't, though. So, either she didn't know or she knew and didn't care.

That's what he'd wanted, wasn't it? For her to move on, find someone else, someone who could give her everything she deserved. Then why did his chest ache like his heart had been ripped from beneath his ribs whenever he thought of her with another man?

He had a sip of coffee, set his cup and toast on the table, and looked out over his lush, green, level backyard. How the fuck had the station found his personal details in the first place? And even more fucking frightening was whether they'd sent any reporters over to spy on him.

After all his hard work to keep hidden, would the "Disabled Cole" story still hit the news and social media, ruin him and the confident, fit, successful-man reputation he'd worked so hard to construct?

His toast and coffee went cold, but he forced them down, like he did the ongoing guilt, anger, and stress. Hope finding out about him through mass media would be devastating. Wrong.

Hence the self-imposed hermit lifestyle— working from home, shopping and paying bills online, forking out exorbitant fees for all his medical and hairdressing appointments to be conducted at his house. The cost was ridiculously high, from a monetary perspective, but worth it to protect his privacy and Hope's feelings.

He screwed up the fancy paper and tossed it in the recycling bin under the sink. Just because he refused to attend the ceremony didn't mean he wouldn't watch the telecast tomorrow night. He had to see if he won. He had to see Hope.

To his great surprise, he made it through his morning physio session without Jeb mentioning *her* once. The post-appointment reduced pain and the accompanying relaxation lasted through to the afternoon session, and he couldn't wait for his mate to push him hard. Physically.

Jeb turned up right at three PM, and Cole led him into the gym. After some warm-up stretches, he had Cole standing between the parallel bars, wearing only his black cotton boxers. It had become his regular afternoon uniform, making it easier for his friend to assess his progress.

"See how long you can stretch it out." He crouched down in front of Cole and palpated his leg muscles, each gentle press eliciting a stab of pain but still no other sensation.

He breathed hard, sweat slathering his skin, the skin he could feel.

"There's good, strong muscle engagement. Can you loosen your grip on the bars?"

Cole's hands clamped down, and his pulse pounded so hard it thumped in his ears. Could he? "Don't know." He had undertaken a lot of risky activities in the past, yet this was the first time he'd experienced paralyzing fear.

"I'm right here. Give it a go. I promise I won't let you fall." Jeb's sturdy gaze and steady voice spurred him on.

"Okay." If he counted himself down, it would give him some time to psychologically prepare. "After three. One." *Fuck.* "Two." He sucked air into his lungs to stop himself from hyperventilating. That's all he needed, to faint in front of his friend. "Three."

He released his grasp, lifting his hands off the

bars for a few seconds, then leaned lightly back on them with his perspiring palms.

"You did it! Well done." Jeb stepped back, still within arm's reach, and assessed him. "Looks like you're taking a good, even amount of weight through your legs and feet. How are your arms feeling?"

"Shaky. But less stressed."

His smile radiated pure joy, as though he was almost as excited as Cole at the outcome. "Excellent. I think you're close to taking a step."

A step? No fucking way. That would be brilliant. No, better than brilliant. It would be fucking amazing. He focused on controlling his breathing, like training for a high-altitude climb. "Even with no sensation?"

"Even without sensation. It seems the nerves controlling your motor function are intact, so all you need to do is rebuild your muscle strength, and watch where you're going. Without sensation, you're going to have to rely more heavily on your vision."

"Don't care. Totally worth it." Cole's legs started to shake, lose strength, putting more pressure on his arms and rebounding to his breathing. "Need. To. Sit."

Jeb's knees blocked his, and his strong, secure hands guided Cole's hips into sitting.

Cole fought to regain even, controlled breaths. He'd done it. He'd stood on his own. Briefly, but it was a start. And all thanks to his mate's expert input and support.

Jeb squatted in front of him. "Great work today. Ready for your massage?"

He couldn't tell whose smile stretched wider, his or his friend's. "Absolutely."

Buzzing with euphoria at his breakthrough, his sense of achievement, Cole almost flew from wheelchair to bed. Once his leg spasms settled he lay on his stomach, arms by his body, head turned to the side. The usual massage drill.

Jeb gently placed his hands on Cole's upper back and curled his fingers over his shoulders, using light pressure with his thumbs, heels of his hands, and fingertips to release tension in Cole's tight muscles.

He began to work his way down, using a combination of pressing and rubbing motions, varying in intensity. "So, the awards are on tomorrow night."

Cole swallowed back the wave of guilt rising in his stomach. "Yeah, that's right."

"Going to watch them?"

"If you were up for an award, wouldn't you?" No way could Jeb have missed his snarky tone. *Shit.*

"Answering a question with a question. I'd say someone's feeling a little uncomfortable. Defensive even."

"I'm fine," Cole said through clenched teeth.

Jeb's thumbs pressed a firm line along the outer edges of Cole's spine. "You know you've fucked up. Big time."

Had he? By refusing to attend the ceremony, he protected Hope and himself. But if that were true, why did he feel so disappointed, so deflated, so fucking weak and stupid?

"I never thought of you as the frightened type. You always took life by the balls."

Jeb was right. Cole had never let anything or anyone scare him, until the accident. It hadn't just knocked his confidence. It had broken it into tiny, jagged shards that felt almost impossible to piece back together.

His friend stopped pressing and placed his hands flat on Cole's lower back. "The true Cole, he's still in here. Somewhere. Beneath the damage." He resumed his physio-manipulation.

"In order to move forward successfully, you have to believe it. You have to realize that what's happened to you isn't you. It doesn't define you unless you let it. Sometimes life deals you a fucked-up hand, but what makes you who you are is how you think and behave, how you cope with hardship, how you treat yourself and others."

And Jeb should know, after the tragic death of his fiancée. He'd experienced pain and loss and grief—not in the same way as Cole, but it still had a significant impact. So much so, he seemed to have gotten stuck in grief, unable to live by his own advice.

When Hope got into matchmaker mode, which had happened frequently while they were together, she offered to set Jeb up with one of her single friends. However, he declined each and every time, saying he was grateful and appreciative but still not ready. But when would he ever be ready to get back into the dating scene, embark on a new relationship? What would be the deciding factor?

Although the trauma of losing his love hadn't affected Jeb's body, the heart-rending situation had impacted on his mind and emotions. He and his fiancée could never be together, whereas Cole still had a chance with Hope. Is that what Jeb was trying to make him see, to reinforce that Cole would be an ungrateful prick if he didn't at least attempt to win Hope back?

Jeb looked him straight in the eye. "Hope rang me, you know."

What? What the fuck? "When? What did you tell her?"

"A little while back, before you got discharged home. I didn't tell her anything specific, obviously. But I wanted to. She's an incredible woman, and I hated not being totally upfront with her. She has a right to know why you called things off. She has a right to know the truth."

Guilt churned in Cole's gut. "What exactly *did* you tell her?"

"That you were okay. She was worried about you. Even after how harsh you'd been."

She was trying to understand. If he'd been in her shoes, he'd have been desperate to try to make sense of things too. "How did she sound?"

"Disappointed, sad, but glad you were all right."

Not just the sexiest, but the sweetest woman Cole had ever known. He'd attempted to reduce her pain by cutting things off without an explanation, short and sharp, like ripping off a bandage.

He'd wanted to shelter her from the knowledge of his disability, prevent additional heartache. But had he inadvertently made the situation worse? *Fuck.* He hadn't foreseen the potential fallout. What had he done?

"Have you ever asked yourself, if the circumstances were reversed, if the same thing had happened to Hope, would you have wanted her to confide in you? Would you have felt obligated to support her, or would you have done it because you cared, because you loved her and wanted her in your life no matter what?"

A rush of words converged in Cole's throat and gushed out like water from a burst dam. "Of course I would've wanted Hope to confide in me, so I could be there for her, to help her in any way that I could. Whether she ended up fully able or not wouldn't have changed my feelings for her."

So why had he assumed she wouldn't feel the same about the changes to him? What made him think if she stayed around it would be out of pity and not love? She wasn't like his well-meaning yet self-absorbed parents, using money as their love currency with little idea of what it took to show they genuinely cared.

"Then there's your answer."

Fuck. Yeah. He'd fucked up. Badly. He should have believed in Hope, believed in what they had, and at least given her the chance to make an informed choice, whether the outcome was in his favor or not. Could he turn things around, or had he left it too late? "You're right. I should've listened to you earlier, but I wasn't ready."

"You are now. So, no excuses for missing any future opportunities. Got that?"

His friend still believed in him, so maybe he did have a chance to make things right. Somehow. "Yes, sir."

Jeb's chuckle vibrated through his large hands and rumbled across Cole's skin. "Good." He finished up the massage and pulled the bedspread over Cole. "It's time for me to get going. I'll be back on the twenty-seventh at ten. In the meantime, if you've got any concerns, call me. Hope you have a restful break and enjoy watching your show."

Enjoy? More like kick himself for not making the most of his opportunities and at least apologizing to Hope.

Jeb washed his hands, collected his physio bag, and left. Although exhausted, Cole pushed himself to shower. Thank fuck his toilet routine was tomorrow. Even sitting on the shower commode for only thirty minutes undid all the physio session pain relief.

His back ached like a bus had slammed into it, crushing the vertebrae and sending aftershocks through his legs and down to the edge of his toes. He'd never shower straight after his physio appointments again. To have any chance of sleeping tonight he'd have to knock himself out with a painkiller and muscle relaxant.

Cole dressed in a clean t-shirt and track pants and transferred back onto his wheelchair. Too fucked to cook, he had a plate of muesli with milk for dinner and parked himself in front of the large screen TV in his cinema room.

A live, Christmas-themed *The Travel Bug* show started and he couldn't turn it off. He had to see Hope. Partway through the program, she sashayed onto the set with a good-looking male co-presenter, and a spear of jealousy jabbed at his heart.

God, she was fucking gorgeous, though a little nervous. Most people probably wouldn't notice it, but he knew everything about her. That manufactured smile and over-wide stare gave her away.

He leaned in to the TV, closer to the stunningly beautiful woman. Dark hair, exotic green eyes, and sexy-as-sin hourglass figure. Nothing had changed ... for her. Not physically. He slumped back in his wheelchair.

Christmas Eve.

A year ago.

He'd stood her up.

Not by choice.

One moment.

Just one moment and his whole life had gone off course like a plane shot down mid-flight.

Crash and crush and crumble.

The show came to a close, but it wasn't enough. He wanted more of her, needed more of her. Fuck, he missed Hope, missed her like he missed his mobility, his mountain-climbing, his freedom.

No more feeling sorry for himself. No more assuming what she wanted, what was best for her. He had to contact Hope. Explain. Beg her for forgiveness. If he didn't try, he'd never know.

It had been a year since he blocked her out of his

life, blocked her number, but he couldn't forget her, couldn't forget it. He grabbed his phone off the coffee table, unblocked her, and typed out a quick text.

Hope, it's Cole. I need to speak to you. Please call me when you get a chance. Or drop by. My new address is…

He sent the message before he could think twice. He'd treated her like crap, so he'd understand if she didn't respond. But this time, he wouldn't give up so easily. He'd keep contacting her until she replied, even if it was to tell him to stop, even if it was to tell him to fuck off.

He doubted she'd tell him to get lost, though, at least not until she had answers. Her curiosity would consume her until she understood what had driven him to call off their relationship.

The next couple of hours, he remained in front of the TV, his mind unable to tune in to any of the programs. Images of Hope and what a fuckhead he'd been swirled around and around in his brain.

Knock, knock, knock.

Cole spun to face the front door. Hope? Couldn't be. She wouldn't come by so late without phoning first … or would she? No. Jeb had probably just forgotten something.

Knock. Knock, knock, knock, knock.

Okay, hang on. "Coming!"

"Cole?"

Hope.

Shit.

His gaze darted around the living room, searching for a MacGyver-style escape option. Sure, he'd invited her to contact him, to come over, but he hadn't thought she'd visit quite so soon.

He thought he'd have more time to prepare. But

how could he ever prepare enough for what he'd put her through? No amount of excuses could compensate for the additional pain he'd caused. He hadn't intended to hurt her, not long term, but the result was still the same.

Either he could make up a bullshit story to avoid opening the door or face his fear. He swallowed the block of stress wedged in his throat. The opportunity had arrived; he had to let her in. He'd promised Jeb. He'd promised himself.

Cole eased the door open, revealing Hope, still decked out in the designer gear she'd worn on the show.

She gasped, slamming her hand to her mouth. "Cole. Oh my … Cole."

Disbelief, concern, pity flitted over her face.

He sank lower into his wheelchair, his condition no longer a secret.

She stepped inside, shut the door, and bent down until her beautiful emerald eyes were equal with his. "What happened? Why didn't you tell me?"

His hand twitched, dying to reach out and touch her. Hope in person was like a just-out-of-grasp narcotic, heightening the craving he'd had for her over the past year. Now that she had come to him, he had to make the most of the situation. He owed her an apology. He owed her the truth.

"I had a fall, coming down Kosciuszko, a few days before…"

"Oh, Cole, I don't—"

"Know what to say?"

She stared at her skyscraper stilettos, then reached for his hand and held it, her heat sending waves of desire through his skin. He'd hoped he'd be immune to her after all this time to allow him to move on if he had to, but his body wasn't on the same wavelength as his mind.

Hope squeezed his hand, and her moist eyes met his gaze. "I wish you'd told me."

"I couldn't. I'm sorry."

Tears erupted onto her cheeks, leaving dark trails of grief. "But we were almost... I could have helped. I could have supported you."

"The accident ruined my life. I couldn't ruin yours too."

"You should have trusted me." She let go of his hand and stood tall, staring down at him, drops of her despair and hurt spotting his pants. "You should have trusted yourself. Look at what you've achieved. You're nominated for one of the most prestigious gaming software awards and you did it all after ... *this*."

She gestured to his wheelchair, his dysfunctional lower body. "What happened to your optimism and sense of adventure, your enthusiasm for life? I loved that about you."

Loved. Past tense. His heart caved deeper into his chest.

She sniffled, sending a fresh wave of tears streaming down her face, leaving tracks of pain etched into her perfect façade. "I saw Brody the other day. I know spina bifida isn't exactly the same as spinal cord injury, but there are a lot of similarities." *So, I understand* wasn't said, but suggested.

"Anyway, for months he's been going on and on about *Intimacy World* and how it's changed his life. He's doing so great now. You should see him. His positive experience is what convinced me to present the award for your category tomorrow night. I planned to thank you even after... For helping my brother."

Not to see him. Of course not. What had he expected after he callously cut her out of his life without any reason? "I'm happy to hear it's made a difference."

"A huge difference. He's been able to stop his antidepressant medication, and he's connecting with people, going out again. Meeting people online and in person."

"That's fantastic." And he really meant it. His game outcomes were exactly as he'd hoped. And Brody was a great guy, an awesome guy. He couldn't think of anyone who deserved happiness more, except maybe the beautiful, caring woman standing before him. The woman he'd hurt. The woman he still loved, would always love.

She swiped at her waterlogged eyes with the back of her hand. "Yeah…"

Her bone-deep sadness crushed his heart. After the accident, he'd broken up with Hope to cut her free. Because he loved her so much, he didn't want her to stick around and suffer.

Until now he didn't realize his assumption had been faulty, skewed, had made her suffer just as much, possibly more. His thinking had been so fucking warped. "About tomorrow night, I won't be there … at the awards."

"Oh … of course." An honest, gut-wrenching, goodbye-forever look replaced the shock and worry on her face. "I should go."

Ah … maybe ending their relationship had been the right decision. He should feel glad, relieved. But he didn't. Not when things had become heartbreakingly clear. "I understand."

It was sympathy, not love.

Chapter Seven
Recommencing the Climb

Christmas Day, and Cole hadn't slept all night. Seeing Hope had reignited all the passion he'd tried to smother, sending his emotions into a torturous tailspin. The tears, the shock and disappointment on her face, the dejected sag of her body, her sudden departure under the weight of his news—all understandable.

Of course she'd run, considering the cruel way he'd broken things off, the insinuation he hadn't trusted her, the fact he was no longer the strong, adventurous, virile man she'd loved.

His phone buzzed and he reached for it on his bedside table. Could it be Hope? Maybe his assessment of her feelings, the conclusion he'd come to last night, had been wrong. Maybe she did still love him and wanted to reconnect. He entered his access code.

A text. From Jeb. Disappointment deflated his heart like a popped balloon.

All ready for tonight? ;-)

No. If he won, what then? How long could he keep on hiding?

Jeb had spoken to him about making the most of opportunities, and another one had presented itself right now. Cole couldn't ignore it, chose not to ignore any of them. Not anymore.

The only way to take a positive step forward required him to push out of his comfort zone. So after sending a quick reply to Jeb, he composed a message to Hope. He'd spent more than enough time assuming, rather than seeking clarity, being sure. He'd spent more than enough time being a coward.

Hey Hope, Thanks again for coming by last

night. It was so good to see you. But that's not why I'm texting. The telecast tonight—come to my place, bring a cameraman and if I win, I'm happy to go live with my acceptance speech. If I lose, I'll do an interview instead. Let me know what you think, Cole x

His head throbbed and his eyes ached with stress and lack of rest. He reread his message, pressed send, and put the phone down. He attempted to turn on his side, a spasm jolting his legs, a reliable indicator that he'd be fucked all day. Stiff and sore and miserable.

At least he didn't have anything planned ... unless Hope took him up on his offer. But what was the likelihood of that? His pulse thumped beneath his skin. What if she did agree? What would that mean?

Would it be purely a business decision, or did it indicate she wanted to give him another chance? Ultimately, if she came over, it wouldn't be until much later. So he had time to get his shit together.

In the meantime, he could do some mindfulness meditation and try to chill, given his parents were still overseas, and Jeb had traveled to his family's vineyard in Rutherglen to catch up for Christmas.

He pressed on his once-hard eight-pack, now-soft two-pack stomach to check his bladder. Distended. Forget getting any more sleep. Time for a catheter. Great. He threw back the bedspread, stretched forward—setting off another spasm—and transferred onto his wheelchair.

While in the bathroom, he decided to do his toilet and shower routine, too, then go back to bed and try to rest. He'd be buggered, but at least he wouldn't have to stress about being ready on time ... if Hope and her crew decided to show.

His phone buzzed with a message from the lady in question, like she had a direct line to his thoughts. His heart rate skipped up to fast and frantic, and he clicked into her text.

Hope: **You don't have to do this.**
Cole: **I want to, need to. It's time.**
Hope: **You're absolutely sure?**
Cole: **Dead set.**

****

Cole had just gotten dressed in his coolest pair of jeans and black shirt, his hands shaking so much it took him triple the time to do up the buttons, when a firm knock rattled the door.

Right at seven o'clock, as arranged. He transferred into his wheelchair, pushed to the door and opened it, revealing Hope all glammed up in a black-and-silver, body-hugging dress. Behind her stood a cameraman with a state-of-the-art camera propped on his shoulder.

She touched Cole's hand and gave him an encouraging and ... was that a loving or sympathetic smile? Sympathy sucked. He fucking hated sympathy, pity. He'd rather she rejected him than feel sorry for him. "Are you ready?"

No. He'd never be totally ready. But how many people were ever a hundred percent ready for change? He nodded, his throat so constricted with suspense he couldn't speak.

Hope pressed and adjusted her earpiece. "Your category's up in the next ten minutes. It'll be first after the ad break."

Cole gestured for them to follow him into the cinema room, and while they set up, he switched on the TV and flicked to the awards ceremony. He kept the sound down low and watched, his mind speeding through possible scenarios and outcomes. Some popular music act finished, and the host announced a commercial break.

A bright light shone over his left side, and he turned and stared into the cameraman's blazing laser beam. Cole lifted his hand to protect his eyes from the glare. The guy fiddled around until he got the lighting just right, and no more black blotches dotted Cole's vision.

In no time, the program returned and a solo presenter stood at the lectern. He launched into the list of nominees, and Cole held his breath. The thumping heartbeats banged so hard inside his chest, he thought his ribs would crack.

"And the winner of the Innovations in Virtual Reality award is…" The guy ripped open the winner's envelope and grinned in that renowned, overly charming showbiz way. "Game software genius and three-time Cosmo Bachelor of the Year, Cole Sparks for *Intimacy World*."

Cole's gaze shot to Hope. Her eyes were shiny with barely restrained tears, but in seconds her face snapped back into her TV persona guise. "And here he is, winner of the Innovations in Virtual Reality award for *Intimacy World*. I'll hand over to Cole for a few words."

Here goes… "Thank you for this wonderful award. I was up against some amazing competition." Surprised gasps and bursts of chatter murmured through his surround sound system.

Cole ignored the anticipated audience reaction and tried to keep focused. He dragged in a deep breath and cleared his throat, silencing the shocked babble. "Many of you know about my adrenaline junkie streak and love of risky pursuits—mountain climbing in particular. But what many of you don't know are the potential side effects when things go wrong.

"A spinal cord injury is so much more than not being able to walk. The loss of sensation causes many complications, some sexual, which drove me to develop *Intimacy World*—a place for people in similar situations to mine—to still find pleasure. And maybe even a little courage and optimism."

Hope's mouth slackened with astonishment.

"Thanks for recognizing my work. I hope it makes a positive difference to people's lives."

Hope's smile radiated awe and heartfelt reverence. "Congratulations, Cole." She turned to look down the camera lens. "Now over to you in the studio, Sam."

The cameraman switched off the spotlight. "And we're done."

"Thanks, Jim. I'll meet you back at the station."

As soon as the guy left, Hope crouched down, teetering on her shiny, stilt-like shoes. "You okay? You know you're going to be hounded by the media."

"I know." He switched off the TV and pressed the control button to open the block-out blinds, letting in the dazzling summer sunshine. "And, yes, I'm okay." Surprisingly. He'd prepared himself to be bombarded by the press. But how about her? How was she doing with all this? Her feelings, her reaction, that's what he cared about most.

"I wanted to apologize about yesterday, about leaving so quickly."

"Nothing to apologize for." It had been a hell of a lot for her to take in.

She stared into his eyes. "Yes, there is. You deserved better. I wanted to come back. I wanted to see you again, wanted to talk about things some more, but … I thought I needed time to process everything. Then when you messaged, I realized I didn't."

She wanted to come back. She wanted to see him again. But he shouldn't get his hopes up about what that meant. "Drink?"

"Love one."

He gestured for her to sit in the closest electric lift recliner. "Eggnog? Made it myself."

Hope put her small, sparkly silver bag between her feet and sat on the edge of the seat, looking tense, nervous. "You? Made something from scratch?"

Something he knew she loved. "Yeah. Rehab was more than just physical. It taught me all about patience, persistence, and true independence."

She smiled and seemed to relax a little. "I'll definitely have to try it then."

He headed into the kitchen, half filled two crystal glasses with his homemade eggnog, and sprinkled the top with nutmeg and cinnamon.

"Do you need any help?" she called out.

"No, thanks. I've got it all under control." Sort of. "You just make yourself at home." He settled the glasses between his legs and pushed back into the cinema room. Nerves tangled around his chest like a noxious vine, strangling his confidence.

He pulled up next to her, put his brakes on, and handed her a glass, trying to keep his hand steady, his self-assurance intact.

Raising his drink, he looked into her bewitching eyes. "To Christmas miracles."

She beamed with happiness and lifted her glass to his. "Cheers."

They both had a sip. Hope grabbed a couple coasters from the center of the coffee table and put her glass down on one. "This is good. Really good."

"That's because I do double the alcohol." He sculled the rest of his drink and placed his empty glass beside hers. "I hope someone's driving you back to the station." He couldn't hold back his devilish grin.

"You're shocking." She swatted his thigh, setting off a spasm. Her terrified eyes darted up to meet his stare. "I'm sorry."

He grasped her hand and held it in his lap. "Nothing to be sorry about. It happens all the time."

She nodded, smiled, but her eyes were glassy. "How are you, Cole, really?"

"Better. Much better. I have a long way to go, though."

Hope glanced down, still holding his hand, then fixed her beguiling gaze on his. "It tore my heart to shreds not seeing you, not even being able to speak to you, contact you this past year." She let out a heavy breath and interlinked her fingers with his. "I know I said I accepted the presenting job to thank you for helping my brother, but it was more than that.

"I'd planned to steal a moment for us to speak in person so I could find out what drove you to end things like you did. Because it seemed so out of character. I just needed to know why, even if we couldn't get back together. Then you surprised me in the best possible way and reached out... So thank you, and thank you for explaining."

"Thank you for letting me. I'm so sorry about the way I handled everything. What I did was unfair to you, and me. I was just so devastated, broken, I couldn't think straight. I really believed breaking up with you would be best, would save you from being stuck in a sub-par relationship.

"I know not confiding in you feels like I didn't trust you, but I do trust you, Hope. I trusted you so much I knew you'd stand by me, and I didn't want to put you in that position. I wanted you to have the best. I didn't want you to be unhappy. I'm not like I was before, not even close."

"What's most important is you're still you on the inside. That's what counts. That's who I fell in love with." Was that a flare of desire in her eyes? She leaned in, pressed her soft lips to his and lingered, a jolt of lust reinvigorating his dormant libido.

The surprise made his brain malfunction.

She pulled back, guzzled her eggnog, and took their empty glasses into the kitchen. She hesitated in the doorway. "I wish I could stay, but unfortunately I need to get back to work." Hope hurried past him, slung the shimmering strap of her handbag over her shoulder, and walked out of the room.

He couldn't let her leave. Not yet. He had to act now; it was his last hope.

Cole followed her to the front door, and she reached for the doorknob.

"Hope, wait." Without thinking, he shoved his feet off the footplates onto the floor, pushed up off his wheelchair armrests, and reached out to her, swaying on shaky legs. "I love you."

She whipped around, her eyes wide, her mouth a big, round O. "You're standing!"

He glanced down. *Shit.* He fucking was, literally standing on his own two feet. He staggered and grasped the armrests.

She shot forward and put a steadying, supportive hand on his bicep. Her gaze dropped to his mouth, then back to his eyes. Mouth, then eyes. Mouth, then eyes. He wobbled, then stabilized himself. Without assistance, he took a stumbled step and kissed her.

She clutched his upper arms and licked the seam of his lips, inviting him in. He didn't hesitate, thrusting his tongue inside her mouth, trying to tamp down the urgency and explore, savor, get emotionally reacquainted. She moaned and he teetered toward her, his legs trembling.

Hope cradled him close, helping him stay upright, and pressed her body against his, her silent, give-me-more tell. And he totally wanted to. But he had to ease back into the physical side of things. His body, his stamina, his spontaneity had changed.

Cole brushed her lips with his, once, twice, then planted one more kiss before collapsing back into his wheelchair. He had to fully disclose to her... She had to know what she was subscribing to if she wanted to renew their romantic relationship.

She crouched in front of him so their eyes were level. "You love me."

"Never stopped."

A huge smile adorned her sensual, kiss-swollen lips.

"Before we take this further, I need to explain a few things. There are no guarantees I'll ever get back to my previous function. Most likely, I won't get anywhere near it. I'm still self-catheterizing to empty my bladder, and my bowels are fucked. Takes me two hours to finish my bowel routine. And my legs are still numb..."

Lines of confusion wrinkled her forehead. "You stood up. Isn't that pretty promising?"

"Yeah, it's bloody exciting. Can't wait to tell Jeb. But..." He caressed her beautiful, high cheekbones, still flushed pink from their kiss. "That might be as far as it goes. I can't feel my cock and I can't orgasm. Believe me, I've tried."

A flicker of hurt chased the hope from her eyes. "You've tried..." With another woman. She didn't say the words, though they were implied.

"Solo. I've tried solo. There's been no one else."

Relief returned to her pretty, accepting face.

Would the sense of relief remain after he dropped

the baby bombshell? "I can get it up, but retaining an erection can be tricky."

"I'm more than happy to help." God, he loved that cheeky grin.

He pressed a kiss to her forehead and held her hands. "You need to know. I may not be able to have kids naturally. Maybe not at all. Depends on how my sperm production's been affected, how my cocktail of hardcore pain meds impact its quality."

Wanting a baby was something she'd made no effort to hide. She'd been upfront with him about her love of children, her desire to start a family. Another thing he'd be asking her to sacrifice.

"Oh." She let go of his hands and stood. A war of emotions battled on her face. Surprise. Sorrow. Disappointment.

"I'm sorry. You don't know how much."

Her emerald eyes glazed with unshed tears and she nodded, still silent.

"It's okay, babe. Whatever you decide." And he meant it. Now that they'd talked, it solidified he wanted her as his life partner, his lover, his best friend, forever.

Ultimately, he loved her so much, he wanted the finest for her, even if that meant he lost her to another man. It would hurt like fucking hell, but he didn't want to stifle her, pressure or guilt her into staying with him and leading a restricted, unfulfilled life.

Hope swiped at mascara-tinged tears that tumbled down her cheeks, and she dropped onto the living room couch nearby him.

His mountain climbing obsession had been his downfall; however, it also taught him all about the importance of freedom and risk, about how to construct a solid base from true love. The foundation of his relationship with Hope had been built on it. It was something they shared. And even though they could no longer share it in the same way, they could apply it to something different … if she chose to take that chance.

He wheeled in beside her, as close as possible. She drew in a deep, stuttered breath and slipped her warm hand around his. "You know how I feel about children…"

Here it comes. Rejection. He braced himself in his wheelchair.

"But I haven't told you how I feel about *you*. Not since…" She motioned from his head to his barely functional feet.

He went to speak, and she held up her hand in a stop signal to cut him off. "I'm not finished yet. Please let me finish."

Cole nodded, and she clasped his other hand. They sat, facing each other, staring into each other's eyes, no longer able to hide their sincere feelings.

"You hurt me. In the way you ended things, that you couldn't be honest with me." She sniffled, her gaze dipping to their interlaced fingers and back to his eyes. "But I understand."

She shook her head. "No, actually, I don't. I have no idea what you've gone through, the physical changes, the emotional, the total disruption and rebuilding of your lifestyle. It must have been—and, I imagine, still is—fucking hard."

She squeezed his hands, her gaze locked on his. "But I can empathize. I can help make things easier."

He smiled. As a friend. That's what she'd offer, because she cared. She cared and she was fucking amazing. And he'd keep her in his life any way he could.

"Because I want to, need to. Because I love you. I haven't stopped loving you. And, yes, I want children, but only with a man I love. And I only love you. So, if we aren't blessed with children, so be it, because the biggest and most important thing is I'm blessed with you."

Had she really just said... All his thoughts evaporated when her lips met his, salt-tinged from her tears. He kissed the pain away, until all that flowed between them was love.

Cole broke the kiss and she whimpered.

A mischievous glint sparked in her eyes. "Your tongue wasn't affected by the accident, was it?"

"No. No, it wasn't."

A slow smile curled up the corners of her lips. "I didn't think so. As I always said, it's one of your greatest assets."

He laughed, the first real, solid belly laugh since he'd been hurt. "I believe you dubbed me Oral King."

"You totally deserved the title. The things you can do with your mouth ... magnificent." Her expression could only be described as contented bliss, a state he aimed to keep her in for a lifetime.

Cole pressed another quick kiss to her lips. "Wait here."

"Okay. I'll just send work a text to let them know I'll be there soon-ish."

He propelled back to his bedroom, opened the top drawer of his bedside table, and pulled out the black velvet box. He placed it between his thighs and pushed back to her, his heart jack-hammering against his breastbone.

She slipped her phone in her handbag and tugged at the hem of her dress, just barely covering her panties. "God, I wish I could strip out of this."

"Me too." He couldn't disguise the roaring need in his voice.

He'd seen her naked so many times he'd lost

count, and yet her cheeks still turned a sweet, virginal pink. He fucking loved it, fucking loved when she blushed.

And he must be a lucky bastard because she did it often, even though they'd shared one hell of a down and dirty sex life … that he hoped to rekindle. Well, as best he could, given his changed circumstances, his restrictions. In this instance, his overachieving tendencies were a huge advantage.

"Later? I can come back after I finish up at the station."

Hell, yes. "I'll be waiting … impatiently." It had been way too long since he'd been able to touch her, taste her, take her to the pinnacle of ecstasy. All the miscommunication, the delays, the wasted time had been his fault, but now he planned to make it up to her and more.

Cole rolled in close, clasped her hand and, with his free hand, plucked the jewelry box from between his thighs. "Not quite on my knees, though it'll have to do." He flipped open the lid to reveal the brilliant cut, solitaire diamond engagement ring, and she gasped.

Her gaze zeroed in on his and held. "When did you…"

"Last year. I planned to propose at dinner after the bridge climb, but then…"

Hope stroked his stubbled jaw, her eyes shining with sadness and deep, heart-seizing love.

"We've been apart too long already. I don't want to waste any more time. I love you so damn much, my sweet, beautiful Hope. Let's climb new mountains together."

He took the ring out of the box and held it up. The spectacular crimson sunset shone through the floor-to-ceiling windows, warm, rich rays of light catching on the diamond and showering the room with a rainbow of sparkles. "Marry me?"

Epilogue
Reaching the Peak

Christmas Day, twelve months later…

Cole kissed his way along his wife's slender neck to her breasts and paused for a suckle. God, he loved Hope's large, erect nipples, like a tempting pair of chocolate bullets. He latched his mouth onto one and tweaked the other, using the pad of his thumb and forefinger, and she moaned and writhed beneath him.

"Stay still or…"

"Orgasm denial, I know." Hope did know. She knew him better than anyone. He was so goddamn lucky. Every night since his proposal, then fast-tracked marriage, he'd had his spirited, loving, spitfire of a wife in his bed. And he still couldn't get enough of her.

He switched nipples and, after a few minutes of lavishing, indulging, slid his tongue to the fleshy inner curve of her breast, bit down, and sucked.

"Cole!"

He pulled back and admired the big red blotch. His mark should turn into quite an impressive love bite. He gave her gorgeous breasts one last admiring glance. Did they seem fuller than usual, or was it just from his extra special attention?

Cole licked along her stomach, eye on the pussy-licious prize.

"I need to taste you too." Her voice sounded on-edge desperate. Like him.

He groaned. They were so fucking in tune. He rolled her onto her side, flipped himself around so his feet faced the bedhead, and propped his head on her exposed inner thigh. She spread her top leg wide, giving him greater access to her pretty, sexy pussy, and nuzzled in close to his cock.

She leaned her head on his bent bottom leg and took him in her hot, moist mouth. He couldn't think, couldn't breathe. But he had to focus, had to get her off first and not prematurely lose his load.

He nestled his head between her thighs and licked, around her clit, between her folds, along her wet slit. God, she tasted incredible. Hot and sweet and sensual. "Mmm ... my delicious wife."

She moaned, wrapped her hand around his hard-on, and stroked, sending an added jolt of euphoria to his cock. "My delicious husband." With her other hand she played with his balls, cupping and rubbing and driving him fucking crazy.

He wouldn't torment her too long today. Or himself. He couldn't. He already teetered on trigger-happy. Now that he could climax again, he struggled to hold off, the renewed sensations almost overwhelming. He needed to be inside her, feel her core grip his cock in shared ecstasy.

Cole trailed his tongue over her opening, thrust inside, then moved his mouth to her clit. His first gentle lick had Hope arching against him. He inserted two fingers inside her and curled them so they stroked her G-spot, then took her engorged nub in his mouth and sucked.

She screamed and bucked against his face, his hand. It almost did him in, feeling her clamp down on his fingers, her orgasmic juices flooding his tongue. But he kept going, teasing out her every last ounce of pleasure, kept going until Hope collapsed against the bed, panting, slaked, boneless.

Fuck, she was beautiful, lying there naked in a heap of bliss. The urgency to be inside her, watch her face and body contort when she came again and again on his cock, made him move as fast as he could, up over her, rubbing himself along her still-sensitive sex.

He leaned down to kiss her, and pain sawed through his lower back and serrated his legs. His face screwed up and he slammed his hand against his sacrum. "You're going to have to jump on this time." He clacked his jaw shut, and his powerless voice hissed through the gaps in his teeth. He sucked in a slow, soothing breath. "My back's fucked."

She squinted, her eyes concerned yet scrutinizing. "You're pushing yourself too hard. Overdoing the physio."

She was right. Ever since the doctor confirmed he'd had a severe case of spinal shock, he'd immersed himself in therapy, desperate to rebuild his strength, his abilities, his independence. And over the past six months, he'd ditched his pain meds, and some of his sensation had returned too.

Patchy sections of skin were still numb, and some even stung, but overall, feeling had improved. Though the most exciting thing—in the last three months he'd been able to orgasm.

Cole rolled onto his back, the pain suddenly ceasing like power to a disconnected electrical plug. He couldn't wait another second for restored skin-on-skin contact, so he reached across and lifted Hope so she straddled his hips.

She shook her head but didn't quite hide her smile. "See, you shouldn't be doing things like that. You don't want to inflame the area and relapse or, even worse, cause permanent damage."

"I know." He traced his fingers along the length of her creamy thighs and hovered near her clit. "I promise I'll be good."

She swatted his hand. "I'm being serious."

"I know. I just want to give rehab my best shot. Try to regain my pre-accident function or as close to it as possible. And before you tell me not to get my hopes up, I'm aware I may not get back to how I was. I realize I may have some irreversible changes, preventing me from mountain climbing. And I'm okay with it." Now.

Having Hope back in his life had helped him get a grip on things, get some perspective that months of solo soul searching had failed to do. It reinforced the importance of having good support, exposure to different thinking, love.

She rubbed his chest, his heart rate now at full sprint. "Good. You know I love you. You, not whether you're Mr. Adventure Man."

"I don't know. You're a pretty big fan of Mr. Adventure Man in the bedroom." He ran his hands over her rounded stomach and stopped on her hips. Hope's stomach had always been iron firm and flat. Flat the whole time he'd known her. Maybe she was bloated or had put on some weight. Not that he cared. She could do with a few extra pounds, fill out those sexy-ass curves to full advantage.

She grabbed his hand, slid it back over her belly, and held it there. "I wondered when you'd notice." Her smile seemed a bit too excited for someone who watched her weight.

Cole could feel the crinkle of confusion on his forehead. She leaned forward, propping one hand on the mattress and using her other hand to keep hold of his over her belly, and kissed the crease away. With soft lips, she kissed his closed eyes, the tip of his nose, his mouth. But before he could plunge his tongue between her sultry, parted lips, she pulled away.

"I have something to tell you."

His eyes snapped open. "Sounds serious."

"It is." But she didn't look worried. She squeezed his hand, still pressed over her stomach. "Mr. Adventure Man has left something behind during one of his escapades."

"Something behind." He couldn't stop the wicked grin spreading across his face. "Did I forget those anal beads again?" His memory flashed straight back to the first time he'd convinced her to give them a go, his mouth feasting between her legs and him pulling out the bumpy thread, one slow bead at a time. The look of pure ecstasy on her face, her unrestrained cries of passion filling the room.

A flush of pink tinged her cheeks. "No. Something that's taken root and won't come out for at least another six months."

The realization hit him like sudden, unexpected rockfall. "You're not…"

"Pregnant?"

His throat tightened with emotion and he nodded.

A smile burst onto her smart, beautiful, pleasure-giving lips. "Yes. Yes, I am. Mr. Adventure Man is going to be a father."

The best Christmas present ever.

Cole placed both his hands over her belly, in awe of their growing child, the Christmas miracle they had created. His gaze connected with hers and he cupped her face, drew her down on top of him so her breasts pressed against his chest, and crushed his mouth to hers.

Hope propped on one elbow, reached between them, and guided his cock inside her hot center.

Should they be putting added pressure on such a fragile, precious gift?

Her lips broke from his, her breathing already labored. "And, yes, it's safe for the baby." It was as though she could read his mind. Read it, and put it at ease. She thrust her tongue back into his mouth and it swirled around and explored his, her sexy hips swiveling, rocking, grinding.

He groaned against her lips, barely able to hold back. He wanted her so damn bad. He needed her so damn much.

Slipping his hand between their bodies, he rubbed her swollen clit.

"Cole, oh God, Cole!" She threw her head back and rode out her release.

Watching his beautiful wife, mother of his child, come apart, combined with the rhythmic clenching on his cock, sent him into a body-shuddering climax.

She fell against his chest, his heart still thudding, his cock still buried deep. He stroked her hair, the silken smooth skin of her back, kissed her damp forehead.

"Mmm…" Her sated murmur hummed through him like a blissful *om*.

If only they could stay snuggled up like this forever. But Hope's family would be arriving soon for Christmas lunch. If he were lucky, there'd still be time for a joint shower. And he was lucky, the luckiest man alive.

He shifted when he wrapped his arms around her, and his cock slipped out. "How are they going to take the pregnancy news at work? You've only been lead presenter on *The Travel Bug* for, what, four months?"

Hope kissed his chest and teased his nipple with her tongue. If she kept doing that, he'd be hard again in no time. "It's still early, so I'm thinking we hold off telling people until things are a bit safer. Maybe around the five-month mark, assuming I'm not showing earlier."

"I agree." The last thing they needed was to get all excited and tell everyone, then lose the baby. Trauma on top of trauma. Much better to be patient and sure.

She stopped her slow seduction and met his gaze. "Though I think we should tell our immediate family. There's no way I'll be able to spend the whole day with mine today and not say something."

"You're the boss."

"Finally, you get it."

Cheeky thing. He slapped her ass, the loud crack ringing in the room.

She squeal-moaned and kissed his mouth, much too briefly. "Regarding my job, the network will be fine. The ratings have been good, so I'm sure they'll work out a way to milk it as much as they can. They'll probably push for some special edition in-home interview with the Sparks, talking about life and our favorite holiday destinations. Oh, I know, I can do a feature story on disability and family-friendly travel spots."

"You've been working in the industry too long. With ideas like that, your manager better watch her back."

Hope nuzzled his neck and laughed, her erect nipples skimming against his skin.

He tipped her chin up so their gazes met. "I love you, my stunningly beautiful wife, amazing mother-to-be."

Hope's ecstatic smile never failed to bring out her exquisite beauty. And he wasn't just referring to the physical. Her true beauty came from the heart. "I love you, my handsome husband, incredible father-to-be."

He kissed her, infusing it with every ounce of his love and passion, and she matched his enthusiasm with every press of her lips, every sweep of her tongue. They were gearing up for round two and...

Hope's phone buzzed, dragging them back from their passion haze.

"You better get it." His voice rasped with lust, belying his words.

Hope's face crinkled up in that adorable, disappointed way like when he threatened orgasm denial, which he was kind of doing right now. But not by choice.

She reached across to her bedside table and read the text message. "Brody. He and his gamer girlfriend are running a little late. They'll pick up my parents on the way through. They won't get here before one."

Brody and his new woman were running late, eh? He bet they were. If she was anything like him, they'd probably been playing *Intimacy World* all morning and lost track of time. They probably got caught up comparing notes on Cole's new patented clit hood and sensor dildo versus the cock sleeve.

He chuckled to himself and checked his watch. Eleven thirty. That meant he and Hope had a good hour to play some more themselves.

"I can't wait to meet her and tell them our news. Though I'm kind of glad they've been held up." Her smile shone with sensual possibilities.

"Me too. Last chance for a joint shower with benefits." He smacked her ass, and she shrieked and jumped up.

"Race you to the bathroom. Winner chooses their pleasure," Hope said, then streaked into the en suite, her gorgeous bare body on display.

Cole never had a chance, and she knew. Using a cane, he could just manage the walk into their shower without a rest stop, and continued to use a manual wheelchair in the community. So, Hope always beat him these days. And he didn't care. It was all about pleasure and love and being together.

And he had nearly given all that up.

Given up Hope.

Out of fear.
Never again.
She was his last and only Hope.
Forever.

The End

SANDRA CARMEL

Limitations live only in our minds.

—Jamie Paolinetti

SANDRA CARMEL

GAME FOR INTIMACY

Intertwined Love, 2

Sandra Carmel

Copyright © 2021

Chapter One
Virtual Connection

B-True: "Oh God, oh God, oh God!"

Fuck! Brody collapsed against his couch, trying to catch his breath, his cock still jerking in his hand from his mega climax. Choosing black leather furniture had been one of his better decisions considering how many times he'd jacked off without a condom, watching porn on his massive screen TV.

Not the fake-tit, over-exaggerated-O, typical shit. His tastes went more European arthouse. Gorgeous exotic women, real bodies, less over-acting.

B-True's post-orgasm panting pounded through his headset, adding to the fucking awesomeness.

B-Brave: "No words."

B-True: "How about a post-coital cuddle?"

God, her husky voice sounded so sassy, so sexy, so hot.

B-Brave: "Sorry. Can't move."

B-True: "Such a guy. Blow your load and straight into sleep mode."

B-Brave: "Ha ha. Sounded like you enjoyed yourself too. Did you use any of the new attachments or rub one out yourself?"

B-True: "Sounded like?"

B-Brave: "Hard to miss all the moans and heavy breathing. But I did promise to show you a good time, and I stuck to it."

A bit like his cum to his dick if he didn't remove the cock sleeve and dispose of the used condom. Bare would be better, but way too messy. And he didn't want to bugger up the sleeve technology. It worked an absolute treat.

If the sensation just from the sleeve rocked his sex life, he couldn't wait to test Cole's patented, touch-sensitive body suit.

B-True: "You definitely did."

B-Brave: "By the way, you didn't answer my question. And I won't give you a free pass on that one, no matter how much you beg."

Probably not one hundred percent true, but she didn't need to know that.

The silence stretched and he could almost hear her biting her lip in hesitation.

B-True: "Rubbed one out."

Now that's all he could imagine. He removed the cock sleeve, grabbed a wad of tissues out of the box on the coffee table, and discarded the condom.

B-Brave: "Hand on pussy?"

B-True: "Actually, more like fingers on pussy."

The scent of his spent seed permeated the air, the dim lighting adding to the sexually-charged atmosphere. He stroked his cock, already as hard as an old-school joystick and he'd only come a few minutes ago.

B-Brave: "Fuck, you're killing me. I could almost go again."

B-True: "Me too."

Shit. They'd chatted for barely a couple months and things had quickly gotten sexual. Probably didn't help playing a game like *Intimacy World*. Problem was he'd become attached. A little too attached. And he had no idea how she even looked, only that she'd recently turned twenty-nine, grew up in country New South Wales, and made a kick-ass fireteam member, not to mention virtual sex partner.

B-True's character remained in a recumbent, blissed-out posture on screen. She looked so deliciously just-fucked, he craved round two but didn't want to bulldoze. It was their first fully intimate time together, and he refused to ruin it by pushing his needy agenda. But that didn't stop him struggling to keep his B-Brave hands off her. It was the closest he'd come to sex in, fuck, over two years.

B-True: "Hey, you've gone all quiet. Everything okay?"

B-Brave: "Totally. Just basking in the afterglow."

And trying to stop thinking about how much he wanted her, beyond the game. So irrational. There may be no spark whatsoever in person. He had no idea if she even looked anything like her super-sexy avatar. If she resembled hers as much as he did his, then the only accuracy lay in her age and coloring—youthful-looking adult with blonde-streaked brown hair and fair skin.

B-True: "Are you going to the PAX Aus convention in Melbourne?"

Nice deflection.

B-Brave: "I've been thinking about it, you?"

B-True: "I'll definitely be there."

Did she ask because she wanted him to attend? Or just out of politeness?

B-True: "If you go, maybe we could meet up?"

A tinge of hope hung on her words. Hmmm … seemed like she did want to make that in-person connection. Now that they'd had virtual sex it could either be fucking amazing or horribly awkward.

He couldn't deny the underlying current of attraction and expectation between them, but what if neither of them lived up to that? Given his situation, he was pretty sure he wouldn't. All the arousal drained from his dick.

B-Brave: "Maybe we should exchange photos then, beforehand, so we know who to look for."

So he could prepare her.

B-True: "Does that mean you'll go?"

B-Brave: "I guess."

B-True: "You could sound a bit more excited."

Part of him was excited, but his logical self stepped in, the weight of reality crushing any lingering, romantic wish.

B-Brave: "I'm nervous."

B-True: "B-Brave. It's just me. It'll be fun. No expectations."

Easy to say, but his heart had already developed an addiction. Had hers? And when she saw him, would it all change?

Probably. But it would be better to know early on. Or so he kept telling himself.

B-Brave: "Okay. I'll book first thing tomorrow."

B-True: "Yay! But no pictures. Let's keep it a surprise. We'll decide on a meeting place at the convention… No, I know, a table at the cocktail event on the Friday night. When they tell you your table number, message me and I'll come to you. My mobile is…"

Swapping mobile numbers. *Shit.* Their relationship had suddenly become really real. Having her number made it so fucking tempting to call just to hear her sultry voice. Or text. He could communicate with her whenever he wanted now. Technically.

No more waiting to see if she'd be online or organizing a game meeting time. It was like having a superpower you knew you shouldn't use unless you had a strong enough reason. Hell. Pure hell. Like making himself go to bed and be responsible when all he wanted was to keep playing the latest game and make it through to the top level.

B-Brave: "Sweet. All saved. I'll send you a test text."

B-True: "Got it! I can't wait."

They wouldn't have to. Not for long. If all went to plan, they'd meet in person in four short days. Should he have told her what to expect? No. He offered to exchange pictures, but she wanted it to be a surprise. He'd definitely live up to that, but not in the way she might have imagined.

Hopefully the sight of him, the reality of his situation, wouldn't send her running the other way. Unfortunately, it wasn't unusual. Even if women didn't run, they immediately allocated him to the friend-zone. It sucked, but at least he'd know where their relationship stood.

No more assuming. No more hoping. No longer could they hide behind their virtual-reality avatars. She'd get to see him and he'd get to see her without the protection of a game screen. And he'd bet his PlayStation 4 and retro game library she couldn't come close to matching his level of revelation.

Chapter Two
Unconventional

PAX Aus, October – Gaming convention, Melbourne

Brody hooked the goodie bag over his wheelchair handles, put his ID lanyard around his neck, and wheeled away from the registration desk into a waiting wall of foaming-at-the-mouth, impatient gamers.

Sardines had it good. The Melbourne Convention and Exhibition Centre was so dense with people—some wearing colorful costumes, representing their favorite game character and taking up extra space—he felt more like a compressed atom. But that's not what made him nervous.

On top of the impending meet-up with his online game buddy and massive crush, B-True, his favorite Aussie model and self-confessed gamer, Beth, was booked to open the convention. And okay, he may have had a secret infatuation with her for forever.

Cam nudged his backrest. "Stop stalling, Brodes, and clear us a path."

"Yeah, wheelchair coming through!" Ben's voice boomed over the networking hum, and several people turned and stared.

Fabulous. Fucking fabulous. Ah … why had he decided it was a good idea to bring his two best mates along again? Moral support. That's right. If he didn't die of embarrassment first.

"Let's check out the stands while we wait for the presentations to start." Cam's face lit up like a kid surrounded by a sea of gifts at Christmas.

As long as they made it to the official opening, Beth's official opening. "Sure. But we can't miss the start."

"More like you can't miss Beth." Ben's eyebrows waggled like a cartoon character bad guy.

Okay, maybe Brody's Beth obsession wasn't as secret as he thought.

They wandered into the cavernous exhibition center, checked out some of the busy stalls—with in-your-face brand promotion banners and paraphernalia—and finally headed into the plenary auditorium. Brody rolled into his designated disability spot, to the far side of the front row in the stalls, super close to the stage. With zero ability to hide.

Ben slapped Brody on the shoulder. "Great seats, man." He and Cam sat in the avocado-green upholstered chairs beside him, but instead of fully checking out the surroundings, they rummaged through their sample bags and compared contents.

Brody's gaze kept drifting to the blue-lit stage where, at any moment, the woman of his dreams would appear. Almost within touching distance. Well, not exactly touching distance, but definitely within easy view. Just thinking she could see him made his heart race, caffeine-overdose style, like when he reached the last do-or-die level of a new game.

In Beth's pictures she always looked so aloof, so inaccessible and yet, something drew him to her. On some subconscious level, he'd connected to an underlying vulnerability she seemed to want to keep concealed.

So similar to his don't-let-others-too-close-to-me, I'll-do-things-on-my-own stance, for fear of getting hurt. Though in his case, he couldn't cover up his main limitation. It was impossible to keep physical disability hidden.

The lights dimmed and the convention convenor

stepped onto the large, luminous stage. He stood at the dais, did a Welcome to Country, and introduced Beth. Fashion images of her flashed up on the huge side screens, and Brody's gaze shot between the pictures and the podium like the ball in an old-fashioned pinball machine.

Ding ding!

All petite one hundred and seventy-three centimeters of her sashayed out from behind the heavy curtain with such a bright, enthusiastic smile, he couldn't help but smile back. In photos she looked beautiful, but in person, stunning. Breathtaking. So alive and engaging.

The convenor gave her the showbiz, double air kiss and she took his place in front of the lectern. "Thank you so much for inviting me to open the PAX Aus convention. It's such an honor and a thrill for me to be here.

"I've traveled the world with my modeling career and it's been amazing, but my not-so-secret passion is gaming. I'm really looking forward to meeting fellow gamers and learning about what's hot and innovative in the gaming scene."

Fuck, she sounded so familiar. Like he knew her. Yeah right. If only... Had to be interviews he'd heard with her on TV, radio, YouTube. Probably a combination of all of the above over the years.

"Wishing you all a wonderful convention and hope you take away lots of great information and make many lasting friendships and memories." Her soft, husky voice oozed sexiness, a bit like ... B-True.

No. No way. If he believed that, he'd hit a whole other level of delusion.

Beth was fantasyland stuff, no matter how much his mind wished she could be B-True. Going by past experience, B-True would most likely be way out of reach too. In reality, someone like Beth wouldn't give him a first, let alone second, glance unless out of pity or political correctness.

Not that he ever even considered his attraction to her as anything more than fascination. He knew what it was—something to enjoy and jack off to in the absence of a real woman, a real girlfriend.

Intimacy World had helped him build his confidence in the game arena, where he felt safe, met people online, *women* online, and had reached the ready point to start getting out there again.

Soon he'd be making a new in-person connection as a result of an online friendship. It probably wouldn't lead to anything more, but without giving it a go, he'd never know.

The convenor handed Beth a bunch of Australian native flowers and she looked around the audience, her gaze stopping on Brody. She smiled, waved to the crowd, her eyes reconnecting with his, then walked off stage.

His heart pounded and the roar of blood in his ears deafened out the clapping. Had his crush on her warped his sense of reality? He had to have imagined her special attention.

Cam elbowed him, his face filled with wonder. "Did you see that?"

Ben's uncharacteristic silence stretched for a whole extra second, his mouth sagging with surprised disbelief. "She looked right at you, dude. Twice!"

And right then, Brody fell a little more in lust with her. He hadn't read into what he'd seen. She'd noticed him. Really seen him. Even if she'd only done it to be PC.

****

After a day of competition gaming at the designated, back-to-back computer corrals, interspersed with break-out information sessions on the latest technology and game developments, Brody's eyes drooped. He was on the verge of falling asleep in his chair. But he had to hold out, had to make it to the cocktail party, where he'd agreed to meet B-True.

He went back to his wheelchair-accessible hotel room, put together his travel, self-propel commode, showered and changed, and met Cam and Ben in the South Wharf Hotel reception area.

All tuxedoed up, well, him in his hipster version—velvet, wine-colored jacket, white shirt, funky tie, and black jeans—he accompanied his friends back to the convention center and found the table he'd reserved, where the pre-arranged meeting with B-True would take place.

No way would he miss it. If he had to risk a pressure injury for spending too many hours in his chair, so be it. He'd come all this way. He'd promised her and, if nothing else, he was true to his word.

The convention committee had done an amazing job converting the venue from simple to chic for the welcome party. The dim, golden lighting created an inviting, sensual feast for the senses, compared to the minimalist, high-tech feel of the daytime program. The unobstructed view of the Yarra river, with colorful lights twinkling across the shimmery surface, added to the impressive, almost-romantic atmosphere.

Scattered across the highly male-centric room, ladies dressed in evening wear, shining like shooting stars. Speaking of which, Beth had been on his brain all day and he hoped she'd make it to the evening event. But he doubted it.

She'd be harassed non-stop by desperate men. Like him. But he wouldn't do that to her. He'd just admire Beth from afar and focus on finding and fostering an attainable relationship. Focus on meeting a woman more in his stratosphere tonight, one he had a chance with.

Plates of finger food made the rounds, but his nervy, knotted-up stomach stopped him from forcing anything down in case it catapulted all the way back up. Instead, he had a drink to take the edge off his anxiety.

A gin man all the way, he sipped on a martini, feeling very James Bond, and chatted to his mates about their plans for day two. And Beth. Impossible not to mention her after their close encounter earlier.

"She always looks so gorgeous in her pictures, but today... Beth in person is just breathtaking," Brody shouted over the loud music, then glanced up into Cam's wide, suddenly freaked-out eyes.

"Thank you."

Oh, fuck. Beth's voice. Unmistakable even amongst the din of conversation and tacky 80s dance tunes. "Beth?" he mouthed to his mate, just to double check.

Cam smiled, his nod almost imperceptible.

Ben just laughed.

Brody clacked his jaw together and tried to steady his suddenly erratic breathing. He checked his watch. *Shit.* Eight already. The time he'd organized to meet his online gamer friend. Beth had to choose right then to come by. What a fucking disaster.

He didn't want to hurry her off, but he couldn't miss the opportunity to meet B-True either. Their pre-planned catch-up had pushed him to fly to Melbourne in the first place.

He swiveled in his wheelchair to face his infatuation. *Whoa!* His mouth went so dry he could hardly pry his tongue off the roof of it to speak. "Hi."

Her warm, brilliant smile nearly knocked him

right out of his chair. Backlit with the vibrant, amber lights lining the entryway, she looked like an angel with a golden, glowing aura. "Hi."

She stood there all soft and stunning and surreal. Like a waking dream, a deep, soul-stirring, spiritual experience. "It seems you've got a bit of an unfair advantage. You know my name, but I don't know yours."

"Brody." God, it was like the cord connecting his thoughts to his speech had been cut. He sounded like a total, inarticulate moron, a fanboy. The exact reason why she'd avoid attending these things. He fumbled for words, her mind probably second-guessing her decision to come over.

"Brody," she said, his name never sounding so bloody good. "Maybe you can help me. This is table sixty-nine, right? I'm trying to find a gamer called B-Brave."

"B-True?" His voice croaked with *no-fucking-way*. Beth couldn't possibly be his online gamer mate, could she? The one he'd had virtual sex with less than a week ago. Scorching heat rushed over his skin like he'd been wrapped in an electric blanket on high. He knew she liked to play, but what were the odds?

"Yes." Her broad smile almost disappeared right off the sides of her face, the joy spreading higher and tugging up the corners of her eyes, like the outcome made her super happy. "You're B-Brave, aren't you?"

Beth stared at him, her hopeful expression suggesting she really wanted it to be true. Which made no sense. Women like her didn't go for guys like him. Maybe in romance novels, but not in the real world. Then again, she was probably just being friendly, making sure she kept up a certain professional image to match her brand, her reputation.

He nodded, still not quite believing the view right

in front of him, *who* stood right in front of him.

Cam clamped his hand on Brody's shoulder. "Nice one, Brodes."

"You hit the lady jackpot!" Ben slapped his hand down on the table. "I'm so fucking jealous."

Beth laughed, and it was the sweetest sound.

Brody shook his head in warning at his friends. "Guys, please."

"It's okay." Her large, chocolate-brown eyes melted his with their intensity. "I'm so glad it's you."

"You are?"

"Yeah, you look like a sweetheart."

Great, totally friend-zoned. Typical. The usual. Able-bodied people didn't seem to get that the disabled population had sexual needs and desires too. "Looks can be deceiving."

"I hope not." Her tone turned serious, like she'd been stuffed around by some dick in the past. And now she used that hurt, wary, vulnerable lens to view others. "There's a real genuineness, a real sincerity to you that my instinct says is true. I hope I'm right. It's very important to me."

No pressure or anything. "Me too." Time to lighten things up a bit, especially while they still had an audience. "Um … can I get you a drink?"

"No. Let me. It's the least I can do to thank you for coming all this way to meet up with me." She glanced over at his mates. "What would you guys like?"

They looked at each other and carried out their trademark silent conversation. Seconds later, Ben said, "Beer for us, thanks."

Beth focused her full attention, like a dual spotlight, back on Brody. He swallowed the crushing boulder of nerves gathering size and blocking his throat. "Ah… I'll have a gin and tonic, please."

"You're kidding. That's my favorite drink." She said it like she'd ticked another sign off the we-were-meant-to-meet list. Or maybe his interpretation had gotten skewed by wishful thinking.

"Mine too."

Beth grabbed a passing waiter's attention and placed the order.

Ben poked Brody in the ribs. "Aren't you gonna offer the lady a seat, man?"

He would, except there were no spare chairs at their table or those surrounding them. "I'd offer you mine but…" He shrugged.

She glanced at his scrawny thighs, strategically obscured under his jeans, and back up until their gazes reconnected. His face had to be the color of a fire truck, and his cock, well… He'd almost had a hard-on from the moment he saw her that morning. Hopefully the bulge was buried in the shadows.

Beth bit down on her plump bottom lip, leaving little white indents of indecision. She went to speak, stopped. Went to speak, stopped, and took a breath. "Is your lap taken?"

Chapter Three
Level One Conquered

Fuck. He shook his head, unable to speak.

"I'm game if you are." Was that a hint of desire in Beth's tone, in her eyes? Had he dropped down into some alternate universe? Things like this didn't happen to him.

Maybe he had bipolar disorder rather than his original diagnosis of depression and had descended into a manic, psychotic break. The mind was a powerful thing; it could make up all kinds of believable shit.

Though, if she sat down, his dick might just burst through his fly. But he couldn't stop her from taking a seat either, didn't want to. He patted his knobby knees. "Let's give it a test run then."

She sat her gorgeous ass on his lap, the massive split on her glittery black dress exposing the olive skin of her long, lean legs, right up to mid-thigh. Breathing became extra hard when she shifted closer to his cock, enabling her feet to hang over the side of his wheelchair.

The drinks came and she leaned forward to retrieve his first, then his mates', then her own, giving him an incredible view of her cleavage. She was killing him. Full on killing him. But in the best possible way. At least he'd die a supremely happy man.

Cam lifted his beer up as though to toast. "To a night of making lifelong memories."

"To a fucking unforgettable night!" Ben's gaze met Brody's, his eyes gleaming with a don't-fuck-this-up-dude look.

Beth turned her beautiful face to Brody and smiled, showing off her flawless white teeth. Up close she looked even more perfect. She raised her glass to his and tapped. "To a great night with a great man."

No matter how much he wished it away, he couldn't stop the blood rushing to his cheeks and cock. He took a large gulp of his gin and tonic and put it down on a flimsy paper coaster. If only he could take a few ice blocks out and cool his face.

"Are you blushing?" Beth put her drink on the table and leaned in close to study his skin. Her smile morphed into a mega grin. "That is so adorable." If she knew he had a raging erection, she might not think him so cute.

Before he could even blink, she threw her arms around his neck and squished him in the most amazing, heartfelt hug. She radiated an indescribable warmth and affection that couldn't be faked. She wriggled in closer, pressing her breasts to his chest, and he prayed she couldn't feel the rock-hard happiness in his pants.

Her hair smelled like an expensive, exotic Haigh's chocolate, and it took all his willpower not to bury his nose in her neck and lick. He wrapped his arms around her slim waist. Surprise at how right it felt, having her cradled in his lap, slammed him straight in the heart.

Brody stared at Cam and Ben and they both charged their beers in a go-for-it-buddy salute and spun in their chairs to start chatting up some ladies at the next table. Leaving him and Beth alone-ish.

Outside of gaming and the usual superficial stuff, what could he speak to her about? They'd never had any trouble talking online, but this was different. In the flesh. No time to contemplate conversation. No ability to hide body language. Their initial chats had happened before he knew she was beautiful, way-out-of-his-league Beth.

"B-Brave, don't worry. It's just me, B-True." An echo of one of the last things she'd said to him when he'd hesitated about them meeting. Beth and B-True were definitely the same person.

To anyone else, Beth's whispered voice probably sounded soothing, but to him it felt like a stroke to his already-aroused cock. And if she wriggled anymore, he'd seriously blow in his jeans like a teenage boy let loose with a lingerie catalogue.

"I'm still trying to get my head around … this."

"Me too. So far, it's pretty awesome." She lifted her head and looked around. "Hey, your friends deserted us."

Leaving Brody no more buffer to fall back on. "Yeah. Pretty poor effort."

"You think so? I'm kind of glad. It gives us more time to get to know each other better."

And more of a chance for me to fuck up.

She kept her arms draped around his neck and looked him in the eye. "If you don't mind me asking, how did you end up in a chair?"

Bizarrely, he preferred it when people were courageous enough to ask him straight out. Most people avoided the topic, as though they thought the subject might hurt his feelings. It hurt more when they avoided the obvious, his chair the mammoth, metal elephant in the room. "Spina bifida. It's basically a birth defect that prevents the spinal cord from developing properly."

"What does that mean for you?"

Now came the part where he told the truth about his condition and solidified his spot in friendsville. Not as a romantic partner. Never as a romantic partner. Not long term, anyway. Maybe a curiosity or fetish fuck, but nothing more.

"Well, I can only take a few shaky steps, so I'm in my wheelchair almost full time, outside of showering and sleeping. My sensation is impaired from around my belly button down and I have less muscle tone in my legs and butt, so I have to be extremely careful with my skin.

"It's really easy to get skin breakdown and pressure injuries if I'm not on top of things, if I don't move off areas often enough. My pressure relieving cushion helps and so do regular pressure lifts."

Her eyes filled with worry, and she dropped her arms from around his neck. "You shouldn't have let me sit on you like this. Shit, I should be getting off your lap right now."

She went to shift forward and he placed a firm hand on her thigh, right on her bare skin. Sharp tingles of lust shot up his arm, and she shivered like she felt it too. "You're fine…" But the expression on her face combined with her body's response suggested she wasn't fine. Flustered, more like it. But from discomfort or desire?

Her usually brown eyes looked like they'd been injected with black ink. "Are you sure?" Dilated pupils, breathy voice. She *was* turned on. *Fuck me.*

"Very. I'll be honest, it's difficult meeting women who can look past my physical limitations. Well, ones I'm interested in. But considering all the potential issues, I'm one of the lucky ones."

"What other potential issues are there?"

His cheeks burned like he'd been branded. But he'd invoke his gamer tag and B-Brave. Being open and honest as early as possible would prevent his heart from getting too involved if she only wanted to remain friends. Or so his rational brain kept trying to tell him.

"Um … sexual. I'm mostly okay. I can get it up and keep it up, but positions are limited due to my reduced mobility, strength, endurance." There, now she'd have to make the final decision about the scope of their relationship.

Normally, when it got to this point, women made up an excuse to leave. But not Beth. She snuggled in closer with a reassuring, almost relieved smile. "Thanks for being so honest. I can't tell you how much it means to me that you felt comfortable enough to share something so personal."

She wrapped her arms loosely around his neck and looked straight into his eyes. "And just so you know, I think you're pretty fantastic. And sweet. And handsome." With each word out of her mouth, her cheeks went from light rosé to deep shiraz red.

"Handsome?" Coming from Beth, a world-class model? Best compliment ever.

"Totally."

Simmering heat flared in his cheeks like he was a bumbling, bashful virgin. Time to change the subject before he made a complete fool of himself and kissed her lush pink lips, right there in public. "So ah … how did you get into modeling?"

"Luck. Right place at the exact right time. I escaped country New South Wales at eighteen and moved to Sydney. I knew I wanted to be a model, but I had no money, no experience, no promotional photos, so I worked in this cool little coffee shop to save enough to get a portfolio done. Then one day a model scout came in for a coffee.

"I had no idea who he was until he struck up a conversation with me, explained *Australia's Next Top Model* was filming around the corner, and offered me a prove-yourself style contract. I could hardly believe it. Before I had a chance to string together an answer, he gave me his card and recommended I do my research. So I did. He proved to be legit, and in less than a week I had agreed to the deal. After that, everything just took off."

"Wow. Your family must be so proud."

Her laugh had more bitterness than concentrated grapefruit juice. "Not quite. We're estranged. They're very ... religious. Judgmental. They never accepted my career choice. Or me."

So sad. Wrong. His family could be full on, but overall they were incredibly supportive and reliable, non-judgmental, just generally awesome. His sister, Hope, in particular had always been there for him.

When he'd wanted to leave his parents' place and move out on his own, she'd supported him. Whenever he needed anything, even just a chat, she always made herself available, despite the demands of her television career. "Oh, I'm so sorry. How about friends?"

She shrugged, a resigned little what-can-I-do lift of her shoulders. "I haven't been in any one place long enough to make any. My apartment's in Sydney, but I'm hardly ever home. I'm flown all over the world for photo shoots. I do meet lots of other models, photographers, makeup artists, hairstylists, designers, but they vary so much from job to job it's hard to get close to anyone. The industry is really competitive, too, so it can get pretty bitchy."

And he thought his life epitomized lonely. Hers may be glamorous and seem cool, but appearances could be deceiving. What she described sounded more and more like a shell of a life. She came across as such a lovable girl that it made the whole situation extra sad.

"But I've got you now, right?" She looked so vulnerable, so unsure, so hopeful. So unlike the confident model she portrayed to the media.

Had her flirtiness been a strategy to secure his friendship or because of genuine attraction? Her body language suggested sexual interest in him, as unbelievable as it seemed, but what the body and mind wanted, needed, could be two different things.

"Absolutely."

She hugged him again and he struggled to suppress a heart-yearning sigh.

The dance floor flashed with tragic 80s-style laser lights, cutting colored stripes across Cam and Ben's faces … and the woman they were busting their best moves with. More like a rubbing and grinding, sensual sandwich than dancing. But she smiled and laughed and twerked like she more than didn't mind the dual attention. His buddies had selected well. They definitely looked like they'd pick up. Lucky bastards.

Brody tucked a sandy-blonde-streaked lock of Beth's hair behind her ear and leaned in, savoring her delicious, sweet scent. "How about a dance?"

She pulled away and stared at him, confusion causing cute little crinkles in her forehead that he wanted to soothe with his lips. "Can you…?"

"Not in the traditional sense."

Beth went to get up, but he held her on his lap. "You can stay here … if you like."

"Oh, I get it. You want to tell everyone you got a lap dance from Beth."

He laughed. "The media would love it. Australia's hottest model, Beth, gives disabled dude a lap dance and makes it the night of his nerdy life."

She kissed his cheek, her lips leaving a throbbing stamp of longing. "You're not a nerd."

"What am I then?"

"Cool. Kind. The best man I've ever met." She answered without even a hint of hesitation.

Fuck. "Wow. Thanks." Okay, that blew her previous compliment not just out of the water, but out of Bass Strait.

"No need to thank me for being your superb self."

He could get used to hearing her talk like this, but

it wasn't a good idea. It got his hopes up, only for them to eventually come crashing down. "Come on, let's go dance."

She stayed sitting on his lap, and he wheeled them onto the packed dance floor. "Eighties music is so cheesy, but great for parties." A gold laser light flashed across her face, making her look like a sun goddess. And he could so worship her, all day, all night.

He gestured to the surrounding gamers. "Especially ones filled with geeks."

She looked at him all stern, but he couldn't miss the upturned curve of her lips peeking out from her fake frown. "Speak for yourself."

Brody did his best wheelchair dance moves, shifting forward, back, to the sides around, while Beth hung onto him, smiling and laughing. It had been the most incredible night of his life. But they'd have to say bye soon and put an end to the fantasy.

He'd had plenty of let downs, but his gut told him this time would be a particularly hard plummet back to harsh reality.

Beth jumped up to get into a few fast numbers and, man, could she move. He could watch her endlessly, his gaze fixed on her like she was the only female in the room. Her presence shone so bright, no other woman registered on his radar.

Although the more upbeat tracks were fun, he thanked the heavens for the ballads that brought her back to his lap so they could cuddle up. They stayed on the dance floor until the crowd thinned out and the DJ announced his last song for the night.

He didn't want to separate from Beth, but he couldn't monopolize her either. Plus he had a full, busy day planned for tomorrow. "It's getting late. We should go to bed." *Oh, fuck.* Was it just him or did that sound like a really bad pick up line?

Beth touched his chest. Her super-soft palm warmed his heart, her energy buzzing like she'd zapped him with a lightning bolt of electricity. "We should." She met his gaze, and instead of the cheek he thought he'd find in her gorgeous brown eyes, they flared with anxiety. "What do you have planned tomorrow?" Someone like her, so famous, so beautiful, so flawless, she couldn't be nervous … could she?

"Check out some more stalls in the morning, go to the Bungie and Epic Games game launches, then hook into the lecture circuit. There's a great session on virtual reality stuff that I'm totally into. Then I'm booked into some gamer events. It's pretty full on. How about you?"

"Nothing lined up. I've got a free day." She hesitated, her soldier-straight teeth biting into her bottom lip. "Mind if I join you?"

Fuck. Really? "I'd love that. Um … where are you staying?"

"South Wharf hotel."

"Me too. How about we meet up for breakfast first, say at seven thirty?"

"Perfect."

The slow song finished and they were the last two left on the dance floor. The overhead lights blasted back to life, making them squint and blink. Staff rushed around clearing tables, the space now deconstruction-zone desolate. "I'll walk you back to your room … escort. You know what I mean. Make sure you get back safely." Fucking hell. Could he sound more fourteen-year-old boy with a crush?

She got off his lap and he felt the loss like he'd been disconnected from the power grid. "Thanks, that's very sweet of you."

Sweet? His motives weren't quite that pure.

Along with ensuring her safety, he hoped to score a goodnight kiss. Something to fuel his fantasies before succumbing to sleep. And seeing her again.

They chatted about games on the commute to the hotel, the easy conversation continuing all the way up in the lift to her room on the twenty-fifth floor. Of course she'd snagged a celebrity-style, one-bedroom suite while he got stuck in a standard wheelchair-accessible room.

Not that he could complain. The facilities provided everything he needed to maintain his safety and independence, and that mattered so much more than aesthetics.

They stopped in front of her door and she turned to face him, her smile warm and sincere. So different from the edgy, sexy shots she was renowned for. But in a good way, like she'd chosen her softer smile especially for him. Fuck, he had to stop letting his wishful feelings delude his thinking.

"I had such a fun night. Thank you," she said, her voice a husky, enticing whisper.

"Me too."

What was the etiquette here? He wanted to kiss her, but being in a chair meant he couldn't be subtle. It made it extra hard to suss out if she wanted it too. It looked more and more like he'd have to ask her directly, ask her permission, which totally ruined the spontaneity and excitement of the moment. Or hope she bent down so he could draw her in.

She fumbled in her glittery black evening bag and pulled out her room key card.

The air throbbed thick and heavy with sexual tension, like sitting in a hundred degree Celsius sauna. "I guess it's goodnight then." But he so didn't want it to be.

"Yeah." She looked disappointed, though maybe it was just him projecting.

"But we'll see each other again in—"

She swooped down, like a determined bird in flight, and closed her lips over his, stealing his words and short circuiting every thought in his head. The kiss made his blood sizzle, his pulse pound. But before he could delve deeper, she pulled back, still within kissing distance.

"Beth." Her name on his lips was half plea, half prayer.

Her pupils mega dilated and her eyes glazed with desire. He imagined his looked similar if not even more trance-like. Before his rational, party-pooper brain intervened, he grasped her face, reconnecting their mouths, and licked across the seam of her lips.

She opened them for him, their tongues entwining, exploring, deep and intense. He hadn't had a lot of experience, but he'd had enough to know this felt right. Beyond right. She had to feel it, too, because no one—no matter how good an actor—could fake that sort of enthusiasm, that sort of attraction. Could they?

The kiss turned tear-your-clothes-off hot, and he didn't want it to stop. But it had to if they didn't want to be arrested for public indecency. And if he followed her into her hotel room, they'd progress from PG to X-Rated.

Not that he didn't crave that. He absolutely did, no question. However, he didn't want her to see him as some pushy, presumptuous guy. In her lifestyle, one-night stands probably happened heaps, but he hoped their hook-up—no, their connection—would be more than that, as ridiculous and unrealistic as it sounded.

Brody ended the kiss and she whimpered.

"I know what you mean." He swept some long, silky strands of hair off her face. "I should probably go." Except the raspy, reluctant tone in his voice said he wanted to stay.

She nodded, her expression an odd mix of sadness and relief.

He rubbed the pads of his thumbs over her flushed cheeks, and she leaned into his hands, her eyes closed, like a cat relishing the tenderness of a trusted master's touch. "I'll meet you downstairs for breakfast at seven thirty."

"Looking forward to it." Her eyes fluttered open, drowsy with leftover longing. Or maybe he'd read into the situation, seen what he wanted to see.

"Goodnight." He brushed his lips against hers one more time, because he couldn't help it, because he couldn't get enough of her, then forced himself to leave.

When he got back to his room, he undressed and transferred onto his travel commode, desperate for a cold shower. Fueling his fantasies was one thing, but he hadn't been prepared for the power of their kiss.

Every cell in him vibrated, wired with the desperate need for release. He wheeled under the chilled water, but it did nothing to cool down his overheated mind and body. Brody needed cold shock combined with manual relief or else he'd get no sleep.

He grabbed his rigid cock in his hand and stroked, already so close. Only a couple more firm pumps and he groaned her name, cum spurting over his fingers in a seemingly never-ending stream.

He collapsed back into his shower commode, eyes closed, dick still jerking in his hand, heart hammering, and allowed the water to rain over him, cleanse him, while he gathered his strength.

Having her so near all night then kissing her was … fucking beyond amazing. Unexpected. Incredible. Torturous. Brilliant.

Beth, B-True, turned out to be his ultimate dream girl come to life. And she liked him. She fucking liked him. Not some fully able, super-hot model guy, *him*. Or so it seemed.

Chapter Four
Level Two Hiccup

The next morning Beth still hadn't fully recovered from Brody's kiss. The type of kiss she hadn't expected. Tender, passionate, a prelude to sex.

Sex. A shiver shuddered along her spine. She could do it … with the right man.

She kept touching her lips and closing her eyes, reliving every hot, phenomenal second. Her mobile buzzed on the bedside table and she reached for it. A text from Brody. A swarm of butterflies flitted and fluttered and flew around in her stomach.

Brody: **Can't wait to see you.**

Beth: **Same. Not long now x**

Only forty-five minutes. She sighed and sank back into the mattress.

Brody had a super cute, hipster-IT kind of vibe going on, but most all, he symbolized safe. So his attentive, confident, forget-her-own-name kiss had been a shock. An unexpected, unforgettable, libido-reviving one.

Beth threw back the covers, slid her hand between her legs, and imagined Brody's mouth on her sex. The warmth of his tongue, the stroke of his fingers, the intensity of his stare.

She rubbed her clit like a woman gone mad with lust and came harder than she could ever remember. Gasping and writhing, she moaned long and loud and collapsed against the bed, her heart hammering. She rubbed her slick folds until her juices absorbed into her skin and her breathing settled.

Even though she'd just had the best orgasm of her life, she still felt horny. She needed a semi-cold shower—otherwise she might dry hump him like a sex-starved rabbit.

No other man had affected her like that. Ever. Normally fear stopped her from flirting, in case the relationship went somewhere uncomfortable. She'd learned to avoid encouraging interest, concerned the more she spoke with a man, the more likely that time would come.

After her cool-shower reboot, she searched through her suitcase for something casual yet sexy, pulled out her *Wanna Play With Me* gamer-girl t-shirt and paired it with leggings and runners. Then she grabbed her bag and took the elevator down to the breakfast bar and restaurant.

The doors opened and she plunged into the sea of people, following the flow into the busy room. The air smelled scrumptious, like crispy bacon, hash browns, and fluffy golden waffles.

After the momentous kiss, she'd hardly slept, unable to believe her gamer friend turned out to be so kind, handsome, wonderful. Not to mention chivalrous and adorable for not pushing her for sex. Plenty of people assumed she'd get it on freely, easily, hooking up with any hot guy she had the opportunity to fuck. But she so wasn't like that. Especially not after…

No. Not going there. She swallowed back the rising stress and scanned the busy room. In seconds she spotted him. Brody stood out, not because of his wheelchair, but because of his hip, unique style.

He looked so appetizing in his open black shirt with rolled up sleeves and white t-shirt underneath, wheeled in tight to the table—near the buffet, thank God. Starving didn't even come close to describing how she felt. Ravenous for food, his company, his touch.

Something about his energy drew her to him,

sending tingles sparking through her body. Tingles of acceptance, appreciation, desire. Although she hadn't known him long, he seemed trustworthy.

So far, he'd been upfront and honest, especially about his disability. She knew how hard that must be, how judgmental people were, how the "wrong" answers could scare people away.

Brody looked up. He flicked his dark brown hair off his face and their gazes met. His elated smile beamed with enough energy to light the room. She stopped in front of him, struck by the realization she'd never felt so valued, so wanted.

His scorching hot stare almost set her panties on fire. "Always."

What? Had he read her mind? She must have looked confused, because he chuckled and gestured to her *Wanna Play With Me* top.

"Oh. Good to know." She bent down, intending to kiss him on the cheek, but couldn't go past his irresistible lips. His cool, minty breath refreshed her senses but did nothing to stop the simmering heat in her blood. "Good morning." And it so was. The best morning she'd had since their recent online sexual experimentation.

He grabbed her waist, warmth seeping through her top to her skin, and cupped her cheek with his other hand, guiding her mouth back to his. Brody's thin black leather bracelets tickled her chin as he brushed his lips against hers with the most caring, heart-seizing kiss.

"Good morning." He flashed her a mischievous, ultra-endearing grin. If he hadn't been holding her, she would have stumbled back.

She rebalanced herself, smiled, and took the seat opposite. "Great spot."

"The perks of being in a wheelchair." Not even a hint of poor-me tinged the sarcasm in his voice. She loved how he could poke a bit of fun at himself. It showed a healthy, strong, together character. Something she aspired to. No wonder she had such an all-consuming attraction to the guy.

He propped his elbows on the white-linen-covered table top, the silver headphones charm on his black necklet swinging forward. Such a gamer nerd. But in the best possible way. "How did you sleep?" he asked. Dark circles shadowed his eyes like he'd been up gaming all night.

"Better than you, by the looks of it."

He laughed, but then his mesmerizing hazel eyes went all serious. "I couldn't stop thinking about you. I hope that's not too full on."

Her stomach fluttered at his sweet, sincere words. Graphic images flooded her brain, showing how he probably dealt with the situation. Oh my... "No. I appreciate the honesty. I kind of had the same affliction."

"Did you?"

The way he looked at her suggested his thoughts had traveled down a similar, totally inappropriate path. Okay, maybe not totally inappropriate. "Yeah, it's like your lips were laced with speed or something and I'm still waiting for the comedown," she confessed.

Brody tapped his lips. "Come and get a top up whenever you need. This is high quality stuff. No bad side effects ... well, except increasing the craving."

She stared at his full, soft lips, her mouth watering. "So increasing the craving."

"Hmmm ... you've got some serious withdrawal symptoms going on—dilated pupils, flushed cheeks, shaky hands. You'll definitely need another dose after breakfast. Doctor's orders."

Brody leaned back, exposing the word *player* written in block letters across the front of his t-shirt. He so wasn't, or at least he didn't seem to be … except when it came to computer games.

Fuck, hardcore flirting over breakfast. How long could they sustain it before… Her stomach clenched, pumping fear into her veins. Maybe she should scale things back. "No Cam or Ben this morning?"

"Ah … no. Too busy." His face went a blazing, ambulance-siren red. "They got lucky last night."

"But I saw them leave with only one woman."

"Yeah. About that. They ah … like to share."

A blast of heat throbbed in her cheeks. "Oh. Right." So much for changing the sexual subject. She fidgeted with the edge of the pristine-white tablecloth. "Good on them. As long as it's all consensual." She had no problems with adults engaging in sexual practices outside of societal norms, as long as they were done with consent.

"I agree."

They took turns filling their plates and, over a mountain of bacon, eggs, hash browns, fruit and oats, she diverted the conversation to a discussion about the day ahead and dinner afterward.

Having chatted through online gaming for a few months helped create familiarity, coziness, and the safer topic soothed the stress that had saturated her bloodstream like a toxin.

"When do you fly back?" She had to know so she could plan.

"Late Sunday night. You?"

"Same. Nine PM on QANTAS." Maybe they could share a taxi and some more steaming hot kisses before boarding.

"No way. Me too."

Destiny, fate. Had to be. The universe seemed to be shoving them together. And it made things, *him*, feel even more right. She pulled her mobile out of her handbag. "Let's do an online check-in so we can sit together. I mean, if you want to."

"Of course I want to."

In less than a couple minutes, she had them all booked in. They finished eating, ducked into the disabled toilet for a heated pash, and spent a relaxed, rest of the day together as promised. By dinnertime they were exhausted and decided to get room service to her suite.

The trip up in the lift echoed with a whoosh and the occasional metal clang in the sudden silence. The first they'd had all day. Outside of when their mouths were busy with other things like eating and kissing. It wasn't exactly awkward, more like buzzing with anticipation ... which created a major dilemma.

She so wanted to be naked with him, take their time exploring each other's bodies, exploring each other, but fear kept blowing in like an oppressive black cloud, drowning out all her excitement.

She should probably talk to him about it, explain her situation, but it was so embarrassing. And what if he didn't understand? They were still in the embryonic stage of their relationship, and she didn't want him thinking it was all too hard and abort before they even really got started, gave things a proper chance to grow.

The elevator pinged. "Here we are." She gestured for him to roll out into the corridor and rummaged around for the key card in her bag, her hand shaking, her breathing quick and shallow.

Brody grabbed her wrist, his touch gentle and reassuring. "No need to be nervous. No pressure. I don't expect anything except for us to hang out. Okay, and maybe a little more kissing." The guy could read her mind.

She let out the breath she'd been holding like a

protective shield in her chest. He made her feel comfortable at every opportunity. Such a good man. The best.

Once inside, she shut the door and he drew her onto his lap so her eyes were almost level with his. "I mean it, you know. If anything I say or do at any time makes you uncomfortable, you tell me and I'll stop."

He spoke like someone who not only knew the meaning of consent but also its importance. Like he understood the ramifications of not getting it right. Exactly the sort of man she needed. But could someone so sweet, so great, so switched on really be true? Or was Brody still on his best behavior?

Beth nodded, unable to steal her gaze away from his kind, spellbinding eyes. She pressed her hand to his chest, as though to stabilize herself, ground her to the moment, check that this amazing man was actually real.

His hands skimmed her hips, his touch whisper-light, and he pressed his mouth against her parted lips. Brody's heart jackhammered against her palm, in sync with her pounding pulse, and a rush of desire swelled in her core.

The tame kiss turned urgent, fevered. She shifted so she straddled him and slid her arms around his neck. He trailed his hands down her back and caressed her butt. Her body responded without consulting her brain, grinding against him in a desperate, wanton attempt to ease the growing ache between her legs.

One of his hands ran up her rib cage and cupped her breast over the thin material of her t-shirt, tentative at first. She arched against him and moaned into his mouth, and his strokes grew bolder, his thumb rubbing her beaded nipple over and over.

God, his touch felt so good, too good. She desperately wanted to strip off her clothes and have his hands and lips and tongue all over her bare skin.

But she couldn't.

That would just lead to trouble.

They could continue doing this, though. Erotic making out. She could finish off with her fingers later. That would keep things enjoyable, safe.

Brody slipped his hand into her leggings, stroked over her panties and groaned. "You're so wet." He said it with reverence, surprise, almost awe. Almost like he couldn't believe he'd gotten her so turned on.

He rubbed over her swollen, ultra-sensitive clit and she nearly shot off his lap. He resumed their passionate kiss, his caresses matching the sensual movement of his tongue, the pre-climactic pressure building and building. She held on tight to him, panting and moaning and writhing so hard against his hand, she thought his wheelchair might tip.

He fingered the lacy edge of her soaked panties and slid underneath, right against her wet pussy. Her head dropped back and he kissed along the column of her throat. "Oh, Brody…"

Her words seemed to encourage him because—*oh God, yes!*—he ramped up the caresses between her legs and slipped his other hand under her t-shirt and into her bra. A surge of heat and megawatt tingles overtook her body, and she teetered on the edge of an explosive orgasm.

Until his finger pressed against her opening.

"No!" Beth pushed at his chest and scrambled off his lap, going from panting with desire to panic attack. She stumbled back and wrapped her arms around herself, gasping for air.

"Beth? Are you okay?" His gentle, concerned voice soothed her raw nerves and filled her to bursting with guilt. He didn't deserve that reaction. He'd only gone with what her body had shown she wanted. What she had shown she wanted.

But Kyle had seemed kind too. Kyle had seemed patient. Kyle had seemed trustworthy.

She shouldn't compare. They were two different people. It was totally unfair and unreasonable to lump Brody into the Kyle category.

She glanced into Brody's pained face, his worried hazel eyes. "Yes. Thanks. I'm sorry—"

"No. I'm sorry. You have nothing to be sorry for. I got carried away. It's my fault. Not yours. Please tell me I haven't fucked everything up."

God, what a caring, considerate man. Too good for her. But she couldn't let him go.

Her breathing settled and she perched on his lap. She held his face between her hands and looked him in the eye. "You haven't fucked things up. Not even close." She kissed his lips, then his crinkled forehead. "Let's order dinner."

After some initial awkwardness, the rest of the night went well. They had pizza and wine and chatted like best friends forever. About the convention, about their favorite games and characters, about the new advances in virtual reality.

It got close to midnight and Brody glanced at his watch. "I better go. How about I meet you for breakfast again at seven thirty tomorrow?"

"I'd like that."

He pushed to the door and paused in front of it as though unsure about the touching etiquette after her earlier meltdown.

Beth twined her arms around his neck. "I really like you. Nothing's changed between us, not from my side." She shook her head. "Actually, that's not totally true. I like you even more than before."

His hands were gentle on her hips, hesitant, so she instigated sitting back down on his lap.

She ran her palms down his chest to his taut stomach and back up, and his grip tightened. Brody had a buff, drool-worthy, not overly built upper body. Exactly what she appreciated in a man, physically. None of that overblown, bulky, body dysmorphia. Beth liked guys who looked after themselves but didn't go berserk. Lean but firm men were her thing, muscular but in proportion.

His skinny, underdeveloped lower body kind of threw that out, well, except his... Jesus Christ, he was blessed with quite a cock. The big bulge pressed insistently against her thigh, making itself known—like something that size could be forgotten.

Most women would be impressed. For most women, his God-given gift would be a massive turn-on. Not for her. For her, a porn-style cock was synonymous with fear, with pain. And yet, she still wanted him.

Brody studied her eyes as though checking she meant what she said. Her expression, combined with her caresses, must have convinced him because he smiled, leaned in, and pressed another tender kiss to her lips. If she hadn't been sitting, she would have swooned. Olden days, 1800s, corseted-women-style swooned.

"You're sure everything's all right?"

"Yes." *With you.* But overall, things weren't all right. And he'd already had a glimpse of that. If she wanted their relationship to have a chance, she had to find a way to sort out her issues before she caused him and herself a world of heartbreak.

****

Brody's last day at the convention with Beth rocked, and the flight back to Sydney only extended the fun. Lots of awesome kissing may have helped. It definitely made him relax a bit after the incident in her suite the night before.

Some bastard must have majorly fucked her over in the past. So he'd do everything he could to show her he cared, that he'd never hurt her. Not intentionally.

After saying their goodbyes to Cam and Ben, he and Beth shared a cab into town. Brody kissed her goodbye with the promise of another catch-up later in the week. Even though things seemed back on track, a hint of weirdness still hung between them.

Maybe he'd read into their attraction and the possibility of a longer term relationship. Maybe Beth just thought of him as a nice guy to hang out with for the weekend and then they'd go their separate ways. She'd return to her glamorous lifestyle and him to his insular IT. He'd stay friends, if that's all she wanted, but with the intensity of their connection, he hoped for more.

Two nights later, while Brody worked furiously on his laptop, trying to solve a security error on his current client's new software program, his mobile chimed. He glanced up and Beth's beautiful face filled his phone screen, stopping all coherent thought. Then seconds into his excitement, he realized it was probably a "I had a wonderful weekend and you're a great guy but we're over" text.

Curiosity got the better of him, and he put his laptop on the couch and snatched his phone off the coffee table.

Beth: **Hey Brody! Hope you're all settled back home. I'm still struggling. I miss hanging out. I miss you. Can't wait to catch up. Let me know when you're free xox**

His stomach flipped and his heart banged in his chest. She'd initiated contact. She wanted to see him.

Brody: **So great to hear from you! How about Friday night? Come over to my place, say 7pm. I'll** cook. **Just bring yourself and limber up your gaming hand ;-) Miss you too.**

    Beth: **Perfect. Can't wait to see you xox**

Chapter Five
Level Two Deja vu

Thank God, Friday rolled around quickly, like the rest of the week had been on fast forward. Brody spent the day finalizing his dinner menu—ensuring both appetizer and main were devoid of garlic—and setting up his apartment for seduction. Or at least a few stolen kisses.

He dimmed the lights in the living area and strategically placed candles leading all the way to his bedroom, to create added ambiance. And, well, to hopefully direct the post-dinner events into a full-blown night of passion. Man, he really needed to rein in his over-eager brain or else risk button fly indents on his dick.

No matter how much he craved Beth, he wouldn't push, just construct an enticing atmosphere and have the universe do the rest. The universe, his genuine charm, and his expert gamer skills. In the end, consent came first.

Living with a disability, he'd experienced occasions where it didn't, and it felt uncomfortable, wrong. Health professionals often assumed they could touch him without asking, without warning. Although they meant well and were trying to assist, the approach was unacceptable.

It created an unequal power play and made him feel helpless rather than empowered. Luckily for him, that power had never been abused. Having Hope as his ever-present support at medical and allied health appointments, growing up, had definitely helped. It scared him to think about how many vulnerable disabled or elderly people had been taken advantage of. So he swore never to put someone in that position.

Brody did some last-minute tidying, unable to sit still, excitement sparking his nerves like lit firecrackers ready to launch. A knock rattled the door, setting off an explosion of fireworks zipping and booming in his stomach.

He glanced at his watch. Seven o'clock. Right on time. Fashionably-late game-playing crap scored no extra points with him. So he was happy she hadn't gone down that route. He loved software games but hated emotional bullshit. He appreciated someone reliable, true to their word, someone who shared his interests.

Closing his eyes, he drew in a deep, controlled breath, then let it out slowly before opening his eyes and propelling to the front foyer. He shook out his shoulders and eased the door open.

Fucking hell. She looked … *fuck*. A dress like that should be banned from public view or else risk a spike in road accidents. No hot-blooded male could ignore that sort of sexy distraction. The short, hot pink little number conformed to her every curve, sending his blood surging south. She looked more alluring than he thought possible.

His eyes must have been close to popping out of their sockets, because she gave him a delighted yet nervous smile and handed him a bottle of wine. "I know you said not to bring anything, but … you were cooking me dinner so…"

"Thank you." In so many ways. He wheeled aside, holding the door open. "Come in. Please."

She stepped inside, then bent forward and pressed a light, affectionate kiss to his lips. Heaven. He'd forgotten just how much she stirred his senses, sent his heart and mind into overdrive. The rush bombarded his body, beating the buzz he got when playing a challenging new game for the first time.

Her sweet, sensual scent swirled around him, conjuring images of her frolicking on the beach, half naked. Hot and summery and deliciously potent. Her presence was undeniably captivating. He couldn't get enough of her, but he needed to pace himself. They had all night.

Brody reluctantly pulled back and gestured toward the focal point of his apartment—a massive wall-mounted TV.

"Wow! What an awesome game room."

"Thanks. I thought we could play later." And, yes, he totally meant the double entendre.

Her eyes went wide with appreciation and maybe even a little lust. "I'd love that!"

Me too. "Take a seat. Dinner's about twenty minutes away. Would you like a wine while we wait?"

"Yes, please. Do you need help with anything?"

"Nope. You just take it easy. Make yourself comfortable." And he totally meant it. He loved having her in his home and hoped she enjoyed it as much as he did.

Brody opened the bottle she'd brought and poured them each a generous glass of red. "To many more enjoyable nights. Together."

She touched her glass to his. "Cheers."

They each had a sip and placed their drinks down on the coffee table.

His gaze reconnected with her big brown eyes. "So, how about a game before dinner?"

"What sort of game?"

"Truth or dare."

She gulped, giving away her apprehension, but nodded. "Okay. You first."

"No, no. You're my guest. Go for it."

"All right." She grabbed her wine, had another sip, and returned her glass to the table. "I dare you to sit next to me."

"Easy." He put his brakes on and transferred onto the two-seater couch next to her.

"Your turn." Her voice sounded all Marilyn Monroe breathy.

"I dare you to kiss me."

She bit her plump bottom lip, her gaze darting between his eyes and lips, then leaned in and pressed her mouth to his for a kiss that went from innocent to erotic. All locked lips, sliding tongues, and wandering hands. Seconds away from ripping their clothes off, or at least that's where his head had gone, the stove alarm went off.

Calling on every ounce of willpower, he broke the kiss and pressed his forehead to hers. "Fuck."

She seemed disappointed, too, but then her mouth curved into a hopeful smile. "We can pick up where we left off after we eat. I don't have a curfew."

So, her mind had diverted down the same deviant path. Excellent start.

Normally he enjoyed food, taking his time to savor the flavors. But not tonight. Tonight he couldn't wait to get dinner out of the way and indulge in a non-food feast.

His dick went battering-ram hard, slamming against his fly with anticipation, making it not only difficult to transfer back into his chair but also to push away from her. However, the sooner he served up their meal, the sooner they could get back to devouring each other.

They sat at the dining table and the conversation flowed, along with the wine. When they finished eating, Beth helped him clean up. Afterward, they returned to the lounge room.

She patted a spot next to her on the couch. "Now, where were we?"

Two great minds, or in their case, dirty minds, really did think alike. Brody did the most lightning-fast transfer ever and shifted in next to her, as close as possible. He cupped her face with his hands and resumed kissing her luscious lips. She tasted like high-end red wine, dark chocolate, and pure sex. Cocaine addictive, one hundred percent bliss.

Her hands explored his chest and moved lower, closer to his about-to-explode cock. "Straddle me." His voice croaked out, desperate with lust and longing.

Thank fuck, she indulged his request, rubbing her panty-covered pussy against his crotch. All he could think of was ripping open his fly and getting inside her wet heat, but he needed to be patient, throw some virtual ice on his wired, overheated body.

His hands didn't seem to get the hold-back memo and roamed under her dress, along her thighs, his thumbs skimming the edge of her panties, desperate to touch her soaked skin.

Her lips moved from his and trailed along his jaw, to his ear, down his neck. "Too many clothes," she murmured and lifted his t-shirt over his head.

Don't blow in your pants, dude.

She continued her arousing onslaught on his chest, sucking and licking his nipples and moving lower. She slipped off his lap and kneeled between his spread legs.

Oh my fucking God. She wasn't going to...

Beth undid his jeans, grasped the edge of his seamless boxers, and glanced up at him with her huge, desire-filled eyes. "Can I...?"

She fucking was. Beth. His dream girl fantasy come true wanted to give him head.

Fuck yes! He nodded, unable to form words.

She tugged at his waistband, freeing his cock, and licked along its length.

Holy fuck.

She kissed the head, swirled her tongue over the slit and took him in, deep. He fought against closing his eyes, determined not to miss one of the best moments of his life. Their gazes locked and he counted back from one hundred in sevens to stop himself from losing it wa-a-ay too prematurely.

His hips thrust forward, the heat of her mouth, the suction of her tongue, the sight of his cock sliding between her lips sending his synapses into stimulation overload. She added her warm hand to caress his balls and he nearly lost control. It rated as the most fucking incredible blow job he'd ever experienced.

Up until then, he'd had a couple one-night stands who had gone down on him, and he'd come, but they hadn't shown even five percent of Beth's passion. Her lips, her tongue, and the fire in her eyes showed she enjoyed pleasuring him as much as he enjoyed the feel of her mouth, the touch of her hands, the electric sensations she aroused in his dick and balls.

He grasped her head, her long, silky hair slipping through his fingers as she worked her magic on his cock. And like an inexperienced pubescent boy, which wasn't too far from reality, he came much quicker than he'd hoped, his climax hitting him like a mega dose of MDMA. But she didn't seem to mind his trigger-happy dick, swallowing burst after burst of his cum and licking him clean.

The jolts of pleasure started to subside and he dropped his head against the back of the couch, his lungs burning, screaming for air like he'd just finished a hundred kilometer wheelchair marathon. Up hill.

He glanced at Beth still on her knees before him looking so fucking sexy. How had he gotten so unbelievably lucky? How had he, a disabled dude, snagged such a gorgeous, giving woman?

She stared at him through her long, brown lashes, her tongue darting out and sweeping over her shiny lips, as though not wanting to miss a drop of his cum. "I've always been a dessert fan. And that was … mmm … divine." Beth's desire-dazed eyes and husky voice made his brain go all primal. He wanted to strip her down and taste every inch of her body.

"Let me return the favor."

She tucked him back in his underwear—her hand on his cock already nudging him toward round two—did up his pants, and joined him on the couch. Obviously, she didn't quite have the same idea.

Beth touched his thigh, making it hard for him to concentrate on anything else. "You don't have to. It was my treat. I wanted to do it."

"I want to do it to you too."

"Next time."

Except, over the next few weeks, she continued to distract him with more mind-blowing orgasms and managed to redirect his advances. He'd snuck in a few touches to her bra-covered breasts and over her damp panties, but that's where it stopped. Frustration station.

His sexual tension got somewhat relieved by her high-class head jobs, but most of the time he struggled with an increasing, severe case of blue balls.

When they weren't in person they chatted on the phone, via text, social media, or playing online games and it was cool. Everything seemed to be going well … outside of her reluctance to allow him intimate knowledge of her body.

The more she wouldn't let him touch her, the

more he craved it, like a sweet on a strict, sugar-free diet. Being refused the chance to even try to please her drove him fucking crazy with unmet need. Somehow, he had to rectify it and soon, before his balls and his composure burst.

Chapter Six
Level Three Success

The week before Christmas, Beth invited Brody to her place for dinner for the first time and he drove over, determined to break through her resistance. But when she opened the door, his gaze collided with a large abstract black-and-white painting of a crucifix.

Hadn't she told him her devout Christian family didn't accept her, that she'd renounced religion? So why have a cross as a center piece in her home?

"Hi." She bit the corner of her bottom lip, her cheeks tinged pink.

He gave her his best, chill-gorgeous-it's-all-good smile. "Hey." He reached around his wheelchair, grabbed the gift bag he'd hung off the back handlebars, and gave it to her.

"What's this?" Her smile widened, and she waved him inside.

"Something I hope you'll enjoy." He rolled through the front entrance and shut the door.

Beth pulled out the little red box and glanced up at him with a quizzical arch in her brow. She fondled the box for a second, then flipped the lid open, revealing the PlayStation earrings he'd agonized over. It had been between those and wireless, discreet earphones.

She lifted out and studied each individual earring, her smile blooming like a spring rose. Breathtaking, memorable, beautiful. "You shouldn't have … but I'm so glad you did. I love them!" She threw her arms around his neck and crushed her mouth to his. "They're perfect," she murmured against his lips, in between breath-stealing kisses.

"I thought they might be." He'd considered

flowers, chocolates, the typical, expected offerings—but none felt right. None fit Beth. Until he found the ideal, gamer-girl gift.

"I can't wait to wear them!" She kissed him again, excitement radiating out of her every pore, then practically skipped into the hollow, open-plan living space. She placed the box on the angular black dining table, the corners so sharp they could cut toughened glass, and turned back to him. "Make yourself at home."

That felt almost impossible when the room had such a minimalist, untouchable vibe. No ornaments, no knick knacks, and only two other framed pictures hung on the large, white walls. One, a black-and-white, high-fashion photo of a woman's face with bright red lipstick, and the other, a portrait sketch of Beth.

He rolled over to the image of her, the one thing that gave away her presence, the one thing that hinted at her personality in this striking but cold place. Her home—more like temporary lodgings in between jobs—seemed to reflect unresolved conflict. Did that internal battle form part of her resistance to a physical relationship?

He fingered the sleek black picture frame. "Where was this done?"

"Paris. By one of the street artists in Montmartre." Her soft, nostalgic tone wafted over him like an expensive perfume. "Have you been?"

"Not yet."

"I'll take you … one day."

His heart leapt in his chest. She saw a future for them. Not just him. "I'd love that."

A high-pitched, persistent beep broke up their cozy conversation. "That's the oven alarm. I better check…" She stepped backward and gestured to a chairless space at the dining table. "That's your spot. I'll be back with the food in a sec."

"Need any help?"

"No. Everything's under control, thanks." She disappeared through a sliding door, her voice trailing behind.

They talked and laughed through a delicious, home-cooked meal and a couple of gin and tonics, then flirted over a decadent taster plate of desserts. The air crackled with sexual tension, and their gazes teased and locked like they were ready to pounce.

Beth pushed her dining chair back and stood. "Come with me." Her inflection made the statement sound almost like a question. Didn't she know by now the power she had over him? That he'd go with her anywhere.

Brody flicked off his wheelchair brakes, left the stark, unlived-in-looking living area and followed her into her warm, candlelit bedroom.

Unlike the other rooms in her apartment, this one had character, embodied Beth. It glowed with a soft, sensual pink and smelled like roses and … patchouli? Essential oils of the aphrodisiac variety, according to his creating-the-mood-for-seduction research.

Her folded doona sat to the side of her queen size bed, with a large white towel rolled out beside it. She'd planned this, planned to get him in her bedroom. Maybe cracking her resistant shell wouldn't be as difficult as he'd assumed.

Beth rubbed her hands together. "Time for you to strip…"

Yes!

"But keep your underwear on and lay on your stomach."

Damn. But at least the situation showed some progress.

He shrugged out of his t-shirt and jeans, setting a new speed record. Transferring onto the towel, he got into position, keeping his head turned to the side so he could watch. She walked up beside him and reached for an aromatherapy oil blend on the bedside table, still fully dressed in her black leggings and tight pink singlet top.

"Uh-uh. If I'm in my underwear, you should be too. It's only fair."

Her eyes widened and she swallowed, swallowed again. She had no valid argument. And she knew. "Okay. Give me a sec." She disappeared and returned in a pastel-pink lace bra and sexy matching panties. "Better?"

So much better. His eyes nearly bugged out of his head like some randy cartoon character. "Oh yeah." Though now his dick strained against his boxers, wedged between him and the bed.

"Ready for your massage?"

"Full body? I have a sore groin that needs some extra special attention."

Her cheeks flushed Ferrari red, even though she'd blown him off more times than his straight-A-maths brain could count. "I'll see what I can do."

She climbed on top of him, perching lightly over his butt, and rubbed scented oil into his skin. Muscle tension evaporated, well, except in one sexually aroused spot.

His low groan filled the super-charged silence. "That feels so good."

"Your shoulders are really tight."

Not to mention the stiffness further south. "Yeah, side effect of sitting in a chair for so long. My computer work and gaming obsession don't help either."

"Well, consider yourself lucky. Now you've got me to give you some relief." Her voice dripped with sensual promise and his dick hardened to a steel rod, ready to skewer her mattress.

She climbed off him with the grace and control of a highly skilled model and gamer. "Roll over."

He did, unable to hide the bulge in his boxers.

She straddled his thighs and massaged his chest, barely concealing a satisfied smirk, the little temptress, then leaned forward and nipped his earlobe. "Hand or mouth. Your choice."

Fuck. "Hand." Mouth would ruin him for the rest of the night. And he wanted tonight to be different, special.

Beth trailed her fingers down his stomach and tugged down his waistband to expose his erect cock. Using one hot, slick hand, she stroked his dick, up down, up down, up down, while the other played with his balls.

Fucking heaven.

She picked up the pace, unmistakable desire turning her eyes almost black.

A few more pumps and he neared the peak. "I'm gonna—"

Beth's mouth covered the head of his cock—her gaze fixing on his—and he came, squirting stream after endless stream down her throat. Her tongue lapped at his slit, clearing the sticky remains of his release, and he sank back against the bed.

"Fucking hell." He couldn't fault her dedication to his dick, her insatiable desire to get him off. But now he wanted the chance to reciprocate. For once. Needed the chance to taste and feel the texture of her pussy with his lips and tongue and make her come.

Brody ran his hands gently down her arms. "Come here."

She planted her palms on each side of his head and he cupped her face. He brought her mouth to his and tangled his tongue with hers in a deep, passionate kiss.

Beth pulled back, breathless, and stared at him with surprise. "I've never been with a guy who's kissed me straight after… It doesn't bother you?"

Tasting himself on her? "No way. It's fucking hot." He pressed another heated kiss to her lips to reinforce the point. "Now it's my turn…"

"No, it's okay." She edged toward the end of the bed, and he sat up and grasped her wrist.

"It's not okay. I'm dying here. I want to do it so damn much."

She picked at a loose thread in the towel right beside his knee. "Seriously, I'm fine. Making you feel good makes me feel good." He didn't doubt she meant that, but honestly, what sane person would pass up the opportunity for an orgasm?

Something major must have gone down in her past, something that took all the joy from such a simple, natural, but unbelievably effective act. And he wanted to be the one to restore her pleasure.

"If you really want to make me feel good…" He brought her hand to his mouth and kissed each of her knuckles. "Then let me see you. Let me touch your body with my hands, my mouth. Let me watch you scream with ecstasy."

Her breathing hitched and her eyes glazed with arousal. She wanted it as much as he did, but that blocker continued to hold her back.

"Let me get close to you."

"I want to…" Her voice trembled more with worry than anticipation.

If she didn't have the courage to confide in him verbally, maybe physically baring herself to him might prop open the door into her mind wide enough to get a glimpse of her fears, her vulnerabilities, to begin to let him in.

"Please let me do this." He teased her palm with an open-mouthed kiss and she shivered. "You can talk to me the whole time. Tell me what you like, want more of, less of. If anything stresses you out, if you want me to stop. Or continue…"

Her teeth clamped onto her bottom lip, leaving white, bloodless indents in the plump, pink flesh. "But you'll want to have sex with me."

Fuck, she didn't just look scared—she looked petrified … about having one of the most incredible, intimate, and what should be brilliant experiences a couple could share. Sex and fear did not belong together. Brody aimed to change that, to undo every bit of hurt the fuckhead in her past had caused, however long it took.

"No. I want to make love to you. But I can see you're not ready. And that's totally okay. There's absolutely no urgency. What's most important to me is that we both want it, both enjoy it."

"Really?" Relief replaced the anguish in her exquisite, expressive face.

"Yes, I swear." Hang on, he assumed all her reluctance to sex related to some earlier, ugly event, but maybe it stemmed from inexperience, performance pressure, fear of failure. How did he ask about her sexual history without sounding judgmental, patronizing? "But to make sure that happens, I need to know … are you … ah…"

"Do I still have my V-card? Not technically."

Whatever the hell that meant. But it did confirm she'd done the deed, somewhat, and it couldn't have been too good. More like memorable for all the wrong reasons. He'd make it his mission to change that.

Brody cradled her neck and kissed her. When he pulled away, that desire daze had returned to her eyes. He reached behind her, his fingers toying with the clasp on her bra. "May I?"

"Yes." Her voice shook with uncertainty. But he'd do everything in his power to make her comfortable, to trust him enough to try again.

Brody slid her delicate lace bra down her arms and tossed it off the side of the bed. God, her breasts were beautiful. High and full with delectable, dusky pink nipples that he wanted to lick and taste. "Lay on your back for me." He could hardly recognize his own voice, all breathy and raspy with want.

Beth swiveled around and lay beside him, her gorgeous sandy-blonde-streaked hair splayed across the pillow. He bent down and kissed along the smooth skin of her throat, across her collar bone, and closed his lips around her nipple. She moaned and pressed into him, and he reached up and rolled her other hard nipple between his thumb and finger.

"How's that?"

"Mmm … good." Beth sank her hands into his hair and tugged, sending a jolt of desire down to his dick.

He continued kissing along her body, over her stomach, her navel, and hooked his fingers in her scrap of lace panties. "Can I…?"

She swallowed. "Yes."

Triumph surged through his bloodstream, the buzz greater than his top-score gaming high. He slid her panties down her long, lean legs and flung them onto the floor. He kissed his way up her calf, to her knee, but before he could go any further, she slammed her thighs together, refusing him entry to her pussy.

"You okay?"

She nodded but kept her legs shut.

"You sure?" The fucking tool who'd screwed with her…

She nodded again.

"Then, relax your legs…" He caressed her thigh with calming, encouraging strokes.

After a few seconds, her breathing slowed and she did as he asked, giving him a glimpse of her neatly groomed muff. "Good, that's good. Now, spread them a bit wider."

Her toes curled and her hands fisted the sheets, but she didn't shift her legs.

"Please. I want to taste you, lick you out, make you come. Have you come like that before?"

"No."

"Has a man ever made you come?"

She hesitated, her face flushing, then shook her head. "No."

What sort of selfish pricks had she been with? "I promise it'll feel good. I'll make sure it feels good."

"You'll just touch the outside, right?" Her soft voice wavered and her worried gaze latched onto his.

"If that's what you want." He'd do anything to put her at ease, to show her this should be fun, exciting, pleasurable. Not something to fear.

"Yes."

"No fingers or tongue inside." He kissed the short cropped hair at the top of her mound.

Her breath hitched. "Promise?"

"I promise."

Slowly, she spread her lovely legs, revealing her pretty pussy, still glistening with arousal. He dipped his head and inhaled her sweet, intoxicating scent. "Can you bend your knees up for me and keep your legs nice and wide? That's it."

And what a view. He was almost ready to come again, just looking at her. Brody got comfortable between her thighs, licked along her seam, and flicked her clit with his thumb.

She gasped and arched up.

"How's that?"

"Oh God. Good. So good."

With a soft tongue, he took his time exploring her folds and circled her entrance, careful not to breach her opening. Her eager moans egged him on, and he trailed his tongue back to her swollen clit.

He alternated between licking and sucking, increasing the rhythm until she cried out in ecstasy. He kept going, lapping at her gush of juices until she came again, thrusting her hips and riding out the rest of her orgasm.

Success! It ranked up there as one of his most proud, memorable moments. He'd not only managed to shift her restrictive, negative assumptions, her apprehension, but he, a disabled dude, not some hot perfect model man, made her come. Twice.

When her muscles stopped shuddering and convulsing, he gave her clit a final kiss and moved up over her body, propping himself up on his elbows. "Seeing you lose control like that is so fucking hot. Makes me want to keep getting you off."

Her sated smile morphed into parted lips and eyes dark and primal with hunger. She gripped his head and drew him down until their lips locked. Some time later, they finally separated to take a much-needed breath.

"Thank you," she whispered against his lips.

"Thank you." And he absolutely meant it. Beth trusting him, giving herself to him, was the best gift he'd ever been given.

He rocked his bulging cock against her pussy, and she rubbed along the length of him, increasing the friction.

They kissed, her beaded nipples dragging deliciously against his bare chest, and he stilled, close to coming.

Beth's face contorted in climax. "Brody!"

Hearing her voice so unhinged, so heavy with passion, pushed him over and he came, hard, thrusts erratic, gasping for breath. He dropped his forehead to hers, and they breathed in each other's recovering breaths. Once his heart rate returned to near normal, he caressed her rosy cheek. "I'll be back in a minute."

Brody levered himself off her, transferred into his wheelchair, and went to the bathroom. He cleaned himself up and stared at his disheveled reflection in the mirror. Not quite sex but still bloody awesome.

He'd been intimate with Beth. *Beth!* The unreachable, out-of-his-stratosphere model. She'd let him see her naked, touch her, taste her. And it was everything he'd dreamed of and more. So much more, so much better.

He splashed his face with cold water. *Take it easy, bro.* He didn't want to scare her off with his protective, you're-mine, caveman male routine. In her industry and with her beauty and celebrity status, she probably got it heaps.

Beth didn't look at him or treat him like any other guy, though. Did his disability make him seem less of a threat, safe? Going by her response, she really liked him, trusted him … mostly. Not even his underdeveloped lower body seemed to bother her. And that was something that usually made him pretty self-conscious.

Her lack of experience with men—a total fucking surprise. He couldn't believe she'd gotten close to thirty without a guy eating her out. Knowing he'd been the first man to give her that pleasure, to make her come, three times now, was a real honor, a privilege.

"Brody, you okay?" Her concerned voice penetrated the bathroom door.

"Yeah, all good." Except she didn't *fully* trust him. She continued to hold back about her past, particularly her sexual history.

The full-on fear when he went anywhere near her slit showed that. If only she'd confide in him, but he didn't want to push. He'd just keep gently coaxing her and hope she opened up, let him help her work on the issue. Together.

Brody propelled back into her bedroom and reached for his t-shirt. "It's getting late. I better go."

She raced to the side of the bed, still gorgeously naked, and snatched his top out of his hand. "No. Don't. I want you to stay." She gulped, her eyes almost pleading. "If you want to."

Fuck, of course he wanted to. He couldn't imagine anything better than falling asleep cuddling Beth and waking up with her in his arms. "You're sure."

"Totally."

Brody transferred back onto her bed, and she snuggled into his side. It felt so natural, like they'd been a couple for years. A loving couple, who could conquer anything. Now he just needed to convince her to believe that too.

Chapter Seven
Level Four Fail

On Christmas Eve, Brody invited Beth over to try out his gamer gift to her and spend the night. They'd almost been inseparable since the lick-out breakthrough at her house. But things hadn't progressed from there, and he hoped tonight would be the game changer.

Then tomorrow, he'd bring Beth to Christmas lunch at Hope's place and make the big-step, girlfriend introduction to his family. He couldn't wait. They were going to love her; he had no doubt.

Sitting on his bed, he put on his best black jeans and runners, transferred into his wheelchair, and went to select a t-shirt. *Are You Game?* sat on top of the pile, the perfect choice for the occasion. Just as he slipped into it, the doorbell rang. Right on seven. He rolled to the door and opened up, his heart just about beating out of his chest with anticipation.

Beth greeted him with a seductive smile and consummate-model pose. In her short red strapless dress with white fur trim and thigh-high, red-and-white stockings, she looked like a sexy Christmas elf. Ready to be plundered. If he physically could, he'd drag her inside and do her up against the door.

His dick rammed against his fly. "Fuck, you look edible."

"You look pretty tasty too." Beth stepped into the front foyer, dropped her small black overnight bag, shut the door with her foot, and leaned against it, her smile wide and devilish. She grabbed his hand, slowly guided it up her inner thigh and … fuck. No underwear. And her pussy already wept for his undivided attention.

He lifted her dress and leaned forward, drinking

in her fresh-coconut, musk-tinged scent. "Lift one leg over my shoulder."

She did as he requested, giving him incredible access to her smooth, hairless mound. Fuck, she'd gone and waxed for him. Best start to Christmas Eve he could ever remember.

Mmmm ... dessert before dinner. He caressed her sleek skin. "Gorgeous. Thank you."

Brody nuzzled the apex of her thighs and licked along her seam. She whimpered and pressed her pelvis into him. Since introducing her to the pleasures of oral she couldn't seem to get enough, which made total sense. Who wouldn't want to make up for lost lick-out time?

He loved her responsiveness, the sexy little sounds escaping her lips, the involuntary rocking of her shapely hips, the blissful contortion of her stunning face when she came. Absolutely loved it.

It turned him on until he could think of nothing else he'd rather do than bury his face between her legs for hours. He just hoped her enthusiasm centered around him and their precious connection more than the physical release.

Brody delved his tongue through her damp folds, licked her entrance and rimmed her back hole, then returned to her clit, swollen and aching for his sensual onslaught. He teased the tight little bud until she begged him to make her come. God, he loved that husky, desperate, pleading tone, like she fully trusted he'd satisfy her needs.

He wrapped his wet lips around her clit and sucked, refusing to ease up until he reached his new goal—making her climax ... multiple times. She gripped his hair and bucked her hips against his face, coming once, twice, three times, coating his tongue and chin with her juices. So fucking hot. He nearly blew without her even touching his cock.

Her leg wobbled, shook, and if not for his steadying hands on her hips, she would have crumpled to the floor, for sure.

"Wow, that was some greeting. I must come over more often." She lifted her leg off his shoulder, bent down and kissed his moist mouth, her breathing still sporadic, her eyes still clouded with lust.

"I agree," he whispered against her lips. "Now follow me."

She helped him set the table and dish out their meals, and after a relaxed, chatty dinner, he escorted her to the living area to chill, game, and make out. In no particular order.

They sat together on the couch, and Beth rummaged through her overnight bag. She whipped out a rectangular, silver-wrapped present and handed it to him. "A little something … for you. Hope you like it."

He stared into her beautiful brown eyes. "I like anything you give me." Time, friendship, love. Fuck, just being with her was a priceless gift.

Brody tore off the paper, revealing a shiny black box. He flipped open the lid and slid the bubble-wrapped contents into his hand. "Finally, a woman who gets me."

"You haven't even seen what's inside yet."

No, he hadn't, on so many levels, yet it didn't stop him from loving the full package. Beth. "Doesn't matter. You had me at bubble wrap."

She laughed, the sweet, melodic sound sending a rush of loving warmth through to every cell in his body. "Come on. Open it!"

"Promise I get to go on a popping frenzy afterwards?"

She tried to tame her smile … and failed. "Only if you behave yourself."

"That's a shame."

Beth laughed again, more of her joy and love infiltrating deep into his heart. "Come on, hurry up!"

He peeled off the protective bubble wrap, revealing a selfie picture of them, on the dance floor at the convention, with Beth cuddled up in his lap, encased in a black frame with *Game On* written in shiny silver letters across the bottom.

Pure, raw emotion jabbed at the back of his eyes. He didn't cry, no matter how tough things got, no matter how angry or sad or elated. He'd never been that sort of guy. Until now.

They looked so happy, so in love, so full of promise. Seeing them together like that provided evidence of their romantic relationship, proof of its existence. It convinced him that what he believed wasn't just a figment of his overactive imagination. Not that he should need proof, but it helped … just like hearing *I love you.*

"So…?"

Shit. How long had he been silent? No words could explain his feelings. He'd just have to show her what her gift meant to him, what she meant to him. He reached up and stroked her pink cheek. He pressed his lips to hers and poured all his hopes, gratitude, and love into the kiss.

Lightheaded from the dizzying intensity of their union, he lifted his head and rested his forehead against hers. "Thank you."

"Thank *you*." Her voice quivered with lingering lust, or was it … more? It definitely felt like more. Passion like that couldn't be faked. Could it? His limited experience made it hard to tell.

He held her face between his hands, brushed a kiss to her brow, her closed eyes, her lush lips. Then he edged forward on the seat, grabbed the gold, gift-wrapped box from under his miniature Christmas tree on the center of the coffee table, and gave it to her.

Her eyes lit up like the Times Square screensaver photo on his computer. She ripped open the present as though she'd never received a gift before and pulled out the newly released clit hood and sensor dildo for his brother-in-law's virtual reality game, the game where they'd first met, *Intimacy World.*

"Not quite the same level of thoughtful—"

"Thank you." Her hands trembled and she wouldn't look at him.

Strange. Sure his choice didn't tug as hard on the heartstrings, but it certainly tugged hard in other areas, baser areas. Or so it was designed to. Although not as sentimental, it still provided the tools to ensure many hours of fun.

He tipped her chin up and studied her eyes. "You okay?"

She nodded but looked far from all right.

"If you don't like it, I can take it back, exchange—"

She slipped her hand around his. "No, it's great. A great idea."

"You're sure? You're not just saying that so you don't hurt my feelings?"

She squeezed his hand. "I'm sure." But she didn't look sure. Something was up and not in a good way. Maybe if they played a game and she tested them out, she'd see just how much they could offer, how they really were the kind of gift that kept on giving.

"How about I grab my cock sleeve and we'll give them a test run."

"No."

His gaze shot back to hers, the vehemence in her

tone a total surprise.

"I mean, I'll try the clit hood but not the other … not yet."

He cradled her cheek and used the pad of his thumb to rub slow, soothing strokes along her skin. "No worries. It's up to you. Whenever you're ready." But when might that be?

They'd been going out close to eight weeks now and couldn't seem to get past her penetration phobia. Without knowing the cause, he had no idea how to tackle the problem, no idea what else to try to get her to positively move forward.

Brody dimmed the lights and loaded *Intimacy World*. He exposed his dick, covered it with a condom, and got his cock sleeve and gloves in place, while she fitted her clit hood and slipped the spare gloves over her trembling hands.

"Ready to give it a go?"

"Yep," she said, though conflict and uncertainty raged in her eyes, making them the color of bitter black coffee.

He started the game and, thankfully, she soon relaxed into it. After several successful missions—dancing competitions, drinking contests, renovating a house, warding off exes—some completed solo and some as their fireteam, their characters made it through to stage five—fucking.

His character, B-Brave, kissed B-True and they quickly discarded their clothes and moved to the bedroom. Some hot-as-fuck foreplay earned them additional orgasm points. Eager to increase his chances of scoring, literally and figuratively, B-Brave lined up his cock and guided it inside B-True. And he felt every tight inch.

So fucking real. He reached between their avatar

bodies and rubbed her clit, and Beth moaned like he'd touched her directly.

B-Brave pumped into B-True, picking up the pace with his cock, as well as his hand on her clit, and she came in the game and real life, almost writhing right off the couch. She looked so fucking gorgeous, he couldn't hold back any longer and lost his load into the condom, the whole time wishing he'd lost himself in her sweet, sweet, out-of-bounds pussy.

They both collapsed against the couch, panting. They'd had virtual sex, but this time beside one another, and it totally transcended awesome. Hopefully soon, he could stop imagining how much more incredible it would be to have real-life sex with Beth and actually know for sure.

Brody removed the cock sleeve, discarded the condom in a tissue, and lifted her so she straddled his lap. "I want you."

He kissed her with the ravenous hunger of a man who hadn't just come moments ago, like he had a sex-crazed fever, his hands all over her body, his cock already hard. Again. He ran his fingers up her inner thighs, removed the clit hood, and stroked the little bundle of nerves.

She arched into him, her breathing shallow. "Brody…"

He unzipped her dress and lifted it over her head, leaving her gloriously naked. He played with her breasts, tugging, nipping and licking her nipples, and continued to tease her clit with his free hand. Her juices coated his skin, so slick, so ready for him that he slid his hand to her opening and thrust a lubricated finger inside.

Her face went from pure elation to outright horror. She pushed his chest and scrambled off his lap, tears tumbling down her face. She wiped at her eyes, but the tears kept coming. "I'm sorry. I can't do this."

No, no, no! Not again. They'd been making such great progress. Her issues ran so much deeper than he realized, had well and truly taken root in her psyche. Brody grasped her hand, entwined their fingers, and urged her to sit back down on the couch beside him. "You don't have to apologize."

She wept and glanced up at him through her waterlogged eyes.

He put his arm around her and hugged her to his chest. "I mean it. It's just ... you were so wet, so I assumed ... but I shouldn't have. I should have checked with you first."

Brody kissed the top of her head and caressed her hair, trying to soothe her, trying to stop her gut-wrenching, body-shuddering sobs. "It's okay. We'll work it out, but ... you need to speak to someone—"

"I'm trying." Her voice was muffled against his tear-soaked skin.

"I hope you know you can talk to me. You can trust me. I want to help."

She tilted her head back until her gaze met his and gave him a quivering-lipped smile. "Thank you. I ... I just ... need more time. But if that's not okay—"

Brody lifted her onto his lap and cuddled her close. "Of course it's okay." No matter the issue, he couldn't lose her, not when he was so deeply in ... fuck.

Love.

Chapter Eight
Stalemate

Brody woke on Christmas morning to the gift of Beth's mouth on his nipple. Sucking, teasing, licking, nipping. God, she had such a talented tongue. Until her, he never knew his nipples were such an erogenous zone. Until her, no other woman had spent the time or the patience to explore his body, to learn what he liked.

She moved across his chest to his other nipple and glanced up. "Good morning." Her voice sounded so sultry he wanted to flip her over and fuck her until she screamed his name. But he couldn't. Not yet. He'd have to settle for some hand and mouth action, which felt great but not quite the same. Not quite so intimate. And with her, he wanted the ultimate in intimacy.

"Not just good. Having you here, in my bed, brilliant."

She flashed him a delighted smile and returned to feasting on his first nipple. He groaned and ran his hands up and down her toned back. Beth continued south and paused over his saluting cock. "You really are happy I'm here."

"So happ—oh."

All coherent thought deserted him, with her mouth around his dick. With her working him from the base, all the way to the top, up and down, up and down, up and down, he struggled to remember his favorite game let alone his own name.

Beth gave the underside of his erection, just below the tip, some extra-special love and his eyes rolled back in his head. That spot, fuck. She knew exactly how to tease it to take him right to the brink. Over and over. Her hands soon joined the sensual torment, one on his cock, one on his balls, rubbing and tugging until he floated at the edge of heaven.

One more labored breath and he let out a long, animalistic grunt, his orgasm exploding through him.

She swallowed all he offered, licked his cock clean, and sat back on her knees. "Mmm … tasty. Who needs breakfast."

"Me." He growled and lifted her so she straddled his face.

By the time they got ready, they were running late. Brody text messaged Hope to let her know, then rang his parents to confirm he and Beth would pick them up shortly.

The car ride went even better than he'd predicted. Beth's media training kept the conversational flow going. No. It was more than that. Her natural warmth shone through. He could tell by the genuine smiles on his parents' faces that they, too, found Beth irresistible.

Brody parked in his sister's expansive driveway, and her husband, Cole, greeted them at the door with his winning, celebrity smile. Such a great guy who'd been through his own personal hell.

If anyone saw him indoors, his single point stick and slow walking speed were the only indicators he'd suffered any trauma. Outdoors, he still used a manual wheelchair, but with each day, he became less and less reliant on it.

"Come in." Cole shook Brody's dad's hand, kissed his mum hello, and waved them through to the kitchen.

Brody rolled into the front foyer and Beth followed, shutting the door behind her and moving to stand right by his side.

"Beth. Breathtaking in photos, even more breathtaking in the flesh. So great to finally meet you."

Cole leaned forward and gave her his standard kiss-on-the-cheek greeting.

"Thanks." She ducked her head, her cheeks turning scarlet. "Great to meet you too. Brody's told me lots about you guys."

Cole smiled that charming, wicked grin of his that had no doubt helped him pull in the ladies in the past. "Not just the boring good stuff, I hope."

She laughed, the sweet sound hitting him right in the heart. "Absolutely not. You created *Intimacy World,* and it's not just good, it's great! Revolutionary."

"Thank you. That means a lot to me. It helped me through…" Cole gestured down his body. "This."

"I know. I saw your acceptance speech on the software awards show. It blew me away. I had to buy the game after that and give it a go. And it totally exceeded my expectations. The Hope-inspired Easter egg was such a cool, romantic touch too."

She sighed. "I kind of got obsessed with playing, trying to find it, and that's how I ended up meeting Brody. Online." Her gaze flicked to him, her smile beaming with excitement and … love? A jolt of unexpected emotion pricked the back of his eyes. Fuck, for someone who didn't cry, he'd almost failed. Twice.

Beth squeezed Brody's hand as though she'd sensed his little *moment* and could relate, but kept her attention on Cole. "I'm sure Brody's already told you our meet cute story, so I won't bore you by repeating the details… But for me personally, since coming across your game, my life's gotten better and better. So thank you."

Cole slapped Brody on the shoulder. "Beautiful, smart, sociable. A highly sought-after package. I can see why you've kept her all to yourself. I would, too, if I were you."

Beth blushed harder, her cheeks turning a deep rosy red, but what woman wouldn't under Cole's approving scrutiny.

"Thanks, man. I knew you'd understand."

A clang, clunk, crash came from the kitchen, followed by a string of swear words.

Hope. Followed by cooing, soothing sounds from his mum, and heavy, hurried dad footsteps. Well, hurried for his father who they always joked was as fast as a tortoise.

"I think that's our signal to join the others," Cole said, his tone rife with wry humor, and waved them ahead.

They entered the super-modern space that looked like a food bomb had detonated. His dad had a broom in hand, sweeping the floor, while Hope and his mum wiped over the kitchen bench and oven.

"Brody!" Hope raced over, flecks of flour splattered across her cheek, and wrapped him in a hug.

"Be careful, sweetheart." Cole sounded cautious, concerned. Strange. The two of them used to climb mountains together, amongst other risk-taking activities, so why would he be stressing about a small kitchen mishap?

Hope rolled her eyes and glanced at her hubby. "I'm fine. Not sure about the fruit mince pies, though."

She kissed Brody on the cheek and he whispered, "Is everything okay?"

"Yes," she said in a back-off, stern tone, then enveloped Beth in a warm, welcoming hug. "I'm so happy you could come today. I've been dying to meet you."

"Me too. Thanks for inviting me."

Hope stepped away and smiled, her sincere, open-hearted, non-TV-presenter smile. "Of course, anyone who's a friend, or in this case, girlfriend of Brody's is always welcome here."

Cole joined them and put his arm around Hope. She snuggled into her husband, looked him in the eye and nodded as though carrying on a spy-worthy, covert conversation.

"We've got something to tell you, but you've got to promise it'll stay just between us ... for the moment," Cole said and kissed Hope's temple. Huge smiles stretched across their faces.

Brody's parents stopped cleaning up and a chorus of "Definitely", "Of course", "Absolutely", and "Cross my heart" filled the room, followed by an expectant silence.

"Thanks, everyone. We'd planned to wait until lunch, but we're both bursting to share our news." Hope stole a glimpse at her husband, then refocused on the rest of them. "I'm pregnant. We're going to have a baby!"

Brody glanced at his girlfriend, unable to stop the joyous smile from taking over his face, while his parents rushed in to congratulate the glowing couple. Beth's eyes looked moist and everyone would assume they were happy, celebratory tears, but he sensed they represented something else.

A sadness. Like maybe she'd never experience that, couldn't experience that unless she worked through whatever caused her fear of penetration.

As soon as his parents moved aside, he rolled up to the ecstatic parents-to-be. "Wow. That's such awesome news, you guys! Congratulations. I'm so incredibly happy for you. You're gonna make the best parents."

After Cole's mountain-climbing accident and what turned out to be spinal shock, his relationship with Hope suffered and they went through some really rough times. But they figured it out, and it rocked to see them rewarded with something so wonderful. Something they thought might not be possible.

"And you're gonna be the most awesome uncle!" Tears spilled onto Hope's cheeks, and she squished him in a super-tight embrace. "Love you."

"Love you, too, sis."

When Hope broke contact he went to shake Cole's hand, and his brother-in-law pulled him into a hug. Somewhere in the midst of the shared moment, Beth appeared, giving her heartfelt congratulations to Cole and Hope, even though they'd only just met, even though it must have been extremely hard for her, given her unresolved issues in the intimacy department. Such an unselfish girl. Another reason why he loved her.

Hope wiped lingering tears from her cheeks. "Okay, enough mushy stuff for now. Let's get lunch started. I'm hungry!"

"She's constantly hungry these days." Cole's tone combined with his sly grin suggested he wasn't just referring to food. Lucky bastard.

Hope playfully elbowed her husband in the side. "Hurry up, Mr. Smart Ass. Instead of standing there talking, show us what you can do."

"I think I might have already proved my prowess," Cole stage-whispered.

Hope squinted her eyes at him but couldn't hide her absolute love for the man.

While Brody's parents worked in the kitchen, finishing some food preparation and tidying up, Beth helped Hope make the salads and set the table on the far side of the back veranda.

Brody carried out a plate of meat on his lap to Cole, aka, master of the BBQ, and decided to use the opportunity to talk to him and get his opinion on the Beth situation. Cole wasn't only approachable and non-judgmental, but also successful and experienced with women. Plus he'd survived severe trauma that had impacted on his own sex life. He'd have some wise words for sure.

Cole took the plate, placed it next to the BBQ, and started filling up the grill. "She seems like a sweet girl." He gestured with the tongs over to where Beth and Hope were laying down plates and cutlery, having a chat and laughing. "You two make a great couple."

Brody fiddled with the zip on his wheelchair bag, his heart rate speeding up to triple time. "Thanks. Ah … about that. I really need to speak to you about something. Something private. Would you mind if…"

"Go for it. Talk away. If anyone looks like coming over, I'll warn you."

Brody sighed with relief. It would do him good to get it off his stress-constricted chest. "It's relationship stuff. Sex stuff."

"My specialty. Dr. Sparks at your service. Ask me anything."

"Promise it's just between you and me. Guy advice stuff," Brody whispered, his voice just audible over the sizzling steaks.

"I promise."

He'd thought about speaking to Cam and Ben as well, but decided against it. Although he considered them great mates, they didn't get the whole celebrity privacy and confidentiality thing like Cole. Not that they'd intentionally say anything to others, but it might slip out in conversation.

If Beth's sexual issue got leaked to the media, he'd never forgive himself. He couldn't risk that happening. He'd hate for her to think he betrayed her confidence. "I need an expert opinion, so I thought…"

Cole's deep blue eyes locked on his. "What's going on?"

Brody looked around and leaned in. "That's the thing. She's a guy's dream. Sexy, passionate. Gorgeous. Loves giving blow jobs. And is fucking brilliant at them. But…" He hesitated, trying to decide the best way to phrase his thoughts. *Just say it straight out, dude.*

"She avoids sex, avoids even letting me touch her slit. It's like she has some sort of penetration phobia or something. Anytime I try and get anywhere near it, she freaks. I'm not sure what to do about it. I want to make her feel good, do what she enjoys but…"

Cole adjusted a dial on the front of the BBQ and turned up the heat. "You need to ask her about it. I know you want to do what she likes, but having such a strong reaction to her boyfriend touching her there, penetrating her, is concerning. Has she had sex before?"

"She said 'technically,' whatever that means. She's pretty guarded about her sexual history."

Tongs in hand, Cole repositioned some T-bones and beef patties and turned the sausages. "Hmmm … I'm just guessing, but it sounds like something's happened to her. Something bad. A bad experience. And it's made her uneasy, overcautious, scared. You're her new boyfriend, so maybe she feels nervous about discussing it with you. Has she got anyone else to talk to, a friend or family member she can trust?"

"I don't think so. She doesn't see her family, and from what she's said, she doesn't have any close friends. I'm not sure whether she's seen anyone professionally."

Cole grabbed a couple of beers from the ice-filled Esky beside him, slipped them in stubby holders, and handed him one. "How about I get Hope to speak to her? She might feel more comfortable talking to another woman."

"I don't know..." Brody unscrewed the top, releasing the bubbling air pressure, and had a big swig.

Cole turned the meat, searing each side. "You know your sister. She's caring and considerate, and she's great at talking to people, extracting information without seeming pushy. And she understands the importance of privacy."

He had a point. Maybe it would be good to get his sister involved. Beth could do with a good friend, someone she could trust, and Hope matched the criteria for the ideal candidate.

"Okay. As long as you don't tell Hope the details. I don't want Beth to think I'm going behind her back to try and get information. And I don't want Hope to feel weird, you know, talking about my sex life. I honestly just want Beth to feel comfortable speaking to someone, to help her sort this out."

"How about I tell Hope that Beth could do with a friend. I'll say she doesn't have any reliable supports, is emotionally guarded, and it's impacting on your relationship. I'll tell her you're worried about Beth's well-being. How does that sound?" Cole removed the meat from the heat and stacked it in a stainless steel pot.

"Great." At least he hoped so.

****

Hope embodied everything her name implied. Christmas Day, they'd really gelled, so when she rang to arrange a coffee catch-up a couple days later, Beth agreed, excited to see her again so soon.

She really needed a woman to talk to, a friend she could trust. Luckily for her, Hope seemed keen to foster an independent friendship, something separate from the relationship Beth shared with Brody.

In the little time they'd spent together, Hope appeared honest, sincere, genuine. And she understood the complexities that came with being a celebrity. If Beth's gut had read her right, Hope would prove to be everything she needed.

She found a corner booth at the back of the busy boutique coffee shop in the heart of Sydney. A few minutes later, Hope arrived, looking perfectly put together, though a little flustered. "So sorry I'm late."

Beth tapped her watch, feigning a stern facial expression. "Five whole minutes. Hmmm … I suppose I can forgive that."

Hope laughed. "Thank you. You're the best." She kissed her hello and sat in the seat opposite. "Have you ordered?"

"No. Not yet."

"Let me."

"Are you sure?" Beth put her handbag on the table and rifled through it to grab her purse.

Hope touched Beth's arm, stopping her search, and she looked up into her waiting gaze. "Definitely. I suggested we catch up, so it's on me. You can pick up the tab next time … when we go for cocktails." She raised her eyebrows, her green eyes sparkling with mischief.

"Ah … aren't you supposed to be avoiding alcohol for the next few months?"

The excitement drained from Hope's face, deflating it like a popped balloon. "Oh, yeah. Bugger. Consider yourself lucky." A cheeky grin returned to her stunning face. "What would you like?"

"A cinnamon latte, please."

"No problem. Be back in a sec."

Rich, decadent browns and golds decorated the minimalist-style coffee shop. The café version of a Ferrero Rocher. One of the benefits of arriving early meant Beth got to choose the booth side while Hope sat in one of the comfy-looking, leather-upholstered chairs with arms.

Fresh coffee and chocolate mingled to create an indulgent, mocha, mouth-watering aroma. The air smelled like pure sin. She'd be the size of a semi-trailer if she worked within a block of the place.

Hope returned and plonked back down on the padded chair opposite. "I ordered us a triple chocolate tart to share. I blame the baby."

Beth laughed, dispelling some of her stress about whether she could not only make a true friend but also keep one. "But I can't!"

"How about female bonding?"

"I—"

She waved her hand. "Doesn't matter. What matters is a contingency plan. All you need to do is work it off at the gym … later."

Beth couldn't argue with that reasoning. "I guess… How are you feeling?"

"Pretty good. Though, from what I've read, I'll start getting extra tired soon. I'm not sure about that. Let's just say, Cole's built up my endurance." A dreamy look floated across her eyes like fluffy white clouds, and her lips curved up in a blissed-out smile.

Heat throbbed in Beth's cheeks. She wasn't used to speaking so candidly about sex-related stuff. "He's a gorgeous man and you're a beautiful woman. It must be hard to keep your hands off each other."

"Thank you. Yes, it's *very* hard to resist him. Then on top of that I have the grueling filming schedule. But I love it." She propped her elbows on the table and leaned forward. "So tell me, how are things with you and my brother?"

How should she answer that? Things were wonderful, yet she knew her little issue had started driving a stake into their relationship, splintering the intimacy they'd built. "Brody's amazing. The best man I've ever known."

"I'm a little biased, but yeah, he is pretty incredible."

"I'm so lucky to have him." He hadn't given up on her, even though she'd held off on sex and remained secretive.

"From what I've seen and heard so far, he's lucky to have you too."

"Maybe…"

"Maybe? What does that mean?" Hope's brow crinkled, her curious green eyes probing.

Beth dropped her gaze to her twitchy hands. "I've got some … issues."

"Hasn't everyone?" Hope really did know from experience. From what Beth had gleaned from media reports and what Brody had told her, Cole and Hope had lived through their own personal nightmare following his accident. And she'd been an amazing support to Brody over the years. If anyone knew about challenging issues, Hope did.

She picked at her nails like a tweaker. "I know but…"

Hope reached across the table and stilled Beth's hand. "Do you want to talk about it? Woman to woman, friend to friend. Maybe I can help."

"I don't know…" But after what Hope had been through maybe she could help. And the more Beth got involved with Brody, the more help she needed.

"I promise whatever we speak about remains between us, unless you give me permission otherwise."

Beth glanced up, her gaze connecting with Hope's. "Thank you."

The perky waitress brought over their coffees and

cake. "Enjoy!"

Hope released Beth's hand, dug her spoon into the chocolate dessert, and scooped a large chunk into her mouth. "Oh my God." She closed her eyes and swallowed, her facial expression like she'd just had the best orgasm of her life. "You have to at least try it."

How could she say no to that? She cut off a small spoonful and popped it in her mouth.

Hope stared at her. "What do you think?"

"Wow. An orgasm for the tastebuds."

"I agree." Hope shoveled another large spoonful into her mouth. "Mmmm… Anyway, where were we? Issues, that's right, and if you want to talk about yours."

Damn. No chance of deflecting with someone like Hope. The media referred to her as the "wall breaker" interviewer extraordinaire. Someone who dug deep into the heart and excavated the truth. How much could she tell her? "Um … well … it's really one main issue and it's kind of personal. Really personal."

"Okay."

"I … I'm not sure what to say, where to start."

Hope abandoned her dessert, reached across the table, and reclasped Beth's hand. "How about you tell me what's worrying you?"

Yeah, how about it. Beth wanted to confide in her so much, but anxiety built a barricade around her vocal cords. She sighed. How could she explain without giving specific details? "I'm worried Brody will leave me."

"I doubt that. I've never seen him so smitten. So happy. He cares about you a lot."

Reassuring. But Hope didn't have the full story. How long could a guy go without sex in a committed relationship? At first she thought his disability would restrict him, giving her more of a buffer. But no. Limited positions due to restricted mobility, yes. Though libido, sex drive, fuck, he was as horny and driven as any healthy, fully functional, red-blooded man.

They couldn't keep going as they were and sustain a long-term romantic relationship. Having a disability didn't mean he didn't have needs just like any able-bodied person. And he deserved to have them met. "Thanks. But ... I don't think it's enough."

"Why? What do you mean?"

"I can't... He's my boyfriend and..."

"And?" Hope's patient gaze and gentle tone coaxed her to keep talking.

"I tense up."

"You tense up?"

Beth stared at the shiny dark wood table top, a sheen of sweat breaking out on her skin. "This is so embarrassing."

Hope squeezed her hand and Beth met her attentive gaze. "Whatever it is, you can tell me and I'll do my best to help." Her eyes were like a truth serum, seeming to drag out what Beth had worked so hard to bury.

Beth glanced down at the reflective, wood-stained surface, trying to gather her thoughts, trying to decide how much to reveal. "If anything, anyone goes near my ... my..." She shifted in her seat, but Hope's hand remained firm around hers, encouraging, reassuring. "Um..." She leaned forward, toward her new friend, and whispered, "My ... opening. It gets... It's so tight, painful."

She could feel Hope's concerned stare studying her face. "Oh, Beth, have you had it checked?"

Her eyes stung and she shook her head, unable to look at Hope. "No. I'm scared, embarrassed."

"I get that. But there's nothing to be scared or embarrassed about. There's help out there."

Beth shot her head up and tried to stop the mounting tears from tumbling onto her cheeks. "Really? They won't think I'm some frigid neurotic freak?"

"Of course not." Hope smiled and the unquestionable kindness in her expression dropped Beth's stress from heart-palpitating high to slight. "I had a friend who had a similar problem. She got diagnosed with vaginismus and now she's cured."

She sniffled. "How?"

"First you need to see your doctor and rule out any physical causes. If it's not something physical, a psychologist can help you sort out any mental and emotional triggers."

"Oh." Could coffee and chocolate curdle, because what tasted scrumptious just moments ago suddenly made her stomach churn.

Could she talk to someone about what had happened? Could the trauma of an event really cause something like this? Could rehashing the past make it worse, inflame an already infected, so far irreparable, wound?

"It's not as scary as it sounds. But if you want me to come with you, give you moral support, I'd be happy to … or Brody. He'll support you, you know. He'd never ever judge. I know my brother. He'll want what's best for you, to help in any way he can. And not just so he can get a bit."

Beth tried to discreetly dab at her eyes with the back of her hand. "Thanks. Yeah, he is pretty wonderful, and you've been so great. Thank you. But I need to do this on my own." She needed to fight and slay those demons and not drag anyone else deeper into her internal battle.

"Only you can decide what's right for you." Hope gave Beth's hand another short squeeze, then let it go and poured them both a cool glass of water from the complimentary carafe on the table.

"In my friend's case, she took her fiancé with her to the counseling sessions and they talked through everything together. The psychologist then gave them homework. She prescribed some specific physical exercises to supplement therapy and assist them to work through the problem as a couple." She kept her tone soft, matching Beth's whisper, reinforcing she understood the importance of keeping their conversation quiet.

"What sort of exercises did your friend have to do?"

"Sexual ones. Her fiancé kept her accountable, in a tender loving way, and assisted her to insert small dildo-like devices during foreplay to stretch her opening so she'd become accustomed to the sensation. Then they gradually worked up to a larger and larger diameter. Basically, until she could take his—"

"I get it."

"She told me having her fiancé involved in her treatment made the whole experience much more fun and helped them to grow and strengthen their relationship. Their sex life is great now and they recently had a baby."

A baby. She'd love a baby, had always wanted one, and being with Brody had only increased her cluckiness. But she'd convinced herself it wouldn't be possible. Not unless she could get over her problem.

The clink of Hope's cup on the table jolted Beth out of her thoughts, and she had a sip of her own drink. "Thanks, Hope. I really appreciate you taking the time to go over everything, to let me know options. I'll think about therapy and confiding in Brody. But for the moment, please don't tell him … or Cole."

"Of course not. This stays between us. Friend to friend." Her sincere look and tone made Beth believe she'd gained a true ally, one who would definitely keep her confidence. She breathed out, relieved, while trying to hold back grateful tears. Not an easy feat when her heart squeezed with unfamiliar emotion. She'd never felt so supported, so understood.

"Let me know how you go, okay? And, as I said, if you ever want to talk more about it, or have me come with you to appointments for moral support, I'm happy to do it."

How things stood currently, Beth had no doubt Hope would follow through with her offer. But would that change if Brody got too frustrated and broke up with Beth before she could make any progress?

Chapter Nine
Level Four Crash

Beth's front door clicked open, and Brody's wheels squeaked on the polished timber foyer. "Beth?"

"In the bedroom." After speaking with Hope, and considering Brody's kindness and patience with her, she decided to put the GP visit on hold and give sex another shot.

The swoosh of his wheelchair confirmed his fast approach. She sucked in gulps of air in an attempt to steady her frazzled nerves. Seconds before he arrived, she struck her best sexy-model pose, showing off her assets in skimpy red lace underwear, ready to seduce. Well, psyching herself up to be ready.

Without even looking, she knew the moment he saw her. His breath hitched, followed by a deep, long, lustful sigh. "You look … wow."

Brody entered her bedroom and she met his hooded gaze. "You can add that into the top three of my favorite welcomes list."

Beth beckoned him forward, climbed onto her bed, and patted the space she'd left in front of her. "Join me?" Would he get her insinuation? She just hoped she could deliver.

He wasted no time undressing down to his underwear, transferred onto the bed and lay facing her, his cock tenting his boxers. The poor, sweet guy. He deserved a relationship where he could fuck his girlfriend. A lot.

She pushed him onto his back, brushed her knuckles over his hard-on, and hooked her fingers into the waistband of his boxers. "You won't be needing these," she said and slid them off his legs.

He groaned and tried to sit up, but she pressed her palm to his chest, keeping him in place. "Just relax and enjoy the show." She needed to control this if she had any hope of succeeding.

Beth knelt beside Brody, unhooked her bra, and slid the straps slowly down her arms. She dangled her discarded bra over his chest, dragged it lightly over his stomach, his stiff cock, and dropped it on the floor. His desire-darkened eyes tracked her every move like a state-of-the-art virtual reality headset, making her panties go from damp to drenched.

She shimmied out of her G-string and tossed him the scrap of arousal-soaked red lace. He caught the tiny bundle of material, brought it to his nose and sniffed. "Fuck. You smell so fucking hot." He closed his eyes and inhaled again, then reached down and stuffed her panties in his wheelchair bag, as though he planned to keep them as a memento.

His words and piercing gaze made her gush with readiness. But would she be slick enough, ready enough to welcome his cock into her body?

Only one way to find out.

She straddled his hips and rocked, his hard-on rubbing her pussy lips and it felt good, sensual, exciting. But she needed more, just to make sure.

She leaned forward, propping her hands on the mattress and angling her breasts over his mouth. "Would you like a taste?"

"Fuck yeah." His mouth devoured one nipple, then the other, back and forth, back and forth, back and forth, making her pussy wetter and wetter, but she needed it dripping.

"Rub my clit. Please."

"With pleasure." Brody's hot breath caressed her breast and he returned to his sucking, now adding his fingers right where she wanted them.

"Yes! Oh God, yes!"

Brody teased her taut, throbbing nipples and rubbed her swollen little bud, and in less than a minute her climax crashed through her in wave after wave of bone-melting pleasure.

Her breathing started to settle and she opened her eyes. He stared back at her with pure male pride. "God, you're gorgeous when you come."

She kissed him, reached between their bodies, and guided his cock to her well-lubricated entrance. Stress-induced dampness slathered her skin and her stomach clenched. She could do this. All the straight women she knew raved about having a cock inside them, about the intimacy, the connection, about the intensity of the orgasm.

Relax. She just had to relax and go with the sensation, open up to him. He'd been nothing but patient and kind and thoughtful and she cared about him too, deeply. So it should be easy, giving herself to the man she loved.

Loved?

Yeah, she loved Brody. No point denying it. She'd do anything for him ... in theory. The true test would be whether she could finally push past this restrictive barrier.

Tentatively, she pressed her pussy down on the firm, smooth head, the tip of his cock breaching her opening. Her muscles spasmed, pain slicing through her core like she'd been stabbed with a blunt, jagged blade.

She jumped off him and retreated to the far corner of the bed, her eyes blurry and stinging. "I'm sorry. I'm so sorry." With the backs of her hands she swiped at the tears streaming onto her cheeks, her chest heaving, her body shaking with restrained sobs.

Brody shifted across the bed until he sat right in front of her. He propped one hand on the mattress and grasped her face with the other, tilting her chin up and forcing her to look into his eyes. She expected to see frustration, anger, but instead they were full of affection, concern. "I'm not going to let you avoid this anymore. You need to tell me what's wrong."

Fear flooded her mind, sending her straight into defense mode. "No, I don't."

"If you want to give our relationship the best chance to work, you do."

"So what are you saying? If I don't tell you, we're over?" Her negative emotions erupted like water from a faulty faucet, impossible to turn off and causing more damage by the second.

"Beth, listen. The last thing I want is to break up with you. I care about you so much it scares me sometimes. But you can't go on like this. It's not healthy. It's not normal. You need to address whatever's going on or you'll struggle to feel fulfilled, to have a successful long-term relationship with any man."

More tears drenched her face, his hand.

"If you can't trust me, can't share yourself with me mentally, emotionally, physically, then the relationship's doomed."

"You're right." God, she wanted to tell him, but the words just wouldn't come, pain and fear censoring her speech.

A relieved smile kicked up the corners of his mouth. He thought she meant she'd confide in him. But would she ever feel totally comfortable letting a man so close? Her trust issues were much more major than she realized. Keeping him as her boyfriend, preventing him from getting the sort of relationship he deserved, was unfair.

Given the fucked up nature of her situation, she couldn't guarantee she'd ever recover. She loved him, felt safe with him, and yet she still couldn't push past her fears.

Beth took a long, slow breath and gathered as much strength as she could to deliver the devastating news. "We're probably not meant to be together."

Confusion ripped the smile from his lips. "What?"

"I think it's best you go." She wrenched her face from his iron grip, grabbed her robe, and ran to the bathroom, her eyes bleary with fresh tears.

"No. Wait." His voice chased behind her and she barricaded herself inside her en suite.

Not even a minute later, Brody banged on the door. "We need to talk about this. It's the only way to resolve it. I love you, Beth. Please." His pained, desperate tone tore through her heart. But their break-up was for the best, no matter how much it hurt.

Defeat poured through her veins like thick, wet, heavy cement. "There's no point. I can't give you what you need." Now or maybe ever.

Chapter Ten
Reboot

Massive, massive mistake.

Her front door slamming shut with Brody's swift departure seemed to score the finality of their split into her soul. Why did she push him away, the one person who constantly showed he wanted to support her, help her? The only man who'd ever said and showed he loved her.

Stupid, stupid, stupid.

Maybe she'd been right all along. He was too good for her. She left the bathroom and slumped onto her bed. But should she really let an incident from the past dictate the path of her whole life? Only she could let her ex-boyfriend, her family, and their fucked-up belief systems win. Why continue to give them so much power?

Her fear of telling Brody the truth stifled her, made her scared shitless she'd push him away. Yet not being honest had done it anyway. What he'd said was spot on. How could she expect to have a successful long-term relationship with someone if she couldn't trust them, couldn't open up, couldn't confide in them?

The next morning she made an appointment with her GP and discussed every embarrassing detail. After a barrage of physical tests, her doctor confirmed no structural abnormalities and no benign or cancerous growths caused her spasms. Which meant her issue was purely psychological. So not surprising.

In some ways it would have been easier to have a physical explanation, something straightforward to treat. But part of her had always known it was much more complex. Although she'd dreaded it, put it off for way too long, she needed the help of a psychologist.

****

Brody knocked on his sister's front door and, in seconds, Hope whipped it open.

"Where's Beth?"

"Hi to you too." Brody wheeled in and gave her a hug. "We broke up."

"What? Why?"

"I'm assuming Cole's here?"

"Yeah…"

"I'd rather just say it once." For days he'd drowned in sorrow, lying in bed and staring at the picture on his bedside table, the one Beth had given him of them cuddled up together at the gaming convention, looking so happy, so in love, so invincible.

Her sexy red lace G-string still sat in his wheelchair bag from their last night together. Although not superstitious, he wanted to believe that keeping part of her close would work like a good luck charm, a talisman, drawing her back to him. But much to his dismay, she hadn't tried to make contact since ending their relationship.

Then he realized maybe Hope could help. She had spoken to Beth, so maybe she knew something, could give him some insider information to understand the situation better and win his girlfriend back.

Brody sat with Cole and his sister at the dining table to eat lunch—not that he could stomach much—and Hope poured him and her hubby a glass of red wine. "What happened?"

"I'm not sure how much to say." He shifted the food around on his plate with his fork.

Hope stared him straight in the eye. "Let me start then. I promised not to go into details and I won't, but basically she told me about her … problem. I suggested she get professional help and recommended she speak to you about it. Did she?"

He put his cutlery down and had a gulp of wine. "No. She refused to divulge any details, even though I did everything I could to reassure her, reinforce I'd support her. I'm not sure if she saw a health professional, but I doubt it."

Cole glanced at Hope and then at him. "Going by her behavior, I'm gonna take a big stab and say she's had a bad experience with a man she trusted and it resulted in trust issues with men ... as well as other complications."

Brody sighed. Helplessness surged up inside him like water from a broken fire hydrant. "I think you're right. But what can I do about it?"

Hope reached across the table and held his hand. "Did you tell her how you feel about her?"

"Yep. I told her I love her and I do. So much. But I also made it clear, sustaining a long-term relationship would be impossible unless she trusted me, unless she could talk to me about the issue, feel comfortable enough to physically and emotionally connect."

"You did the right thing," Cole said.

Hope glared at her husband, then focused her frank gaze on Brody. "It's not as simple as that. I think you've frightened her. I think she's taken what you've said as an ultimatum or even worse, just another guy who prioritizes sex above everything else."

That's what he loved about Hope; she wouldn't just take sides with him. She'd tell him how it was, make sure he saw the full perspective.

"You know I'm not like that, though."

"I know, but does she?"

Cole finished his last mouthful of stir fry and propped his forearms on the table. "You have a right to have your needs met too. For a relationship to work, it's not all about catering to one person. Compromise is required on both sides, but there are also deal breakers. And I'll be honest, if I couldn't make love to my partner, no matter how much I loved her, the relationship couldn't last."

Not even Hope disagreed with that. The only way he'd get Beth back was if she took some steps to resolve her fears, to show Brody she trusted him, that their relationship was important enough to fight for.

****

Brody turned off the stove and glanced at his mobile. Nearly seven. Where was Hope? Normally she arrived early for their catch-ups. Maybe Cole had made her run late. What was he thinking? Of course Cole had made her run late. He couldn't keep his hands off her, and not just his hands.

Brody chuckled. He couldn't be jealous. Not when his sister was such a great person. She deserved to have a man who loved her as much as Cole did. Brody just hoped that someday he'd be as happy in love.

At the very last minute, Hope had called and requested beef ravioli with a Bolognese sauce—Beth's favorite—for an impromptu dinner. Given her pregnancy cravings, he'd gone out of his way to please her. No, it wasn't just that. He couldn't resist spoiling her when she'd been such an amazing, consistent support in his life.

The doorbell rang.

"Coming."

He reached the door, pulled it open and ... it wasn't Hope.

Beth.

Fuck.

His heart seriously stopped. Then kicked into a rapid, thundering rhythm.

"What are you doing … oh. Hope's not coming, is she?" His sister had set him up. And he owed her, big time.

"No. Can I come in?" The pleading look in her eyes broke his heart. Did she really think he wouldn't want to see her, wouldn't want to let her back into his life?

"Of course." He gestured for her to enter.

"I hope you're not angry."

"Not at all." How could he be angry? The woman he loved had returned and stood within touching distance, wearing the PlayStation earrings he'd gifted her. But he'd let Beth talk, give her a chance to explain. He couldn't allow himself to get his hopes up in case nothing had changed.

Her big brown eyes stared at him with soul-deep sincerity. "I owe you an explanation and an apology."

If he left it up to instinct, he'd hug her, soothe and comfort and forgive. But that wouldn't resolve anything. The only way to positively move forward required her to prove she acknowledged the problem and had taken action. "Have a seat."

"Thanks." She sat on the living room couch, where they'd made out too many times to count.

"I've been seeing someone."

His heart sank into his chest as though swallowed up by quicksand. *Oh.* She'd come to tell him thanks, but she'd moved on?

She must have seen the confusion and sadness in his eyes, because she smiled and blushed. "A therapist. I'm seeing a psychologist who specializes in sexual health and well-being. About my … penetration phobia. And it's helping."

"That's so great. I'm really happy to hear it."

She crossed her legs toward him and looked him

in the eye. "It's all thanks to you. Losing you forced me to face my fears, to work through my trust issues with men."

Brody transferred onto the couch beside her and held and squeezed her hand. She squeezed back. "The thing is, I love you, Brody. I do trust you, and I want you back if you'll have me. But before you answer, I need to tell you what started this, what created the complex layers, the … difficulties."

He nodded, his resurrected heart thundering beneath his breastbone.

"After my year twelve graduation, I went parking with my boyfriend. Things got heated and we started to have sex, but I changed my mind. The religious beliefs I'd grown up with made me feel really confused. So many contradictory emotions swirled around in my head, I wasn't sure whether to keep going or stop. But he kept going, kept pushing, and I tensed up. I can still remember the pain…"

She slammed her eyes shut and shook her head. Brody caressed and massaged her hand between his, trying to show her through his actions he'd stand by the woman he loved. He'd give her whatever support and encouragement she needed. She took a couple of slow, controlled breaths and refocused her gaze on his.

"I cried and screamed and finally managed to push him off me. I jumped out of his car and ran home, but instead of comforting me, my parents blamed me for being too easy and called me a slut. A *slut*. Guilt and shame churned in my stomach, making me sick. For what I'd done, for what I'd allowed to happen.

"Then when I told them I wanted to be a model, that was it. The sour cherry on top. It reinforced their already negative opinion of me. They refused to accept or support my career choice, making it clear they saw it as the devil's work. So I ran away."

"Beth, I'm so sorry." He wanted to hold her close, allow all the pain to drain out of her body. But not yet, not until she finished saying what she needed to say.

She touched his cheek, her fingers so light, yet the sensation reached right to his heart. "It's not your fault. So not your fault. I kept everything bottled up, too ashamed to speak about it, wondering if maybe their words held some truth. Then when I started getting a name for myself modeling, I worried my past would come out and I'd be branded as a cock tease or a tramp or frigid.

"And I didn't want to be tainted by any of those assumptions. I just wanted to be me. It took me a long time to realize not even I knew who I was. Not really. I'd hidden a huge part of myself away, built up walls to protect my most vulnerable parts.

"Until you pushed me to step back and focus, really focus and evaluate everything, I hadn't gotten the significance of B-True. It wasn't just a character name or a plea to others. It was a subconscious calling for me to be integral, to be fully real."

Smart, insightful, and so damn sexy. "I'm so proud of you. You're such an amazing woman." He cupped her face and brought her lips to his in a loving kiss.

Beth pulled away and stared into his eyes. "Does that mean you'll take me back, as your girlfriend?" She sounded so scared, so hopeful, so sweet and innocent.

"Girlfriend? No."

Her beautiful face dropped, but he wouldn't leave her hanging, wouldn't let her mind jump to false conclusions. "I was thinking more … fiancée."

Her eyes widened and her mouth slackened in shock. "Fiancée? But…"

"But what? It's simple. We love each other and we want to be together."

She threw her arms around him and sobbed into his shoulder. But this time with happy tears.

Epilogue
Breaking the Final Barrier

"Look what I dug out." Beth's saucy smile peeked over the back of Brody's couch, and she lifted the sensor dildo he'd bought her last Christmas. That still hadn't been used.

He shut the front door, propelled over, and transferred onto the seat beside her. She shifted closer and loosened his tie. "How did the meetings go?"

"Not bad. They seemed to like me. Looks like I'll probably pick up a couple big IT support contracts."

"Congratulations." She planted a celebratory kiss on his lips and broke away mid tongue tangle, her suddenly serious gaze probing. "They better not interfere with our honeymoon."

"No way." He and Beth hadn't had sex yet, but they were getting there. In less than a month they'd arrive in Paris, then travel to Italy's Dolomites, where he hoped to spend most of the time enjoying the view, buried deep inside his new wife.

"Good." She slid his paisley silk tie from around his neck and brushed her lips against his ear. "Not sure about you, but I'm feeling a bit playful. Game for intimacy?"

His breath caught in his throat and he nodded. When she instigated sexy times between them, it never failed to render him speechless.

Beth clicked the game remote, and the start screen of *Intimacy World* brightened the softly lit room. The sensor dildo sat between them on the couch. Her eyes moved from it to him and she held out the removed, over-priced silk tie Cole and Hope had bought him last birthday. "Tie me up."

His cock jerked in his pants before he could even register the implications. Tying her up meant her putting total trust in him and her pleasure. It meant giving him full control, for the first time, to touch her however he chose, wherever he chose, including dildo play.

Fuck if his dick didn't pierce his black jeans to touch her. But she hadn't asked for that. Not yet. And he would respect her silent but clear wishes.

She held her wrists together behind her back and he took his time winding the smooth silk tie around them, tightening the bond.

"Undo my dress." Her raw, breathy voice rasped with desire and anticipation.

Button by slow button, he revealed more and more of her flawless skin, naked breasts, and smooth, glistening pussy.

Before he got too carried away, he glanced up at the game, chose B-True solo mode, keeping his character, B-Brave, in auto, and selected a bondage scene. He played the game until B-Brave bound B-True and they were ready to do the deed.

Brody attached the clit hood to Beth's hairless little nub and fingered the sensor dildo, ready to rub it over her pussy lips, then fuck her with it after she'd come.

While B-Brave licked out B-True on screen, the sensation tapping directly into her clit, he dropped his head to her breast and took her erect nipple in his mouth, palming and squeezing her other breast with his hand to add a bit more spice.

"So, so good." She arched up into him, her moans needy and desperate and close to climax.

Her gaze shifted between him feasting on her breasts, and the high-quality, almost real-looking sexy images on screen. Without headphones on, all he could hear were Beth's whimpers and heavy breathing and the wet lapping of his tongue on her aroused body.

His aching cock chafed against his jeans, desperate to burst out and thrust inside her before he blew. But he'd just have to redirect all his longing into Beth. She'd put her trust in him, and he'd do all he could to prove his worthiness. Right now, that meant concentrating on her pleasure.

Sweat dampened her skin. Her face crinkled up and she cried out, her hips bucking with her release. She looked so fucking hot, so fucking gorgeous.

He stopped sucking on her pointed pink nipple. She slumped against the black leather, still panting, eyes closed. The scent of her arousal made him so fucking horny, but patience was the name of this intimacy game.

Brody nibbled her earlobe. "Ready for round two, or do you need me to pause?"

Her eyes opened, still dazed and glassy post orgasm. "I'm ready."

"You're sure."

She stared back at him with true conviction. "Very."

Brody picked up the sensor dildo and rubbed it through her pussy lips, coating it in her juices and mimicking B-Brave's cock on screen. He focused on her face, determined not to miss even a hint of discomfort. He wanted this shared experience to be positive as much as she did.

B-Brave positioned himself above B-True, his cock poised at her entrance. Brody cut his gaze back to Beth and she smiled and nodded, answering without him asking. He pressed the head of the dildo to her opening and eased it inside. She tensed and he stopped about an inch in. He bent down and kissed her parted lips.

"Keep going," she murmured, barely breaking the

kiss. So he did, resuming their pash and slowly sliding the dildo all the way in.

He leaned back enough to see her eyes. "Okay?"

"Yes. Keep moving."

To maximize the effects of the game, the instructions recommended inserting the dildo, attaching the clit hood, and leaving them in place. The technology then gave the sensation of movement when the character touched themselves or another character touched them. But his beautiful Beth pushed herself and it was so impressive, so fucking sexy.

He slid the dildo almost all the way out and back in, their stares remaining locked.

"Faster." Her husky, breathy voice sounded on-edge desperate.

He obliged and she rewarded him with a look of wondrous ecstasy. "More." She moaned and moved her hips, meeting each of his thrusts.

In the game, B-Brave and B-True went at it hard and fast. Beth's sudden scream tore his gaze from the screen in time to see her bucking and shuddering with bone-deep satisfaction.

He kept up the thrusts until she came down from her extended high. When she flopped against the couch, he removed the dildo, placed it on a clump of tissues on the coffee table, and dove in for a full-on kiss.

She pressed into him, matching his desire, his urgency. "How you going?" he managed between breaths.

"Out of my mind if I don't touch you this second."

Her wrists. *Fuck.*

He undid the tie, brought her hands around to her lap, and rubbed the red marks on her skin. She snatched her hands from his grasp, undid the buttons on his shirt, and ran her palms over his bare chest. After what they'd just experienced, she only had to keep up her caresses for another minute and he'd come.

She seemed to sense his thoughts and dropped her hands to his fly, plucking at the buttons on his pants and freeing his erection. She flicked off the clit hood and straddled his hips, pressing her breasts into his face and rubbing her pussy along the length of him. "I want you."

He groaned, the raw sound rumbling up from deep in his chest.

With one palm pressed to his shoulder, Beth braced herself, reached down with her other hand to stroke his cock, then guided him to her entrance. He grabbed her hips and she took a couple of breaths, her eyes on his the whole time. Then she lowered herself onto him, super slow.

Tight, so tight. Add the fucking incredible friction and he had to count backward from a thousand by sevens to stop from blowing like an inexperienced teenage boy.

She lifted her lower hand onto his other shoulder, sank all the way down, until he filled her to the hilt, and they both sucked in a big breath. "Okay?" He had to check, had to be sure.

"So okay." She slid up along him, her channel hugging and squeezing his dick, and back down, each time increasing the pace and the fucking awesome sensation. He slipped his hand between them and thumbed her clit, rubbing in rough circles.

"Brody! Oh God, oh God, oh God!" She clung to his shoulders, her nails biting into his skin, and her core clenched and released his cock as she rode out her climax.

He stilled, his orgasm tearing through him, shooting cum deep inside her. She fell against his chest, her head nuzzling his neck, cradled in the crook of his shoulder, her erratic breaths cooling his sweaty skin. He caressed her hair and kissed her temple, then reached up under her open, crumpled dress and stroked her back. "Fucking amazing."

"Mmm…"

"I'm assuming that's a good mmm…"

"Totally. I think that last orgasm wiped out my brain cells."

He laughed and kissed her again. "I love you so fucking much."

She glanced up. Her rich brown eyes shone, still glazed with the after effects of their lovemaking. "I love you too."

He slid out of her and she winced. Concern stabbed his heart like an upthrust sword.

"It's okay. It's okay," she said, as though seeing his distress. "I expect it to still hurt a bit … until I get used to it." Her sexy little smile suggested she looked forward to fitting in more practice. He couldn't be more on board.

"You know, I almost look forward to going to work, knowing I'll be coming home to that sort of welcome. Hint hint."

Beth laughed, and the melodic sound hit a happiness chord that seemed to further unite their souls. She kissed him, sweet and tender and way too short. "There's something I wanted to speak to you about."

"Was that some sort of serious-topic foreplay?"

She laughed again. "You could say that. You see…" The heat of her palm on his chest made it hard for him to think straight. He still struggled to believe they'd actually had sex. What if he woke up now and it was just some erotic dream? A fucking great erotic dream but…

Beth studied his eyes. "Hey, are you listening?"

"To you? Always."

"Good answer. Okay, so, I got a new contract today."

"That's brilliant. Congratulations!" He squeezed her into a tight hug and gave her a quick kiss.

"Thanks. But it's not for modeling … exactly."

"Oh?"

"I'm doing a campaign." She hesitated, a fresh flush of scarlet tinging her cheeks. "To raise awareness for vaginismus. To let women know not to be ashamed, to talk about it, because there is treatment available. Successful treatment."

He smiled, joy tugging the corners of his lips so wide, his face ached. "That is so awesome!"

"You're not embarrassed about me doing this? How it might impact on you, us?"

"You're going out with a dude in a wheelchair. Most people don't even see me as a sexual being, let alone think I have an interest in or, heaven forbid, actually have sex. So, no, I'm not embarrassed. I'm proud. What you're doing is fantastic. Challenging and breaking down barriers takes a lot of guts. But it can be so rewarding, liberating."

She twined her arms around his neck and snuggled into him. "Thanks. Your support means so much to me."

"As yours does to me." He kissed her forehead, her nose, her lips. He'd always thought love and happiness linked strongly to appearance, physical ability, but that was all superficial stuff. Meeting Beth made him realize appearances were deceiving.

What many people saw, including him, was a virtual reality, not real life. A constructed view of made-up rules and assumptions. Trying to compare led to unrealistic expectations and even more toxic, counter-productive rules.

Experiencing true love and happiness came down to breaking through the mind games. Thoughts, emotions, and the end behavior—that's what created it. That's what kept a person open to opportunities, willing to compromise, willing to connect, willing to grow and improve.

Beth climbed off his lap, held and tugged his hand, her open dress framing her sublime, marble-smooth body. But it was her words, her actions, her sexy, loving smile that exposed her beautiful mind and deepened his attraction.

"Come on, B-Brave, let's go to bed. If you're good, you might even get lucky. Again."

With Beth, he was more than lucky. He was sure.

With Beth, he'd always be game for intimacy.

With Beth, he'd reached the top level. He'd won the grand prize.

Love.

The End

SANDRA CARMEL

What's meant to be will always find a way.

—Trisha Yearwood

SANDRA CARMEL

DANCE OF LOVE

Intertwined Love, 3

Sandra Carmel

Copyright © 2021

≈⌢·· ♦ ·· ⌢≈

Chapter One
Taking a Chance

"Issy's arrived."

Jeb's heart rate went from steady jog to flat-out sprint. Knowing he'd see his sexy little power-pack patient in just a few minutes did that to him. Every. Single. Time.

"Thanks. I'll be out shortly." He put the phone down and tried to control his hammering heart and some anatomy further south. What was it about her?

He'd met, and put his hands on, plenty of attractive women during his physio career, but none had sent him into such a turned-on state. Not like this. Just hearing her name gave him a hard-on. No one had done that since…

Nope, he refused to go there. Refused to descend into that dark place. Closing his eyes, he did some slow, deep yoga breaths until he got his heart beating at a somewhat normal speed.

Jeb pressed his palms flat onto the smooth, cool desk top and stood up. He adjusted himself and strode out of his treatment room, down the corridor, and into the waiting area.

His eyes zeroed in on Issy sitting amongst the sea of clients, her wispy, asymmetrical haircut cool and unique. Just like her. God, how many times had he imagined running his fingers through the silky blonde strands. "Issy? Come on through."

She glanced up from her phone and smiled. And what a fucking seductive sight, her pouty pink lips saying "kiss me, I know you want to." Fuck, did he want to, but she was so off limits. Issy had to remain a fantasy. Maybe if he repeated the phrase over and over, like a mantra, he'd believe it and finally convince his dick.

The tempting woman got up, graceful as ever, and made her way to him, a seriously stunning, petite little package. He towered over her at 195 cm. She'd be lucky to reach 155 cm and weigh more than fifty kilos. He could practically bench press her one-handed.

"Hi, Jeb." That sultry voice, it did things to him, struck some resonating chord deep in his soul.

He pushed the door open and waved her through, ahead of him. His gaze drifted to her toned little ass. *Control yourself!* If he didn't, he'd be forced to work on her with a massive boner. And wasn't that just the most uncomfortable, unprofessional thing ever.

Her wild hair and sensual strut totally matched her personality, going by their conversations over the past six months. Maybe it was the hands-on treatment, but as a physio people seemed to open up to him, tell him their worries, their desires, their secrets.

He didn't reciprocate, instead keeping his heart padlocked and protected. He'd become a master at focusing on others and distracting them from delving below his safe, superficial surface. All part of being professional or so he tried to believe.

She walked into his treatment room and took her usual seat by the window overlooking The Rocks. She knew the drill.

He sat opposite. "How have you been?"

"Great. You?"

"Same." His standard, guarded, me-physio-you-client answer. "How's the hip and knee?"

She leaned forward in her seat, her big jewel-blue eyes sparkling like the sun reflecting off the ocean outside the window. "Better, thanks to you."

"Good to hear. So what can I help you with today?"

"I need a thorough physical review to make sure I'm ready to return to training." Her smile suggested things other than physio treatment. Sexual things. Or maybe it was him wishing so hard, he'd read into her body language.

He fucking had to stop his dick railroading his rational thinking. He glanced at the Sydney Harbour Bridge, hoping the big sturdy steel structure would give him strength. As much as he wished he and Issy could get together, even if she proved to be equally attracted to him, they couldn't act on their feelings. "Have you been doing the exercises I prescribed?"

"Yes, and I haven't even felt a twinge."

"Excellent. Okay, hop onto the plinth, lay on your front, and I'll check things out." If only he could check things out in a much more up-close-and-personal way. *Stop it.*

He sucked in a long, steadying breath and slowly blew it out. "I'm going to start with your glutes." Before he touched anyone, especially in such a usually off-limits area, he made sure he always gave them a heads-up, obtained their consent.

"Go for it."

He pressed around her hip and butt, watching for any signs of discomfort and feeling plenty of his own, in the groin region. The woman was pure sculptured beauty. Trim, firm, yet curvaceous. *Concentrate.* "How does that feel?"

"Wonderful."

His hands agreed. "Good. Did you end up doing that audition?" For some renowned overseas contemporary dance company, from memory. Who was he kidding—he remembered every single word she'd ever spoken to him, like some obsessed, infatuated teenage boy.

"Yes."

He dug into her butt and she moaned.

"Sore?"

"No, feels great."

He rubbed and activated some pressure points and she moaned again. Would she sound like that during sex? *Fuck, fuck, fuck.* "How did the audition go?"

"Perfectly. No pain, and I just found out this week, I got accepted."

Great way to tame his over-eager cock. His heart sank to the pit of his stomach, but he forced what he hoped passed as a cheerful tone. "Congratulations. When do you leave?"

"I fly out to New York in a month."

"A month?" That kept things real. And gave him an end date. Forced him to move on from his infatuation. "You must be ecstatic."

"Yeah, it's pretty awesome. Exactly what I've been working towards. I've dreamed of joining them for years. Even though I'll hate leaving Sydney, there's no way I could turn down such a fabulous opportunity."

Of course she couldn't. He understood that logically, but emotionally…

"What are you doing Friday night?"

"Friday night?" Nothing. After work he went to the gym and then home. No dating, no dinners, no pubs, no clubs, just his regular routine and the odd catch-up with his good mate, Cole.

"Yeah. Are you free? I'm having some celebratory drinks with friends and so, I hoped you'd come."

Me too. "I shouldn't. I'm you're treating physio. It's unprofessional. But thanks for asking."

She sat up and stared into his eyes, her face so close he could almost feel her breath on his skin. "It's not unprofessional if we end our client-physio relationship."

She must have seen the confusion in his eyes and continued. "This is my last session, so after today, you're no longer officially my therapist."

Oh. "True."

She grabbed his hand, her gaze fixed on his. "Come on, please. You've helped me so much and I'm so grateful."

Grateful. A friend. Nothing else. Of course. What did he expect? She was breathtaking, bubbly, full of life, whereas he didn't even know how to flirt. "I don't know."

Her eyes pleaded and her mouth stretched into her characteristic sensual smile. "Please. I want you there. You're incredible. And I want everyone to know."

If any other woman had given him that compliment, it'd just about confirm her interest. Not with Issy. She treated everyone the same, from what he'd seen. And she went through men like used, discarded tissues. But even knowing that didn't stop him from having a massive crush on her.

"Thanks. You're too kind."

"Not at all. It's the truth." One of the things he loved about her. Loved? What the fuck? Appreciated. Yeah, appreciated. He admired a person who could speak openly. He wished he could, but he had too many soul-destroying secrets.

"I'll think about Friday, but I'm not promising anything."

She smiled like she knew she had him, knew he'd already given in. Her confidence and charm were almost impossible to resist.

"Now, stand up for me and walk toward the wall."

She did as he asked and he tried to focus on her muscle engagement, her gait pattern, but couldn't help appreciating her lithe physique. "Good. How do you feel?"

"Strong, free. No stiffness or pain."

"Come and stand in front of me. Bend over and touch your toes." Mmm … he could never get sick of that view. *Fucking stop.*

She looked at him between her legs. "What do you think?"

What did he think? He'd love to push her up against the wall, kiss her hard on the lips and sink into her. He cleared the lust clogging his throat. "The alignment looks good."

"Please tell me it's massage time now?" Her eyes flashed with mischief.

"Hmmm … well, seeing you've been doing your exercises and this is your final session, sure." Like giving her a rub down was doing *her* a favor.

Her sapphire-blue eyes lit up and she smiled. She effortlessly lifted herself back onto the plinth and sat, swinging her smooth, toned legs and waiting for further instructions.

"All right, top off, lie face down, and undo your bra."

She did as directed and he rubbed some massage oil into his hands and placed them on her upper back.

"Mmm..." she groaned and he hadn't even started pressing around yet.

He ran his hands up her fair skin, curled his fingers over her shoulders, and used his thumbs to manipulate the muscles in her neck. "So tell me, any man news?"

"No."

The tension he hadn't even realized he'd been holding drained from his body. "No? It's been over a month. What's going on? Lost your touch?"

She laughed. "Not sure. Maybe."

He found a knot in her trap and pressed.

"Oh God, yeah, that's it. That's the spot."

His imagination went wild. He wanted to close his eyes and succumb to the daydream of him and Issy writhing and naked but forced himself to drag his attention back to the present, reality. No matter how tempting, he had to remain clear-headed, appropriate.

He kept pressing and kneading and the muscle tension released.

She relaxed into the plinth. "Actually, there's this guy..."

Fuck, he knew it'd just be a matter of time before she got more seriously interested in someone. Probably a good thing. Definitely a good thing. "Yeah?"

"Yeah. I've had my eye on him for a while, but I'm not sure he's interested."

The correlation between relieving muscle tightness and freedom of expression fascinated him.

Relaxation seemed to release a person's inhibitions. Some people laughed, some cried, and others spoke openly. Would she reveal the identity of this mystery guy who'd caught her attention? "Why don't you ask him? You don't seem the shy type." Why was he encouraging this?

"I'd planned to, but now that I'm going..."

"You could just have a fling." She did that all the time, had expressed to him in detail about her various conquests, highlighting her casual-sex history. So why not indulge now?

"Not with this guy. I'm pretty sure he's not the fling type."

Oh. Fuck. This *was* serious. He swallowed the fireball of jealousy and disappointment rising in his throat. "But you don't definitely know. Just ask him. You might be surprised." He grit out every supportive, go-for-it-with-this-guy word, but he cared about her, ultimately wanted her to be happy. And if that meant she hooked up with another man, so be it. Even if it hurt.

"Maybe. I'll think about it." He dug into the muscles along her scapulae and she whimpered. "You have to come on Friday, please."

If she was so interested in this other guy, why did it matter whether Jeb came to her drinks? It didn't make sense unless she wanted him there for support. But could he stand by and watch her pick up someone else?

What if the dude didn't show? Should he have a crack? After today he'd no longer be her physio, and she'd leave the country soon—if things didn't work out, it wouldn't matter. So what was stopping him?

Fear. Plain and simple. He wanted her to like him. He wanted her to stay. But he couldn't guarantee either. He'd just turned twenty-eight, and she was the first woman he'd desired since... Even more reason to push past his fears and reservations or he'd remain afraid and regretful and celibate for the rest of his life. "Okay."

"Okay?" She sounded surprised and totally rapt.

"Yeah, just let me know where and what time." If things didn't pan out with her, he may meet someone else who could end up being the true love of his life. It was all about taking measured risks, making the most of each situation. Or so everyone said.

He finished the massage. She fastened her bra and sat up, looking relaxed and dreamy. "Give me your mobile number and I'll text you the details."

Jeb recited it to her, and she sent him a test text.

She squeezed into her body-hugging top, hopped down onto the floor in front of him, and tilted her head up until their gazes locked. "Thanks, Jeb. For everything. I'll see you Friday." Her silver tongue ring glistened and set his heart racing.

He'd never been a piercing type, but something about that stud made him think dirty, X-rated thoughts. Like how it'd feel if she sucked his dick into her mouth and blew him off. He took a long blink and tried to regain some control over his hyper-aroused body.

Fuck. Had he done the right thing accepting her invitation? She stirred up his libido, his emotions, just from her close proximity. What would happen when the work boundaries were removed?

What would happen if he had to stand by and watch or, even worse, help her hook up with some other guy? Maybe he should have kept things professional, less complicated, less likely to lead to heartache.

Jeb refocused on her irresistible eyes and the way she looked at him, all happy and hopeful, he couldn't change his mind about attending. It wouldn't be fair to either of them. He couldn't continue to let his heightened anxiety sway him from making personal connections with women, couldn't let guilt and unease keep winning.

Going ahead with this would be stressful—his heart ramped up to overdrive just at the thought—but he refused to be flaky, refused to go back on his word. He'd made a promise, and now he had to make the effort to see her. It might be his last chance.

Chapter Two
Getting Close

Issy slipped into her sparkly silver sling-back sandals and did a little victory dance. Finally, she'd convinced Jeb to come out. And she couldn't wait to see him.

Her mobile rang and she rushed into the living room. Jeb had better not be piking. She'd sensed his hesitation like it was a living entity creating a barrier between them. She snatched her phone off the coffee table and glanced at the screen.

Mum. Great. Just what she needed. The woman seemed to have a sixth sense when it came to spoiling Issy's fun. She debated whether to answer, but decided to get it over with now rather than send her mum to voicemail and stress about returning her call later.

Issy slumped onto her couch, head in hand. "To what do I owe the pleasure?"

"Hello, darling. Can't I just check how my daughter's going?"

No. She only ever rang when she wanted something. "What is it, Mum? And please make it quick. I'm on my way out and don't want to be late." Issy eyed her most recently completed WW2 model plane, the B-17D Flying Fortress "Swoose" sitting proudly in her display cabinet by the window.

It never failed to calm her: choosing one, making it, remembering the wonderful times she'd had sharing the experience with her WW2-mad dad. He'd always been her rock, grounding her even in death.

"Before you desert your mother and take off overseas, I hoped you could do me a favor."

Issy's mother, on the other hand, was the total

opposite, like now. She'd gone straight into battle with the big guilt guns. Her mum must really want this *thing*. Who was she kidding? Her mum always wanted things over people.

"I thought you were happy for me? Didn't you always want me to reach an elite level? The only way to do that is to go overseas. Australia doesn't have the same opportunities or reputation." She'd let her mum get to her again. The urge to explain herself always hovered on her lips. Flying to the other side of the world suddenly seemed like Issy's only viable option, not just for career advancement but to keep her sane.

"Darling, you know I'm proud."

But. With her, there was always a but.

"But I'll miss you."

She'd miss the attention. She'd miss taking all the credit, basking in all the glory for pushing Issy into dancing in the first place. "And?" Issy's leg shook. Speaking to her mum consistently brought on a bout of anxiety. Like a boiling kettle, the building pressure needed an escape.

"You know Gerry from The Sydney Morning Herald? He wants to write an article, a mother-and-daughter piece."

And there it was. She wouldn't miss her daughter. She'd miss the limelight. "I'm flat out. I've got no time to come up to Byron Bay just to do an interview for the newspaper."

"I can come to you, stay at your apartment for a few days, spend some quality time with my only daughter."

No. No fucking way. Her mum had always been a manipulation expert. Nothing had changed. And Issy refused to play into it.

Being away from her mum had helped combat

falling victim to her scheming ways, but Issy's stomach still roiled with unease at causing her disappointment. "Sorry, Mum, it won't work with my schedule. You'll just have to do the interview on your own."

"But he wants a picture of us together. And we can't use the last one. So out of date. We need something new, fresh. And heaven knows, I need time to oversee your hair and makeup, make sure it works, plus allow enough time to do my own.

"Looking great doesn't just happen, you know. I don't just wake up like this. The least you can do is accommodate me. I'm sure you want both of us to look our best. It reflects well on you. Don't forget how much time and money I spent getting you to where you are."

You owe me wasn't said but implied.

Did she?

She kind of did, but how many times could her mum use that excuse. Forever? "All right, I'll think about it. I'll see what I can do and get back to you. I need to go now." Issy hung up. Why couldn't she just tell her *no* and stick to it? Her mum had a way of burying herself under Issy's skin, like a leech, sucking out all her energy, all her happiness, all her life. "Arrggh!"

She fell against the backrest, closed her eyes, and breathed. Slowly in, super slowly out, until her heart returned to a somewhat regular beat. She opened her eyes, and her gaze landed back on the model airplane. "Miss you, Dad. So much."

She wiped a stray tear from the corner of her eye, plastered a smile on her face, and slipped her phone into her miniature glittery bag. She refused to let the conversation with her mum continue to ruin her mood.

In only a couple hours or so she'd see Jeb, assuming he didn't wuss out. Would he wear his usual physio-style uniform—long shorts, runners and a tight-fitting T-shirt with that sexy-as-fuck, bleeding-heart tattoo peeking out from under his left sleeve—or would he dress up? It didn't really matter. What mattered was him making an appearance and hopefully showing interest beyond physio-client, beyond just friends.

Excitement swelled inside her, like that moment just before she performed on stage in front of a packed house, eradicating the remnants of guilt, fear, and frustration left lingering from her mother's phone call.

Even if Jeb didn't make it, she'd dance the night away with her good friends and have a blast. She couldn't control what he did, but she could control her own actions and state-of-mind. Or so she liked to think.

The sunny afternoon transcended into twilight when she left her Bondi apartment and took the train to LEAP, her favorite underground club in Darlinghurst. She strutted down the red-lit bluestone alley, leading to the cool, cozy little members' bar, straight past the pack of people milling around at the front of the club, trying to get in, and sought out her security guard mate. Sure enough, he had her up-to-date guest list, with Jeb at the very top.

Perfect.

The bouncers pushed open the engraved silver double doors. She stepped into a hot, throbbing wall of sound, the pounding bass shaking every cell in her body. She loved it, couldn't get enough, couldn't wait to get out on the dance floor and join the writhing, sweaty bodies dancing to the edgy techno beats.

Unable to tame the achingly wide smile on her face, she went straight to the bar and bought a Fluffy Duck while waiting for her friends to arrive. While waiting for Jeb. How would he look out of his work clothes? How would he look out of clothes full stop? Going by the glimpses of his ripped abs under his T-shirt, pretty damn delicious.

When he'd been treating her, she'd almost caved to her craving and asked him out but knew he'd consider it unprofessional. He wasn't uptight, but he had a by-the-book style. She respected that, so had avoided putting him in a compromising position. But it hadn't stopped her fantasizing about the buff, broad-chested giant of a man. Having his big, strong hands on her during her treatment sessions hadn't helped.

So many times she had to stifle a moan or else risk him knowing how she felt. Plus, she hadn't wanted to make things awkward, especially if he didn't reciprocate her interest. Though something, a gut instinct, told her he did, in his own weird way. He definitely wasn't like the usual guys she met. She flirted, they flirted back and bang, in the bedroom.

Strobe lights flashed across the crowd, followed by a plume of strawberry-scented smoke. She sipped on her drink, her body moving to the music, desperate to expend some pent-up energy.

Soon.

Patience.

The song changed to an old trance favorite, taking her on a nostalgic journey back to when she'd arrived in Sydney and started making a life for herself. Besides dancing, she'd met some great people and couldn't complain about her sexual encounters. She'd had some fucking fantastic experiences.

But Jeb was different. Special. Part of the appeal probably had something to do with his lack of responsiveness, the challenge of winning him over. Should she pursue him, though, considering she'd be leaving soon? Was that fair? Like she'd said to him in their last session, she didn't think—actually, she was pretty sure—he wasn't a fling type. Not that she admitted she'd been referring to him.

"Hey, Issy!" A couple air kisses and full-body hugs from her two male, super-hot, super-platonic contemporary dance troupe mates, Jimmy and Dan, and they dragged her onto the dance floor. Okay, not exactly dragged. More like tried to stop her from stealing the show with her resurrected flexibility and accompanying no-holds-barred dance moves.

Thanks to Jeb.

Any little thing reminded her of him these days. So unlike her. She'd never gotten this stuck on a man in, like, ever.

Five songs and one wine later, the dance floor was crammed. Two twenty-something women still managed to squeeze in next to her. "Oooh, check *him* out."

Issy followed their line of sight.

Jeb.

Her heartbeat sped in response. He'd come. He'd actually come. A fiery bolt of energy zapped through her like she'd downed three shots of Chartreuse. She kept dancing, swiveling and grinding her hips, pumping her hands in the air, sweaty, breathless.

Jimmy leaned into her ear. "Just going for a bathroom break. Dan too. You okay on your own for a few minutes?"

She nodded, unable to tear her gaze away from Jeb. The big hunk of a man surveyed the dance floor, searching for her, like he knew that's where she'd be. She closed her eyes and kept moving, her pulse pounding in time with the dark, dirty beats.

"Issy?" Jeb's deep, alluring voice breathed sizzling hot air in her ear and sent tingles skittering along her spine.

She spun to face him, beckoning him to bend

forward. "Dance with me." His fresh, clean, outdoorsy scent wound around her and made her drunk. On him.

He pulled away just enough to make eye contact, his lips within licking distance, and shook his head. "I don't dance."

"You do now." She flashed him her most seductive grin, grabbed his hands, and pressed them to her hips.

He froze.

Shit, had she pushed him too far? He looked totally frightened, scared shitless. She studied his eyes. They'd gone from almost silver to just about black, which fit with fear.

Or desire.

His eyelids dropped to half-mast, and his gaze shifted between her eyes and her mouth. Not fear, definitely not fear. The guy was turned on. To the max. That little revelation ramped up the sexual tension between them to super-charged.

So, not only *she* felt the potent magnetism. Her lady bits rejoiced. But should she encourage it? Why not? He knew she was going. He could say no to her advances. If she didn't give things a go, she'd never know.

She slid her hands onto his narrow hips and guided them to sway in sync with hers. After a good minute, he'd gotten into the intimate groove. The guy could move. She tilted her head back and smiled. "That's it."

God, she felt so small next to him. Even in heels, the top of her head hardly reached his collarbone. She'd never been with such a huge, powerful man. Standing near Jeb made her feel feminine, sexy. Fucking him would be … interesting. Hopefully, she'd find out just how interesting tonight.

More people crowded onto the dance floor, pressing them together. Holy fuck, he throbbed against her, thick and long and enormous. And she didn't mean his height. When God gave out Jeb's genetics, he'd gotten *way* more than his share.

She rubbed against his snug denim jeans, ran her hands up his glowing white shirt, and twined her arms around his neck.

Jeb swallowed, his Adam's apple bobbing like a nervous tic. "We should go get a drink." He stepped out of her grasp, grabbed her hand, and led her to the bar before she could protest.

Had she misread him? His aroused state proved he wanted what she did—bodies didn't lie. But then he broke away. Why? Issy hadn't hidden her attraction to him. She'd shown him the total opposite.

He let go of her hand and leaned in close to her ear. "What would you like?"

Your mouth between my legs. You inside me. Either, both. "Soda water, please."

"Not drinking?"

"Soda water's a drink."

He laughed. "I mean—"

"I know what you mean. I want to stay in control, remember every moment. Between us."

He stopped laughing. "O-kay."

"You know what? Don't order."

His brow crinkled with confusion. "What? Why?"

"Come back to my place."

He shook his head, conflict turning his eyes defensive, gunmetal grey. "I can't."

A male rejecting an obvious offer for sex? That was a first. "Yes, you can. I'm inviting you."

His gaze dropped to his feet. "Thank you. I appreciate it. It's just..."

She slid her fingers along his stubbled jaw and tipped his chin up until their eyes met. "Just what? You're not interested."

He chuckled, an anxious, stressed sound. "It's not that."

"Then what?"

"You wouldn't understand."

"Try me." And she totally meant that literally and figuratively.

His crooked, twitchy-lipped smile suggested he got her double meaning. He studied her face, his expression turning serious. "I'll come on one condition."

Ooh, that sounded like a challenge she could only accept. "Okay, spill."

"We just talk."

Talk? She'd practically thrown herself at Jeb, given him the green light for a fuck, and he wanted to talk? Since when did a virile, hot-blooded man pass up guaranteed sex? It just didn't make sense.

She stared at him, trying to comprehend, trying to make sure she'd heard right. "You want to ... talk?"

He shoved his hands in the front pockets of his jeans, highlighting the huge, persistent bulge behind his about-to-split fly. "Yeah."

She'd really hoped to get laid tonight. But not with just any guy. She wanted Jeb, had wanted him almost from the moment she'd met him. It had been ages since her last hook-up, and she shook with withdrawal and aching need.

However, even though his body contradicted his words, practically pleaded for her touch, he'd slammed shut that window of opportunity, much to her massive disappointment. It didn't deter her, though. It made her want him more.

Curiosity drove her to accept his proposition.

Maybe she could change his mind. Ultimately, she wanted to hang out with Jeb, and she didn't want him to leave alone or with anyone else.

"Okay. Let's go." Once they were in a quiet space together, it would be easier to convince him they should take things further. Or so she hoped.

His gaze met hers, his almost-silver eyes full of surprise and a strange combination of stress and relief. No, more gratitude. *Interesting.*

Issy scanned the club and couldn't spot her friends, so she sent them a quick text to let them know she'd decided to head home. She threaded her arm through Jeb's and nudged him toward the exit. "Come on."

****

Fuck, when Issy had told him about a man she'd been interested in for a while, he never thought she'd meant him. But her words and actions tonight had made it pretty bloody clear. They stepped out onto the busy street and into the cold, sobering air. Not that Jeb had had much to drink. Maybe he should have. Loosen him up a bit, lower his inhibitions.

Intoxicated or not, he had to tell her. Now. Explain things, explain his hesitation. Conflict warred inside his head. Part of him had wanted her to say, "Don't worry about it. Forget the whole thing. No hard feelings. See you later," while part of him had hoped she'd agree to just chat. Now he questioned whether spending more time with her had been the smartest decision.

The closer their bodies, the longer they spoke, the more he wanted her. Preferably naked. But she needed to know his situation first, and even then…

What would happen if she accepted him, still wanted to go through with spending the night together, having sex? What if it was everything he imagined, but it didn't work for her? Or even if it did and she enjoyed it, she'd be leaving the country for who knows how long. Maybe forever.

Not the best start to a relationship, if she even considered their interaction a relationship. From the conversations they'd had, she didn't do long term, and he wasn't an affair guy, but maybe he should give it a try. With her. The only woman he'd fantasized about since... Ultimately, if this was the only way he could have Issy...

They reached his car, neither of them saying a word since leaving the club, his dick refusing to acknowledge the message to retreat. Jeb subtly adjusted himself. "This is me." He walked her around to the passenger side of his Subaru Forester and opened up.

She faced him, her back against the closed door. "You okay?"

With her in that super-short mini skirt and white, almost translucent skin-tight singlet top, so sheer her breasts may as well have been bare, he couldn't be totally sure anymore. Moments into meeting her, she'd stirred up the sense of equilibrium he'd painstakingly erected. "Mostly. You?"

"Intrigued more than anything." She glanced at his junk, then slipped into the passenger seat.

They drove to her place in silence, well, except her instructing him on where to go. With each second secluded in such close quarters, sexual tension charged the air, until it turned nuclear-bomb explosive.

He parked out front of her contemporary new apartment block in Bondi and kept the engine running, ready to escape.

She stared him straight in the eye as though reading his plan to flee. "I thought you said we could talk."

"We can."

"Then come up."

He edged toward his window. "I don't think that's a good idea."

She shifted forward, cornering him in his own car. "Why not?"

Because she'd work out his whole confident-guy thing was a well-constructed façade. "It's complicated."

She cast her eyes slowly over him, lingering on his crotch, then his lips, then his eyes, her spellbinding stare penetrating beyond his concrete-solid barriers. "Jeb, let me make this clear. You come up to my place and you're gonna get laid. No maybe, no teasing. I'm a sure thing. And I want you. I've wanted you for months."

Fuck if that didn't make his heart nearly burst right out of his chest. He glanced at his fidgety hands, heat flooding his cheeks. Lucky the darkness hid his embarrassing blush. He wanted her, too, so much he could barely keep his hands off her, but... "I shouldn't."

"Shouldn't is a bullshit word. We definitely should. There's an undeniable chemistry between us. So don't you dare try and tell me there isn't. It's something else. I've been totally honest with you. Now be honest with me. What's stopping you, Jeb?"

He met her probing gaze. "My fiancée."

Chapter Three
The Proposal

"Fiancée? Why didn't you tell me? You never, ever mentioned her in six months. I wouldn't have come on to you if I knew you were already involved with someone." Issy buried her face in her hands. He could almost feel her distress.

Shit. He'd fucked up, majorly. "Issy, it's not what you think. I *had* a fiancée."

Her gaze reconnected with his. "Had. So, you've split up."

"Not exactly."

"Not exactly?"

He hesitated, his jaw muscle twitching, stress morphing into guilt. "She … died. The night before we were meant to get married."

"Oh my God, Jeb." Issy reached out and touched his hand. "I'm so sorry. What happened?"

He *really* didn't want to talk about it, not in-depth, but he'd steered the conversation in this direction so couldn't back out now without an explanation. "We had a fight. I tried to stop her from leaving, but she took off and got killed in a car accident, going home from my place."

Issy rubbed up and down his arm with reassuring strokes. "It's not your fault. You know that, right?"

Logically, yes. Emotionally, not really. But he didn't want to go into it any further and absolutely kill the mood.

She must have seen the doubt in his eyes and continued. "I'm sure you're sick of hearing this, but it was her time."

He stilled her hand and pinned her with a

frustrated scowl. "You're right. I am sick of hearing it."

She slid her hand out from under his and pressed it on his knee. The simple move somehow diffused all his negative feelings. "I'm not saying the whole thing wasn't difficult. It must have been horrible, awful. I honestly can't imagine how tough it would have been. And I get that you would've experienced a shocking amount of grief and probably survivor's guilt too."

She didn't know the half of it. His parents and twin sister had been supportive, but he couldn't look townspeople in the eye, couldn't deal with their judgment, the pity, the anger. "Yeah, the family vineyard where I grew up, a place I'd always loved, didn't feel like home anymore. I couldn't move on in Rutherglen, so I relocated to Sydney."

Where no one knew him or what had happened. To start fresh. "For five years I've poured myself into my work, hoping it would help me progress. And it has, but not relationship-wise. Since she passed away, I've hardly even been tempted by another woman."

"And now?" Was that hope he saw in her big blue eyes?

"Temptation isn't the issue. It's…" How could he explain it? Get her to understand.

The truth. It was the only way forward. No hints, no assumptions, no self-protective lies. "My fiancée and I had a pact."

"What sort of pact?" Issy's unblinking, genuinely interested gaze encouraged him to continue.

"To wait until we were married to ah … take things further physically."

"So you guys never…"

"Had sex? No. I wanted to, but holding off was important to her and I loved her so…" He averted his eyes and stared at his suddenly super-interesting lap.

"Since I lost her I haven't... There's been no other woman." Years of guilt and fear ate at his insides and boxed him into a solo existence.

"Are you talking serious relationship or no woman at all?"

His pulse pounded so hard, he could almost hear the blood rushing through his veins. "None at all." He glanced up and braced himself, ready for her rejection.

Her eyes widened and her jaw slackened with surprise. "You haven't had sex. Ever?"

He tried to swallow the spiky-massage-ball lump in his throat. "No."

"But you're so confident, gorgeous, sexy."

"Thank you." Nice to know he'd hidden his virgin status well. Though, it could set up false expectations, giving him less buffer in the bedroom. Not far off where he'd gotten to right now.

"I just ... it doesn't make sense. I mean, it does, from what you've told me—but it doesn't. How old are you?"

"Twenty-eight." Would she judge him, think him strange, repressed, frigid?

"Wow. I really am shocked. It's so unusual these days."

"I know." He lifted her hand from his knee and placed it in her lap. "I should go."

She kept hold of his hand and squeezed. "No, you shouldn't."

"I won't be able to please you. I don't know what I'm doing."

She went silent, her eyes searching internally, most likely trying to find a nice way to back out, following his confession. A way to let him down easy. It was probably for the best, even though his body thrummed with need, strongly disagreeing with his rational brain.

Her gaze snapped back to his. "I'll teach you."

"What?" The total opposite of the response he expected.

"I'll help you through it, give you tips, pointers." Her smile grew with each second, as though the idea was brilliant beyond belief. "I've never been with a virgin before, so this'll be a first for both of us."

He stared back at her in amazement. "It doesn't bother you?"

"Of course not. Why should it? Chemistry, passion, and connection are the keys to making sex an incredible experience, not the mechanics alone."

"But you're leaving soon."

"In four weeks. Plenty of time for you and me to fit in lots of hands-on sex education. I can put together a short but intensive practical course on how a woman can please you and you can please a woman."

"You'd do that?"

"You say it like it's a drain on me, a huge sacrifice. It's so not. I'm going to love every second."

She looked serious. And interested, really interested. "Every second, eh?"

"Yep. I just feel sorry for the women of Sydney. Once I leave and let you loose in the dating world with your master toolkit of strategies and techniques, there'll be broken hearts all over the place."

Including his. But he shouldn't think about that when he'd been offered the proposition of a lifetime. It might be his only chance to sample the woman he'd been lusting over for months and learn some skills at the same time. She could help increase his confidence to move forward positively and be sure of what he could offer, once their fling-of-sorts finished. Better to have had a taste than nothing at all. Right?

He could do this. Or at least give it his best shot. If he said no, he'd never know.

Jeb cupped her face and kissed her, clinging like he'd been thrown overboard into a sea of stormy, turbulent emotions and Issy was the single, life-saving raft.

He pulled back to take a breath, her dazed expression mirroring exactly how he felt. "Okay."

Her wishful gaze met his. "Okay? So you're coming up?"

"Not just coming up, following through."

She smiled, relief and excitement evident in her eyes. "Excellent. Come on."

Jeb turned off the engine, jumped out, and joined her on the passenger side. Issy reached for his hand, intertwined their fingers, and led him to the lift. She pressed level ten and, as soon as the doors shut, pounced on him.

Arms around his neck, her lips on his, she pressed against his torso and practically scaled him like a tree. And it felt phenomenal. The urgency, the absolute unmistakable desire.

He clamped his arms around her, his palms supporting her taut ass, and held her so close their bodies almost melded into one. He'd definitely made the right choice. He'd never been so turned on in his life.

The elevator ride to her apartment was a short, metallic-grey blur fueled by lust and anticipation. When they reached her floor, she broke the kiss, her luscious lips swollen with passion. She slid down his body, adding delicious friction to his hyper-aroused state, making his dick impossibly harder, and grasped his hand, leading him along the dim corridor.

She unlocked her front door and gestured to her cozy, two-seater couch. "Take a seat."

Her place smelled like one of those high-end candle stores—rousing, inviting, stimulating.

She let go of his hand, dumped her bag on the coffee table, and headed into the open-plan kitchen. "What would you like to drink?"

"What have you got?"

"Beer and a pretty well-stocked bar."

"Vodka and soda?"

"Coming up."

He sat on her comfy couch, his back to her, his hard-on still raging. Fuck, he needed to get some control or risk blowing prematurely in his pants. And wouldn't that be bloody humiliating. As a fucking adult, surely he could hold things together, at least until she touched him again.

He closed his eyes and concentrated on his breathing. In out, in out, in out.

"I'm back. Did you miss me?"

He snapped his eyes open and they locked on a totally naked Issy carrying two drinks. *Fucking hell.* His eyes just about bugged right out of his head, and his mouth dropped open, but he couldn't speak. Could hardly think. In clothes she looked sexy as all fuck and without them… *Jesus*.

Graceful and elegant as ever, she placed their drinks on the coffee table, then came and stood between his legs, radiating pure self-assurance and sensuality. So fucking beautiful, toned, balanced. Petite and small breasted but curvaceous. And her whole package absolutely worked, particularly on his libido.

He tried to stop ogling her, but it was impossible with her so close. He wanted to touch her everywhere but couldn't decide where to start.

She palmed his cheek. "I think you need to let go before we continue lesson one."

His gaze raked up her body and fixed on her mesmerizing eyes.

"Have you ever had a blowjob?"

His dick slammed against his fly and he shook his head, the idea rendering him speechless. The thought of her mouth christening his cock… Fuck. If he didn't start reciting exercise plans for his nursing home clients, he'd be in trouble.

"Let me show you what you've been missing." She knelt between his legs, unbuttoned his jeans, and freed his cock from his boxers before he had a chance to come to grips with what she'd promised.

"Just as I imagined. Huge, like the rest of you. Mmmm…" Keeping her sparkling sapphire eyes on his, she dipped her head and licked the eye of his cock, lapping up the pre-cum already leaking from the tip.

He groaned. Fuck, her eagerness, her warm wet tongue, the mind-blowing acupressure effect of that silver stud. It all did things to him. Delicious, exciting things. He couldn't imagine what it felt like to have her whole mouth wrapped around him, her whole sweet, slick pussy.

"You're going to want to make sure your partner's nice and wet before you attempt to get this monster inside her." She licked around the head, and his hips bucked up off the couch.

He always thought it'd feel good, had pictured and jacked off to the explicit images heaps of times, heard his friends talk about it in detail, read about it, but nothing had prepared him for the actual, real-life act. Then again, maybe that said more about the person giving the blowjob. Their experience, their knowledge, their passion.

Issy's tongue worked him like she savored his texture, his flavor, like she'd been hanging out for such a rare treat. She sucked him into her mouth, his dick disappearing between her full, giving lips the fucking sexiest sight.

Her next head bob took him deeper, his cock hitting the back of her throat. She hummed with approval, nearly sending him over the edge, but he willed himself to hold back, to extend the pleasure as long as possible.

He grasped her head, massaging her scalp, slipping his fingers through her lustrous blonde hair. And that's when she gripped him with one hand, her mouth sliding up and down, her other hand caressing his balls.

Lost. He was lost, shooting his load before he could even warn her he'd reached climax. She didn't seem to mind, though, lapping up and swallowing his powerful spurts of cum as though it tasted like the finest quality chocolate.

He dropped his head back, gasping for breath, trying to recover from his epic orgasm. Either she rated number-one cock-sucking queen, he was well overdue for release, or both. "Fuck."

She climbed onto his lap and kissed him. He could taste himself on her lips, but instead of grossing him out, it spurred him on. Made him want to go again. He gripped her hips and pulled her against his renewed erection.

She gasped. "Already?" she whispered against his lips.

"Yeah. I've had to struggle through your treatment sessions with a hard-on for the last six months."

"Really? Good to know." She kissed him again, slow, sensual, intense, then pulled away. "But never forget to factor in your partner's needs, not just your own."

Made perfect sense, logically, though with his body in desperate need of another orgasm, he struggled to consider much more than giving himself some relief. However, from what he'd learned so far, mindset, more than anything else, separated a great lover from a substandard selfish one.

He dropped his gaze to her pert little breasts, the nipples jutting out like mini musk sticks. And he fucking loved musk sticks. He leaned forward, took one nipple in his mouth, and sucked.

She moaned and ground her hips against his dick.

"You like that."

"Yes!" Her big blue eyes met his, glassy with lust.

"So I passed the 'factoring in my partner's needs' test then?"

A huge smile spread across her stunning face. "So far so good. But this isn't a short sprint. This is a mega marathon. You need to consistently give your partner your full attention, work out what gets her going."

"How? What's the best way?"

She kissed his forehead and undid the buttons on his shirt with nimble fingers. "Like with anything, it's a combination of factors. Asking questions, the person's body language, their physical responses, their breathing, the sounds they're making."

Issy pushed his shirt open, pressed her palms to his bare chest, and kissed along his jaw, down his neck, across to his earlobe. Every cell in his body vibrated with need. "For example, I know you're aroused and enjoying yourself because you're participating, your pupils are dilated and your cock, well, it's as hard as a ballet barre."

If he didn't say something, distract himself in some way, he'd come before he could glide into her slick heat. "Okay, my turn." He shrugged off his shirt, threw it onto the floor, and ran his hands over her skin, making her shiver. "I know you're into what we're doing because you're moaning, grinding your hips into mine, touching me, wet for me."

"Exactly." She rubbed her breasts against his pecs.

"Fuck, I want to be inside you so bad."

"Just what I wanted to hear." With pure, dancer-style poise, Issy stood and reached out her hand. He interlocked their fingers and she tugged, helping to lever him into standing, then led him into her bedroom.

She released his hand to pull her red doona back and got onto the bed, flashing him a great view of her flawless, rounded ass. He stared, transfixed, as she lay in the center of the mattress and spread her sexy-as-sin legs, giving him a breath-hitching view of her pink, wet pussy. Somehow, she still looked as classy and elegant as ever.

She touched her breasts and ran one hand between her legs. "Are you coming?"

At this point, he couldn't imagine what would stop him.

****

Jeb's intense gaze between her spread legs made her tingle all over with want. He licked his lips like he intended to feast on her, and she almost suggested his first lesson focus on eating her out.

But given his admission about needing inside her ASAP, she doubted he'd have the patience to give oral his best go. He needed a good fuck before he could concentrate enough to master the finer aspects of sex. To become a sexpert.

A jolt of jealousy stabbed her stomach at the idea of him pleasuring other women. Which did not make any sense. She never worried about that stuff. She threw herself into whatever good times she could share with a guy and moved on to the next one.

She had no time to think about the complexities of that now. Sex awaited with a super-hot man.

He stripped off his pants, using that masculine, sexy bend and kick-off combo, totally taking her by surprise. Not that she expected a shy, meek man, but definitely some hesitancy, given his lack of sexual experience.

Jeb, however, oozed confidence, his almost-silver eyes glimmering like a starving man that only she could give sustenance. Only she could give satisfaction. Talk about a massive ego stroke. His appreciation made her feel bold, powerful, respected.

Not once had any of her previous lovers ever made her feel this cherished, this desired. Maybe because she'd never been with a virgin. She'd never been with a man so desperate to get a bit. Her gut clenched as though absolutely refuting the idea. The connection between her and Jeb felt so much deeper than just an animalistic urge.

What was wrong with her? She shouldn't be acknowledging let alone fostering a bond between them. Their time together had to be light-hearted, physical fun. Nothing more than that or they'd both get hurt.

He approached the bed, and fuck, his body. Ripped, muscular, strong. Wide shoulders, powerful legs, washboard abs, tapered hips and a trail of golden hair leading to his cock, proudly jutting out, commanding her attention. Add his perpetual tan—a real one, from being active in the sun—and he looked like a Greek god. She wanted to drop to her knees and worship him.

Again.

But there would be plenty of time for that later.

Jeb moved above her, propped his elbows on either side of her head, and took her mouth in another electrifying kiss. She'd always enjoyed kissing, but usually got all antsy and impatient to move on to more exciting stuff. Maybe because she'd mostly had short-term affairs rather than relationships. A pleasure-seeker by nature, she didn't believe in wasting too much time on things that weren't exceptional.

But with Jeb ... wow. The way he caressed her cheek and neck and tenderly swept her hair off her face while he explored her mouth. Swoonworthy. Slow and sensual soon escalated to deep and desperate, like turning the dial on the stovetop from simmer to full heat.

She could kiss him all day, all night, and not get bored. Maybe he'd perfected the art with his fiancée, considering just about everything else was restricted. His now tragically dead fiancée.

The poor, sweet man. Her death had also killed off his pursuit of naked pleasure and kept him stuck in personal purgatory. For way too long. But Issy would help him work through it. If all went to plan, they'd both enjoy the journey.

Part of her already wished she didn't have to leave so soon. But she had to. Nothing would change her mind. She'd passed up the opportunity of a lifetime for a man, and it had been a massive mistake.

No way would she ruin a second chance at reaching stellar career success. She'd dreamed about it forever. This time, she couldn't let anything or anyone distract her from her goal. No matter how tempting.

His broad, toned chest pressed against hers, his heart thundering, his breath pounding against her lips, her jaw, her neck. He planted open-mouthed kisses along the way, continuing his slow seduction down to her breasts.

Although barely a B cup, he stared in awe the way most men drooled over a D cup. Generally a confident person, the one thing she'd always felt a little self-conscious about were her less-than-ample breasts. Great for dancing, but not so much for attracting guys.

Except Jeb.

He studied her, touched her, kissed her like she was something special. Her heart swelled until it almost burst with love.

Love?

No.

Ridiculous.

It had to be a side effect of the intense lust building between them like an enormous ball of unspent sexual energy. Deep inside, her core coiled tight, desperate to come, so near the edge of pleasure, which might also have something to do with her unusual, lovey-dovey, over-the-top feelings.

He kissed his way down her stomach, but she grasped his face and encouraged him back up her body.

She reached between them and stroked his cock, which was already seeping pre-cum, and his growl of protest transformed into a groan of ecstasy. The sound of his raspy, rumbling voice flicked a point-of-no-return switch inside her and, like an addict, she needed more. She needed him thrusting deep and hard and fast in her pussy. "Condom. Have you put one on before?"

That seemed to drag him out of his sensual intoxication and sober him right up. All the composure drained from his face, his breathing strained. He swallowed loudly, once, twice, three times, his Adam's apple bulging and retracting.

His gaze drifted up to hers, wrinkles of pain and mortification forming around his eyes and scoring his forehead. "No. Sor—"

"Nothing to be sorry about." She flashed him her most reassuring smile and touched his cheek, which had already gotten rougher with renewed stubble. If he had no idea about condom usage, she had to include it as part of the intensive sex-cation lesson plan and teach him an efficient, effective technique. Not putting one on correctly could lead to significant life-changing results, like playing a form of sexual Russian roulette with a cock instead of a gun.

The last thing he needed was to sow his wild oats and have them sprout into an unplanned family. Unease roiled in her stomach like spoiled chicken, and a jolt of jealousy burned all the way into her heart like reflux. The idea of him with other women… God, what was with her overly-sensitive reaction? She had to be PMSed.

Issy reined in her runaway feelings and focused on the task of teaching successful seduction. She reached into her top bedside drawer, rummaged around, and grabbed a foil packet. She tore the edge with her teeth and took out the condom. "Let me show you."

He sat back on his legs. Even with the unwelcome break in events, he'd still managed to sustain a healthy erection. Like a true sex god.

"Pinch the tip and place it on the head of your cock." She demonstrated and, once it was in place, re-engaged eye contract. "And leave a little bit of space at the top to collect cum. Making sense so far?" She hoped she didn't sound condescending, but it was important he got this right.

He nodded. "Yep."

"Good, because it's your turn next time."

He smiled at that like he was as rapt as her there would be a next time.

She pulled his foreskin back and rolled the condom over his rigid shaft, all the way to the base, or as close as she could. He really was massive, all over. Just the thought made her pussy weep. How she loved having him in her hands. Her heart just about leapt from her chest. "I've heard it's more comfortable pulling your foreskin out of the way. How does that feel?"

"Good." He pressed her back to the mattress, with revitalized confidence. "We ready to go?" His voice strained with urgency. She could totally relate but...

She placed her palm against his chest, in a hang-on-a-sec gesture. "Almost. One more thing."

"Okay." His stare said *hurry up and get to the point.*

"Once you come, hold onto the rim of the condom and pull your cock out before it goes soft or else semen can leak out. Believe me, you don't want to risk that."

"No." Though the way he looked at her suggested he wouldn't mind risking that with her. Not surprising. She'd be his first, so he probably had extra strong feelings, like she'd had after her first time. An added attachment connected to the whole experience.

It had nothing to do with her specifically, which should be exactly what she wanted, yet the thought had her heart plummeting into her stomach like an elevator car with a severed cable.

No time to try to make sense of her scattered emotions. She'd save that for when she was next alone and had a few moments to reflect. At present there were more pleasantly distracting needs.

Jeb stared at her with such intensity, it short-circuited her brain. She closed her eyes in an attempt to re-engage her mind and impart any last, important messages before she got thoroughly lost in him.

"Oh, and always be careful not to spill cum on your partner, unless she likes that sort of thing. And throw the used condom in the rubbish, never the toilet." Not too bad. She was surprised she spoke any sense, with such a potent, irresistible man above her, ready to fuck.

She slid her eyes open and he leaned in, his lips hovering over hers, his breath hot with promise. "Okay, enough talking."

Chapter Four
The Deal

Jeb crushed his mouth to hers before she could carry on in teacher mode, before she could continue her lecture. Thank God, she didn't resist. He teetered on the edge of blowing his load. He had to get inside her this second or he'd totally embarrass himself.

Propped on one elbow, he ran his hand over the swell of her beautiful breast and trailed his fingers lower, but she stopped his progression, stopped all thought, by wrapping her small, smooth hand around his cock and stroking.

"Fuck, Issy," he hissed out, hoping she heard the if-you-do-that-again-I'll-come warning in his tone. Even through the condom, her touch drove him completely out of his mind.

Issy must have understood his silent threat because she positioned his dick at her entrance and thrust up, enveloping him in hot wet heaven.

She moaned and arched into him, her erect nipples scraping against his chest and further ratcheting up his pleasure. He eased out of her tight channel, the friction so much more incredible than he ever imagined, and pumped straight back inside.

He leaned on both elbows and his primitive instincts took over, thrusting like a man gone wild.

"Jeb, oh God!" She raked her nails down his back, gripped his ass and rolled her hips, matching his pace.

A growl emerged from his chest. He couldn't hold on any longer, his cum spurting into the condom in stream after never-ending stream. His thrusts turned erratic. Then, blissfully drained, he fell against her, breathing hard.

Her skin smelled like summer, all sultry and tropical and spirited—his personal holiday paradise. He could drink in her scent for days and still want more.

The orgasm haze lifted. Fuck, he had to feel like a dead weight. Issy was such a tiny little thing yet so sassy and sexy and strong. He went to move and stopped. What had she instructed again? Oh yeah… He reached between where they were still joined, held the rim of the condom, and reluctantly eased out of her. "I'll be right back."

"Don't take too long." Her eyes remained closed and a smile lifted the corners of her lips. Not quite the satisfied smile he'd hoped to see.

Oh fuck.

Fuck.

He'd broken the number one, cardinal sex rule. Please his partner. Guilt chewed up his insides and spat out the short-lived euphoria. What a colossal screw up. And after she'd agreed to help. She had to be so disappointed, maybe even regretful. *Shit!*

He didn't consider himself a selfish guy, well, not these days, not since the incident with his fiancée. In fact, he had made it his mission never to return to his old self-absorbed ways, never to relapse. So if he was integral, as he aimed to be, as he hoped others believed, he'd make sure not to repeat the sexual faux pas in future.

Jeb hurried into the en suite, switched on the light, and shut the door. How many times had he heard how important it was to get a woman off at least once before penetration? However, in the heat of the moment his mind had gone AWOL. He'd been totally overtaken and compelled by physical need.

He'd fucked up so majorly. The tally so far—his two mind-blowing orgasms to her zero. He leaned against the vanity and shoved his hand through his hair.

Not on, not on at all. He wanted to please his partner, not just himself. Otherwise it defeated the purpose of interacting with someone else.

But before he could apologize, before he could attempt to somehow make it up to her, he had to dispose of the used condom. Careful not to catch any stray hairs, he removed the rubber, wrapped it in a tissue, and dumped it in the bin next to the toilet.

He quickly cleaned himself up, took a couple of deep, centering breaths, and returned to her still lying on the bed, all stretched out and looking like a wet dream.

He couldn't stop staring, couldn't get his fill of her. He already craved the press and friction of their skin, the tight grip of her pussy milking his dick, the deep, unwavering eye contact, allowing only honesty. Had he fucked up his chance for round two or would she forgive him?

Rejoining her on the bed, he pressed a gentle kiss to her forehead.

Issy opened her eyes and smiled.

She wasn't angry? Or could her reaction be the eerie calm before the devastating storm? "I'm so sorry."

"For what?" Little lines of confusion marred her smooth brow.

"Losing control."

She held his face between her palms and brought his mouth to hers in a delicate yet toe-curling kiss that ended way too soon. "Totally understandable, given the circumstances."

"Not sure I agree with that. I promise it won't happen again."

She pushed him onto his back and hovered over him. "Good, because I only give out one free pass."

He laughed. Thank God.

Her expression shifted into what he was starting

to recognize as lecture mode, and she held her finger up in a listen-and-listen-good motion. "It's kind of an unwritten rule that guys get their female partner to come before themselves. I know it's a bit sexist, but that's just the way it is."

Her lips curled into a sly smile. "Not that I'm complaining, and I don't think you'll find many women who would."

"Yeah, I can't see many turning that down."

"But, believe it or not, many guys, well, the good ones, equally enjoy getting their woman off." That's definitely what he aspired to.

She relaxed against him, one leg hugging his hip, her fingers tugging at his little thatch of chest hair, her breath brushing his collarbone. "The best lovers will give their partner one or two orgasms before even having sex and then make sure she's about to come before giving in to their own climax."

Jeb played with her hair and anchored his free arm on her lower back, holding her tight and determined to make sure she believed in him, believed he'd learned his lesson. "I know. I'm sorry. It was selfish. But I'll make it up to you, I promise."

****

"What did you have in mind?" Normally, she wouldn't be so forgiving of her lovers, but poor Jeb. He'd been through so much. His eyes, his words, his body language proved he was remorseful. And he trusted her to help him understand the sex and dating world.

It must have been hard to admit his lack of experience. But he did, opening himself up and making his heart vulnerable. So much to admire.

"Whatever you want." The fierce determination in his tone confirmed he meant what he said.

"Whatever I want. Hmmm..." She tapped her

fingers lightly against her jaw.

Jeb tilted her chin up so she looked straight into his concerned eyes. "Tell me what you want, what you need."

He looked so sweet and serious she wanted to wrap him in a hug and never let go. Her oxytocin-addled brain really needed to shut the fuck up. Her body, on the other hand, still screamed for release. Might be time to really test the guy.

"Your mouth between my legs." She loved good oral almost more than penetration. Though, most of her partners had failed to deliver. To be fair, the relationships, if they could be called that, were short lived so both parties tended to focus on getting their own needs met. The men she hooked up with were just lucky she got off on giving head.

But even if Jeb sucked—she stifled a laugh at the clever little double-meaning—she could teach him to be a master. If that meant she had to allow for plenty of practice, she didn't mind one bit.

A dirty smile slid onto his lips. She hadn't expected that, especially from a guy who'd just discovered the joys of sex. Had he been thinking of having a taste? If so, it was an excellent start.

Some guys couldn't even get their heads around the concept, yet were happy for women to suck their dicks and then not kiss them. Losers. Totally selfish, narrow-minded losers.

Jeb tipped her onto her back and slid down her body, his chest hair tantalizing her skin and setting her endorphin receptors firing. He positioned his face right at the apex of her thighs, his gaze fixed on hers, and inhaled long and deep. The look of approval—no, unadulterated pleasure—in his eyes made her heart pound its own thumping, techno beat.

"You'll need to guide me." His burst of hot breath against her mound surged her need higher.

"Go with your instincts. And whatever you do, do it with passion. A woman can tell if you're not into it."

He licked his lips. "Oh, I'm into it. Your scent alone is driving me crazy."

At the rate her heart hammered beneath her ribs, if she didn't climax soon, she'd have a cardiac arrest. But what a way to die.

Jeb planted a kiss on her inner thigh, then the other, so close to the target, yet not close enough. She grasped fistfuls of her fitted sheet to stop herself from grabbing his head and pulling his face to her pussy. *Give him a chance.*

He pressed a soft kiss to her mound, then kissed lower and lower, missing her clit. He'd certainly got the teasing aspect right.

The need to come had gotten so strong, she wouldn't last more than another minute before she shoved her hands in his whiskey-gold hair and sped up the process.

As though reading her mind, he moved all the way along her folds and explored around her entrance with his tongue.

"You taste so fucking good." He said it like he hadn't ever sampled anything so exquisite.

Her body arched up into him. "More, please." Had she really just said that, begged? She didn't beg. What was he doing to her? Outside of turning her upside down and inside out.

A proud, relieved smile formed on his lips and he dove in deeper, this time capturing her clit in his warm, wet mouth.

"Yes!" She nearly came right then, but instead, decided to give him more practice and draw out the spine-tingling pleasure.

Initially, he sucked softly, sussing out how much pressure to use, but with each of her breathless moans, and positive encouragement, he grew bolder. In between sucks, he licked her sensitive nub and lapped up the fresh flow of fluid on her folds. Like a sexpert.

Jeb was a natural cunnilinguist. And what a skill to have. She wove her fingers in his hair. He lifted her legs over his shoulders, not once interrupting the glorious rhythm. He gripped her hips like a pro, muscles flexing in his arms, and his skin shimmered with a sheen of sweat. She could watch him eat her out for hours and never get sick of the show.

Three more flicks of his tongue and she came, just about saw stars, and he hadn't even fingered her pussy. His mouth alone, the mouth of a virgin, sent her straight into nirvana. If she hadn't experienced it herself, she'd never have believed it possible.

She flopped against the bed, all loose-limbed and sated, and glanced up at him. His mouth and chin glistened with her juices and it made him look so delectable, she wanted him again, her own private, sexy-as-fuck pin-up guy. Before she could pull him down for a kiss, he beat her to it, smashing his lips against hers. Tasting herself on him was the sexiest thing.

Confidence, with a hint of dominance, infused his deep, long kiss. Her favorite combination, never failing to press all the right buttons.

He pulled back to take a breath and touched his forehead to hers. "How did I do?"

"Brilliantly."

He grinned, understandably pleased with himself. And so he should be. His technique rocked.

"I do have a suggestion, though. Next time, try using two fingers to test my wetness, and then pump them inside me like they were your cock."

He sucked in a shaky breath, as though her words were an aphrodisiac. They had a similar effect on her too. But she'd leave the physical lesson there tonight. Let him process everything. They had all month to consolidate his skills. They had all month to thoroughly enjoy each other.

"It adds to the intensity of the orgasm and to your experience as well."

"Okay. What next?"

Fuck, this man was like an Eveready battery—he could go all night. So unusual, in her experience. As a professional dancer, her stamina outdid most people she knew. But not Jeb. He needed a break, though. She didn't want him to feel too overwhelmed. Better he practice and master a few things than scramble to do too much half-assed.

Now that she'd recovered, and her logical brain started working again, she too craved rest, snuggled in his big strong arms. "Sleep."

"Sleep? Oh." He went to get up.

She grabbed his hand. "Where are you going?"

"You said you want to sleep. So, it's time for me to go. Although I've never done this, I understand that part."

"No, you don't." She tugged on his hand, and his penetrating eyes met hers. "Because I want you to stay, to sleep together."

"You do?" He sounded surprised, like he couldn't believe what he'd heard.

"Yes."

She yanked him closer and could almost feel the tension in Jeb's body dissipate.

He lay on his side, next to her, leaning on his elbow, his head propped on his hand. "So how is all this going to work? I think we need a clear plan. That way, we both know where we stand and there are no assumptions, no unrealistic expectations."

Virile, mature, and captivating. He really did tick all her perfect-man boxes and then some. When it came to romance, she rarely made plans, choosing to just go with the flow. So this was all new. Good new, explicit new.

Clarity helped reduce anxiety and define what they were embarking on together.

Clarity helped retain logic and prevent her heart getting involved … or so she hoped.

How could they best make their arrangement work? The more frequent access they had to each other the better. *Oh. Yes!* The ideal solution popped into her head. Would he go for it? She faced him, mirroring his position, and met his curious gaze. "We have four weeks so, to make the most of it, I think you should move in here, with me."

"Oh, um…"

"Remember, we both have work/training, so it makes sense to take advantage of any spare hours. And it's easier to do that if we're both staying in the one place." Was she trying to convince him so he'd get the best out of his lessons or for her own selfish reasons?

If she stood back and objectively evaluated her suggestion, it would allow him more opportunities to learn. Plus, she got to enjoy a sex-fest with a passionate, gorgeous man.

"Uh, yeah, I guess that makes practical sense. But what if we drive each other nuts?"

Or fall deeper, get more attached, which was probably the more concerning outcome. But they'd have rules. Rules would keep them safely within the boundaries. "We'll renegotiate the terms."

His gaze was probing. "You're sure."

"I wouldn't have suggested it if I wasn't. But it's up to you."

"Okay." A slow smile crept onto his lips, and his eyes danced with mischief. "I'll think about it."

Chapter Five
Fear of Heartbreak

Issy woke up sprawled across Jeb, his large warm palm splayed along the dip in her lower back. With her face buried in his neck, she was surrounded by his enticing, fresh pine scent. It all felt so good, so comfortable, so right.

In the past she'd avoided sleepovers—after the-ex-who-shall-not-be-named screwed her over—to avoid complications and lingering emotional entanglements. But this was all about practicality. Right?

"Is it normal to enjoy cuddling after sex, to feel this connected?" His husky voice, still heavy with sleep, sent shivers of longing rippling down her spine.

She didn't want to lead him on, have him think their relationship had long-lasting potential, but she had to answer him honestly. "No, but it could be because of the situation. You had years of built-up sexual tension, so I'd say last night bombarded you with endorphins." Though, it didn't explain her feelings of a deeper connection.

"Oh, yeah." He sounded deflated, disappointed, and it hit her in the gut like a prize-fighter punch.

She lifted her head and met his gaze, desperate to make him feel better. And herself. "We have bucket-loads of chemistry. That definitely plays a part." She smiled, hoping he could see the truth in her words, her sincerity.

He obviously did because he smiled back with rejuvenated happiness. He brushed her hair from her face. It had to be sticking up everywhere. Not that he seemed to care. The look in his eyes said he wanted to devour her, in the best possible way.

Jeb cupped her cheek and brought her mouth to his, their lips meeting in a tender, all-consuming kiss. She shifted until she straddled his narrow hips, pressing her breasts against his sturdy, rugged chest.

He trailed his hands down and gripped her butt, his big cock rubbing between her legs. She broke the kiss before they got too carried away. "Aren't you forgetting something?"

He palmed his cock. "This," he pressed the head against her entrance, "belongs in here, buried to the hilt."

How could she concentrate and be responsible when he spoke like that? "Yes, and we'll get to that. But first, I need you to show me what you learned last night."

"Okay, um…" His gaze drifted to the ceiling, as if he were deep in thought.

A sensual smile slid onto his lips, and his piercing eyes refocused on hers. "How would you like it? In your mouth? Inside you? Or would you prefer I bury my face between your legs and go from there?"

What was it she wanted him to demonstrate again?

His expression changed from seductive to eager student. "Is that right, me checking on your needs?"

God, he was so adorable. And hot. "Yes, excellent work. We haven't really touched on dirty talk yet and you're already a champion." The more time she spent with him, the more he proved himself to be a natural in many areas.

His smile went from tentative to beaming. "Thanks."

She stroked the scruff on his cheek and imagined how it would feel to have the now bristly, close-cropped beard scrape her inner thighs as he licked her out.

Later.

Patience.

She still needed to give him a chance to redeem himself. "This morning, I want you inside me. I want you to make me scream."

Hunger flared in his eyes, turning them to molten silver.

She ran her finger along his chiseled jaw, down his neck, over his muscular shoulder and onto his brawny chest. "But before you do that, there's one thing you've forgotten."

His brow furrowed in concentration, and she could see the moment the answer registered. He reached over to the top bedside drawer and pulled out a condom.

"Perfect. You're quite the advanced student."

"I've always excelled at my favorite subjects." Then he demonstrated that by his faultless condom roll-on technique.

He grabbed her hips and guided her onto his cock, and she pushed down until he was fully seated. Oh God, the angle electrified the nerve endings in her core, setting them aflame. "This position is great for so many reasons. Can you name some?" Her voice sounded breathy, needy, contradicting her number one priority.

Fucking Jeb wasn't like her usual random hook-ups. In so many ways. For one, they'd agreed on terms, a verbal contract. The sex had an agenda way beyond pure pleasure. She owed him. She'd promised to teach him, based on her extensive experience, and aimed to follow through, no matter how much her body yearned for release.

"Now?" Poor guy was probably more desperate than her to orgasm, but holding back would not only help him learn the broader dynamics, but also develop his stamina, his endurance, his ability to control when he came.

Her base instinct screamed for her to shake her

head and say *forget about it, let's fuck*, but somehow her rational mind held firm. "Yeah. Patience pays off, I promise." Or at least she hoped he'd agree.

He dragged in a shuddered breath. "Okay, well, I'm liking the view. A lot. Ah … I can touch you just about anywhere. All over. And I really want to. Another big win." His hands twitched on her hips as though struggling to stay put. "And I can watch your reaction, your enjoyment, and kiss you while you sink down on my dick."

Her heart thudded so loud it surprised her he couldn't hear it and see the beats banging against her chest. "Anything else?" She gently undulated her hips, squeezing her pelvic floor muscles.

His eyes rolled back and he groaned.

That probably wasn't fair. The man emitted so much sexiness, she kept forgetting he was a beginner. "I'll give it to you. This time."

A sly smile slid onto his strained face. "I hope so."

She squinted her eyes at him in mock sternness. "I see I have a naughty student on my hands."

"Not just on your hands."

She laughed.

"Oh please, miss, tell me there's some kinky punishment."

God, he was so gorgeous and funny and provocative. "We're never going to have sex if we keep going like this."

"Oh yes, we are. I won't let you leave this bed until you're panting and writhing and screaming my name, as requested."

Holy. Fuck.

Time she sped things up before she came prematurely. And undid all her good role modeling. "One of the best bits about this position is it gives the woman more control. She can adjust the angle to make sure your cock hits her G-spot, her clit rubs against your pelvis or she can play with it for her pleasure and yours, and the rhythm moves at just the right pace. It pretty much guarantees an earth-shattering climax. Every time. While you just relax back and enjoy the show. It's a win-win."

"Show me." His half-mast, desire-filled eyes locked on hers, his voice deep and raspy and a massive turn-on.

Issy planted her palms on either side of his head. She leaned down and kissed his mouth, his perma-stubble scratching against her skin in the most erotic way. He grasped her face and delved his tongue between her lips, stroking it against hers, exploring, while she played around with the angle where they joined.

His cock hit the jackpot. With each grind, she rubbed her clit against his pelvis, lighting her up inside like the Las Vegas strip.

Issy broke the kiss and leaned right back. Confusion etched into his handsome face until she grabbed his hands and pressed them to her breasts. In an instant, his expression turned to mega appreciation.

"You're stunning." His voice cracked, giving away how much he fought to hold back. Not only a sweetheart but also a fast learner.

No need to torture him or herself any longer. She propped one flat palm on his chest, his heartbeat thumping against her hand, and picked up the thrusting pace, their skin slapping, the scent of joined arousal thick in the air. With her free hand, she reached between their bodies and stroked her clit.

A gruff growl of approval rumbled in his throat. His sensual caress of her breasts turned rough, primal, and she loved every second. Her moans grew louder, rebounding off the walls as he tugged on her nipples. Hard.

She came. Oh God, did she come. Euphoria flooded her veins and she cried out his name, over and over.

Just as the waves of bliss began to ebb, he flipped her onto her back and pounded into her. She hooked her legs around his waist, his body now creating the perfect amount of friction to restimulate her clit with every thrust. The second orgasm snuck up and exploded in her sex, her core contracting rhythmically on his magnificent cock.

"Issy!" He stilled, his face contorting with pre-release pleasure, then slammed into her with fast, spasmodic pumps. His motions slowed and he gave one last sexy grunt and collapsed on top of her, his head buried between her shoulder and neck.

His breath whooshed fast and hot against her cooling skin. "You okay?" he murmured near her ear.

"More than okay. Much more. You?" She stroked his damp hair, like burnished gold in the lamplight.

"Yeah. That was incredible."

"I agree."

Jeb continued to pant, the heavy puffs of air scorching her shoulder. "The connection, it's so deep. And I don't just mean physically. It's all-round addictive."

"Yeah, sex is like an illicit drug. Once you have a taste of the good stuff, you want more and more and more."

His body tensed. "Shit, I must be squashing you." He went to get up before she could reply, stopped, then shot his hand between them and grabbed his cock. "Better take care of this." The expression on his face looked relieved with a hint of proud-I-remembered.

Jeb eased out of her, holding the base of the condom. "Be right back," he said, his cheeks flushed from their strenuous activity. It only made her want to jump him again.

She stretched out on the bed, some muscles already aching in the most wonderful way. Sex, like dancing, was a full-body workout. She couldn't get enough of that sort of exercise and accompanying soreness.

A few minutes later, Jeb rejoined her on the bed and enveloped her in his warm embrace. She hadn't wanted to cuddle since she ditched the ex and Jeb came on the scene. Being wrapped in Jeb's arms felt good, no, great, comfortable, safe. She didn't want to move. Ever.

Ridiculous. PMS had to be playing full-on havoc with her mind. She never got all sentimental and mushy over a guy. But there was something special about his touch. It emanated not only attraction and desire but also tenderness, love.

Her eyes stung with sudden moisture. What had she done? Her proposal was supposed to be a no-strings, fun few weeks and already she felt a strong pull to him. She hadn't planned on feelings getting involved. But since being intimate with Jeb, her emotional tap had gone from leaky faucet to broken, gushing fire hydrant.

The situation was so screwed up. Why did they have to meet now? Conflicted feelings swirled in her heart, contaminating her head. She couldn't get too close and miss such an awesome career opportunity on the hope their budding relationship bloomed. She couldn't give up a definite for a possible.

She had to uphold their teacher/student agreement, keep things light and superficial. So they could both move on successfully. But if that were the best option, why did her heart feel as though it had been ripped from her chest, stomped on, and pulverized into a bloody red pulp?

****

Issy hobbled into training on Monday morning, sorer than she'd ever been from a sex session. But then again, this was the first time she'd had a three-night sleepover filled with hours of fucking. Memories flooded her mind. She couldn't stop the smile from spreading across her face, the concentrated heat flaring in her core.

She dropped her bag at the back of the room, found a spot in front of the wall of mirrors, and tried to stretch—struggling in the most rewarding way.

Jimmy stretched toward her. "So, who's the guy? You looked super cozy on Friday night."

"That would be Jeb—"

"The physio? Fuck. Who wouldn't want that man's hands on them?" He finished his stretch and twirled her to face him. "And going by that smile, you've had more than his hands on you."

She blushed.

She never blushed.

Jimmy's face broke out into a super-wide smile. "I knew it! So, are you seeing him again?"

Issy moved into her next sequence of stretches. "Yes."

Jimmy shifted in front of her, mirroring her movements. "You like him. *Really* like him."

"Yeah."

A concerned crinkle scrunched up Jimmy's olive-skinned brow. "But you're leaving."

"Exactly."

The resident Nazi-style choreographer glided into class. "Two more minutes, then move into your positions and we'll take it from the top."

The chatter dwindled, each dancer making sure

they warmed up thoroughly or else risk potential career-ending injury. The type that had led her to Jeb, though in her case she'd gotten lucky. On both fronts.

"Does he know?" Jimmy whispered.

"Yeah."

Dan pushed in between them. "What's going on?"

"Issy's got the hots for her physio friend."

"The guy on Friday night?"

"That's the one." Jimmy bumped Dan aside and pinned Issy with his scrutinizing stare. "So what are you gonna do?"

She dropped her gaze to the gleaming timber floorboards. "Go."

"Really? Even though you care about him?"

"What else can I do?" Her head shot up and met Jimmy and Dan's stares, like dual laser beams scanning her thoughts, her heart.

Jimmy thrust his hands on his hips. "Plenty. Don't delude yourself into thinking this will be the same as moving on from your usual fuck-and-run men. Don't pretend you'll get over Jeb like the others. You've been talking about him for months and every time you do, you get this dreamy look in your eyes."

Dan stepped forward, accepting the conversational baton and running with it. "It's never happened with any other guy."

Jimmy turned to Dan. "Not since..." Thankfully, he stopped himself. After her freak out last time he mentioned her bastard of an ex-boyfriend, he knew better than to speak the dickhead's name aloud. "And even then, you never showed half this enthusiasm."

He refocused on Issy. "Forget trying to play down your feelings. There's no way this Jeb guy is just another one of your flings. I can see right through your bullshit."

"You don't understand. I can't stay—"

"I stayed for Shelley and have absolutely no regrets." Dan puffed out his chest with unmistakable pride. But he and Shelley were so in sync, like a well-choreographed routine. They'd been inseparable almost from the moment they met eighteen months ago.

Shelley had interviewed him for the newspaper after his show-stopping solo performance in Sydney, right at the peak of his career, before he was supposed to jet off to London. But instead of leaving to climb the broader ladder of opportunities, searching for greater and greater career success, he chose love.

He chose relationship success with his soulmate. Now, they were only a few weeks away from becoming first-time parents. Things didn't work out so white-picket-fence for everyone, though.

"I know. You guys are the perfect happily-ever-after story. But you're the exception rather than the rule. I can't pass up this offer. I can't reject it like last time. I'm lucky to have a second chance. Some people never even get a first."

The choreographer clapped her hands. "Positions please."

Jimmy held Issy's shoulders, his fingers digging into her tight muscles. "And some people never find true love. What's more important to you—career or the right man?"

He left her standing there with the question ping-ponging around in her brain and took his place on the far side of the room.

True love? Sure she cared about Jeb, but it was way too early for the "L" word. Okay, she'd thought it, but not seriously, so why Jimmy would suggest... Oh yeah, of course, he'd gone all relationship whisperer on her, tapping into her *real* feelings. Supposedly.

She absentmindedly shook her head and wandered into her designated spot to start the routine. It seemed unbelievable, yet Jimmy had been scarily accurate with other dancers' love lives. It didn't mean he was right this time, though.

Love didn't have any guarantees. Her heart had already learned that and frequently relived the soul-crushing memory, determined to never again travel down that road of hurt.

Chapter Six
Irresistible Offer

"Cole's arrived."

"Thanks, I'll be out in a sec." Jeb tore his gaze from the tranquil ocean out his office window and hung up the phone, his hand shaking.

Why was he so nervous? He and Cole had been mates for years. They'd hit it off Jeb's first year out of uni.

Cole had had a mountain climbing incident, and Jeb had helped him recover. Cole continued to come back to him whenever he needed treatment, and they hung out as well. But never as much as the past year, after Cole had the accident that nearly left him permanently paralyzed.

Jeb closed his eyes and did a thirty-second meditation. Even though they'd forged a strong friendship, he'd never told him everything. Would his best mate look at him differently? Did it matter? He needed advice, and Cole was the perfect person to provide it given his history with women, with trauma and its impact on sex.

In the waiting room, he spotted Cole, sitting right in the front row, engrossed in his phone, cane hooked over the back of his chair. His heart rejoiced seeing his good friend using a walking stick now instead of a wheelchair. For short distances, anyway.

"Cole, come on through."

Slow and cautious, his mate stood, got his balance, slipped his phone into his man bag, and met Jeb at the waiting room door. "Hey, Jeb. Thanks for squeezing me in."

"Any time. You know that." Jeb led him down

the corridor to his treatment room. "Take a seat."

Cole chose the bridge chair, as always, and hung his cane and bag on the backrest. Jeb sat opposite him. "So how are you feeling?"

"Not bad. The burning pain seems to be lessening, but I'm still getting the 'recovery' pain."

"Yeah, unfortunately it's part of the process. Are you taking regular rest breaks?"

"Ah…"

"I'll take that as a *no*. Why doesn't that surprise me?" Jeb couldn't hide the smile on his face. His mate had always been such a high achiever, creating his own successful game software company by the time he reached twenty-five. Not even his accident changed his drive, his passion. "Any improvements with your function?"

Cole flashed his trademark charming smile, all straight white teeth, with a clear edge of control, confidence, dominance. No wonder women fell for the guy. Not that he took any notice these days, with his stunning wife, Hope, in his life. "I'm getting more sensation. I can feel my cock again, orgasm regularly. And the best thing—Hope's pregnant."

"That's fantastic. I'm so happy for you both." The guy bloody deserved it and more, so much more after the hell he'd suffered.

"Thanks, man."

"When's she due?"

"End of June."

"So, she's over halfway?"

Cole averted his eyes, shifted in his seat, and glanced back up, his gaze weighed down with guilt. "Yeah, I wanted to tell you earlier, but we decided to hold off until she'd safely passed the miscarriage danger zone. Sorry, mate."

"Nothing to be sorry about." After the trauma they'd been through, it made total sense they'd wanted to wait, to ensure they could announce some happy news.

"I thought you'd understand."

"Absolutely."

"Oh, um … and I got on the treadmill, but I kept the speed on slow."

"I told you to hold off on that."

"Not so understanding now, huh?"

Jeb conjured up his most stern, I'm-extremely-disappointed look. "Cole."

Another wave of guilt crashed onto his friend's face. "I know. I just wanted to see how I'd go."

"And?"

"I didn't fall off." Not even the traumatic event stopped his mate from being a risk taker, always pushing right to the brink of a boundary. Although professionally Jeb had to caution him, personally, he admired it.

"So what did you want to work on today?"

"Sexual positions. I want to build up my stamina and add a bit more variety into my sex life. Don't get me wrong—I love Hope riding me—but I hoped you could help me tweak a few other positions to minimize my pain so I can give her a break from doing all the hard work. She's getting tired more easily, just generally, and I want her to keep enjoying our lovemaking, find it a welcome release and not a chore."

"Right. Ah…" Heat rose up Jeb's neck and continued onto his face. Normally, he had no issues going through safe sexual positions with clients, but today, with his confession paused on his lips, it added another dimension, another agenda. "Let's warm you up a bit. Then we'll go through some options. How does that sound?"

Cole shifted forward and scrutinized Jeb's skin.

By now he imagined it had turned a telling, bright cherry red. "Mate, are you okay?"

He forced what he hoped passed as a convincing smile. "Yeah, of course."

"Bullshit. Something's up. We've been friends too long for me not to notice."

Something was up all right. It had hardly gone down since Friday night.

"Spit it out, Jeb."

Now that the segue had opened up, and Cole was unlikely to back down, he may as well take advantage. "Okay. I need your advice."

"Sure. On what?"

"Start doing your stretches and I'll fill you in."

Cole sprang—well, more like a rusty spring—into standing and moved to the mini gym area. He stopped on the mat in front of the parallel bars and commenced with a calf muscle stretch.

Jeb followed him over and propped against the nearest wall. Cole pinned him with his CEO, no-nonsense stare. "I've held up my end of the bargain. Now it's your turn."

Here we go… "I'm not sure where to start."

Cole's lips curled into his characteristic smart-ass smile. "The beginning's always good."

"Right." Jeb's nerves were so rattled he couldn't even muster up a you're-hilarious eye roll.

His mate stopped mid-stretch, his smile fading. "This is really serious."

"Yeah, well, to me."

"No more stalling, then. Let me help."

"You keep stretching. I'll keep talking."

Cole's smile returned as he moved onto a hamstring stretch. "Sounds fair."

Jeb cleared his throat and a path for his thoughts

to hopefully flow. "You know I lost my fiancée a few years ago."

"Yes, a tragic accident." His best friend knew all about those, having come close to death himself.

"Since then, I've been struggling."

"I'm not surprised." Cole finished his stretch and leaned back against the parallel bars. "Going by the look on your face, your slumped shoulders, you're still carrying some guilt."

"I am."

"Have you spoken to anyone about it? A professional?"

Jeb went to cross his arms, but stopped himself. He needed to be open and confront his fears or he'd never fully recover. "Early on, yeah. It helped, but the feelings have lingered."

"And held you back, stopped you from moving forward, stunted your growth."

"In a lot of ways, but particularly with women."

"I see."

"Actually, you probably don't. Not fully. Not yet." He pushed off the wall and walked to the window. The wind had picked up, tossing turbulent waves around like the stressful thoughts in his head. "I wasn't interested in anyone, haven't been interested in anyone for a long time. Part of me didn't think I deserved happiness, but I won't go into that. Maybe another time."

"Definitely another time."

Jeb glanced at his friend. No way Cole would let him off the emotional hook after that admission. "Fine. But right now, it's not what I want advice on. I've met someone. Actually, I've known her a little while now."

"The dancer."

Fuck, he knew the guy was talented at reading people, but… "How did you…?"

"You never saw your face when you spoke about her. So what's happened? You still treating her?"

"No."

"Have you asked her out?"

"She asked me out."

Cole moved into his quad stretches. "And? Come on, mate. Stop keeping me in suspense."

"We caught up Friday night and things developed."

"Developed how?"

Jeb propped his butt against the window sill. "This is where it gets a bit weird."

"Sounds intriguing. Kink-like. And you know how much I love kink."

Jeb laughed. "Oh yeah. It's never been something you've tried to hide."

"True."

Cole had always been approachable, trustworthy, candid about sex. So Jeb probably should have confided in him earlier, seeing he considered the man his best mate. But, even though he'd shown a history of non-judgmental behavior, Jeb worried about his reaction once he told him the absolute truth. "Anyway, um, she made it clear she wanted me to go home with her, pretty much guaranteed sex."

"Sounds perfect so far."

Yeah, to a normal guy. "But I was hesitant."

"Because of the guilt?"

He fiddled with the cords hanging from the waistband of his long shorts. "That, and I was nervous. Really nervous. She's very sexually open, and I worried I wouldn't stack up in the lover department."

"Why would you think that? You're an attractive guy. You look after yourself, and you're great with your hands, attentive, thoughtful, interested."

His stomach churned with growing stress. Would his friend still accept him, respect him, once he admitted his little secret? "Thanks. But I'd never done *that* before."

"A one-night stand?"

"Not much more than making out."

Cole stopped mid-stretch. "Hang on, hang on. Let me get this right. You've never done more than make out?"

Jeb nodded, embarrassment heating his cheeks. Every time he went to confide in his friend in the past, he'd faltered. Then Cole got hurt and had much more important things to deal with.

Cole dropped his bent-up leg to the ground and stared, as though trying to get his head around Jeb's revelation, as though not sure he'd heard correctly, as though not believing it could be true.

"My fiancée and I had agreed to wait. And then she … and I never…"

"So, you haven't had a blowjob, haven't tasted pussy, and have never had sex." His tone held no judgment, just plain curiosity, putting Jeb a little more at ease.

"I hadn't until Friday night."

Cole grabbed his cane and came to join him by the window. "How did it go?"

"Great. She's incredible. Sexy. Passionate. I can't get enough of her."

"I hear a 'but'."

"She's leaving in a month."

"Oh."

"Yeah."

"So, what's the story? Where did you leave things? Are you planning to keep seeing each other before she goes?"

"Yeah." Fuck, how did he explain the rest of their agreement without it sounding totally lame, pathetic? All he could do was be honest, upfront. If Cole didn't accept it, didn't accept and support him, maybe he wasn't a true friend. "We set up a deal for the next four weeks. For her to teach me. A full-on, practical, sex-cation program."

"O-kay." Cole shifted his weight from one foot to the other and back again, a slight clammy sheen to his skin. He could almost conceal the grimace on his face but not his clamped teeth, a total giveaway his pain levels had hit close to an unbearable ten.

"How about we sit down before you pass out?"

"How about you stop deflecting and keep explaining?"

Jeb brought over the two closest chairs and angled them toward each other, still with views of the harbor. "How about both?"

"Deal."

They sat and Cole leaned back and waited. His silence technique had been one of his most successful strategies when doing business, negotiating deals. Got people talking to fill the space. Agree to things.

Now that Jeb had firsthand experience of it, words banked up in his throat, ready to purge. "So far, the sessions have been brilliant. I've already learned heaps and, fuck, what guy wouldn't want to have heaps of sex with a beautiful woman, even if it has a time limit."

"But we're not talking about any guy. We're talking about you." Cole's calm, interested tone snuck into Jeb's brain like a covert search party looking for answers.

"I want the sex. Of course I want the sex. With her. I'd be crazy not to. She's smart, skilled, amazing. And now that I've had a sample of the high-grade stuff, I can't go back. But it's more than that. I'm falling for a woman who's made it clear there's no relationship future. I'm setting myself up for heartbreak. Again. And I don't know what to do about it."

Jeb stared at his hands clasped tight in his lap. "I know it probably sounds ridiculous having such strong feelings for her already, but they're there. I can't ignore them. Maybe it's because she's my first. I don't know. I hoped you could help me make sense of it."

Cole slapped a warm hand on his arm. "You've done the right thing, talking about this with someone you trust. I am someone you trust, right?"

So Cole to inject light humor into the situation, ease the intensity. "You know you are. No need to fish for compliments."

"You know what I love? Outside of Hope, you're the only person who calls me out on my shit. I appreciate it a lot. Thanks, man." His mate's grin settled into a grateful smile. "But back to this woman of yours. You may not have gone out until now, but you've known her for months. Sounds like you'd already started to connect along the way, so falling for her is totally feasible.

"There's nothing wrong with what you're feeling. What you need to work out is where you want things to go from here. I can give you my opinion, but only you know what's right for you, what you can handle."

"I'm conflicted, Cole. Part of me wants to stop things now before my heart gets too involved, and part of me wants to stick things out to see how compatible we are and convince her we're meant to be together."

"It's a tricky one, but I agree it's a great opportunity to find out if you are actually suited. You may not be, for anything more than a fun fling, and then it'll be easy to move on. If you do have something deeper, then you have some leverage to fight for the relationship. Doesn't mean she'll see things the same way as you, though. Ultimately, spending more time with her is a risk. So you need to ask yourself—is she worth it?"

Chapter Seven
Love or Lust?

Jeb stepped into his bare-bones apartment, closed the door, and leaned back against it. He fumbled in the front pocket of his shorts for the fiftieth time today and fingered the spare key to Issy's place like it was some sort of lucky charm.

The look in her eyes and that knowing smile as she'd dropped it into his hand that morning suggested she believed he wouldn't wuss out. What did Cole call the pull a woman had on a man? Muff struck. Yeah. Now Jeb understood it, too, that profound, mysterious womanly power.

But it wasn't just the sexual attraction, the promise of more mind-blowing sessions. He enjoyed her frankness, her vast knowledge, her easy company. One thing he knew for certain—Issy was absolutely worth the risk, even with only a slim possibility of long-term relationship success.

The only way to increase his chances entailed him accepting her offer to move in with her for the month. The more time they spent together, the easier it would be to bond. Or repel. Going by their interactions so far, he'd bet on bond.

He pushed off the door, packed some clothes and toiletries, and drove to Issy's place, his stomach in nervous knots. The whole situation demanded taking a big step. A huge step. The intensive sex crash course had propelled him from prep to university level in three days. Pleasure turned out to be an effective motivator to fast-track learning. Go figure.

On the ride up to her floor in the elevator, his phone buzzed. He whipped it out and laughed at her cheeky text.

Issy: **After a day of weighing up pros and cons, my guess is you're either at my place or on the way. I'm right, right?**

Jeb: **In the lift up to your apartment as we speak. Maybe you should have gone into fortune telling instead of dancing.**

Issy: **Considered it. Didn't pay as well, not to mention no audience adoration. Anyway, just letting you know I won't make it home til after 9.**

Jeb: **No worries. Have you had dinner?**

Issy: **No, I'll eat later.**

Jeb: **Okay, see you when you get here.**

It had just ticked over to seven o'clock, which gave him two hours to prepare something for them. He exited the lift, entered her apartment, and dropped his bags in her bedroom.

Returning to the kitchen, he had a quick search of her cupboards and fridge. Hmmm ... given the timeframe, what food she had on hand, and factoring in an active job like hers, the answer pointed to pasta.

Once he'd pulled out the required ingredients, he got started on his special vege-and-meat themed Bolognese sauce. While it simmered away on the stove, he took a self-guided tour of the rest of her home. The place had a sleek, contemporary design, with a light and airy, open feel. Just like Issy.

Her apartment reflected her personality perfectly. Unlike his flat. He'd moved in more than a year ago and still hadn't unpacked all the boxes, still hadn't decorated. Just didn't have the motivation, the enthusiasm. A shelter, a hideout more than a home, it provided a secure place to eat and sleep and recuperate. Nothing more.

Jeb wandered into the spare bedroom—a simple double bed, a chest of drawers, decorated in whites and rich walnut tones. Obviously a spot she didn't venture into too often. A bit like a B&B. No real personality. A true guest room.

In the lounge, however, a range of books lined the inbuilt shelves on the left of the faux fireplace. He studied the spines—photographic books on dancing, with a range of artistic shots of well-known performers such as Rudolph Nureyev, Mikhail Baryshnikov, Anna Pavlova, Margot Fonteyn, Isadora Duncan.

Isadora.

Issy's full name, according to her physio file.

He'd have to ask her about any link.

The rest of her library sported a range of genres from mystery to thriller to romance, autobiographies and dance craft. On the right of the fireplace, certificates, awards, and trophies filled the shelves. Impressive. Not that he doubted her skills for a second.

He ducked back into the kitchen to check on the sauce and put some pasta on to boil.

Opposite a huge window overlooking the beach hung a spectacular black-and-white photo of Issy mid-leap, framed in black. The setting sun sent soft rays of amber light shining through the window and glinting off a display case, drawing him across the room to investigate.

Instead of dance-related paraphernalia, it showed off intricate World War Two model airplanes. Absolutely not what he'd expected. Had she made them? A display case suggested significance. Had she inherited them from someone close? What was the correlation?

Whatever it was piqued his interest and drove him to further suss things out. He never would have associated dancer with WW2 buff. Not that he didn't expect her to have depth. No way could he be so attracted to—so interested in—a vapid, high maintenance, superficial woman.

How little he'd noticed over their weekend together. Not surprising given he'd hardly left Issy's bedroom. He'd been burning up with Issy fever. She'd become the center of his universe, all he could see, hear, smell, feel, taste, their sexual synchronicity totally overpowering.

Issy's place radiated so much drive, so much energy, so much warmth. He couldn't get the cute little quirky woman out of his mind, out of his heart. He had it so fucking bad. If he didn't get some semblance of control over his emotions, he'd develop unrealistic, unhealthy expectations that could only lead to disappointment.

At the end of the month, she'd organized to leave. She'd been totally upfront about that from the start. So he couldn't expect her to give up her dream to pursue a budding new relationship.

However, he could work on convincing her to give them a chance, reinforce that her going didn't have to mean breaking up. It wouldn't be easy, not when she'd insinuated she didn't want more than a short-term affair. But he was up for the challenge.

Their physical connection couldn't be faked. Could it? His little experience with women meant he had no idea. From what Cole had said, it'd be in Jeb's favor to stick things out, to give his heart and soul to whatever it was they had to reinforce they could make a go of things, somehow. Assuming their month together ended up a success and they didn't drive each other insane.

He re-entered the kitchen, strained the pasta, stirred it into the sauce, and washed up the dirty dishes. Perfect timing. Only thirty more minutes until Issy arrived. Images of their reunion set his thoughts alight and blazed through his body.

How could he make her welcome home special? How could he demonstrate his difference from the other men she'd been with? When it came to sexual relationships, romantic relationships in general, he still lugged around his L plates.

Candles? Dim lighting, mood music? What would she like? Something that showed he got her, he cared. A soothing bath? *Yeah.*

He entered her bathroom and searched for a bath bomb, scented bath salts, something relaxing. In the cupboard under the vanity he found patchouli-scented candles and bubble bath.

When the bubble bath solution hit the steaming water, an erotic, earthy aroma held in the humid air. It mixed with his excitement and reacted to his chemistry with Issy, further stimulating the idea they could have a serious future.

Jeb propped his butt against the basin, drinking in the nasogasmic scent. He could dream, hope, at the very least, aim to make the most of this once-in-a-lifetime experience. Whatever that may be.

He'd never believed in love at first sight, or in this case, love at first fuck. But like Cole had said, even though he and Issy hadn't dated, they'd already known each other for six months. Enough time to develop rapport, to develop feelings.

So maybe his reaction was normal. Maybe he'd feel like this every time he slept with someone. Because he'd already realized he couldn't just have sex, couldn't just have a quick fuck. Not if there were no other deeper feelings. He could only connect with a woman he cared for, truly be intimate, make love.

Make love.

Had Issy made love with all the men before him? Or had she just had sex? Did she define sex and making love differently? To him, sex was a primal act, to slake an urge, to satisfy a need. Jeb had his hand for that. If he chose to sleep with someone, it would be because he wanted to share something more meaningful, something soul deep.

Given that, he couldn't imagine making love to anyone except Issy. But as they spent more time together, would his overwhelming feelings for her settle? Would he get to a point where he'd be able to move on armed with more skills and confidence to take into the next relationship?

Maybe. But what would happen if he didn't? What if he only wanted Issy? He'd already lost one love. Could he survive losing another?

****

Issy nudged the front door open, her arms loaded up with recycled shopping bags filled with groceries. For the two of them. "Jeb?"

The door shut behind her, and she glanced into the kitchen. A pot sat on the stove, possibly pasta sauce going by the hint of oregano and basil in the air. She took a deep breath, let it out, then took another, not wanting to stop sniffing the sensational aroma. She'd lucked out—a yummy, considerate man for a month, who could not only burn up the sheets with some hot, sweaty sex but also cook like a Michelin star chef.

"Issy?"

He appeared in the hallway, freshly showered and looking like a runway model. Tall, built, imposing. His wet whiskey-blond hair had turned a dark malt color, and drips of water trickled down his neck and onto his bare chest. A white towel hung low on his hips and showed off the happy trail leading to his covered cock. Fuck, he was so mouth-watering. Man-ificent.

"I'm really glad you decided to stay." The joy

rising up inside her overflowed, surprising her with its intensity.

"Me too. Once I commit, I try my best to stick to my decision."

Good to know. "Let me put these away and—"

"I'll help you." He walked over and grabbed the collection of bags hanging on her forearms.

"Oh, and hello." He bent down and pressed a kiss to her lips. Not full on, more tender, affectionate, loving. The simple gesture stirred up things in her, emotions she should be avoiding.

He pulled back and smiled. "Dinner's already done, by the way."

The whole scene seemed so domestic and surprisingly good, comforting.

No.

"Thank you. It smells divine." No guy had ever done that for her, not even… No. No, no, no, no, no, no, no, no, no.

She walked into the kitchen. Spotless, totally spick and span, outside of that one pot on the stove, wisps of steam curling out through the gap in the lid. "You cooked and cleaned up?"

"Of course. I'm pretty well housetrained, you know." He lifted the multitude of bags still dangling from his muscular arms, his tattoo drawing her attention. But she refused to stare, refused to ask him about it, even though she was terribly tempted, in case it brought them closer. Knowing her luck, it would strengthen the already developing bond between them and make it heaps harder to leave him behind.

"Now show me where this stuff goes." Jeb's sensual voice snapped her out of her head and back to the moment, her gaze shooting up to his face. If he kept up that sexy-as-sin grin, he'd weaken her defenses to the point he could persuade her to do almost anything.

"Most of it lives in here." She gestured to the kitchen cupboards and gave him a little overview of what was stored in each.

He disentangled himself from the bags, popped them in a pile in the corner, and got to work. Not only drop-dead, ovary-exploding gorgeous but also proactive, thoughtful, sweet. She couldn't help but fall a little more in love with him.

Love. What the fuck? She couldn't let her feelings get involved. Not again. How many times did she have to repeat it to herself? Falling for another man and staying would mean career suicide. She'd barely survived last time.

This was a fling. A fling and an opportunity to help a wonderful man. That's all. Or so she kept trying to convince herself. Her rebellious heart refused to concede.

As Jeb put things away, his muscles bulged and slid beneath his golden skin. She couldn't stop staring, wishing his towel would drop to reveal more of his masculine splendor. After such a full-on day, she was ravenous for food, sure, but for him, more. Yeah, that's what she had to do—focus on the lust, the sex, the physical pleasure. Nothing deeper.

She slunk up behind him, running her hands over his broad back, and he froze. Even with him facing away from her, she could hear his shallow, labored breaths, imagine the rapid rise and fall of his chest.

She tugged on the corner of his towel and it fell to the floor. He spun around, desire swirling in his hooded, silver-tinged eyes. They peered right into her, as though able to read her most secret thoughts.

Issy broke eye contact and touched his chest, his heart pounding, the dark blond hair tickling her palm and bombarding her brain with insatiable longing.

He cupped her face with his big hands, tilted it up, and crushed his lips to hers. She could scarcely breathe, could hardly think, she wanted him so much. Their tongues tangled, their hearts beating as one. He walked her to the closest bench, as though he really could tune into her thoughts. How could something be so fucking scary and exhilarating?

He yanked off her runners, pulled down her leggings and panties in one swift move, and lifted her onto the cool stone surface.

Before she could pull his mouth back to hers, he dropped to his knees and trailed his tongue along one inner thigh and then the other.

"I need a shower." Although she loved a man's mouth between her legs, she wanted to make sure the working conditions exceeded standards. And after her sweat-drenching day of training, she couldn't be sure.

"Later." He kissed her mound, her folds, her opening, then spread her legs wider. "Mmm ... you smell fucking edible."

Okay, then. No need to worry. She grasped his head and he swooped in, licking her seam and thrusting his tongue inside her core.

She tugged on his hair. "Oh God, Jeb."

He tongue-fucked her like a pro. Other men had done it before, too, but never with so much passion. Jeb kept going and going, until she almost came. He pulled back and she whimpered. "Please."

He'd taken her to pleading point again? No one else had done it once, let alone twice, but he'd driven her so out of her mind, she needed release like she needed to breathe.

The pleased look on his face could have been mistaken for smugness, but he wasn't that type. He was proud. Proud of his ability to turn her on, particularly being a novice. He dove back in, sucking her clit into his mouth, tantalizing it with his tongue. God, it felt so good, amazing, the perfect combination of lick and suck.

She skyrocketed toward climax. He thrust two thick fingers inside her and flicked her thrill switch. Bright white stars exploded behind her eyes, making her nearly pass out. She bucked against his hand in a fucking frenzy, riding out wave after wave of body-shuddering bliss.

Finally, she returned to earth and let go of the death grip on his hair. "Sorry."

"Don't be sorry. I liked it."

So he enjoyed a bit of pain. Like her. So far they really did seem aligned. She wasn't a strict BDSM girl, but she enjoyed aspects. And it appeared he did too.

He stood between her legs, his cock rubbing against her still-sensitive sex.

Her eyes zeroed in on his. "I'm on the pill and I'm clean."

"So?"

"You don't need a condom unless you want to go get one."

She seriously hoped he agreed with her thinking. She'd just orgasmed, but she still craved the smooth, solid feel of him.

"No, I trust you." He lifted her singlet top over her head, unhooked her bra, and slammed his mouth on hers, his lips drifting down to her jaw, her ear, and along her neck, to her breast. He took turns, licking and sucking on one nipple, then the other, driving her mad with need.

"Inside me now. Please!"

He repositioned himself, his cock nudging her entrance. Jeb's lips captured hers right as he thrust inside her. She'd never had sex without a condom. She'd never wanted to before. But with Jeb, things were different; she had full faith in him. And her heart swelled, knowing he had full faith in her too.

He slid out, then back inside her with a raw, primitive grunt. She wrapped her arms around his neck and crossed her ankles around his waist, angling their connection until he stroked her G-spot. "That's it. That's it!"

With their lips locked in a deep, passionate kiss, she met him thrust for thrust, his pelvis rubbing deliciously against her clit. And she came, squeezing his cock in rhythmic contractions.

Jeb only lasted two more pumps and growled out his release, his cum coating her core. Part of her crazily wished she'd conceive. Ridiculous. She'd avoided relationships to pursue her career. A baby would totally fuck it up. And yet, the idea of carrying Jeb's child…

No. She couldn't let her mind even consider traveling down that path.

He stayed inside her and dropped his head onto her shoulder, his recovering breaths pelting against her damp skin. She didn't want to move, didn't want to disrupt the strong connection between them. But if she stayed in his embrace, she'd get too attached. Part of her already had.

She wriggled back. "Mmm, I was wondering what to do for an appetizer."

His gaze slid lazily over her body and locked on her eyes. "Best entree I've ever had. Remind me to come to this restaurant again. And again. And again."

She pressed a kiss to his lips. "Sure thing."

Jeb chuckled, registering her double meaning. Then he lifted her off the bench and strode out of the room.

"Where are we going?"

"Bathroom."

"But what about dinner?"

"It can wait a few more minutes."

He entered her en suite, the scent of patchouli heating her insides, reinvigorating her lust. He'd only recently given her back-to-back orgasms, and she already hungered for more.

She slid down his body, his rejuvenated erection rubbing against her stomach. Then he stepped into the bath, steam rising up out of the water, and held out his hand. She gripped it and he steadied her as she joined him. Jeb sank into the water and pulled her down between his legs, her back resting against his chest.

She lay her head on his shoulder and, after soaping up his hands, he gave her the most sensual wash she'd ever had. She whimpered and squirmed against him, his cock growing harder.

Issy couldn't leave him like this, all hot and bothered when he'd been so accommodating of her needs, so she lifted herself up, angled her pelvis, and impaled herself on him.

He groaned and gripped her hips. She rode him, slow at first, then picked up the pace to match his escalated breaths. Grabbing one of his hands, she brought it to her clit, his fingers circling it without her having to explain what she wanted.

"Jeb!"

Three more thrusts, combined with his frantic rubs, and she came.

"Issy, ohhh … Issy!" He groaned and followed her over the edge.

She slumped against him, post-climax aftershocks still fluttering in her core, his cock still jolting. Still inside her, he massaged her breasts and kissed a line along her neck and shoulder. She couldn't have felt more appreciated, more loved.

No.

She hurried into standing, water crashing off her and splashing onto his surprised face. "We should eat. It's getting late."

She grabbed a towel from the cabinet below the vanity, dried herself off, and raced from the room.

A couple minutes later, he joined her in the kitchen. "What was that?"

"Me enforcing the boundaries."

"I see." But did he? He turned away from her before she could read his facial expression, pulled two plates from the cupboard, scooped out a serve each of pasta, and carried their dinner to the pre-set table.

They ate in awkward, tension-filled silence, the unspoken confrontation deafening.

She kept glancing up, but his gaze remained fixed on his food.

If she wanted him to stay, if she intended to teach him more, she had to get the balance right. Her recent stunt had hovered way too close to rejection. She had to keep him interested, engaged, while guarding her feelings and not encouraging his. Easier said than enacted. But she had to try.

Partway through eating their meals, she lifted her leg and stroked his cock with the ball of her foot. Jeb just about choked. She struggled to hold in a laugh, nearly spitting out her mouthful of food.

That seemed to shift the mood in a more positive, salvageable direction. Thank God.

He stared at her with steel-hard intensity. "If you don't stop that, I'm going to bend you over the bench and fuck you so hard you'll forget your own name."

Her eyes went wide and her heart raced. Where the fuck had that dominant caveman vibe come from?

She'd noticed hints of it in his voice, his words, but nothing so overt. Until now. His tone seemed to reach deep into her pussy until she was so wet she swore she'd stain the dining chair.

She quite enjoyed a good pounding, a bit of rough sex. With the right man, an attentive man attuned to her needs, a man she could trust. Like Jeb. Exactly like Jeb. Instead of overthinking it, Issy concentrated on the moment, holding his gaze and rubbing the arch of her foot up and down his growing length.

His eyes went black with desire. With his gaze locked on hers Jeb stood, pushing his chair back with so much force it toppled over. He grabbed her with his long sinewy arms, threw her over his shoulder, and stalked into her bedroom. A man on a fucking mission.

Lowering her onto the mattress, face down, he then pulled her hips up, spread her legs, and moved between them. He held her wrists behind her back, adrenaline pumping through her veins in anticipation, and plunged into her.

She moaned and pushed back, loving his take-charge attitude and the sensation of him buried deep. "Jeb, oh God."

"Oh yeah." He picked up the pounding pace, and in less than a minute they came hot and hard. She collapsed onto the bed, with him on top. And, surprisingly, the heat and heaviness added to her blissed-out state.

Eventually, he shifted and lay on his back.

She snuggled into him. "You're such a gorgeous, sexy man, a good man."

He stiffened.

"Yeah? Does a good man fantasize about restraining his partner and fucking her until she can hardly move?" His tone sounded full of pain and self-loathing.

She pushed up on her elbow and looked into his troubled eyes. "He does in my world. I love being restrained and fucked until I'm boneless, by the right guy."

His gaze penetrated straight into her soul. "Am I the right guy?" His expression, his voice, suggested there was so much more to his simple question.

But she couldn't give him or herself false hope. "Yes, and others like you."

A shadow of a smile barely lifted the corner of his lips, let alone reached his eyes. "I understand." Then he rolled on his side, away from her, and went to sleep.

Or pretended.

Either way, his actions spoke louder than any words—she'd hurt him, again, and he needed space. At least he didn't leave. Like she would. Soon.

Chapter Eight
Sexual Discovery

Jeb woke up alone in Issy's bed. He had to snap out of his somber mood. Her honesty had been one of the things he loved and admired about her, but obviously not when it was something he didn't want to hear.

She'd done the right thing, sticking to what they'd agreed on—keeping the boundaries in place and focusing on having fun while he learned, discovered.

He rolled onto his back, her vacated spot still warm, which meant she hadn't gotten up too long ago. Would she return or had she decided to leave him alone for a while longer? If she didn't make an appearance in ten minutes, he'd go seek her out.

Jeb folded his hands behind his head and stared at the shadows dancing on the ceiling. They still had close to four weeks together, so he had time to win her over or at least give it his absolute best shot. The worst thing he could do was rush it and push her away. If he bulldozed ahead, it might scare her and she'd probably sever their agreement. Then he'd have no chance.

The sound of water splashing in the sink had his gaze darting to the en suite door. Seconds later Issy eased it open and her eyes met his.

She smiled. "You're awake."

"Yeah."

"How did you sleep?"

"Okay. A bit disturbed."

"Same." She approached the bed, climbed back onto her side—*her side*, like he had a side—and sat cross-legged facing him, still gloriously naked and tempting. "Look, I hope what I said last night wasn't too harsh."

"I'm sorry if I overreacted. I get that you're making sure we stick to the rules, to protect both of us."

"Exactly. So are we cool?"

"Totally." Sort of. He smiled and beckoned her under the quilt. "Snuggle before breakfast?"

"I'd hoped for a bit more than a snuggle."

"Great minds definitely do think alike."

She draped half her body over his and trailed a line of soft, enticing open-mouthed kisses along his shoulder and up to his jaw.

His cock responded like she'd kissed him along it instead. Time for a chat to take his mind off his growing need to come. "So tell me, Isadora, what's the history of your name?"

She paused between kisses. "What made you ask about that?"

He ran one hand over her upper back and the other over her butt and thigh, her skin like high-quality silk. "Your book collection."

"Ah." She nipped on his earlobe and sucked to soothe the sting, the delicious, stimulating side effect seeming to have a direct line to his dick. "It's all my mum's fault. She named me after the famous dancer, Isadora Duncan, hoping it would guide my path, make me successful."

"It seems to have worked." His erratic breathing made his voice sound raspy, staccato.

"Yeah."

"You don't sound too convinced."

She pulled back and angled her head until she looked into his eyes. "I do love dancing. Now. For a long time, I hated it. Mum was a total stage parent, and it put me under a huge amount of stress. Destroyed every ounce of fun."

He stopped his hands roaming over her beautiful,

distracting body. "So why stick it out? What changed?"

"I showed some natural ability, ended up getting lots of praise and attention, and here I am."

"Do you see your parents much?"

She averted her eyes, interlinked her legs with his, and rested her head in the crook of his neck, her palm over his heart. "Dad died when I was ten, and Mum... I moved away when I turned eighteen."

Oh. Shit. Way to kill the mood. "I'm sorry about your dad." And the angsty, tenuous relationship with her mum.

"Thanks." Her voice had gone quiet, her tone heavy with sadness. She'd lost her father and, by the sounds of it, her mother, too, to some degree. The woman sounded self-absorbed, incapable or unaware of how to offer the emotional support her daughter needed.

He should change the subject, find a safer topic, give her a reprieve from the pent-up grief. Their time together was supposed to be easy and carefree, after all. "Tell me about the World War Two planes."

She tensed. "What's with all the questions?"

So much for finding a safer topic. "I'm trying to get to know you."

"I'm not sure that's a good idea."

"Why?"

"You know why."

Ah, because it meant getting closer, developing a deeper intimacy. Exactly what he wanted and exactly what she intended to avoid. "We're friends, aren't we? And I don't know about you, but I enjoy learning about my friends."

She propped her chin on his chest and gave him a reluctant smile. "You're good."

He couldn't stop the massive grin stretching across his face. "Good? I thought you said I was great."

She shook her head and laughed. "The planes were my thing with Dad. Mum hated it."

The universe really didn't seem to be on his side this morning.

Issy combed her fingers through his wispy chest hair, over and over. "I think she was jealous. Dad and I got on so well. She couldn't understand my fascination with war stuff.

"I was an only child and a tom boy. She worked hard on converting me into a girly girl, a daughter who aligned more with her values, her interests. And after Dad died, I guess I kind of caved. I couldn't deal with losing two parents. I'm just lucky I ended up enjoying dancing."

"Lucky for audiences too. You sure can move. You're brilliant at what you do, a true star. I bet it makes your mum proud."

She stared at her fingers entwined in his chest hair. "Not entirely. She envisioned ballet for me, not contemporary. She expected tutus, beautiful, elegant dresses and mixing in posh circles, whereas I was attracted to raw, primal, natural. Less mainstream. It wasn't until I started getting a name for myself that she came around. But whatever I do is still never good enough. She's always pushing for me to do more, better."

Had she injured herself trying to impress her mother, seeking her approval? "What does she think about your upcoming move overseas? She's gotta be rapt."

"She is…"

He tipped her chin up so their eyes met. "But?"

She sighed, as though trying to expel years of stored, negative energy. "Mum's always got something to complain about. Too far away, don't I love her enough, why settle for this dance company when I should be at that better one instead. She always finds something."

"You must be under enormous pressure."

"More from her than the fickle competitive world of dancing, believe it or not."

"So moving away…"

"Was the best thing I ever did. Phone calls and texts can still be difficult, but it's heaps easier to communicate with her that way than face to face."

"Have you told her how you feel?"

The look on her face spelled horrified. "No. No way. The relationship is strained enough as it is."

"Maybe that's because she doesn't understand your needs."

"She doesn't understand anyone's needs except her own."

"If no one's ever pulled her up on her selfish behavior, she probably doesn't realize the hurt it causes."

"Come on, how could she not know?"

The million-dollar question. From what he'd seen, it all came down to a person's foundation and personality. "Not everyone has that capability, that insight. Some people need more clarity, more boundaries to know the best way to behave, to get the best outcomes."

"Ugh." She flopped onto her back and covered her eyes with her forearm. "I don't need this. If I want psychoanalysis, I'll hire a professional."

"I'm just trying to help." And he absolutely was. He wanted to eradicate any non-dancing reason she had for leaving and to strengthen her supports in Australia. Because he cared. Above all else, he wanted her to be happy.

Issy lifted her arm and peeked at him. "I know." The repentant look on her face said, *forgive me.*

Nothing to forgive. He rolled onto his side and peered into her eyes. "One last question. How often do you visit?"

"I travel to her place in northern New South Wales once or twice a year, and she comes here when she can fit me in. Usually between high-powered boyfriends," she said, bitterness leaching into her tone.

Issy touched his shoulder. "Sorry. Old habits and all that." Her small, gentle hand traveled down his arm and she interlaced their fingers. "Thanks for trying to help. I honestly do appreciate it. You're a great guy, and you make me feel good. No. Awesome."

"I do?" Even after he'd grilled her?

"Yeah, no bullshit."

"I'm glad. You make me feel pretty awesome too."

She shifted so she faced him, her big blue eyes sparkling with friskiness. "Two horny little peas in a fun, non-judgmental pod."

He laughed. "Fun is right. I don't think I've ever had this much fun in my entire life."

****

Golden rays of dawn light streamed through the bedroom window, spotlighting Jeb. It had been five mornings in a row now and she still hadn't gotten sick of such a sublime sight.

With all they'd done, and his consistent ability to pick up and build on each intimate lesson, Issy couldn't quite believe he'd never had sex before they'd hooked up. He didn't come across at all like a virginal type. A shy, nerdy, awkward guy fit that stereotype. Jeb, on the other hand, was all man. Cool, handsome, confident. He reinforced the importance of never assuming.

However, lying beside her—with his eyes still closed in sleep, his angular jaw relaxed—he looked serene, boyish, sweet. She skimmed her hand across the dusting of caramel-colored hair covering his broad chest and lightly traced the muscle definition in his pecs, his stomach. He groaned and shifted onto his side, exposing his left bicep and that intricate tattoo.

His breathing drifted back to slow and steady, and she carefully adjusted her position until she could study the tribal black and red bleeding-heart design. For months she'd wondered what it meant. If she had to guess, she'd bet the heartrending situation with his fiancée had something to do with it.

For all its beauty, the design exuded a sense of sorrow and loss. Issy had given up on trying to remain aloof, distant, her curiosity pushing her to find out the details. Like he'd said, at the very least, they were friends, and friends cared about and were interested in each other.

Ever since that conversation, that realization, she'd been waiting for the right time to ask him about it. But what signified the right time? So far, a high percentage of their days and nights together got filled with more pressing, primal needs.

She glanced at him, his eyes now wide awake, assessing. Her inhalation of breath caught partway down her throat, and she stifled a cough. "How long have you been…"

"Watching you watching me?"

"Ah, yeah."

"A few minutes."

Issy's gaze returned to his tattoo, like it had some magical magnetic power. "It's beautiful." Beautiful, yet with an undercurrent of grief. Like him. "Is it for her?"

"My fiancée?"

She nodded, irrational jealousy stealing her words.

He rubbed over it, his glacial grey eyes turning distant, nostalgic. "I got it a few months after … as a sort of tribute."

"Did it help?"

"Not really. But I'm glad I did it, marked a special spot for her to be with me. Always." He scrutinized Issy as though to check he hadn't upset her with his honesty.

She forced her most convincing I-get-it-and-I'm-okay smile, even though her heart contracted, wishing he had such strong feelings for her. Which totally didn't make sense considering she didn't want or need any romance-related complications. Not now.

He took her hand and placed it over the tattoo, then trailed her palm across his chest to his heart and held it there. His big, warm hand pressed down on hers in the most tender, affectionate way.

Her heartbeat shot up to a fast-paced tempo and his did, too, as though their bodies were so aligned, they functioned as one. "But, as you've shown me, I'm still alive and I need to make the most of that, push through even when it gets difficult. If I don't, I won't be honoring her memory or being fair to myself or anyone else."

"And that would be a waste, an absolute waste. A tragedy. A man like you deserves the best, not living life like a loner."

"I didn't believe that. Not for a long time." He interlocked his fingers with hers, keeping their joined hands over his heart. "Things with my fiancée were complicated."

"Complicated how?"

He closed his eyes and exhaled. "You know how I told you we'd agreed to hold off on having sex until we got married? What I didn't mention was I started to struggle with that. I willed time to speed up so the wedding would happen and we could finally fully connect."

"That's understandable. You were young and eager and wanted to be with the woman you loved."

His eyes snapped open and locked on hers. "Exactly. But I took things too far."

"I don't believe that."

"It's true." He swallowed loudly, once, twice, his gaze unwavering, as though searching for any discomfort in her demeanor. Searching for any hint that would make him think twice about being one hundred percent open.

She must have passed the test, because he cleared his throat and continued. "The night before the wedding, she dropped by my house for a visit and when we kissed goodbye, things got a little heated. I grabbed her wrists, pinned them above her head, and we kept kissing. Then, suddenly, she broke away and shoved on my chest. She was so angry. I tried to console her, but she stopped me from coming any closer. As though I was a bad guy, abusive. Like she was frightened. Of me. Her fiancé. I felt like absolute crap. She blamed me for being too rough, too pushy, and stormed off."

"Oh, Jeb."

He stared at the ceiling, his eyes focused inward, reliving the horrible event. "I followed her to her car and tried to apologize, but she refused to listen and sped down the street. I called her, but her phone rang and rang and rang and went to voicemail. I kept ringing back, determined to sort out the situation and make sure the wedding went off without a hitch. I couldn't sleep. I had to speak to her, but she wouldn't respond. Then the doorbell rang. I rushed to answer it, thinking she'd come back, thinking we could resolve things, but it was the police. They told me she'd died in a car accident and that it looked like she might have been texting or holding the phone to make a call."

His gaze met hers, his eyes glassy, full of unresolved guilt.

"It's not your fault. What happened was out of your control."

"But if I hadn't tried to call her…"

"You don't know what she was doing with her phone. And even if she had reached to try and answer it or turn it off—which she shouldn't have even attempted while driving—it was her choice. No one else's. No one forced her."

"I tried to force her to have sex."

Rubbish! No wonder the poor guy had stayed celibate for so long. He hadn't only lost his fiancée and his self-confidence. He believed he was a monster. "No, you didn't. You said she responded positively at the start, and as soon as she revoked her consent, you stopped. There's a massive difference between having dominant tendencies, enjoying being in control, and forcing someone against their will. You're a good, considerate man, Jeb, with a lot of love to give. Don't you dare believe anything else."

The black cloud of guilt and shame seemed to clear from his face. "Thank you." He leaned in and kissed her, his lips expressing the words, the feelings he didn't say. The depth of their connection was undeniable and totally scary.

But she couldn't ignore it or avoid it this time. Not after what they'd both shared. They'd made themselves vulnerable, laid themselves bare, literally and figuratively. And she wanted him, needed him more than ever.

In one swift move, she repositioned herself so they were in a sixty-nine position.

His erection sprang to life and she took him in her

mouth, right to the back of her throat, the needy groan coming from his lips nearly pushing her into a premature orgasm. Issy kept up her adoration of his dick and he reciprocated, his tongue delving between her folds, exploring.

It felt so fucking good, wonderful, and she never wanted it to stop.

Pre-cum leaked from his large cock and she licked it off, reveling in his response, the way his shaft throbbed in her hand, telling her he was close. Like her.

He kept up his passionate assault, and in seconds she came on his tongue.

Jeb grunted, his release flooding her mouth, and she swallowed every delicious drop. And after that, she could no longer deny, he'd now officially infiltrated her body, mind and soul.

Chapter Nine
Career Conflict

Jeb had hardly slept and never felt better. He kissed Issy's temple, slid out of bed, and headed for the en suite. Living with Issy, making love to her... Fuck, he'd never felt so alive. He'd always thought she was phenomenal and now he knew for sure. She encapsulated everything he needed in a woman. Sensual, intelligent, talented in many, many ways.

They'd made it into their third week, and he loved her even more. Not good. So not good. For his heart, his mental and emotional health. He'd set himself up for another massive love failure. But he couldn't help it. He found Issy impossible to resist.

The bathroom door creaked open, letting in an arc of sunlight, framing Issy in the soft, early morning rays. He never thought it possible, but she looked even more enchanting, heavenly, like a goddess.

She smiled and sashayed over to him, all confidence and assurance. She excelled at practicality, at sex, but what about emotions?

Opening the shower door, she joined him under the spray. "You should have woken me up."

"You looked so peaceful, I couldn't."

"I want to make the most of our time together." In other words, nothing had changed. For her, anyway. She still planned to leave. He didn't hold that against her. He'd just hoped things would be different. He'd just hoped the time they spent together reinforced their relationship was worth fighting for.

Silent, hopeful expectations could fuck with your head, though. Part of him had believed she'd feel like he did, especially after their intense, deep and meaningful confession sessions. But assuming she'd come around was unfair. He knew the rules going into their arrangement and had to respect them to the end. That didn't mean he'd give up on the possibility of continuing and growing their relationship, not while there was still a remote chance.

Jeb angled her face up and pressed his lips to hers, trying to pour all of his desire, his love, his devotion into the kiss. Trying to show her how much he cared, how much he wanted her, needed her in his life in a permanent way.

She responded with such raw passion, a passion that couldn't be faked. Or so he assumed. What experience did he have? He was going off a vibe rather than data.

Issy wrapped her arms around his neck, rubbing her beautiful, naked body against his, causing him to almost overdose on lust. No, not pure lust. Lust tangled together with love.

They'd had sex too many times to count, but it still wasn't enough. God, he craved her, and not just physically. She was like a happiness drug that required constant top up. Physically, mentally, emotionally, spiritually.

The water pelted down on them, and he spun her to face the wall. She pressed her outstretched hand against it and dipped her back in the hottest pose. He had to fight off the urge to come.

Jeb ran his hand along her arched back, moved in behind her until his dick prodded her entrance, and thrust into her delicious depths. Every time they made love felt sacred, so much greater than pure carnal contact.

Her core gripped him and she squeezed, driving him even more insane with desire. She moaned, his name a plea on her lips, and pushed back against him. With one hand, he cupped her breast and with the other, he sought out her clit.

He tweaked her nipple and rubbed her swollen little nub and she made the sexiest sounds, desperate, wanton sounds, taking him right to the edge of release.

"I'm close."

Thank fuck. He was only just holding on, but he wanted her to climax first. "Come for me, Issy." His voice sounded strained, frantic, vulnerable.

And it worked. She screamed out his name and bucked against him, her core contracting over and over, igniting his own orgasm. His thrusts became erratic as stream after stream of cum poured into her, his stunning, irreplaceable Issy.

They rode through their release and he collapsed against her, holding her tight, upright.

"Wow."

He kissed the crown of her head. "Yeah." With her, always wow. Not that he could compare to any previous conquests, any previous encounters. Yet, this felt right. Though, according to her, it could only be temporary.

"I should get to work." He didn't want to go. But, although eager to spend every last precious moment with Issy, he had other responsibilities. His clients counted on him.

"I know. Me too." She whirled around and the look on her face spelled disappointment mixed with pure and utter love. Or maybe it was just him wishing so hard he couldn't decipher hope from reality.

****

Their second-to-last day together had arrived. Over breakfast—when they finally got to it—Issy sat on Jeb's lap, unable to bring herself to break the connection. This man was a standout. Rare, unrivaled, exceptional.

No matter how many times she'd tried to play it down, it didn't work. He'd weaseled into her heart, and she couldn't extract him.

Bacon, poached eggs, mushrooms, and avocado, and he'd served them up exactly how she loved. Had sex exactly how she loved. Conversed exactly how she loved.

For the duration of their agreement, he'd cooked for her, challenged her, supported her. Everything he'd done seemed to bring out the best in her, and she'd become a better person as a result. No one had ever made that effort. No one had ever spent the time. No one had ever gotten her like he did. He valued her and what she had to offer, accepted her quirks and insecurities.

"You're an incredible man, Jeb. Whatever woman you choose is so lucky." She took a deep breath, trying to fight the tears storming her eyes. She didn't want to let him go, but she had to.

Long distance relationships were hard, almost impossible in her line of work. And it was unfair to expect him to wait on the off chance she ever returned. She couldn't expect him to follow her when she wasn't willing to make that sacrifice.

He hugged her tight. "And you're an amazing woman."

"Thank you. You don't know how much it means to me to hear you say that."

"I have an idea."

Did he? She glanced up, her eyes searching his. "Really?"

"Yeah. Our situations are different, yet the same. We both craved acceptance from those closest to us, understanding, and the people in our lives tried their best, but it wasn't enough. Their own needs took precedence. Don't get me wrong, they didn't mean it. They just had their own issues to deal with and struggled to get past them, if they ever did."

Spot on. Not only a good listener, but also he constantly proved he understood her. "You're right. So right."

He tucked a loose lock of wet hair behind her ear. "They had a self-preservation agenda, but it's wrong to blame them. That's our expectations talking. I honestly think they didn't know any better. I reckon they did what they did because they believed it was for the best."

She focused on his handsome face, examining every little detail. One of the last few times she had to study him, appreciate him. "You're not only sexy and smart but also wise. You've taught me so much."

"And you, me." He kissed her forehead, the tip of her nose, corner of her jaw, and last but never least her lips. Although passionate, always passionate with Jeb, so much more meaning infused their meeting of mouths. Affection, tenderness, love.

Guilt tore through her. Had she been selfish? She should have anticipated him getting attached. And her too. But it was harder on him. So much harder. Cruel. She should have called the whole thing off earlier, as soon as she saw the signs.

He'd fallen for her and didn't even try to hide it, pouring his feelings into his tone, his attention, his touch. However, she'd remained guarded, in self-preservation mode, to protect her own heart.

Yet, her internal angst couldn't stop her responding to him, returning his passion. Could he sense her conflict? Could he tell he wasn't the only one who'd fallen in love?

He broke the kiss but remained close, his breath buffeting her skin, his gaze raking over her face. "You're so beautiful, inside and out."

Mounting tears stung the back of her eyes and she glanced down. "Thanks, I um … need to get going. It's my last day. I need to say goodbye."

She slipped out of his grasp before he could say another word, clutch her to him, and change her mind.

****

That night, no matter how hard, she needed to make her last moments with Jeb special, lasting. She walked in the front door and he stood in the kitchen, by the stove, making them another meal.

What a marvelous man. She'd been so lucky to have him, even for a short time. And she needed to appreciate all they'd shared. The memories would take her through to forever.

Best she tried a light-hearted approach before she burst into tears. "Honey, I'm home."

He whipped around, but instead of going along with her joke he strode over, picked her up and pressed her to him, his lips devouring hers. By the time they pulled apart, she was breathless, needy.

"Jeb…"

He kissed her temple. "Dinner's nearly ready."

"Thank you. And dessert?"

"Muff burger?"

She laughed, but it sounded stilted and tinged with sadness. "Whatever you want."

"No. Whatever *we* want. What do you want, Issy?"

Such a loaded question. Him. Him and dancing. But she couldn't be greedy. Or unrealistic. "To make you feel good, confident." She rubbed her palm up and down the cotton T-shirt hugging his chest like a second skin. "There are a couple more positions I think you should experience, have in your sexual repertoire. For the right woman." And God, did she wish it was her.

He smiled, but it stalled on his lips. Had he been testing her, hoping she'd admit she was the right woman and she only wanted him? Because she did. But she'd learned she couldn't have her fancy cake and gobble it down too.

"You're going to love both, I promise."

Jeb picked her up and carried her to her bedroom. "Tell me about these positions," he said between soul-stirring kisses.

"The first one is most guys' favorite." She reluctantly broke the kiss, stripped off, and climbed onto the bed. "Doggy style." She moved onto all fours and glanced over her shoulder.

He'd discarded his clothes and stroked his cock, staring at her with such intensity, such love, her eyes teared up. Her gaze darted back to the headboard, and she tried to reinstate some control. Tonight, their last night together, was supposed to be fun.

His big hand on her back made her shiver. But not from cold, from the pure love and promise of his orgasm-inducing touch. He pressed an open-mouthed kiss to each butt cheek and slid his tongue along her seam, her whole body shuddering in response. His mouth left her skin and she whimpered. She pushed back, his cock spearing into her, and didn't stop until he filled her fully.

He groaned, one hand holding her hip and the other finding her clit. Slow thrusts, soon turned fast and wild, his cock striking her G-spot over and over and his fingers playing her clit like a sexual virtuoso.

She couldn't stop the needy sounds coming from her throat. They seemed to spur him on, his thrusts losing their rhythm, his grunts becoming more guttural, a sign he would lose his load any second. And she couldn't wait. She came hard, squeezing his cock again and again and again until he let loose.

They rode the waves of euphoria right to the end, Jeb collapsing on top of her, his breath hot against her ear. "Fuck."

"I told you you'd enjoy it."

"Yeah, right again." He kissed her neck, slipped out of her, and lay on his back.

She crawled up him and snuggled in along his delectable, muscle-sculpted body, her head resting on his chest. The scent of clean male sweat, potent with pheromones, wafted up from his heated skin. And fuck, did she love it, love him. She couldn't deny it, at least to herself. Issy squeezed her eyes shut and wished things were different. But they weren't.

With one hand, he caressed her hair. With the other, he drew light lines on her lower back, making her feel loved, treasured. "It's not my favorite position, though."

"It's not?"

"Nope. You riding me is my favorite because I can kiss you, see your face, every little expression of pleasure, and not only our bodies but also our eyes, our hearts, and our souls connect."

Her eyes burned. This man... "Ah, you say that now, but you still haven't given anal a go." She had to deflect or else break down in tears.

"Anal?"

She tried to ignore, tried to shove aside the stabbing, don't-end-this sensation behind her breastbone, pushed up onto her elbow, and stared into his curious, eager eyes. "Some women love it. And I'm one of them."

"How much different can it feel to regular sex?"

Not that what they'd been doing could be considered regular. More like spectacular. "A lot. It's not just a sexual act. It's a trust thing. You'll see." She teased his lips with nips and licks and moved in for a long and languid kiss, rubbing and tugging his nipples until his cock returned to rigid.

She reached into her top bedside drawer and pulled out a tube of lube. Grabbing a pillow, she lay on her back and tucked it under her sacrum. "Now, before you plunge in, you need lots of lubrication, preferably a combination of saliva, mickey juice, and the bought stuff or else there's too much friction. In a bad way."

"I think I get it." He moved his head between her legs, bringing her super close to orgasm with his mouth. Then he trailed his tongue to her back hole and rimmed her, like he'd read her mind. The guy had done his homework.

"I'm so ready," she said in between frenzied panting.

"Me too." Using his thick fingers, he spread some of her juices onto her back hole and added a generous amount of lube, the shock of coolness on her heated skin making her shudder. He lubed up his cock and pressed it against her puckered opening. His solid gaze met hers. "Ready?"

For him, always. "Yes."

She lifted her bent legs over his shoulders, and the head of his cock breached her rear entrance.

"Okay?"

"More than okay." She'd always been more of an anal girl, loved that initial thrust, the tightness, the fullness. But with Jeb, it was so much more than just the physical sensation.

He cautiously slid all the way in and stopped. "All right?" His strained tone gave away his need to get into a rhythm. But he held off, just as she'd instructed.

"Yes!" What a sweetheart. Her star pupil. No. They'd gone beyond teacher and student.

He gripped her hips and soon found a steady, enjoyable pace for both of them, going by their chorus of sighs and groans. "Issy…"

"Yeah, I know." And she did know. They both felt it, that deeper connection. But it didn't change what would happen next, didn't change the fact their relationship had an end date. Though she wouldn't let that ruin the moment.

She clamped her hand around one of his biceps and reached between them with her other hand, finding her clit and giving it a flick. Five strokes later she came, clenching his cock and crying out.

A low rumble morphed into a roar as he threw his head back and climaxed, still managing to control his thrusts so he wouldn't hurt her. And yet, here she was hurting him, inflicting invisible wounds, but with much more painful, emotional scars.

He didn't deserve it. She didn't deserve it. But what other choice did she have? Give up a fantastic career opportunity, again, for a guy she'd known even less time than the ex-who-shall-not-be-named, on the hope, not the guarantee, Jeb was the one. She couldn't take that risk.

Her gaze met his penetrating stare. That look, like she'd spoken her thoughts aloud and he wanted to convince her to take a chance on him. But he didn't say anything, just pulled out and hauled her into his arms, kissing her like he wanted to fuse her into his memory, like he never wanted to let her go.

Chapter Ten
Saying Goodbye

Early the next morning, Jeb slipped out of bed to have a shower before he packed and got ready to leave. He didn't want to, but the longer he hung back, the harder it would be to say goodbye. More like farewell.

His eyes stung, but he refused to let any tears fall. With every second that passed, it looked more and more like he'd fail his quest to keep her; however, he didn't want Issy to remember him as an unappreciative, bad loser. Their time together had been outstanding. They'd shared so many life-changing experiences, and he had to let her know so they could part on a positive note.

He crept toward the en suite and reached for the door knob.

"Come back to bed." Her voice had that husky, just-woke-up-from-a-night-of-full-on,   down-and-dirty sex sound. Which, of course, was exactly what had happened. At least no one could ever take the memories away from him.

"I'm just going to have a quick shower." And use the alone time to get his thoughts in order to deliver his last-hurrah speech.

"I'll join you."

"You just rest. I'll be back soon."

"No way." The rustle of sheets followed by that familiar bed squeak reinforced that Issy refused to leave him alone. "There's something else I want to show you."

Something else? Fuck. Issy's imagination, creativity, and passion seemed to come together to create endless possibilities. The sex options were much more fathomless than he'd ever realized. So he'd be a closed-minded idiot to knock her back. Plus, it would give him more to store away in his fucking-amazing memory files.

She touched his back, the sudden heat of her hand striking his skin like a lightning bolt of lust. He swung around, and with the soft lamplight haloing her naked body she looked like an angel. A sexy-as-fuck angel. Instinctive, Neanderthal desire took over his brain and he hoisted her over his shoulder.

She gasped, but he kept up his stride into the shower. Not only Issy could play the sexual surprise game.

Once he'd regulated the water temperature, he slowly slid her down the front of his body, his persistent hard-on growing impossibly harder just from the friction of her skin.

Her huge eyes had almost turned black, with only the outer rims remaining blue, and like a solar eclipse he should have known better than to stare. But he couldn't tear his gaze away from the remarkable woman, the woman who had successfully given CPR to revive his love life and was now discharging him back into the world.

His last-resort speech better be pretty awesome if it had any hope of convincing her to stay. If not physically, maybe she could at least agree to them remaining together, long distance. Until they could review all options and sort out something more certain.

Jeb backed her into the steaming water and drenched them both with the cleansing drops. They took turns washing each other, sensually soaping up and massaging the bubbles into one another's skin until they'd disappeared, extending the foreplay, the build-up, the finish line.

She stepped away from under the spray and crooked her finger to encourage him forward, the water sluicing down his back. What could she possibly have planned? He thought they'd covered most things during her condensed, experiential sex course, but it seemed he still had more to learn. Just like life.

To be successful he had to continue to grow, not stagnate. Luckily, he'd always loved learning, though this subject had been a standout, an absolute pleasure.

Issy knelt before him and looked up through her long blonde lashes, a cheeky smile curving her luscious lips. A blowjob? Nothing new about that. Not that he was complaining.

She leaned forward and licked the swollen head of his cock, which was already covered in pre-cum. Her tongue ring did sensational things to his nerve endings before she took him all the way into her mouth and sucked.

Fuck. Deep throating. She'd done that to him too. And he fucking loved it. His hips had an almost irrepressible urge to thrust on their own, but he wouldn't give in to it. One of the key messages she'd taught him was the importance of control.

Being such a motivated learner, he nearly had it mastered. It helped that holding off heightened the mind-blowing power of the experience. Nothing provided quite the same level of incentive as the promise of an earth-shattering orgasm.

A growl rose up out of his chest, her hand and mouth working his dick like a state-of-the-art head job machine, bringing him to the brink. His shallow, quickened breathing seared his airways and … she eased off. *Fuck.* He groaned with frustration and she smiled up at him.

"Do you trust me?" she asked in between consolatory little licks and sucks.

Issy embodied sex kitten, and a totally irresistible one. "Of course."

She reached around to the vanity, pulled a tube of lube from the drawer, and squeezed some onto her fingers. "Now just relax. You're going to love this."

Before he could ask what "this" was, she'd returned to sucking his dick and wiping his mind of all coherent thought. His body throbbed and tingled and ached with the need for release.

She squeezed and stroked his balls, pushing him closer. He gripped her head, and she reached her lubed-up hand behind him and up to his... *Oh fuck.*

Issy coated his asshole, the cool lube combined with her unexpected touch making his muscles tense.

She eased his dick out of her mouth and glanced up at him, her tongue darting out to lick the head. "What did I say?"

What had she said? He could hardly think with so many conflicting sensations swirling around his body and over-stimulating his brain. "Ah..."

"To relax, remember. I promise to make it good. No, great."

And he believed her. She hadn't let him down yet. Not sexually, anyway.

He forced in a few slow, meditation-style breaths, and she got back to work on his dick, his balls, and his ass. Once she'd greased the hole right up, she added some more lube to her fingers and pressed against the tight muscle until it gave way and let her in.

One of his hands slapped against the wall to steady himself, and the other stayed threaded in her wet hair.

A little moan escaped her lips. "How's that?"

"Strange. Stretched."

"But not painful." It sounded more a statement than a question. She would know exactly how it felt, being a self-confessed anal girl.

"No."

"Good." She eased one finger in and out, in and out, in and out, until his sphincter loosened, slipped in a second finger and stilled. "How does that feel?"

"Full. And a bit like I need to piss."

"Perfect. Now just let yourself go."

So he did. And man, what a fucking ride. She increased the pace and depth of her dual finger thrusts, while stroking his balls and sucking him off and, suddenly, lightning white sparks dazzled his vision and pleasure exploded inside him like an active volcano, spewing cum after burst of cum down her throat.

The orgasm seemed to go on and on and he lost time, almost blacked out from the intensity. He hadn't even realized he'd closed his eyes until they cracked open and her upturned exquisite face met his gaze with a breathtaking smile.

"All recovered?"

"I don't know if I'll ever fully recover from that." He shoved his hands in his soaked hair. "Fuck."

She laughed, the cheerful, sweet sound soon to be relegated to just another memory.

"Get up here."

She stood with her usual grace and elegance and he hoisted her body against his for a deep, open-mouthed kiss.

Several minutes later, she broke apart from him and looked into his eyes, unable to hide the shimmer of moisture. She smiled, but her lips trembled with a stifled sob. "Something to remember me by."

So many things he could never forget.

They shut off the water, dried themselves in contemplative silence, and returned to bed. Lying on their sides, facing each other, she wound her leg around his waist, tenderly kissed his lips, and they made bittersweet love. Afterward, she fell asleep curled against him. He held her tight and stared at the ceiling, unable to get any more rest.

What was he going to do without her? Returning to a hermit status wasn't an option, would undo all her good work. He couldn't do that to Issy, couldn't be so ungrateful. Yet loving another woman even twenty-five percent as much as her didn't seem possible. And even if it was, he couldn't settle for a second-rate substitute.

As soon as Issy rolled over, out of his grasp, still snoozing, Jeb slipped out of bed and gathered his things. He'd originally planned to come up with a speech, a last-ditch effort to win her over. But what would he say to convince her to stay in a committed relationship with him?

Thoughts jammed his brain, but nothing sounded right. That's when he lost his nerve and decided to leave her a note and sneak out instead. It would suck spending their precious last moments in a potentially messy, highly emotive confrontation.

Jeb took one final long look at the special place they'd shared for the past month. He didn't just focus on the physical shell, but the whole loving, educational, soul-discovering environment.

He couldn't believe how much he'd grown over their intensive four-week journey. Sure, he knew more sexually, but he'd also learned so much about himself. His wants, his needs, his desires, who he wanted to be, where he wanted to head.

He'd redeveloped his motivation, his passion for living. He couldn't go back to trudging through an empty existence day after day, not acknowledging his hopes and dreams and ultimately wading through time, waiting to die.

They'd had an unforgettable night, and morning,

an extraordinary month, the perfect ending to their time together. If there was such a thing. If nothing else, they'd gone out with a bang.

Taking light, quiet steps, which was far from easy given his oversized build, he picked up his bags and dumped them by the front door. He surveyed the living area, making sure he hadn't forgotten anything and saving as much info as possible into his mind to recall later.

Before he could compose a goodbye note, she appeared in the bedroom doorway, her short blue satin dressing gown hanging open, revealing a tempting sliver of her body, her eyes still heavy with sleep, her blonde hair sticking up in the cutest, sexiest way.

She glanced at his bags and back at him. "Where are you going?"

"Home."

"But I don't leave until tonight. Stay. Please."

The begging tone in her voice nearly broke him, but he had to remain strong. Not once had she suggested taking things further, trying to problem solve how they could continue being a couple.

As much as he wanted to enter into a committed, permanent bond, she obviously didn't, even though he saw glimpses of deeper feeling in her beautiful blue eyes, could feel it in the way they made love. But unless she felt how he did, could acknowledge and accept it, could admit it out loud, their affair had an expiry date.

Today.

She joined him by the front door, and he swept a few loose strands of hair off her stunning face. "I can't. Just like you can't."

"No, Jeb. You don't understand. Not fully. You know I already passed up an awesome career opportunity for a man, one I thought I loved, but what you don't know is he left me less than two months later."

Shit. No wonder she'd struggled with developing emotional intimacy. But association didn't equal fact. Her ex had done her wrong, but it didn't mean Jeb would. "I'm not him, Issy."

She shook her head. "I know. But what if things still don't work out. I can't risk choosing a possible relationship for a guaranteed positive career move. Not again."

"You're right—I don't understand, not after what we've shared, but I won't press you. You need to feel it too. You need to do what best suits you." It didn't mean he wouldn't express his gratitude, though, his sincere feelings. "Whether or not you feel the same as me, I want us to part on a happy note."

She frowned. "Happy note?"

"Yeah." He swallowed the fit-ball-sized lump jamming his throat and forced a smile. "These past few weeks have been incredible, one of the best months of my life. I've learned so much. Not just about sex, about myself, intimacy, connection, love."

"What are you—"

"I can't go without telling you how I feel." Now that she'd caught him, he had to make himself vulnerable and speak from the heart. He had to give their relationship one last shot. He had to try to somehow prove he wouldn't do what that dick of a guy had done. "I know we haven't been involved long, but it's been intense and amazing and ... I love you."

Her eyes welled up. "Don't, please."

"I'm not doing this to guilt you into staying. I just want to be honest. I owe you and myself that. And I want the best for you. So go do your thing. Maximize the opportunity. I won't hold you back. I'll never hold you back because I love you." If she loved him as well, he'd given her the perfect opportunity to say so, to tell him they'd find a way to make their relationship work.

Her bottom lip quivered and she broke eye contact, her gaze darting everywhere except his face.

A bad sign. Either she didn't love him or she did but her feelings weren't strong enough to change her mind about moving on. Both options hurt, both meant heartache. However, it was better he knew now rather than later.

The silence dragged on.

And on.

And on.

The death knell, announcing the end of their relationship. Time to put her out of her misery and put his on hold.

Jeb cupped her face, his thumbs caressing her cheeks. "They're so lucky to have you. I hope they appreciate not just your talent, but you. You're so sweet and beautiful, a once-in-a-lifetime woman. I'm so glad our lives intersected, so privileged to have shared and experienced something so special. I'll never forget you."

He kissed the top of her head, soaking up her unique, intoxicating Issy scent, savoring the silky texture of her hair for the last time.

She threw her arms around his waist and held him tight. "I wish things were different." Her voice muffled against his T-shirt.

"Me too. But they're not." Unless she admitted she loved him and suggested an alternative to splitting up.

She lifted her head, her eyes blue in every sense of the word. Her body language suggested, on some level, she wanted to stay. Stay and explore this bond between them. But she wouldn't. Not his determined, driven Issy.

He planted a loving kiss on her lips. "Let me know once you're settled, how you're going. If you want." A growing wedge of grief blocked his throat. He swallowed once, twice, three times, but it wouldn't shift.

She nodded and sniffled and his own chest tightened with restrained tears. He had to go before he got all misty-eyed. After rubbing her back with a few soothing strokes, he stepped away, picked up his luggage, and faced her one final time.

Issy sucked in a sob-like breath and gave him a watery smile.

His heart broke. It wasn't supposed to end this way, both of them pining for each other but not willing to take a leap into the relationship unknown. Though he had ventured partway, offering up his heart. Obviously, the gesture still wasn't enough of a promise.

Her ex had screwed her over bad, romantically and career-wise. So Jeb got it, got her resistance, her reluctance. Once bitten, and all the associated baggage. When he reviewed their time together, he thought he'd shown her he wasn't the same, that he'd support her, wanted the best for her, that she could trust him with her heart.

He turned away from her and went to walk out the door.

"Jeb?" She touched his arm and he hesitated.

"Yeah?"

She came and stood in front of him, her eyes sad, worried. "Look after yourself."

"You too." He brushed his lips over hers because he couldn't resist one last taste, then headed toward the lift and didn't look back.

Just as he reached the elevator, the doors opened and he hurried inside. He pressed the ground-floor button, dropped his bags by the back wall, and slumped against the hard steel.

He'd done everything he could. Ultimately, she'd needed to reciprocate in some way for them to have a chance. Her body language suggested she cared about him a lot, but she hadn't confirmed his assumption with words, hadn't been forthcoming about her feelings. So, he'd had to let her go. And in the process, lost the love of his life for the second time. Maybe it would be third-time lucky?

****

After Jeb went, Issy intended to go back to bed and sleep, but all the crying made that impossible. She hadn't been prepared for him to take off so soon. She thought they'd have a bit more time. But then again, what difference would that have made? She was still going.

Just as she was about to leave for the airport, her mobile rang. She plucked it from her bag, hoping it was Jeb, but no such luck. She should have known it would be her mum. The woman had a knack for always calling at the worst possible time.

She stabbed the green call button. "Mum, I can't do this right now."

"Do what, darling? Can't a mother ring to wish her daughter well."

"Of course. If that's what this is."

Silence. Which meant Issy had hit that familiar nail on the predictable head.

"Look, I have to go. I need to get to the airport. My plane goes in four hours."

"This will only take a few minutes. You never got back to me about doing the mother-daughter story. But being my organized, resourceful self, I've arranged for Gerry from the paper to do a conference call interview before you jet off. Although it's far from ideal, he said he can use one of our older pictures together. You know the one on opening night when you played lead in that vulgar, almost-naked—"

"Enough." Issy sat on her bed and dropped her head into her hand. "There's always a problem, isn't there? You can't just be happy for me or my achievements. It always comes back to you and how it impacts on you. And you know what? I'm sick of it. I'm not going to let you make me feel bad. Ever again."

"Isadora—"

"Don't you dare full name me." She jolted up ramrod straight, but instead of going off on an over-emotional tirade, she kept her voice calm but firm. "And don't even try to fear or guilt me into doing what you want. You're a master manipulator, and I won't fall for it anymore."

"This is—"

"Not what you expected? Frustrating? Confronting? Well, get used to it. I'm living my life for *me* now. The irony is I was actually starting to consider giving up this unbelievable US opportunity and staying, but you've just reinforced how essential it is that I see it through. Not only for the career kudos, but also for the personal benefits. For the first time, I'm taking control of my life."

Well, except the Jeb situation. But no decision was perfect. There was always some sort of fallout, compromise. And her mum had just convinced her that she'd made the right choice no matter how heartbreaking. "It's time for you to do the same, Mum, and not rely on me. You need to stop all the game-playing."

"Issy—"

"Or you're going to be on your own."

"Issy, please let me speak." Her mum's imploring tone sounded the most genuine she'd ever heard.

"Okay, say what you need to say and then I have to hang up."

"I'm sorry, darling. You never told me you felt this way. I didn't realize. I just got carried away. I thought I was helping."

"Helping yourself."

A heavy sigh traveled down the phone line. "I deserve that. And I can't say I haven't enjoyed the attention. But, Issy, please know I love you and I want you to be happy. I obviously haven't always gone about it the best way, but I promise to try and change my approach."

The remorseful tone in her voice made Issy almost believe her mum meant what she'd said. Had Jeb been right? Had her mum really not realized her negative impact? Had she plowed ahead with her selfish ways because she'd been indulged too long and lacked clear boundaries? More importantly, would she follow through on her promise to do things differently now? It sure sounded like she'd try. But only time would tell.

"I hope so, Mum. I really do."

Silence and—was that a stifled sniffle from her hard-ass mum? Maybe an old leopard really did have the potential to change its lifelong spots.

"Well, I suppose I better not hold you up any longer. Have a safe trip and let me know once you arrive. I'm going to miss you, darling."

"Thanks, Mum. I'll be in touch soon."

Issy hung up and for once, the conversation with her mum hadn't left a revolting taste in her mouth. Being straight up instead of using her usual snarky approach and dancing around the truth regarding how she felt seemed to work.

Her confession appeared to be the antidote to her mum's usually poisonous words. Just as Jeb had suggested. *Jeb*... She sighed. Helping her even in his absence. Forever imprinted in her soul.

She lugged her suitcase and carry-on luggage into the living room and flopped onto her couch. Her Uber should arrive in the next five minutes. She plucked her phone from her bag to check on the car's progress and accidentally clicked on her gallery app. A selfie of her and Jeb, all ecstatic smiles, filled the screen. She traced his face with her finger.

Maybe things between them didn't have to end permanently. Jeb wasn't her loser of an ex-boyfriend, as he'd reminded her and repeatedly proven over their time together. And the clincher—he'd told her he loved her with unmistakable sincerity. Unlike her ex, who, when she reflected back, had been an expert at fake-but-believable charm.

That didn't mean things would definitely work out between her and Jeb, hence why she'd still chosen to accept this amazing dance job and go now, but leaving didn't have to signify the end.

She shouldn't give up, couldn't, not when her feelings were equally as strong. When she arrived in the US, she'd make it a priority to search for opportunities to reunite them.

Her mobile buzzed with a text to let her know the Uber had arrived. She put her phone in her bag, grabbed her things, and locked up her apartment. Thank goodness the couple she'd arranged to rent her place would be moving in within the next two weeks. The additional income would come in extra handy. And give her peace of mind.

A ray of hope sparked in her heart. The cloud of heaviness weighing her down seemed to lift. With a lightness in her step, and feeling stronger than ever, she took off on her new overseas adventure.

Chapter Eleven
A Spark of Hope?

After six grueling but brilliant weeks of rehearsals in New York, the boutique, highly regarded dance company Issy had become a part of arrived in Hawaii. Finally. Somewhere she had always dreamed of visiting.

The moment she stepped off the plane, she got leid, literally had a lei hooked over her head, and breathed in the tropical floral fragrance. Paradise. For one. When it should have been two.

She and her dad were supposed to go together. To Pearl Harbor. But their dream trip had never eventuated. Now she'd have to do it on her own, fit it in somewhere between rehearsals and shows, which seemed to be the key recurring theme in her life. Her first free day and she'd go to honor her father, if nothing else.

She had kept herself open to ways of possibly rekindling her relationship with Jeb; however, so far, Issy had come up with nothing. Until she did, she preferred to keep their communication brief, through texting. She didn't want to string him along and give either of them false hope.

After an intense but seamless dress rehearsal in the sumptuous, antique-gold Hawaii Theatre, Issy showered and changed, slung her bag over her shoulder, and bolted out of the dressing room, still wired. She ran straight into the lead choreographer, who looked even more frazzled.

"Tell me you know a good physio." Her eyes searched Issy's, desperate, hoping, wishing.

How Issy felt about Jeb. *Jeb.* Not just a fantastic physio, a wonderful man in so many ways. "Ah, yeah.

But he's in Australia."

The tiny, toned woman huffed out a frustrated sigh. "I knew it was a long shot, but I had to try."

"Why? What's going on?"

"Chuck's resigned. Personal reasons. And we need a replacement ASAP. Someone who can accompany us on tour."

Could this be the opportunity Issy had been searching for to get her and Jeb back together? She missed him like fucking crazy, but should she ask him whether he'd consider the job? Relocate? For her, after she'd left without admitting she loved him too.

Since she'd been away she realized, more than ever, how much she wanted him in her life, needed him. She had to take the risk and make contact to at least let him know about the position. The worst thing he could say was *no*.

"I'll ask my physio in Australia and see if he can suggest someone." Hopefully, he'd nominate himself. Hopefully, she hadn't left her run too late.

That night, after dinner, she sank into her comfy couch and picked up her mobile phone to text Jeb. Her heart banged against her ribs. What if he said he wasn't interested? What if he said he couldn't help? Wouldn't help. What if he confessed he'd found someone else and moved on?

She'd deserve it.

Issy gulped down half her mega glass of white wine and waited for its calming effects to seep into her mind and body.

Issy: **Hey, Jeb, I've found you the perfect job. How would you like to come to Hawaii?**

Jeb: **The perfect job as what? Pool boy? Gigolo?**

Her stomach sank, like she'd swallowed a cement

sack of guilt. Is that what he thought? That she'd crushed every romantic bone in his body and taught him to be a player, an emotionally-detached sexpert. That she didn't have a heart, hadn't developed feelings so deep they pierced her soul, hadn't fallen in love.

Of course he'd believe the worst. She'd walked away without hesitation, without revealing how much she cared, unlike him, who'd made his feelings Swarovski-crystal clear.

Issy: **I'm serious. There's a physio position available to tour with the company, starting in Hawaii in two weeks.**

Jeb: **And?**

Issy: **I'd love you to apply. You'd be perfect.**

Jeb: **Is that all?**

Issy: **No.**

Jeb: **What else?**

Issy: **I miss you.**

Jeb: **I miss you too.**

Did that mean he still loved her? She had to tell him how she felt while she had the chance and hope he was still interested.

Issy: **But it's not just that. I want you here with me. Need you here.**

One minute, two minutes, three minutes. Ten minutes went by without a reply. *Fuck.* What was he thinking? She finished the rest of her wine, never taking her eyes off her mobile phone. Each second that dragged by made a snail's pace seem like the speed of light in comparison. Time seemed to power down to super slow-mo, like a slug on valium.

Her phone screen lit up.

Jeb.

Finally.

I can't promise you anything, but I'll see what

I can do.

What the hell did that mean? Would he apply for the job himself or suggest someone else? Had he given up on her? He said he missed her but didn't say he still loved her or even comment on her confession. She'd lost her right to press him, so she just had to be patient and not lose that lingering thread of hope.

****

Issy's phone buzzed on her nightstand. She reached for it in the dark, her heart racing, praying it was Jeb.

No, Jimmy. Her best dancer friend from Sydney. She sank into the mattress and lifted her mobile to her ear. "Hey, girl, how's Hawaii?"

Issy tried to infuse excitement into her tone. "Incredible."

"It doesn't sound incredible."

Shit. She couldn't even conceal her true feelings from her people-whisperer friend over the phone, nine thousand kilometers away. "The dancing is great, everything I'd hoped."

"But it's not enough. Not what you thought it would be."

Yep, she may as well not even bother trying to hide anything from him. She got comfortable under her quilt and prepared to spill her guts. "No. I thought it'd be the answer to my happiness."

"Dancing, all on its own, can't give you that."

"So I've learned."

"For you, dancing is an escape, a regular hit of pleasure to avoid intimacy."

The deep-rooted truth of his statement slammed into her solar plexus like a steel-fisted punch. And she couldn't help but jump to her own defense. "But I love dancing, the freedom of expression—"

"I know, and you're elite. No question. Though, underlying that, dancing's your emotional crutch. You only started to please your mum, desperate for her to accept you, and since then it's filled the gap in your heart, giving you an excuse to keep your distance, especially from men, to stop you getting hurt. But it was only ever temporary, a short-term solution until the right person arrived. Then Jeb came along—with the correct chemistry—and dissolved your avoidance, eroded the delusion."

His words were like an axe splitting open her psyche. Thoughts bled out, about losing her dad, about her constant fear of losing people she loved, about preventing anyone from getting too close, to protect herself.

And yet in doing that, she pushed people away, sacrificed any chance of relationship success. *Fuck.* Taking a risk and feeling some love was so much better than living in fear and being numb and alone.

She'd made a mega-huge mistake. Much bigger than she'd originally thought. Possibly irredeemable. Hopefully, Jeb would forgive her, give her another chance.

Her eyes stung with mounting tears. If only she'd worked all this out earlier. "Thanks for giving me a reality check. I've fucked up, Jimmy. I never realized the importance of letting people close to me, creating connections and developing strong bonds with others, the added joy of sharing my success with someone I care about, someone who's important to me, someone who loves me."

"You do now. So what are you going to do about it?"

"Well, I messaged Jeb—"
"And?"

She squeezed the air out of her tight lungs. "I told him about a physio position to work with the dance company during the US tour. He said thanks but hasn't confirmed whether he'll follow it up or not."

"Have you let him know how you feel?"

"That I miss him, that I need him. Yes."

"But not that you love him."

"No, I…"

"It's okay, baby, don't stress. You'll both work it out, if it's meant to be."

****

Jeb stepped into his favorite bar to meet Cole after work. He scanned the expansive space and found him in a booth seat near the back, already nursing a red wine.

He ambled over and placed his hand on Cole's shoulder. "Congratulations again, mate."

He glanced up and smiled so wide, Jeb thought the guy's face would split in two. "Thanks, man."

"How's the little one settling in? How's Hope?"

"They're both doing great so far, thanks. We're not even sleep deprived yet. Mind you, they've only been home from hospital one day."

"Give Mireya some time," Jeb said with a smirk and sat opposite Cole. "Let me know when I can visit. I can't wait to meet her."

"Will do."

The waiter came around shortly after and took Jeb's drink order.

Cole propped his elbows on the table and leaned in. "So what's been happening with you?"

Jeb fiddled with the paper coaster, avoiding eye contact. "Same. Eat, work, sleep."

"Have you been getting out?"

"No."

"Heard from Issy?"

"Yeah."

"And?"

"I'm confused."

"Confused about what?"

"She messaged me about a physio job to travel around with her dance company. And that she misses me, needs me. Apparently." His gut wanted to believe she'd fallen as hard as he had. But he didn't want to get his hopes up. Maybe she just planned for them to extend their affair. He would have been surer of her intentions if he'd heard her tone and not just read her words.

"That's great. Have you applied yet?"

He shook his head. "No."

"Why not?"

"You haven't finished your treatment, and now with the extra demands of a new baby—"

"Don't worry about me, mate. I'll be fine. I'm pretty much in maintenance now anyway. And if I really get stuck, you'll only be a phone call away."

"I guess."

"There's something else, though. And please don't give me a pathetic excuse like you can't get the time off work."

"Don't sugar-coat it. Tell me what you really think." Jeb couldn't hold back the sarcasm, even though he appreciated and admired Cole's candid, no-bullshit approach. Ultimately, and most importantly, the guy wanted to help.

"Ah, of course, you're afraid." Like always, he'd cut right to the raw emotional core.

Jeb's beer arrived and he gulped down half of it in one swig, grateful for the mini reprieve. "Well, yeah. What if she still wants to move on at the end? It's a real possibility. I'm better off trying to find someone else here, now, aren't I?"

Cole's captive gaze pinned him like a fly in a spider's intricate web. "Are you? Or is that your fear talking again?"

He swallowed back the rising unease in his throat. "I don't know."

"If you love her like you say, then you'll do your best to give things a go. That way you'll have no regrets. You'll know you've done everything to try and make it work. If your relationship doesn't survive after that, you're just not meant for each other."

Jeb nursed his beer, staring into the dissipating foam on top. "Logically that makes sense, but emotionally…"

"I know it's not easy. Not after what you've been through. But if you don't try, you'll always wonder what could have been. Remember I nearly fucked everything up with Hope. Every day, I'm so thankful I took your advice and risked my heart."

"Thanks, mate. As always, I appreciate your honesty. I'll give it some serious thought."

Jeb went to have another drink of beer, but his friend grabbed his wrist in a firm, listen-to-me grip. "No, not serious thought. You're past that. You need to take action. Your decision could be the difference between living a solo life and sharing love with your soulmate."

Chapter Twelve
Fulfilling a Dream

On Issy's day off, she caught the bus from Ala Moana to visit Pearl Harbor, something she could finally tick off her bucket list. During the one-hour trip, she stared out the window, thinking about the dance routines, opening night, her dad, and Jeb, the lush scenery passing by in a blur of greens and blues.

All week, she'd had her phone almost glued to her side, desperate for contact from Jeb. He'd sent a few short texts, but mentioned nothing more about the job or visiting or anything else relationship-wise. And she couldn't do a thing about it except keep busy, distract herself, hope, and pray. She wasn't religious, but she'd been doing a lot of that lately. Anything that might help them reunite.

The bus stopped and she joined the rest of the tour group as they trickled off and boarded a boat across to a white beacon sitting atop a calm cerulean sea. Such a serene scene. So different to how it would have been close to eighty years prior.

Stinging hot tears welled in her eyes. She'd prepared herself for a hard-going, heart-wrenching experience. The loss of her dad and the whole Jeb situation only added to her anguish.

Once inside the bright, sunbathed building, Issy walked up to the wall memorial and read through the huge list of names, mourning for those who had lost their lives, the unresolvable heartbreak. And all because Western society strove for a better, safer life, a more peaceful existence.

Although connected to tragic memories, exploring this meditative place somehow encouraged self-reflection, self-cleansing and, strangely, a sense of peace. The tour ended too quickly, her red, puffy eyes not quite recovered by the time she arrived at the dance studio, so she threw herself into the super-tough rehearsal before anyone could notice and ask what was wrong.

The choreographer looked all smiles, which seemed odd given there'd been no mention of a replacement physio. Either she was extremely happy with their performance or the physio position actually had been filled and the announcement not made yet. Issy was too afraid to ask.

At the end of the exhaustive session, Issy stared at the confronting wall of mirrors. Sweat glistened on her exposed skin. Dark smudges made her eyes look hollow, tired. Her energy levels slumped, her body just functioning on the last dregs of fuel.

Thoroughly drained, she forced a cheery bye to the rest of the troupe, refusing their offer of celebratory cocktails in preparation for their upcoming opening-night show. She just wasn't up to it. She needed some time to recuperate. She needed Jeb. And until she had at least one of those, preferably both, she'd be a downer, ruin the joy, the festive spirit.

The more time she spent with her dance mates, and the longer she'd been separated from Jeb, the trickier it became to keep up a front. She could tell by their concerned expressions and coaxing questions that some of her new friends had worked out she hadn't been herself, especially over the last few days. Definitely not the excited, sky's-the-limit dancer they'd first met.

Her friends left, taking their warmth and acceptance with them. She shivered, still unable to shift her gaze from her reflection. Even her dancing gear reflected her dark state of mind. Normally, she chose bright pinks and primary colors, but today she'd subconsciously chosen all morose, grieving black.

Issy loved the new project, the other dancers, and usually a good, challenging training session lifted her mood. But lately nothing worked. Well, her visit to Pearl Harbor temporarily helped, but she couldn't sustain a sense of peace when unresolved restlessness bubbled below the surface. She was more troubled than she realized if such an awe-inspiring, tropical paradise couldn't break her out of her funk.

What really rammed it home was her career goal had lost its shine. It no longer held the same appeal since she'd left Jeb behind. She needed him by her side to give it full meaning, to complete the picture, to share this long-sought-after achievement with someone she cared about, someone she loved. She still adored dancing, but, as Jimmy had highlighted, she'd also used it as a form of escape.

Escape from the disappointment of a failed first love.

Escape from committing her heart.

Escape from hurt and soul-deep exposure.

An escape from the world, reality.

Dancing had never let her down. It positively challenged her, consistently gave her pleasure. But Jeb had grounded her, shown her the benefits of being vulnerable, allowed her to love, not just chase a momentary high, not just run and hide.

Although she had more sexual experience, he'd trounced her in the emotional maturity department. Her fear had prevented her from speaking to him, instead cowering via text. But if she were serious, she should call.

She needed to tell him, not just insinuate *I love you*. And if it came down to it, if it meant resurrecting their relationship, she'd give notice at the end of the tour and pick up her career back home. She'd now officially established a name for herself in the dance industry, but finding a lifetime love was something else entirely. The time had come to try her hardest to win Jeb back.

The more-than-doable idea—the possibility of success—injected her with renewed energy. Issy rushed over to her gear and dropped to the floor. She pulled up her leg warmers, put on her runners, slung her bag over her shoulder, and hurried to the door.

She stopped, turned, and had one last glance at the empty room. She excelled at dancing because of her dedication and love of it. So, if she invested the same devotion in Jeb, why shouldn't she excel with her win-him-back mission?

Issy reached up and switched off the light.

"Wait." A deep, husky, out-of-breath voice. Jeb's voice?

It couldn't be him, could it? She had to be imagining things, too caught up in her thoughts and entangled emotions about the guy.

She spun around, her eyes widening in shock, her bag dropping along with her jaw. He stood before her, flushed and sucking in air, like he'd run up the five flights of stairs. "What are you doing here?"

He chuckled. "Great to see you too."

She launched herself at him, her arms winding around his neck, her legs wrapping around his waist, her head buried in the crook of his neck.

He held her against him in a tight, loving hug. "I got the job."

She pulled back. "You got… Oh my God!" She kissed his delectable lips over and over and over. "This is so incredible! I can't believe you didn't say anything."

"I wanted to be certain they'd hold my physio position in Sydney, which they have for a year, arrange for someone to rent my flat in the meantime, just in case, and ensure it was all official."

"You had nothing to worry about. You're process driven, clear-headed, sensible. You'd work it out. And let's face it, no one would have been able to compete with you for this role. You're amazing at what you do."

A fresh wave of pink darkened his tanned face. "Thank you."

Issy caressed his heated cheek and stared into his penetrating eyes that shone like polished silver in the low light. God, she loved him so much. "It's not just that, though. You're one-of-a-kind, loving, inspirational. Outside of my dad, you're the first person to truly care about me, believe in me, want the best for me. It means so much. I can't thank you enough."

"You don't have to thank me." He tucked a few wisps of her hair behind her ear, his touch warm and tender. His earnest gaze reconnected with hers. "All I ask, all I've ever wanted, is your love."

"And you have it. I love you, Jeb."

****

At the end of the opening week of shows, which Issy totally blitzed, she had her second day off. Their first day off together. Jeb had spent the night celebrating with her in all sorts of X-rated positions, fantasy stuff. When they finally made it out of bed, they decided to cool off on the pristine white sands of Waikiki Beach.

Issy lay on her stomach on her beach towel, bikini top undone, soaking up the sun. And God, did she look like every straight, hot-blooded man's dream woman. He sure couldn't get enough of her.

Jeb body-surfed a small wave back to the shallows and stepped onto the shore. He dragged his hands through his drenched hair and made his way back to his stunning girlfriend, his dunk in the ocean only half successful at cooling his overheated body.

He crouched beside her and her eyelids flickered open. "Stop making me wet."

"Can't promise you that."

She attempted to swat him with her closest hand, but missed by a mile.

"You're pinking right up. Join me under the umbrella for a minute and I'll reapply your sunscreen." Any excuse to get his hands on her super-smooth skin—and, okay, he had another more life-changing agenda.

"Oh, thanks." She did up her barely-there bikini top and sat with him under the shade.

Jeb grabbed the cooler bag and rummaged through it, his heart hammering.

"Didn't we put the sunscreen in the beach bag?"

"Yep." He found what he was searching for and hid it behind his back, trying not to grin like an anxious, excited idiot.

She stared at him, her brow creased with confusion. "What's going on, Jeb?"

He kneeled beside her, and she leaned back on outstretched hands, her beautiful bronzed body on show. He didn't mind at all because she was his. And would be permanently. He hoped.

Jeb's stomach jittered with nerves, but he wouldn't wuss out now. He'd committed. He had to follow through. He had to know. "Issy, I have something to ask you?"

"Sure, go ahead."

He brought his arm forward and opened his palm in front of her face, revealing the trademark Tiffany and Co aqua ring box.

Her hand flew to her chest, her gaze darting between his eyes and the box. "Oh my God. Jeb?"

"Open it."

She shifted forward and flipped open the lid, the solitaire diamond ring sparkling. He'd known it was perfect the second he saw it, couched in plush black velvet. Her gaze met his, her eyes moist. "It's so beautiful. When did you…?"

"Buy it? Before I left Melbourne."

"You knew you wanted to do this before you left?"

"No. I knew you were the one not even a week into our *arrangement*."

"You did?" A tear slid down her cheek.

He wiped it away with the pad of his thumb. "Yeah."

She laugh-sniffled. "You know what? Me too. I just had to find a way out of my maze of fear."

"So, does that mean you'll do me the honor of wearing my ring, of agreeing to be my wife?"

"Yes! Absolutely, yes!" Before he could slide the ring onto her finger, she snatched it out of the box and did it herself. Forever the independent woman, a woman who knew what she wanted. One of her most endearing, most attractive qualities. "I want to be with you always." She flung herself into his lap and wouldn't stop kissing him.

He held her face between his hands and pulled back, her sultry breath caressing his lips and tempting him to reconnect. "Ah, as much as I'd like to continue this, we're in a public place." His voice sounded scratchy and raw with need.

Her bright sapphire eyes danced with joy and desire. "Then let's go."

And they did.

Together.

The End

EVERNIGHT PUBLISHING ®

www.evernightpublishing.com